The Straw that Broke the Camel's Heart

J. Gunter

Copyright © 2022 by J. Gunter.

ISBN: 978-1-957009-46-9 (sc)

Library of Congress Control Number: 2022917016

All rights reserved. No part of this book may be reproduced, stored, or transmitted by any means—whether auditory, graphic, mechanical, or electronic—without written permission of both publisher and author, except in the case of brief excerpts used in critical articles and reviews. Unauthorized reproduction of any part of this work is illegal and is punishable by law.

For Kestrel—

Who Never Was

CONTENTS

Michelle's Plan

Michelle paused briefly outside building where she worked. She very slowly and intently surveyed the parking lot even though she knew exactly where her car was parked and at only ten minutes after five on this summer afternoon it certainly wasn't dark. Activity in the lot made it look like a hive of brightly colored bees departing on their individual nectar expeditions. Michelle made no effort to walk to her car, she just stood there as if her shoes were part of the sun-baked concrete sidewalk.

Her briefcase suddenly seemed so heavy that she wasn't sure she could manage it. Her shoulders sagged even more as she stepped off the curb and started toward her car. Michelle's mind was traveling at warp three but her concentration was almost nonexistent. She was momentarily jarred back to reality when a bright red Miata stopped in front of her, blocking her path.

Michelle instantly recognized Shelley who worked down the hall from her sitting behind the wheel. "Michelle," she said, "some of us are going to PJ's for a drink. Want to join us?"

Michelle hesitated as she tried to get her thoughts focused enough to make an intelligent answer. "Thanks, but I think

I'll go on home. For some reason I'm really tired," she finally replied "Okay, but if you change your mind, come on over. We'll probably be there 'til who knows when." Then, with a wave, Shelley was gone. When she got to the parking lot exit she turned right and in a matter of seconds had disappeared behind a hedge of tall redtips that separated the parking area from the street.

With an audible sigh Michelle continued her trek across the parking lot. For a moment she regretted parking so far away from the other cars. She had always tried to be careful where she parked and because of this habit her car doors still looked nearly new though her car was several years old. The only spot that even showed was a tiny scuff on the right door from some inconsiderate clod but it had neither been dented nor was the paint actually chipped.

"I never noticed how far apart these lines are," she thought to herself. Michelle switched hands with her briefcase and wondered why it was so heavy and why she had even bothered to bring it with her. It really would have been simpler if I had just left it behind but it's too late now, she decided.

With what appeared to her to be an Olympian effort she finally made it to her car. As she inserted the key into the lock Michelle noticed that a rather large bird had blessed the hood after eating some kind of berry. She stared at it for a few seconds, too tired to be anymore disgusted, and thought, "That pretty much sums up my life."

Opening the door, she sat down on the soft, gray seat fabric. Michelle twisted at the waist, legs still outside the car, and dropped her briefcase on the right seat. She then pushed the top of the case forward and laid it gently down. She turned back to face the front and, putting her hand on the steering wheel for support, she raised her legs and spun around under the wheel. Closing the door, Michelle just sat there, no movement, no nothing, she just stared through the windshield into space.

The temperature inside her car was approaching one hundred twenty-five degrees and it seemed to engulf her Michelle thought, "I bet this is what a potato feels like when it's been sentenced to be baked in a preheated oven." Suddenly she realized something was crawling on her. Pulling the top of her blouse away from her, she peeked down and discovered a rivulet of perspiration tracing her sternum and disappearing between her breasts. Much relieved, Michelle continued to look out the windshield as she tried to collect her thoughts.

"Damn, it's hot in here," she thought. Though it had taken a while to do so, it finally registered with her that she could start the engine and turn on the air conditioner. She put the key in the switch, turned it, and the engine spun into life. It smoothed out immediately and she punched the a/c button. An initial blast of hot air rushed out at her from the heat soaked air ducts but after several seconds it started to cool. Michelle lowered the windows slightly to let the hot air escape as the cooler air pushed in. Her car was much more comfortable now so she fastened her seatbelt and moved the shifter into Drive. She eased across the parking lot toward the street where she turned left and accelerated toward her home on the east side of town.

The drive home took her about the usual twenty minutes. When Michelle arrived at her driveway she slowed and turned in. She stopped in front of her garage but did not open the door. Instead, she put the shifter in Park and turned off the engine. Michelle didn't get out of the car immediately, she just sat there staring out the windshield at the garage door. It was almost as if her mind, or what was left of it, had become detached from her body. She took a deep breath and let her upper body sag back against the seat. Just before she closed her eyes, Michelle thought, "I think the garage door needs painting."

Her house shaded her from the late afternoon sun so the inside of her car was still pleasant from the air conditioner. Turning her head slightly to the left, her eyes focused on a pine cone. It was about fifteen feet away and was just lying there by itself on the neatly cropped grass. It would have been a blemish on the yard except that the soft gray brown colored cone blended so nicely with the dark green grass. About four feet from the cone was a cluster of bright yellow evening primroses. Their half-dollar sized blooms seemed to Michelle to be tiny radar antennae as they tried to track the journey of the sun across the sky.

With a great sigh, she finally opened the door and climbed out of the car. Michelle started to reach back in for her briefcase then had second thoughts. I won't need it tonight and besides, I'm too tired to carry it, she decided, as she turned and walked slowly across the yard. When she got to the front porch she grabbed the black wrought iron corner post and pulled herself up. She wasn't sure there was enough energy in her legs to climb the three steps from the walk to the porch without a helpful tug. Then, Michelle walked across the porch passed a bright red geranium, opened the front door, and went in.

After being outside in the heat the house initially seemed too cool for her but she knew that after a few minutes her body would adjust and the temperature would be much more pleasant. To the right of the front door there was a wall mounted coat rack. It wasn't very large, only about twenty inches long, with four evenly spaced shaker pegs protruding from it. On the peg closest to the door Michelle hung her purse. It was a small leather bag, earth tones in color, and though it wasn't heavy, she was greatly relieved to get it off her shoulder.

Michelle walked slowly across the living room, her feet making an almost imperceptible sound on the carpet. As she moved, her fingers fumbled with the buttons on her blouse. By the time she had walked down the hall and into her bedroom she had the front completely unbuttoned.

To the right of the large walk-in closet door was an oak dresser with a tall mirror on it. Michelle usually dressed and undressed in front of it. Her rationale for this was, if she did not like what she saw, probably no one else would. Though she had finally reached the point that she really didn't care a great deal anymore what other people thought, she still cared what she thought, sort of.

Stopping in front of the mirror, she stood there and stared deeply into her own eyes. Her eyes slowly traced the lines of the reflection. Looking back at her was a tall slender woman. Michelle had never tried to fool herself, she knew that she wasn't beautiful but she also knew that she was reasonably attractive. On a good day she imagined herself to possibly even be a seven. On a great day when her biorhythms were peaking she thought that she just might be an eight, maybe even an eight plus. However, tonight she was much too tired to play the numbers game, besides that, it didn't matter anymore. After tonight there would be no more games, numbers or any other kind, it would all be history.

Michelle pushed her dark brown hair back and continued to stare deeply into her brown, almond shaped eyes. The woman looking back at her from the mirror certainly wasn't even a seven this evening though the potential would have still been obvious to an observer. There was no vitality in her eyes and she thought it very strange that they could be empty and yet, at the same time, filled to overflowing with sadness.

Moving across the room, she continued to remove her clothes and carefully place them on the back of a chair. When she had finished she walked into the bathroom and turned on the shower. Michelle adjusted the water temperature and stepped in. The water felt good and she immediately turned the shower head to let it drum down on the back of her neck and shoulders.

With a tremendous sigh she let her head sag forward until her chin was almost touching her chest. As she stood there Michelle tried to put her arms around herself as if she were getting a hug but, try as she might, it just wasn't the same. Finally, she gave up and reached for the soap.

Michelle continued at a leisurely pace, there was really no reason to hurry and she had no plans to leave the house that evening. After she had washed all the soap off she continued to stand there for several minutes just enjoying the luxurious feeling that the hot, cascading water gave her. Finally, assuring herself that she had enough to last her a lifetime, Michelle turned the water off. Before she dried off she reached for her bottle of baby oil. After putting some in one hand, Michelle rubbed both hands lightly together and then she rubbed them all over her still wet body letting the oil and water mix briefly before she dried. Though numerous people had complimented her on the softness of her skin, she had never divulged her simple, inexpensive secret. Doing it in this manner left her skin soft and smooth but not oily and it was a feeling that she greatly enjoyed. When Michelle had finished with the towel she hung it over the shower rod and walked back into the bedroom where she once again stopped in front of the large mirror on her dresser.

Looking into the mirror she saw the same reflection she had seen earlier, only this time the grime of the day had been washed away. The same empty eyes looked back at her as she stared deeply into them. Michelle had been blessed genetically. The bridge of her nose was slightly higher than normal but it was straight and narrow. The slight deformity that she had at times observed in others of where the nasal cartilage joined the bone was not even noticeable in hers. Her cheekbones were high and the lines around her eyes only showed when she smiled and up until recently, she had done a lot of that.

Michelle's fingers were long and slender and had she pursued music seriously, they would have certainly been an asset. Her arms were not big, however, like the rest of her body, they appeared as if they engaged in regular exercise. Though her breasts were not large, they were high and firm.

They had not yet begun to sag and the dark nipples always protruded slightly like she was almost sexually aroused, but not quite. Her stomach was flat and tight and there was a smooth flare toward her hips. Michelle's legs were slightly longer than normal for someone her height and the distal end of the thigh just above the knee was only slightly larger than the top of her calf just below the knee. The many years of running had given her calf muscles a slight diamond shape and it had also helped to keep her ankles slender so it was easy to see her prominent Achilles tendon. Michelle was outwardly very attractive but only she could see the inner scars that disturbed her so and only she knew the wounds that each scar covered.

As she stood there gazing in the mirror the figure looking back at her began to blur. A large tear started to form in each eye causing the light to refract at odd angles and that caused the reflection in the mirror to become distorted. Blinking the tears away, Michelle decided that the figure in the mirror and reality had a lot in common, they would each become distorted when viewed through a tear. With that thought she opened a drawer in the dresser, removed some underwear and slipped it on. Then she walked over to the closet and got out a lightweight sweat suit and pulled it on. Her nipples started to protrude more as the material rubbed against them as she moved around the room.

It suddenly dawned on her that she was hungry so she padded quietly down the hall and into the kitchen to see what she could find that would make a fitting meal for such an occasion. As luck would have it, in the freezer she discovered a rather large piece of Black Forest Cake and nearly half of a New York style cheesecake. Normally, Michelle ate desserts very sparingly, if at all, but tonight would be different. She would pull out all the stops. "So what if my cholesterol and fat meters shoot into the danger zone," she thought, "who gives a damn? I certainly don't. Move over pig out city, here I come."

Placing the two items on the kitchen table, Michelle turned to get a fork. What's missing, she wondered. Then it came to her, she had nothing to drink and there was nothing but sweets on the table. Reaching up into a cabinet she removed a large jar of cashews that was still over half full. Michelle put it on the table with the other two desserts and then removed a water glass from the dish drain. Going to the refrigerator, she removed a half gallon of white wine and almost filled the glass with it. Michelle left the bottle sitting on the table just in case she wanted more and she wasn't the least bit concerned about a hangover.

Judging everything to now be in order, Michelle sat down at the table, picked up her fork and began to eat. First she took a bite of cheesecake, then a bite of Black Forest Cake, and then two cashews. This would be her pattern as long as the three items lasted. The only thing that did not have a particular sequence was the wine. Sometimes she took several bites and then a sip, sometimes she took a sip after each bite, and more than once she took several sips between bites. Consuming this many calories and this much fat and sugar would normally have repulsed her but tonight she was neither repulsed nor concerned. Michelle caught herself grinning when she decided that she could never eat enough of this kind of food to die of natural causes.

After she had eaten everything she had put on the table, Michelle finished with an apple. Dropping the core into the trash, she topped off her glass of wine and carried it with her back to the bedroom. She placed the glass on the night stand and stepped into the bathroom where she flossed and then brushed her teeth. "Mom would be proud," she thought, "faithful to the bitter end."

Michelle's Thoughts

At the age of twenty-nine Michelle had attended the party of a friend where she had met roger. He was fivers older than she was and displayed a lot of self-confidence combined with an effervescent personality. Most people. especially women enjoyed being around him because of his charm and wit. She had been quite surprised, and not just a little pleased, when he had offered to get her a glass of wine and then engaged her in light, but stimulating, conversation.

Though he did live up to his reputation of being a charmer, Michelle was in no hurry to do anything she might regret. Whereas she had a tendency to be quiet and pensive, he, though not loud, liked to be the center of attention. This made for a contrast in them that seemed to be complementary.

Roger had called her the next week to see if she would join him for supper and a movie. They had seemed to hit it off quite well and over the following weeks they grew rather fond of each other. Michelle was still proceeding with a certain amount of caution when, about four months after they initially met, he had called her and asked her to go out of town to attend a weekend seminar with him. Surprised at her own willingness, she had immediately replied that she would love to go with him.

Later, after much thought about what would probably happen, she still wanted to go. Michelle knew her feelings were growing stronger for Roger and she found these feelings simultaneously exciting and disconcerting.

While he attended meetings during the day, she read, swam, and just relaxed. After dining that evening, what she thought would happen, did, and she loved it. After it was over, as they lay there holding each other, he told her that he loved her.

With the passing of time they grew even closer and their relationship continued to blossom. To Michelle it seemed as if she were living in a dream world. She was almost like a little girl as she floated along through her everyday life.

A little over two years after they had met, Roger asked her to marry him. Though a little scared of the entire situation, she had been giddy with the excitement of thinking that someone really wanted her. Not just a temporary want but something permanent. Though it was almost overwhelming, she had managed to keep her emotions under control enough to help plan their small wedding.

Since she had fewer possessions than Roger and his apartment was larger than hers, she moved everything either to his, now their, place or put it in storage. Realizing they needed more space and the tax advantages of home ownership, they eventually started a house search. They had already given up one Saturday morning and had started back home when she suggested they turn down a quiet, tree lined street on the edge of town.

There it was, seeming to be just waiting for them, a medium size brick ranch with an acceptable front yard and an enormous back yard. The previous owners had taken good care of it and it was in their price range. Neat patches of flowers were blooming in several places around the house. There were trees in both the front and back yards and by the curb was a small pile of dead branches that had recently been put there for the garbage men to pick up. They were both ecstatic and, after a tour by the very pleasant owners, they knew they would find a way to purchase it.

Several weeks later they had moved in. Roger had even carried her over the threshold and presented her, as the lady of the house, with a rose and some champagne. Michelle's fantasy world was continuing and she had been very happy. She enjoyed working in the yard and in the flower beds. Sometimes Roger helped her but it was mainly on the weekends and she noticed that he never really seemed to be putting all his energy into his efforts.

As the months went by his efforts around the house became fewer and fewer and when he did help her it was never voluntary. Her exuberance for their life together no longer seemed to be carrying over to him. She often suggested that they go to bed early but he rarely complied with her wishes. Even when he did, something was missing. Michelle began to question herself as to whether or not she was enough woman for this man she had married.

To try to stem the growing doubts about herself she enrolled in a health club to firm up even more and to lose the four pounds she had slowly gained since they had gotten married. She bought new clothes, new very sexy lingerie, even changed her hair style, but nothing seemed to have any long lasting positive effect and they continued to slowly drift apart.

One warm Saturday afternoon while she was pulling some weeds from the flower beds, Roger pulled into the driveways as he returned from a trip downtown. He walked over to her and stopped just inches from her outstretched fingers as she supported herself with one hand while pulling grass with other. She remembered all to well how he had just stood there, not saying anything, as if he were trying to summon up the courage to say whatever was on his mind.

When his words finally tumbled out they were rapid fire with short pauses in between the phrases. The way he spoke reminded her of a machine gun firing with each tenth bullet pulled from the belt just to remind the gunner of what he was doing. Though his voice reminded her of bullets firing, what he had said had the impact of a bomb going off. He had thought long and hard about his decision and had come to pick up his personal belongings. He was going to stay with Randy, a longtime friend of his whom Michelle had met but didn't know very well, for a few days while he looked for another place to live. She could have the house and everything in it. He wanted only his pre-marriage belongings, his clothes, and his attorney would be in touch. Then, he turned and walked inside.

Too taken by surprise to speak and too devastated to cry, Michelle had simply continued to weed the flowers. Much later Roger had come out carrying two enormous suitcases and a few boxes. He placed them in the trunk of his car and then returned for several armloads of assorted items. Neither had spoken during this time. When he had finished, he just stood by his car and looked at her. Michelle stopped weeding long enough to meet his gaze. Still without speaking, he had gotten into his car and driven out of her life. She had simply finished the flower bed she was weeding and gone inside for a drink of water.

That evening while eating supper the reality of what had happened finally hit her. After many tears she realized that she would rather be alone by herself than alone with somebody. She also decided that even though she and Roger had lived in the same house and slept in the same bed, that for the last year she had been alone and had simply been denying it. As she thought about it Michelle wondered how it had lasted as long as it had. After a rather large glass of wine and with mixed feelings of sadness and relief, she got up from her recliner and went to bed.

It had been a slow recovery from this blow that life had dealt her. She had sought refuge wherever she could find it, mainly from trying to stay as busy as possible, being away from home as much as possible, and usually, too much wine in the evening.

Though Michelle knew she could not drown her memories, she especially liked the buzz the wine gave her. Finally deciding that she did not need to consume so many calories for such a light, foggy feeling, she started ordering a different drink each time she went wherever alcohol was being served. One evening she discovered that a gin and tonic, when made with Tanqueray and two pieces of lime, was much to her liking.

Now she could stop experimenting and get down to the business of what she really liked to do, letting an alcoholic fog slip quietly over her mind and temporarily deaden the pain in her life. Nearly every night she got into bed with dulled thought processes and when she closed her eyes the bed would begin its slow revolutions. Sometimes it seemed that the bed would spin lazily upward and she would begin a journey that took her away from her cares.

These journeys usually ended with her falling into a troubled sleep. She never really understood how she always ended up back in her bedroom after floating through space but she always did. Invariably, three or four hours after her bed had lifted off, she would pop wide awake and toss and turn until nearly time for her to get up. Then she would usually fall asleep again for a short, troubled nap that lasted till her alarm clock jarred her awake.

In the evening Michelle would often sink into a faraway place in her mind. There, oblivious to her surroundings, she would stay as long as possible. Though she still went to work each day she spent less and less time fraternizing with her friends. Her gin and tonic drinks were no longer the standard bar size. It was not uncommon for her to mix them in a water glass and then sit in the dark with her foggy mind racing even though she was unable to concentrate on anything. To avoid having the spell broken, she would usually take a telephone off the hook and journey through the silent darkness until it was time for her to go to bed.

This became the status quo of Michelle's life. Monday through Friday she worked. When she got home from work and the weather was nice, she worked in her yard. If she had no desire for yard work, she would go to the park or go do the stores at the mall. Anything she could think of, she did, it made no difference, she had to stay busy. When she ran out of something to do she would again seek refuge in the silent darkness with her industrial strength toddy.

After months of this kind of existence she had been almost dragged to a party by one of her friends. She had not wanted to go. She had not one iota of desire to change her evening routine but Mary had been adamant to the point of literally grabbing her by the shoulders and giving her a good shaking. Finally, Michelle had told her yes, more due to the fear of suffering whiplash than to any real desire to attend.

It was the first time in ages that she had dressed for any reason other than work and she had to admit that it did make her feel better. Michelle put on some black slacks that she especially liked because they fit her as if they had been tailor made. Her silver earrings were very delicate and dangled about an inch below her ear lobes. Her dark hair and eyes were in stark contrast to her blouse. Each one seemed to make the other stand out even more. Slipping on a pair of black, medium heeled pumps, she decided that she was ready to party--at least for a little while.

When Michelle arrived at Mary's several guests were already there, some she knew but most of them were strangers. As she made her rounds chatiing with the different people she had a strange feeling that someone was watching her. Though she noticed no one staring at her, the feeling was there just the same. As Michelle moved around the room the feeling stayed with her even though she continued to be unsuccessful at pinpointing the source of this odd sensation. While chatting with the different people her eyes searched the room but to no avail. Michelle was just finishing the last sip of her glass of white wine when a strange voice said, "Allow me."

Turning toward the voice, she discovered a rather tall man looking at her and holding the very bottle from which she had earlier poured her drink. Holding out her glass, she said, "Thank you." He filled her glass and set the bottle on a magazine on the sofa table next to them.

"I'm Paul," he said quietly.

"I'm Michelle," she replied.

Continuing, he said, "I haven't seen you at any of these parties before. Are you new in town?"

"No, I just don't go to parties much anymore," she answered with a shy smile.

"They're more fun than just sitting at home," he added. "I suppose they are," Michelle said. "Excuse me. Oh, thanks for the wine."

As she moved away from Paul, she thought, "Not bad." She could feel his eyes on her as she walked across the room toward Lisa. More than just wanting to talk with Lisa, Michelle wanted to observe this new found acquaintance from a better vantage point. As she and Lisa talked she watched Paul move around the room visiting with other guests.

He seemed to be sure of himself and, whether laughing or talking, he did it quietly. She noticed that each person with whom he spoke always laughed before Paul moved on. What is he telling all those people she wondered?

Occasionally, she would catch him watching her. Instead of looking away, he would just make some facial expression to acknowledge her. Once, he even wiggled his nose in a way that reminded her of a rabbit. This action had totally disarmed her and she, in turn, had acknowledged with a smile.

"Who is the guy in the dark blue short sleeve shirt? That Paul guy," she finally asked Lisa.

Glancing the way Michelle was facing, Lisa replied, "Paul somebody. Why?"

"I was just curious," Michelle answered. "He got me a glass of wine a while ago and I have no idea who he is. He seems to know everybody."

"Yeah, he's been coming to the different parties for the last several months. I think he works with Ed at R and D Torque. I think someone said he moved here last year from somewhere in the mid-west, maybe Tulsa. Anyway, he always seems real nice."

Michelle continued to watch him interacting with the different people. He was taller than she by about six inches so that made him over six feet tall. His clothes hung nicely on him and she imagined that he visited the gym on a regular basis. His smile was quick and he seemed to laugh easily. She was slightly surprised when she discovered herself wishing that he would come over to talk with her again.

About the time Michelle had this thought, off in a far corner of her mind a subconscious memory circuit closed and she suddenly became very tired. She could almost feel the energy draining out of her and she had a sudden desire to be home in bed, away from parties and people. Her shoulders slumped perceptibly and the small, half empty wine glass in her hand felt as heavy as if it were made of lead and contained mercury. She quickly set it on a lamp table to keep from dropping it and took a deep breath to try to regain her ebbing energy.

All the deep breath seemed to do was to exhaust her even more. She looked around the room for some convenient place to sit but all the seats were occupied. Starting for the door, she was thankful that she had left her purse in the car. As Michelle moved across the room she tried to avoid eye contact with anyone out of fear that someone might try to engage her in conversation. She no longer cared if she were being watched or not. Now, her primary goal was to avoid everyone and to make it out the front door as quickly and as inconspicuously as possible.

Finally, she was successful and since she was not carrying her handbag, no one thought she was leaving. Though the fresh evening air was appreciably cooler than the inside air had been, it still did not revitalize her. As she continued toward her car her movement was more of a shuffle than a walk, so much so that, had someone been observing her in the dim light, she would have easily been mistaken for someone either quite elderly or infirm.

Reaching her, car at last, Michelle fumbled with the key and finally got the door open. She peeked in the back seat as she got inside and then closed and locked the door. Closing her eyes, she let her head fall back against the headrest and took a lung-fillingg deep breath. Instead of starting her car, Michelle just sat there with her head back and her eyes shut while she struggled to find enough energy for her drive home.

After several minutes of just sitting there like that, she decided to attempt the drive anyway, liking that option better that sleeping in her car. In an almost mechanical state she started the engine and pulled into the street. A block and a half later she turned on the headlights.

It wasn't a long trip back to her house, only about twenty minutes, but she was greatly relieved when she turned into her familiar driveway. Stopping as close as she could to the front door, Michelle got out, locked her car doors, and then walked slowly inside. As she closed the front door she kicked off her shoes and made her way to her bedroom where, without undressing, she fell face first on her bed narrowly missing a coat hanger she had forgotten.

Before going to sleep she tried to replay in her mind all the events of the evening but nothing seemed to fall into place. Her thought processes seemed to be reaching the red line but none of them was really coherent. She pictured herself being involved in a fast-paced conversation with a group of people where only she and one other person spoke English. Still trying to fathom what was going on inside her head, Michelle sank into a restless sleep with dreams in vivid colors but nothing she would remember upon awakening. Suddenly she jerked awake, startled back into reality by a loud noise inside her head.

After Michelle had slept fitfully for about two hours she finally got up brush her teeth and remove her clothes. Getting back into bed, she thrashed around for a while before finally slipping into the stranger world that is found only between being awake and being asleep. As she perceived her body starting to relax and her breathing becoming deeper and more regular, she knew sleep was almost in her grasp. Once again her body suddenly jerked awake, having been jarred back to reality by a sudden loud noise that came from somewhere deep inside her mind. With her heart pounding and her body trembling she continued to lie there trying to collect her thoughts and push away the too real terror of this recurring dream. At last her exhausted mind and body could take it no more and sleep helped her to once again escape reality.

Several days had passed since Michelle attended the party at Mary's house. As she sat in her large oak rocker watching the final rays of the setting sun make different shadows on the floor and wall, the telephone rang. Instead of getting up to answer it, she just let it ring. In trying to escape, she had also turned off the answering machine so no one would expect her to return a call. After several rings the phone went silent and she continued to just sit there in the dimming light, still watching the shadows.

The sun had long since faded, taking the shadows with it and leaving only the darkness behind with Michelle still sitting in the rocker. The quiet of the room was suddenly interrupted again by the ringing telephone. To avoid being disturbed later, she decided to answer it. Even as she picked it up she had a strange, unexplainable feeling that she would be far better off to just let it ring. She answered with a barely audible, "Hello." audible, "Hello."

On the other end a voice that she recognized but could not place, said, "Michelle, please."

"This is Michelle," she replied quietly.

"This is Paul. We met several weeks ago at Mary's party. I poured you a glass of wine," he continued.

"I remember," she went on, "you had on a dark blue shirt."

"One and the same," he said. "You slipped away rather suddenly and I didn't have a chance to chat with you anymore. Do you think we could continue our conversation Friday evening over supper?"

Michelle was just beginning to become aware of what was taking place and now she was faced with having to make a decision. Here was a man who numerous people found interesting and he was expressing a desire to get to know her better. At the party he had seemed pleasant enough and, though she had been polite, she certainly had done nothing to invite his attention. Though her interest in dining with him, or anyone else, was certainly not at an all time high, she could think of no real reason to decline his offer. "Besides," she thought, "since I didn't tell him my last name, he had to do some inquiring. I guess initiative should be rewarded." In a quiet voice she answered, "Okay. What time?"

"Great," came his reply, "I'll pick you up at seven, if that's okay. Bye."

As she hung up the phone Michelle began to wonder what she had gotten herself into. While her heart was saying, "Go for it," her mind was saying, "If you're not careful, you're going to step in something and track it inside on the white carpet." "It's only an evening," she thought, "and, if it sucks, it wont be the first time and probably not the last. Who knows, he might be just what I need to get my life kick started again." With that thought on her mind she walked through the dark house toward her bedroom. She finally went to sleep and tonight there were no dreams of any kind. any kind.

Michelle went about her usual activities in the usual manner. She discovered that if she were not actively engaged in a task of some kind that her mind began to wander and she would lapse into a daydream about the approaching Friday evening rendezvous. Though still very hesitant and unsure if her decision had been the correct one, she found herself looking forward to the upcoming event. She had even decided that she might enjoy it.

That Friday when Michelle got home from work she had a mild case of anxiety. It had been quite a while since she had been out on a real, live date and though she was excited about it, she was at the same time uneasy. After all, she had only met Paul once and really knew very little about him. She wondered what his expectations of her might be.

Trying to stifle her negative feelings, she stepped into her closet to choose her attire for the evening. Since she had absolutely no idea where they would be going for supper she was at a loss as to what to wear. Finally deciding that it was better to be overdressed than underdressed, Michelle made her choice. She chose a cobalt blue dress made of peachskin that hung nicely on her slender curves and was hemmed slightly above her knees. To accentuate it, she chose a silver necklace that hung slightly below her throat. The necklace consisted of three small balls on a delicate chain with the center ball being a little larger than the one on either side. For her ear adornment Michelle chose a pair of small diamond studs in white gold.

Removing the dress from the closet, she hung it on the top of the closet door frame and went into the bathroom and turned on the shower. As she showered she discovered that the combination of the hot spray on her skin and the yet unfolded mysteries of the upcoming evening quite stimulating. The slick, soapy lather enabled her hands to slide easily over her breasts and her firm stomach. She had her eyes closed when she turned to face the cascading water and discovered that when it splashed on her chest that there was a pleasant tingling in her nipples. As Michelle ran her fingers over them they became more erect as the blood supply increased until they were protruding like tiny, pink stumps on the side of a hill. "I better get this out of my mind now," she thought, "but if it happens later, I'll just have to cope with it." When she had rinsed all the soap down the drain, she turned off the water and reached for a towel. It felt good as she rubbed it over her skin. So stimulated was she that her nipples were still erect as she dried her upper body. They tingled even more when she rubbed the towel over them. "I have got to relax," she mused, "I've been out before, this is nothing new." Still, she was beginning to become more excited about the upcoming events of the evening, it had been a very long time since anything like this had happened to her. As she slipped into her clothes Michelle glanced at the clock. She nearly panicked when she realized how much time she had spent in the shower.

Michelle had just finished combing her haird and was reaching for a bottle of Jontue spray when she heard a knock on the door. Automatically, she looked again at the clock, it showed four minutes after seven. Slipping on her shoes,

Michelle walked quickly down the hall toward the front door. She hoped she didn't overpower him since the alcohol had not yet completely evaporated from the cologne. "Rats," she thought, "I probably smell like a street walker."

Not knowing whether or not Michelle had heard him knock, Paul had just raised his hand to knock again, only this time a little harder. As his hand came forward, Michelle pulled the door open with a jerk. They got to know each other for the second time as the knuckles of his right hand landed with no sound at all on her left breast.

After knocking the first time and not getting a response, Paul had started looking around admiring the flowers in Michelle's front yard and on the porch. When he drew his hand back to knock the second time he fully expected the door to remain stationary. When his hand went too far forward he turned back to see what had happened to the door. He had turned his head back to face the front about the time his hand had landed. There they were, for all practical purposes, strangers, except he was trying to get a resonant sound from her upper left chest.

As they stood there looking at each other Paul turned a flaming red and withdrew his hand. Neither spokem they just stood looking at each other. Suddenly, thinking of how ridiculous this must look, Michelle erupted in laughter and Paul joined in. When they had regained their composure he said, "Does this mean we know each other?"

Still trying to maintain her composure, she replied, "Yes, but not in the Biblical sense." Michelle stepped back and invited him in, closing the door behind him.

"I'm really sorry about our meeting a moment ago," Paul said.

"Don't worry about it," she replied. "Just be glad I wasn't in a wheel chair knocking on your door and have it happen to you." Picking up her purse, she said, "I'm ready."

They walked to Paul's car and got in. As he drove, Paul went over his plans for their evening and asked if she had a preference in cuisine. Deciding on Chinese, he drove to the Rangoon Room. They went in and were seated, by request, in a corner booth that had no one sitting close to it. He struck Michelle as an intelligent individual who was obviously skilled in the art of conversation and though he tried to engage her in one, with some degree of success, Michelle was still reticent. Part of her was enjoying the evening immensely but a distant part of her was unwilling to fully participate. That part of her was sending a message that said, "Be careful. You've been through this before and it doesn't matter that you want someone special in your life, no one wants you. Remember, whatever he does to you, you deserve for not learning the last time. Proceed with caution."

As the battle within her raged, Michelle responded to the conversation according to which side was winning at the time. She would go from being a chatterbox to being very quiet and pensive. If Paul perceived anything unusual, he did not let it show. It just appeared to him that, at times, she wanted to talk and at other times she wanted to listen. Not having any idea why, he simply accepted it as normal ebb and flow of conversation.

When their food came and they began to eat they both seemed to relax a little more. Michelle discovered that she was really enjoying his company and she made a sincere effort to push away any thoughts of the things that Roger had said and done. "I've really missed this," she thought, "I wonder if there's hope after all?" After her second glass of sweet plum wine the circuit that controlled the warning signal in her head finally disconnected.

They sat and talked for a long time after they had finished eating. Michelle was becoming much more relaxed and found herself laughing more than she had in months.

She had just taken another sip of water and, after setting her glass back down, she let her hand linger by the glass. Suddenly, she felt Paul's fingertips touching hers, then she felt a sudden pounding in her chest. "What in the world is wrong with me," she thought, "I'm not some sixteen-year-old out on her first date." Even though she had to admit that she did kind of feel that way, she was not totally displeased with the feeling. She responded to his touch by putting two of her fingertips on top of his. Their conversation had almost come to a standstill as they just sat there playing their fingertip game and looking at each other. The initial pounding of her heart had quietened enough that she was no longer afraid Paul could hear it, and for this, Michelle was indeed thankful.

When the waitress came by and refilled their water glasses they hardly noticed, they were much too absorbed in each other. The fingertip game had advanced to the point that Paul's fingers alternated between overlapping hers all the way to her knuckles, to him tracing random patterns on the back of her hand.

Michelle just sat there feeling the different sensations caused by his fingers and wondering why it felt so good to be touched by another person. As if to make a point, he would sometimes squeeze, ever so slightly, harder. At other times she could barely feel them at all as if there were only a tiny bug disturbing her normal tactile tranquillity. Her nose started to itch slightly and she struggled against it for fear she would sneeze. That, she was afraid, would have been disastrous. What if it woke her up, or much worse, what if it woke Paul up? "If this is a dream," she thought, "please let me sleep on."

Just below the surface of her mind feelings that Michelle had not had in months had begun to bubble. It reminded her of watching a pot of water as it was just beginning to boil, first one tiny bubble would leave the bottom and rise toward the surface, then another, and another. About the time Paul slipped his fingers under her hand and raised it, putting his fingers between hers and giving them a squeeze, the water of her emotions started to boil over once again. She squeezed his hand and was nearly overwhelmed at what went through her mind.

Suddenly, as if he had touched an embedded splinter in her finger, Michelle withdrew her hand. The movement had happened so quickly that it startled them both and also embarrassed her.

"Did I hurt you?" Paul asked.

"No," she replied, "I banged my hand yesterday and it has a tender spot but it's okay now."

Michelle really had hurt her hand the day before but that was not what had caused her to suddenly jerk it back. A distant memory of similar pleasure that had led to so much pain had manifested itself in the tiny bruise on the back of her hand. This memory had caused a circuit to close and the much longed for high that she was experiencing started flowing away like raindrops from a summertime shower into a storm drain. She felt it overwhelming her and she was powerless in its invisible grasp. As Michelle sat there she knew that she was becoming more and more exhausted with each passing moment. There was no trace of the former smile that had been on her face, now there was no expression at all. Her blank look would have made an old time poker player proud, does she hold a pair of two's or a full house?

In a quiet voice she said, "I think we should go. It's been a long day and I'm really tired."

Paul's sudden disappointment flashed across his face and if Michelle had cared, she would have seen it. However, tonight she was too tired to observe anything that required any perception. She just wanted to be home in bed, alone.

As they rose to leave Paul reached for the check and they walked without talking toward the front of the restaurant.

When Paul stopped to pay the cashier Michelle walked closer to the front door and stood there with her shoulders sagging and her head down as she looked into the street. Nothing she saw really registered, nothing she saw really mattered.

Michelle suddenly became aware of Paul standing beside her and they moved toward the door which he opened for her to pass through. It was obvious to him that she was preoccupied with something but he was hesitant to inquire. When they got to his car he unlocked her door and she got in. As soon as she sat down her head went back against the headrest and she closed her eyes. "If I can only make it a little longer," she thought, "I'll be home in bed."

During the drive across town to her house Michelle initiated no conversation and she spoke only in response to Paul's efforts engage her in one. When they arrived at her driveway he turned in and stopped behind her car. "How are you feeling?" he inquired.

"I don't feel especially bad," she replied, "I suddenly just got so very tired. Actually, I feel beyond tired, somewhere in the exhausted range."

Paul got out and started around the car to open her door. Michelle was no longer interested in his being polite, she simply wanted to go to bed. So, with that thought in mind and because she opened her own door most of the time anyway, she pushed it open and was already standing by the car when he got there.

"I was going to do that for you," he said.

"I know you were," she replied, "but I'm not paralyzed, I'm just tired." Had Michelle been fully aware of what was happening she would have considered both her action and her statement strange since she really did like being treated like a lady.

When they got to the front door they paused. After earlier events of the evening the silence seemed awkward.

Michelle put the key in the lock and gave it a turn. She did not quite push the door open, she just released it from its lock. Turning toward Paul, she said in a quiet voice, "Thanks. I had a great time and I really do wish I felt better."

"Is there anything I can do for you?" he asked. "No."

"Shall I call you next week?" he inquired.

"Please do," she answered, "maybe by then some of my energy will have returned. Goodnight."

"Goodnight."

Michelle turned and entered as Paul walked back to his car. When she finally made it to her bedroom and her bed it only took sleep a few minutes to overtake her.

Several days had gone by when Paul called her again. They talked for a while but her side of the conversation would not flow. Finally, sensing things were not going as well as he had hoped, Paul decided to take a chance. He went ahead and asked her to join him for a weekend movie and, after what had happened, he wasn't terribly surprised when she declined. Her answer had been very non-specific, just a simple, "I really better not. Maybe in a week or so I'll be more up to it."

After she hung up the phone Michelle continued to sit in the lengthening shadows. She knew something wasn't quite right in her life but she was also unsure as to exactly what to do about the situation. Though she longed for a special someone in her life to fill the big empty spot in her heart, she was having a real problem making the effort to find that someone, or, to let that someone find her. "How stranger," she thought, "here is a guy who appears to have a lot going for himself, seems pleasant and intelligent, has an obvious interest in me, and I really don't seem to care."

Though Michelle's mind was constantly racing, she was concentrating on nothing. The sun dropped over the horizon to shine its light on people and places that were at least as far from Michelle as reality was but that really didn't bother her. She just sat there in the darkness with the only sound being a slight squeak as she rocked that came from where the back of the chair joined the seat. In her bedroom her clock made its friendly, rhythmic ticking but she was too far away to hear it. Other than that there was no sign or sound of life.

Several days passed with Michelle's daily routine being very much the same. On work days that's just what she did, she got up and went to work. At the end of the day she drove home and changed clothes. She alternated between lying on the couch and sitting in her rocking chair. Occasionally she would listen to some quiet music and at other times she simply enjoyed the silence. To avoid the outside world from which she was trying to escape, she would simply take a phone off the hook and not put it back on till the next morning. Her only activity was watching the shadows lengthen across the floor. About the time most people would have been starting to party she would get up and walk through the darkness to her bedroom where she would formally go to bed.

The weekends varied only slightly since she did not have to go to work. Those days she usually slept late, if possible, and lounged around the house in one of her numerous sweat suits. If she needed something from the store, she went to get it and returned as quickly as possible to her solitary existence. Though she was well aware that something was not quite right in her mind, she was simply too tired to care.

Upon awakening early one Saturday morning Michelle noticed a change inside her head even before she got up. She reached over and put the telephone on the small table by her bed back on its cradle. Lying there she stretched like a large cat and then relaxed once again. The sun was trying to brighten the room in spite of the venetian blinds and curtains over the windows. In the quiet she could hear the birds chirping in the shrubs that were close to her bedroom. Something really has changed, she decided, but I'm not sure what. Then it dawned on her, her energy had returned and she felt as if she were starving. Pushing back the cover, Michelle got up and walked to the windows and pushed the curtains aside and opened the blinds to let in more light as she gazed outside at another lovely morning.

Michelle slipped into a long, dark blue terry cloth robe as she walked toward the kitchen, detouring only to push open more windows. Unlike recent mornings when it really did not matter to her whether she ate or not, this morning she was ravenous. She reached into a cabinet and pulled out a box of Oreos. As Michelle looked at the box she smiled and thought, "Ahhhh, the staff of life." Popping one into her mouth, she then poured herself a large glass of cranberry juice.

She proceeded to remove eggs, milk, and some sharp cheddar from the refrigerator and started to prepare an omelet. When it was nearly finished cooking she put two pieces of bread in the toaster. She was just sliding the omelet on a plate when the toast popped up. Her hunger was such that she had to make a conscious effort not to gobble her food. When it was all gone she reverted to her attack on the Oreos. Several cookies later Michelle closed the box and returned the remaining milk, eggs, and cheese to the refrigerator and got out a large red apple. As she ate it she walked through the house opening more curtains and blinds to let in the light.

Michelle had just finished the apple and had washed the juice from her fingers when the phone rang. It had been so long since she had heard one ring at home that it startled her. She picked it up and heard a vaguely familiar voice, "Michelle?"

"Yes," she replied.

"This is Paul," the voice went on, "are you okay?"

"Oh, hi, Paul," she answered cheerily. "Yes, I'm okay. Why wouldn't I be?"

"I was beginning to wonder. I've tried several times to call you but never got an answer."

Michelle paused for a moment as she tried to think of a suitable explanation to his statement and then responded, "I kind of needed to escape for a while so I've been hard to reach. I just needed to get away," she went on, but what she didn't tell him was that the place she went to was somewhere inside her mind.

"Well, I'm glad you're back," Paul said. "Would you like to go out and play this evening?"

Without hesitation Michelle replied, "I'd love to. How about around seven again?"

"I'll see you then. Bye."

Michelle returned the phone to its cradle and just stood there as if in a trance. Her energy level that seemed to have been reborn this morning now surged even higher. She thought, "Somebody wants me," but she refused to dwell on it. As Michelle went about tidying up the kitchen she caught herself humming a song from once upon a time. She still wasn't sure why she felt so good, she was just glad she did and, for a change, she was really looking forward to the coming evening and being with another person.

While Michelle had been dwelling in a far corner of her mind, most of the normal household chores had been put on hold. While the clothes washed and dried, she dusted and vacuumed. Long before these tasks were finished the sun had dried the dew from the grass and it was ready for a much needed mowing. When the inside work was done Michelle went outside to her tool shed and rolled out the mower. She gassed it, checked the oil, and gave the cord a tug. It wasn't long until she was enjoying the smell of new cut grass and the faint odor of the mower's exhaust.

Michelle really didn't know or care why she enjoyed these simple things, she just knew she did.

By early afternoon she had finished the yard work and went inside for a snack. When she had finished a bowl of soup and a tomato and cheddar sandwich she was tempted to continue working around the house but she decided not to do it all at once. She still wanted to have some energy left for whatever the evening might have in store. So, with that in mind, Michelle sat back in her recliner and forced herself to relax and to take a short nap. She remembered what had happened before when Paul had taken her to supper and she was not impressed with her conduct. This evening she determined, things would be different; she would try to be much better company.

After Michelle woke up from her nap she decided not to continue with anything else that would tire her any more. It was now mid-afternoon and she saw no reason to continue with work in the house or the yard. With that in mind she thumbed through several old magazines and quickly got bored. As she pondered what to do to entertain herself for a while before starting to get ready for the night out she went into one of the spare bedrooms where she had set up her music stand and kept her flute. Though she had not felt like playing for several weeks she did manage to stumble through some haunting melodies that were slow and in a minor key.

Not knowing quite what to expect for the evening, Michelle tried to dress so she would be acceptable in most potential situations. She had slipped on a pair of black wool blend slacks and topped them off with a plum colored blouse made of silk. Her earrings were white gold studs with a small black onyx set in the center. Adorning her slender neck was a delicate white gold chain that held a black onyx teardrop also set in white gold.

At four minutes after seven Michelle was on her front porch watering her geraniums when Paul pulled into her driveway. Looking his way when she heard him, she smiled, waved, and continued to water her plants. He got out of the car and walked over to her, arriving just as she was setting down the sprinkler can.

"Beautiful plants," he said, "almost as much as you." With that, Michelle blushed and smiled demurely.

"Thank you," she replied softly.

Michelle opened the door and stepped inside, inviting Paul to follow. He complied and after looking around, said, "Nice house."

"Thank you. Let me get my purse and I'll be ready to go," Michelle said as she started walking down the hall toward her bedroom. She disappeared and Paul was left alone in her large living room. While he was waiting he walked around looking at the numerous pictures that were hanging on the walls.

One that he found particularly intriguing depicted a rather large black and white cat sitting on a blue hassock. In the background, reaching toward a plant, was a very pale, almost raif-like, cat. He was still contemplating the painting when Michelle returned carrying her handbag." Like it?" she asked.

"Yes, very much," he answered. "It's different. Is it titled?"

"Not really." Michelle replied, "at least not by the artist but I call it 'Miss Kitty and Shadow'. It was painted by a friend of mine several years ago."

Paul took one last look at the picture and then turned to follow Michelle as she walked toward the front door. They stepped outside and she closed the door behind them. With a push and a quick turn of the knob she ascertained that the door was secure and they proceeded down the sidewalk toward Paul's car. He opened the door for her and then went around to the other side and got in. Backing into the street to turn around, they were soon headed toward whatever the evening would hold for them.

As they drove slowly down the street Paul asked her about the neighborhood, how long she had lived there, and numerous other questions about herself. Michelle answered each question readily and, even though much information was being revealed about herself and very little about him, she was enjoying being out of the house for some reason other than work. She was even elated that someone seemed to care enough to try to learn more about her. Michelle even interjected her answers to Paul's questions with comments about a particularly pretty patch of flowers or a nice house they passed.

Their conversation was still flowing easily when Paul suddenly said, "Where are we going?"

"I haven't the foggiest," Michelle replied. "I'm just riding along enjoying the scenery. Anyway, I thought you had everything figured out."

"Actually," Paul continued, "since we had Chinese last time, let's eat another country tonight."

"The whole thing, including the highways and parking lots?"

"Oh, no, we won't eat them. It takes them forever to get tender. We'll only eat the good stuff."

They both laughed and as if that light-hearted exchange had been a signal, something happened inside Michelle's head but this time it was something good. She knew that tonight would not end like their last encounter had.

They continued across town talking less than they had been but they were communicating more. As a subtle invitation Michelle put her left hand on the console. She was still looking out the window moments later when she felt Paul's hand close around it and give it a light squeeze.

Michelle responded by squeezing his finger with her thumb.

Michelle was no longer looking out her window. Now, she was facing straight ahead and she had her eyes closed. Her mind started to relax and she was simply enjoying the touch of another human being. "It's been so long," she thought, "this feels so good. I've missed it."

Paul's voice jarred her back to reality when he said, "Here we are at the country of the night, Luigi's Café Italiano, I hope their roads and parking lots are microwavable." They were still laughing as he pulled into a parking place.

Michelle waited for Paul to come around to open the door for her. When he had done so, she swung her legs around and extended her right hand so he could further assist her. The slight tug Paul gave her as she stood up was irrelevant in her mind, it wasn't forceful and she wasn't an invalid but the touch of his hand, that was what she craved. Michelle had nearly forgotten how it felt to have another person touch her and she suddenly found herself fighting off distant stirrings of loneliness.

Paul closed the door and they started toward the restaurant entrance. As they walked Michelle let her hand brush his and he responded just as she hoped he would. His hand closed around hers and gave it a playful squeeze.

At the corner of the building was a small garden with multicolored petunias growing in it. She deftly steered Paul away from the path toward the entrance and started walking beside the restaurant toward the flowers. "Let's look at these little guys before we go in," she said cheerily.

As they paused to contemplate the flowers, Michelle bent down and ran her fingers very lightly over a bloom. It was very soft and delicate with a faintly sweet fragrance. "Aren't they beautiful?" she said quietly.

"Yes," Paul answered, "they are."

The pastel blooms were beautiful and they had a fresh, clean scent but that wasn't the real reason Michelle wanted to look more closely at them. She was simply using looking at the flowers as a ploy to keep her hand in his for a few extra moments. Suddenly she had a thought that simultaneously slightly unnerved her and also made her chuckle inwardly. "What if he thinks I'm some clingy bitch who tries to stick to a man like already chewed bubble gum does to a shoe sole in the summertime?" Mustering her courage, she slipped her fingers out of his hand and feigned adjusting a button on her blouse. With that, she said, "Shall we?" and started toward the door.

As they stepped inside they were greeted by the hostess who ushered them to a corner booth. They sat opposite each other and casually perused the menus the hostess had left. Michelle held her menu in front of her as if she were sincerely trying to decide what to order and to the casual observer that's what it appeared she was doing. Unseen was her mind that was traveling at light speed. Michelle still had not recovered from the touch of another person and, though she was elated, she was also slightly confused as to why it had felt so good. Her spirits that had been sagging for so long now seemed to be soaring. She felt slightly giddy at the possibilities of what the night might have in store for her.

A strange voice jolted her back to reality. "Good evening. I'm Rob and I'll be your server tonight."

Looking up from the menu she saw a medium built man in his early twenties standing there smiling. Sudden impulse made her want to say, "This is Paul and I'm Michelle and we'll be your patrons for the evening," but prudence kept her from it.

The voice continued, "Have you made your selections, yet?" That's when it dawned on her that she had been sitting there for several minutes holding the menu without reading it.

As a pained expression came over her face she heard Paul say, "Give us a few more minutes, please."

Rob departed and Michelle began to seriously study the menu. When he returned in a few minutes they were both ready with their choices. Rob wrote them down and disappeared through a set of louvered swinging doors.

Michelle and Paul continued their small talk and though Paul had his hands on the table, she kept hers in her lap. After an expected wait of several minutes Rob returned with their food and placed it before them. Only then did Michelle venture to put a hand on the table and that was done with a certain shyness. Though she wanted very much to continue playing the finger games they had started earlier, she was now reluctant to do so.

As they ate their conversation slowed. They stayed mostly with the trivial subjects since it was apparent that neither of them had any real desire to settle world issues and they found laughter in places that it would normally have been well hidden.

Communication seemed to be taking place whether they talked or not. It appeared to Michelle that feelings were being exchanged, that both she and Paul were on the same wavelength. Sensing this, she decided to let her feelings flow but to proceed with utmost caution—she hoped. "I've been there before," she thought, "and the pleasure just isn't worth the pain."

Paul continued to eat at a regular rhythm but the time between Michelle's bites had begun to lengthen. Instead of eating, she had begun to toy with her food as if she were totally preoccupied with other thoughts, and she was. He finally noticed that Michelle had nearly stopped eating. He stopped and put his fork down. "Are you okay?" he inquired.

"Oh, yes," she replied. "I feel fine and the food is very good. I just sort of drifted away."

"Oh. Well, you did have a far away look and when you stopped eating I thought you might not feel well."

Michelle smiled at him. "I feel the best I've felt in ages, thank you," she said softly.

Rob returned to see if everything was satisfactory and then slipped quietly away. They each returned to eating and more small talk. Their talk was getting smaller, or at least less frequent. It finally dawned on them that they had both stopped eating and they had even stopped talking. They were just sitting there gazing into each other's eyes as they communicated. Michelle became aware that her breathing had slowed and deepened.

This rare moment that can only be understood if experienced and never, ever explained, was brought to a rather abrupt, unromantic ending when Rob said, "Anyone care for dessert?"

Trying not to let a totally embarrassing moment get completely out of control, Michelle said, "Yes. I really would like a piece of key lime pie, please."

Rob replied, "Okay, and you, sir."

"Let me think about it for a moment, please."

As Rob departed Michelle said, "Don't you want some dessert? They look delicious."

As Paul looked into her eyes he said barely loud enough for her to hear, "I'd love some dessert but what I really would like to have is not on the menu." Caught completely off guard, Michelle said with all the innocence of a small child, "And, what's that?"

Now it was Paul's turn to be caught off guard and he almost laughed out loud. As he put his hand on top of hers he did not speak, he simply mouthed one word, "You."

Michelle just sat there motionless feeling his hand on hers. A single thought raced through her head and she hoped there were no cracks in the floor close enough for her to fall through. She could already visualize the headline on the front of the Enquirer, "Woman in coma able to eat and talk." "What a moron he must think I am," she thought. Her mind raced on, "Does he really think I'm that desirable?" However, that thought made her tremble ever so slightly.

Michelle remembered similar situations with Roger from once upon a time. Though the thought that Paul found her attractive excited her, she could not forget what had happened the last time someone else had said those things to her. These thoughts tended to unnerve her just a little and she had to struggle to push them aside. "Why be so concerned about this?" she thought, "we hardly know each other." However, she had to admit that his hand really did feel good on hers.

She was much relieved when Rob returned with her dessert. Now she could move her hand away from Paul's and not have to risk either an explanation or looking stupid. Michelle took a small bite and savored it. "Very good," she said, "want a bite?"

Paul nodded and said, "No, I'll just sit here and watch you eat."

Michelle was in no hurry to finish eating. Not only was the pie quite good, she was trying to collect her thoughts. Inside her head, if not a battle, at least a fire fight was being waged between the euphoric feeling of the moment that a man found her desirable and old memories that made her feel totally inadequate and undesirable. Michelle had no idea which side would be victorious and she decided that she really didn't care about the outcome. Whichever way it ended would be fine with her, she would simply savor the moment.

She continued to nibble on her dessert and Paul continued to watch her. His gaze made her slightly self conscious but she decided not to let it bother her. She finally finished the last bite and put down her fork. "That was very good," she said, "you should have had some." Taking a sip of water, she said, "I'll be right back." Then she got up and walked toward the powder room.

As Michelle walked away from him, Paul watched her move. "She must take a lot of exercise," he thought, "she looks very firm and bouncy." Then he noticed something else that had so far escaped him, Michelle was ever so slightly bowlegged. "She could probably outrun me," he mused and he was right about that, she probably could have.

In just a few minutes Michelle returned and sat down. Having carefully flossed and reapplied her lipstick she was no more confident about smiling and talking. Though she had no idea in which direction the evening was headed, she had no desire to be a turn-off due to something stuck between her teeth. Deep down she hoped Paul felt the same way.

As she sat back down Paul said that he was next and he got up and departed. He returned shortly and asked if she were ready to leave. Michelle nodded and got up. As they walked toward the door Rob saw them leaving and waved. They waved back and then stepped outside into the parking lot. There it occurred to her that Paul must have paid for supper during her absence.

The sun had nearly set while they had been inside and the cooler evening air felt great to them. They walked toward his car without speaking, each caught up in just enjoying the evening. They went to her side of the car and paused while Paul opened the door. As she started to get in Paul suddenly whispered softly, "Wait." Michelle paused to see what was wrong and when she did so, he leaned forward and kissed her very lightly right on the tip of her nose. His action seemed to be as much of a surprise to him as it had been to her.

Neither pursued the moment, mainly because of the openness of a very private situation. She got in the car and, after he closed the door, Paul went around to the other side of the car and got in. He looked at her and said, "Now what?"

"How about a walk in the park?" Michelle replied. "That sounds like fun," he responded as he backed out of the parking place. Paul pulled into the street and headed toward Mimosa Park on the edge of town.

As he drove, Michelle looked out the window at the lengthening shadows. Without turning to face him she said quietly, "Thanks for supper, it was very good. Maybe we should come back and eat that country again, minus the roads and parking lots, of course."

"Of course," Paul said as they both laughed.

The park wasn't crowded when they arrived which was just what each of them had been privately hoping. They got out of the car and walked toward one of the paved nature trails. Their hands brushed as they walked and just a moment later their fingers were interwined as they continued slowly along. Being away from large areas of concrete and pavement made it even cooler than they thought it would be and they found it to be a most pleasant atmosphere. There was just enough breeze to stir the leaves. The night bugs had started their evening symphony that was added to by the calls of the few evening birds.

Neither of them had spoken for several minutes, they were seemingly entranced by the sounds and feelings of their surroundings. Though they had not been previously walking very rapidly, they slowed even more. Without realizing what she was doing, Michelle laid her head against Paul's shoulder. When she did this, Paul turned her hand loose and put his arm around her slender waist, pulling her even closer to him. She responded by putting her arm around him.

There were some mimosa trees in bloom growing along the pathway and the sweet smell of their flowers only added to the ambiance of the evening. One of the trees had its branches growing over the walkway and under this tree they stopped and listened to the night as they inhaled the sweet smelling air.

As they stood there just enjoying the moment, Paul suddenly turned toward Michelle and put his other arm around her. He pulled her tightly against him and laid his cheek against the top of her head. Her hair was very soft and smelled fresh and clean. Michelle responded by tucking her head on his right shoulder and putting both her arms around him.

As they stood there Paul started to sway slightly from side to side and Michelle followed his lead. It was almost as if they were doing some sort of dance except that their feet were not moving. As they swayed there Paul became aware of the light pressure on his chest from Michelle's firm breasts. He held her even tighter and she reciprocated by pulling him closer. Their eyes were closed and neither had spoken for quite some time. There seemed to be a mutual understanding that the moment would disappear forever if either spoke.

Michelle could not believe how good it felt to be held like this. Part of her feared that Paul would loosen his hold on her or say something and ruin the moment while another part of her was becoming very concerned and at least a little frightened.

There was a battle beginning to take place inside her head. One side was telling her to throw caution to the wind and go for the gusto. The other side was whispering very quietly, reminding her of how her involvement with men always turned out. She had no idea which side was right, what the outcome would be, or why. All Michelle knew was that this felt so good. With that in mind, she tried to hold Paul even tighter.

Though the moment truly was wonderful and Michelle was totally absorbed by it, her mind started to wander. She began to think about how it would be if they were glued in this position and she could not decide if that would be a good or bad thing. The more she thought about this scenario the more her mind drifted into how they would be able to do everything that needed to be done. As Michelle visualized trying to mow the grass like this, she got tickled. "That would be a strange tango," she thought, "even with a dip at the end." It no longer mattered to her that she desperately needed to be touched in this manner and as she tried to hold back her laughter, she started to shake. Finally, unable to control it any longer, Michelle began to laugh. Knowing that she had spoiled the moment for both of them, she quietly said, "I'm sorry."

Paul loosened his hold on her and took a small step backward. When Michelle felt him do this she relaxed and also stepped back. They were still holding hands and Paul was wondering what had happened to her. He had been struggling to keep his feelings in check and had been fighting a losing battle. He wondered if Michelle had felt his futile effort and had gotten tickled over it. As he was just about to be embarrassed over his inability to better control his passions and apologize to her, Michelle looked up at him and said in a soft, sheepish voice, "I really am sorry but I just couldn't help it. I started thinking about how we would do stuff if we were glued in this position and I was dealing with it pretty well until I pictured us trying to mow the grass. It was sort of an elongated tango and that's when I lost it."

Paul just stood there looking her in the eyes as she spoke. Finally, after Michelle had asked him to please forgive her, he once again pulled her to him and held her close. Then, as he visualized what she had told him, he also got tickled and chuckled quietly. "I can see how that would be a sight to behold," he said, then added, "what about washing the car or cooking? What if you tried to sew something? Wouldn't that be a hoot?" He held her even tighter and continued to laugh. Michelle was greatly relieved that he wasn't upset with her for destroying the moment and she snuggled even closer against him.

"I really am sorry," she whispered.

"Forget it," he responded, "we'll have other moments like that, I hope."

Michelle had been doing just fine controlling herself until Paul added the "I hope." Upon hearing that, she trembled slightly and was acutely aware that he had felt it because his arms tightened around her even more.

Though she was definitely enjoying what she was experiencing, Michelle had become aware of caution flags that were waving inside her head. Paul's statement that he hoped they would have other special moments made her happy and filled her with excited anticipation just thinking of the possibilities. However, she also too well remembered how her other affairs of the heart had always turned out. Michelle knew she wasn't rich, nor did she consider herself to be exciting and she certainly did not consider herself to be beautiful. Being aware of her imperfections made her wonder, even as Paul held her close, whether this was a smart thing to do or not.

Michelle wanted very much to love someone and to be loved in return by that person but the last lesson she had learned about love had not been a kind one and this was the reason she found herself in this dilemma. Not wanting Paul to turn her loose but yet not being totally comfortable with what was going on inside her head, she whispered, "Let's walk some more."

"Okay," he replied and they unwrapped their arms from each other. They once again started their slow stroll along the nature trail. Now, just holding hands, Michelle felt a little more at ease. She knew she needed time to think about what she was feeling and thinking. Pushing all these thoughts from her mind, Michelle said, "What a beautiful evening."

"Yes," Paul replied, "and you are, too."

Instead of responding, Michelle pretended to be lost in thought. She wasn't quite sure what to say so she just continued to walk, feeling her hand being squeezed ever so gently by Paul. As they continued their slow journey along the trail Michelle wondered why Paul appeared to be interested in pursuing a relationship with her. Why had he made his earlier statement comparing her to the evening? "Do I really want to get another knife in the back and go through all the same old feelings again?" she wondered.

Having been to the park numerous times in the past, Michelle knew where the trails went. She also knew that if they strayed from the trail and went to their right for about forty yards that they would come to a cluster of mimosa trees surrounding a small gazebo. It would be a much more secluded spot and, if no one else were there, they would also have a place to sit. Without fully understanding why, she suddenly veered to her right and gave Paul's hand a gentle tug. He followed without speaking and in just a few yards they were in much darker shadows as they walked silently across the neatly cropped grass. "Damn," thought Michelle, "I wonder if he thinks I'm just another cheap floozy who can't wait to be in the dark with a man?" Pushing this thought from her mind, she continued to lead Paul toward the gazebo.

After they had walked over half way to their destination Michelle suddenly stopped. Paul took another two steps before he realized she had intended to stop. When he turned toward her he saw that Michelle had her head tilted back, gazing up at the night sky. In the dim light he could make out a big smile on her face like a child who had never witnessed a really dark place to view the stars. He stepped behind her and put his arms lightly around her waist. Paul felt Michelle relax against him as he joined her in looking up into the heavens.

Neither had spoken since they left the path and neither seemed to be in any hurry to do so. Michelle put her hands on Paul's and they just leaned against each other as they continued to look upward. After several minutes in this position Paul moved his hands and she felt him turning her around to face him. He pulled her close to his chest and, since her face was still tilted upward, Paul decided to follow up on the parking lot kiss that had been on the tip of her nose. As he pulled her to him she felt soft but at the same time firm and though he certainly wasn't cold, the warmth of her body melted into him and felt good. He leaned forward slightly and kissed Michelle lightly on the tip of her nose again. Then on her forehead, several times from one side of her face to the other. Michelle still had her eyes open but she closed them when Paul moved his lips down and kissed her softly on her eyelids. She trembled slightly and began to hope that he wouldn't stop there, and he didn't. He left a trail of kisses down her left cheek to the corner of her waiting lips but he didn't touch them. He simply moved to the right side of her face and started kissing down that cheek once again stopping at the corner of her mouth. Then he kissed the tip of her nose again.

Michelle wanted and needed more. About the time Paul was nibbling lightly on the tip of her nose for the second time, she put her hands behind his head and pulled his lips down to hers. His arms tightened around her and she reciprocated by holding him closer. Their kiss started lightly at first but became more of a kiss of passion as the tips of their tongues touched. Paul dragged the tip of his tongue along the inside of Michelle's upper lip and felt her body tremble from head to toe. After two or three minutes of tongue exploration he pulled back from her. Michelle tucked her head on his shoulder and, as he held her close, Paul could feel her chest heaving against him as she tried to regain her composure. Finally, her breathing became slower and at a more regular rhythm. "I think we better walk some more," he said as he loosened his arms from around her.

Michelle hesitated before she let her arms relax. Without looking at him and almost embarrassed, she said softly, "I think you're right." They continued their slow walk in the dark toward the gazebo. As they approached it Michelle was really hoping that no one else would be there. This time her wish was granted. They climbed the two steps from the grass to the floor and walked around inside the railing looking at the different views of the darkened park as the moved. Though the moon was late in its first quarter it was still bright enough to cast soft shadows on one side of the octagonal sitting area. It was in this shadowed area that Paul sat down and pulled Michelle gently down until she was sitting on his lap. He had his arms around her waist and she responded by resting her head on his shoulder.

There was still silence between them as they sat there mesmerized listening to the night creatures making their beautiful music. Michelle put her lips very close to Paul's left ear and said in a whisper that only he could hear, "I'm sorry I was such a bitch when we went out a few weeks ago. I didn't mean to be but sometimes my mind gets very cluttered and my thoughts don't make any sense at all. I'm glad you didn't give up on me."

When she had finished whispering these words, and since her lips were already close to his ear, she started kissing it very softly. Then she tugged lightly on the lobe with her teeth. Michelle wasn't quite sure what she wanted Paul to do but when she nibbled on his ear he had tightened his arms around her. Suddenly, before she realized what she was doing, Michelle planted a deep, passionate kiss right in the center of Paul's ear and ended it with a flick of her tongue as she felt a shudder course through his body. Feeling that response, she started to slowly tease him once more. His arms tightened around her even more and she could feel pressure on the side swell of her left breast.

Just for a moment Michelle struggled with whether or not to stop teasing his ear in hopes that his hand would venture no farther or whether to continue teasing him and hope that he would continue to explore her body. She didn't have to wait long for the resolution to her dilemma. As her tongue continued to trace the curve of Paul's ear, his hand moved slightly upward and gently cupped the entire softness of her breast. As he lightly fondled her he found the erect nipple and softly rolled it between his finger and thum. Then, ever so gently, he tugged on it. Michelle's concentration on his ear had been shattered and she just sat there relishing the touch of another human being. Paul's touch was so tender and sensual that she wasn't sure she would say "No" if he tried to lay her down on the picnic table they were sitting by. She wanted him to unbutton her blouse and put his hand inside it. As if he had been able to read her thoughts she felt his fingers release her breast and fumble briefly with a strategically located button. "I've got to stop him now," Michelle thought but she couldn't bring herself to say or do anything except tighten her arms around him. Michelle felt his warm hand close around the thin material of the bra and she trembled again. She had worn a bra that hooked in the front and in just a matter of moments she felt Paul's fingers undoing it. "It's too late now," she thought as she felt the thin material separate and her breasts escape their restraint.

Michelle knew her breathing had changed perceptibly and when Paul's strong hand cupped the soft, bare flesh a low moan escaped her before she could stifle it. No longer was her head on his shoulder, she had tilted it back as she tried to get enough air and to thrust her breasts forward in a subconscious act of submission. Michelle felt another button being undone and her blouse pulled open even more. The night air rushed across her damp chest and she tingled with anticipation. Paul had started to kiss her throat and he was slowly working his way down toward her chest. Michelle hoped she knew where his exploring lips would end up and she didn't have to wait long to find out. She felt his breath on her left nipple, then, the entire end of her breast was engulfed in a white hot mouth that made her tremble uncontrollably with excitement and desire. Michelle wanted to say something, she wasn't quite sure just what, but something. However, her mouth was so dry and her brain so overloaded with sensations that nothing would come out. Paul's mouth made soft sucking sounds like a hungry baby as he moved from one nipple to the other. He didn't just suck them, he licked them, he kissed them, he flogged them with his tongue while keeping the end in his mouth and rolling the nipple.

Michelle had become oblivious to her surroundings and she knew that whatever Paul wanted to do, she was game. His lips and tongue had just finished another assault on her right nipple and she was vaguely aware that her left hand had started sliding down his chest to what she knew would be waiting when the reverie was broken.

"Here, Rusty. Come here, boy," broke both the silence and the passion of the moment. Paul and Michelle were both jarred back to reality instantly as they looked in the direction of the sound. They could barely make out the shape of another person about thirty yards away and a small, light-coloredred dog that was frolicking close by. Not knowing which way the person was going next, Michelle fumbled to rehook her bra and get her blouse buttoned. They sat there quietly trying to compose themselves as they waited to see what would happen.

While they were getting their clothes straightened out the dog continued to approach the gazebo. When it was about ten yards away they could see it well enough to tell that it was medium size and it appeared to be a part collie mix. It sensed their presence but wasn't sure what to do about it. With tail wagging, it slowly approached the steps. The dog's owner was also coming toward them as he continued to call and whistle. Just as Paul started to speak to the dog it gave a low "chuff", turned, and bounded back toward the shadow figure that was calling it.

"Maybe we should continue our walk," Michelle said in a low voice. She viewed Paul's nodded agreement with mixed emotions. What he had been doing to her had felt so good and it had been much too long since anyone had touched her. Not wanting to seem like she was an easy conquest, Michelle got up and walked toward the steps. Paul followed and put his left arm around her as they descended the stairway to the grass. The stranger and his dog were no where to be seen or heard and there was no sound except the night creatures making their nocturnal music. As they started their slow walk across the grass, Michelle whispered, "It's been a fun evening."

"Yes, it has," Paul replied quietly, "I know it has to end but it really has been nice. Would you like to do it again sometime soon? We could go to a movie or just continue our tour of the park, or both."

"Actually," Michelle replied, "I would like that very much. Do you have any idea what time it is?"

Paul squinted at his watch in the dim light then answered, "It appears to be pushing eleven thirty."

"Maybe we should set sail back toward the car," Michelle said, "I had a busy week and a busy day. Besides, at midnight I turn into a pumpkin."

"We don't want that to happen," Paul replied, "there may be someone out here with a pie fetish."

Michelle laughed. Though she really didn't want the evening to end, she knew she needed to have time to think about everything that had happened. The entire evening had been such fun for her but, deep down, she was also troubled. The things Paul had said and done to her, she had enjoyed, even needed, but she could not escape the memories of how these things always started out, or how they always, without fail, ended. Michelle knew she simply needed to get away from Paul for a while so she could clear her mind and try to put things in perspective. As much as she wanted to throw all inhibitions and caution to the wind, she was more than slightly unnerved at the prospect of putting her emotions in the hands of another person. As they continued their slow journey toward the parking lot Michelle put her arm around Paul and said, "I guess we better call it an evening, though it was a fun one."

Their walk to Paul's car had been an intentionally slow one, more of a directional dance than a walk. When they finally arrived at the parking lot, instead of getting directly in the car, Paul leaned against it and held Michelle gently around the waist. He swayed slowly from side to side and she followed his lead. Finally, with a long sigh, Michelle whispered, "I really better go."

"I know."

Paul fumbled for his car key and opened the door for her. Michelle got in and reached over to unlock the other door. Paul got in, started the engine, and rolled slowly across the parking lot and into the street. Michelle put her hand on his seat and pushed her fingers slightly under his leg. Though they rode in silence to her house, they were still communicating.

Paul turned down the street where she lived and said, "Almost there with time to spare. Bet you would make a cute pumpkin."

"Just don't make me into a pie. I burned my hand on the oven when I was little girl and I'm still very careful around them."

Reaching her driveway, Paul turned in and stopped behind her car. He got out and, as he was coming around to help her, she opened the door. Michelle put out her hand which Paul took and gave her a slight tug to help her up. She stood up and lightly sagged against his chest. "Thanks," she said, "this has been the nicest evening I've had in a long time."

"I rather enjoyed it myself," Paul whispered, "let's do it again sometime soon."

"Okay. Call me. Sometimes I'm hard to catch, as you discovered, but I do return calls. Sometimes it just takes a while."

"I'll buzz you next week if that's okay."

"Next week is going to be hectic but we can give it some thought."

Michelle pushed herself gently away from Paul's chest and, taking him by the hand, started walking toward the front door. He followed and in just a moment they stepped up on the front porch. Michelle found her key and opened the door, then she stepped back toward Paul. "I'll talk to you soon," she said as she gave his hand a squeeze. Then, she opened the screen door and stepped inside. Michelle turned and gave him a big smile, "I had a fabulous time. Thanks. Goodnight."

"I did, too. I'll call you. Goodnight." Paul turned and started down the walk as Michelle watched him. He was getting into his car before she finally closed the door.

Without turning on a light she made her way across the living room and down the hall to her bedroom where she pulled the bathroom door nearly closed before she turned on the light. After her eyes adjusted to the dim light she pushed the door open wider and let mre indirect light flow into hanger and hung it over the closet door. Michelle kicked off her shoes and undid her slacks, then leaned against the chair as she pulled them off. She placed them on a hanger and also hung them on the trim across the top of the closet door next to her blouse, then she went into the bathroom to wash her face. When that task was completed she applied a light coat of cream to her face, brushed her teeth, and finished getting ready for bed.

As she lay in bed in the quiet of night Michelle replayed the events of the evening. She thought at length about what Paul had done to her while they were at the gazebo and she knew that the dog had most likely saved her from making a fool of herself. It became increasingly apparent to her that she wanted and needed more of that and that one evening in the near future they would be at her house or his house and there wouldn't be a dog to start barking. "Should I have invited him in?" she wondered, "he could be here right now driving me wild." As that thought was going through her mind Michelle became aware that she had unconsciously moved her feet apart. Realizing what she had done and what it meant, she felt her face flush with embarrassment. "Damn," she said out loud, "I guess that's what I've been missing. Maybe I am a trollop, at least at heart." After a few moments Michelle continued talking out loud to herself in the dark, "One day soon I know it will happen. Should I hold out and play hard to get? Maybe I should let him chase me in a chaste way. That's it, the chaste chase." At that, she laughed. "That's a joke. If it hadn't been for that damn dog he would have probably peeled me like a banana and banged me like a drum on the picnic table. Chaste chase, my ass, and he knows it."

Michelle stopped talking to herself and tried to relax as she listened to the rhythmic ticking of her striking clock. "Do I really want to go through this again?" she wondered. "I don't seem to ever learn. Sometimes I think my back must have 'knife holder' written on it. If I go through with this, I know I'll lose in the end. Don't know how, don't know why, I just know I'll lose. Is my heart up to getting smashed again? Why do I have to take this affair of the heart bull as such a personal thing?"

As Michelle continued to think about her potential situation she noticed that she was having more and more trouble collecting her thoughts. Her breathing smoothed out and she felt herself relaxing. She opened her eyes and peeked at the digital clock. It was 3:21 and she noticed that she had worked the sheet off of her and that her shoulders were cool. Pulling the cover back up to her neck, she snuggled among the pillows and was soon gone again to the world of sleep.

The next time Michelle woke up the room was filled with a very subdued light that told her Sunday morning really had arrived. Not wanting to get up quite so early, she positioned a pillow over her eyes and eventually drifted back to sleep.

When she opened her eyes again the room was filled with light and she decided not to fight it any longer. As she finally fot up she glanced at her striking clock. It showed twenty minutes after eight. "Good," she thought, "I can have breakfast and get ready for church without having to hurry." Slipping on her bedroom shoes, Michelle stepped into the bathroom to get her robe and to splash some cold water on her face. Now that she was really awake she wondered about what to do for breakfast. Only slightly hungry, she decided on a bowl of cereal and an orange. As she prepared her food she found herself wondering what Paul was having, if anything. Was he even out of bed? Does he like cereal? Does he have to eat something animal before he considers it a meal? As she ate, Michelle couldn't get all these questions about him out of her mind. She struggled with the question of how she should proceed with what appeared again to be the beginning of letting someone into her life. She had always thought someone would want her but after the breakup of her marriage she had begun to wonder. She continued to nibble as she found herself simultaneously excited and, yet, petrified at this possibility. Michelle finally became so engrossed with these thoughts that she stopped even attempting to eat. Letting the spoon clink on the side of the bowl, she sat there staring into space as she continued to ponder her situation.

"Why can't I view this as the game it is?" she wondered. "It's just a game, it really has no meaning but I always seem to take it seriously even though no one else does. I know what will happen so why go through it again? I guess there's really not that much difference in the optimist and the fool, neither has learned that it's not going to work out but for some unknown reason each one keeps trying. I wonder if my heart can stand another smashing because this time will be a good one."

Michelle picked up the spoon and started once again to eat her cereal. She finished what was left, washed out the bowl, and placed it on the counter. She was unsure why these thoughts troubled her so. In the back of her mind she had a foreboding feeling that she should simply play it safe and let the love games become ancient history.

As Michelle walked back down the hall toward the bedroom she untied the belt on her robe. It draped open slightly and she ran her hands over her stomach and felt the bottom of her ribs. From there her hands trailed upward to her breasts and paused. She touched her nipples and found them slightly sensitive. Remembering last night and how they had gotten this way made her shudder lightly. "I want someone to touch and someone to touch me," she thought. "I'm screwed. Whichever way I go, I'll lose. If I don't go with this, I'll miss some really fun things with someone I really like. If I do go with this, I'll end up with another knife in the back and something tells me that this knife will be by far the biggest and the sharpest. I know better, I'm just screwed."

Michelle walked into the bathroom and brushed her teeth. The entire situation continued to trouble her. She wanted to trust Paul and to care about him but she also wanted him to feel the same way about her. Though she was by no means desperate, Michelle simply thought it would be nice to love and to be loved. Glancing at the clock she knew that there was no reason for her to hurry. "I need to go for a run," she thought, "maybe that will help clear my thoughts."

Michelle put the robe on the bed and gathered up her running gear. After dressing, she sat down on the bedroom floor and did some stretching exercises. The more she stretched, the better she felt. Her thoughts started to drift into the anticipated run and that relaxed her even more. She finally stood up and sinished stretching. Now, all the morning kinks were gone and she was ready for the streets. Michelle slipped out the back door and hid the house key under an out of the way flower pot, She then walked around to the front of the house and down the driveway into the street.

As she headed away from her house she started to become more a part of this activity that she had done since she was a little girl. After about a quarter of a mile she noticed her breathing changed and she felt even more relaxed. As Michelle glided along she listened to the birds chirping and saw an early rising butterfly sail across the street in front of her and she watched it perch on a bright flower. A few people were out walking and she noticed that everyone seemed to be in a good mood. "How could they feel any other way on this magnificient morning?" she wondered.

Michelle felt a big smile come across her face as she ran. It was something that happened quite often because of her fondness for this activity. She waved at an elderly couple walking a small, brown dog. As she reached the halfway point she increased her pace very slightly. After a two minute period at that pace she slowed to her normal speed. Her house came into sight and she knew that another enjoyable play period was nearly over. Upon reaching her driveway Michelle slowed to a walk and continued out the street past her house while her body returned to normal. As she walked she continued to enjoy the peacefulness of the morning. When her breathing slowed Michelle's thoughts began to return to what was troubling her. Her breathing had nearly returned to normal when she turned and started walking back toward her house. "I know better," she thought, "I just don't ever seem to learn. If I do this again, how high will the price be for losing one more time?"

When she returned from church Michelle removed her dress and hung it on the top of the closet door. After putting on a pair of summer weight sweat pants and a tee shirt she pondered what she should eat. In spite of the beauty of the day and the thoughts of the recently heard sermon, Michelle was still troubled. As she puttered in the kitchen she had trouble concentrating on preparing her food. Thoughts of how other men had treated her in the past kept rearing their ugly heads to haunt her. She kept thinking about the events of the evening before and she knew she wanted more but as she wondered about those things, she became more and more agitated. She became acutely aware of the battle that had begun to rage inside her head and knew that the tension on the mainspring of her biological clock was becoming less and less with each passing day.

Walking into the living room she sat down in her big recliner and pushed it back. Michelle closed her eyes and let her thoughts wander. She pictured herself in a family setting with Paul beside her. After she fantasized about that scene for a while she added a small, dark haired little boy toddling about. Then she added a little dark haired girl playing with him. "A family," she thought, "of my own."

As suddenly as the idyllic scenes had materialized they were gone and were replaced by a deep feeling of sadness that she neither understood nor was able to fight off. Thinking about how these things had always turned out for her in the past, Michelle felt large tears form in her eyes. "I wish love wasn't such a personal thing for me," she thought. "Why can't I view it as the adult bed game it is instead of thinking it means something and always ending up with a knife in the back? What a dumb bitch I must be if I go through this again. Whatever happens to me, I deserve it for being stupid. I should know better."

The tears that had been forming in her eyes had finally grown so large that they could no longer hold their position. Almost simultaneously they slid down her cheeks and landed quietly on her neck. "Whichever way I decide," she thought, "I'll lose. It's just a matter of how much." That was the last thing she remembered as she slipped silently into a troubled sleep.

About a half hour later Michelle roused from her nap. The same thoughts that had troubled her earlier were still with her. She shifted slightly in the chair and tried once again to relax. Thoughts of how love should be kept running through her mind but they were always closely followed by the thoughts of how it really is. Her foreboding feeling simply would not go away. "If I try to have a go at this, against my better judgment, I'll deserve whatever happens. I know better," she kept thinking, "if I do, when this one blows up, it's going to be a bad one. I know I won't come out unscathed but I wonder if I'll even survive." With that thought Michelle drifted back into her troubled sleep.

Michelle awoke with a start and looked around, then she realized the phone was ringing. She picked it up and mumbled, "Hello."

"Michelle, it's me, Paul."

"Oh. Hi," she said as she tried to collect her thoughts.

"Did I wake you? You sound sleepy."

"I was kicked back in my big chair relaxing. I haven't done late hours in a long time so I'm sort of out of practice."

"It was a little later than I normally stay up, too, but it was still fun. Sorry I kept you out so late."

"It really wasn't that late. I guess we're just a couple of old fogies. I did have a great time but I ate too much and I'm paying for that today."

They chatted on for a while and Michelle overcame her initial grogginess and their conversation had an easy flow to it. After they had talked for about twenty minutes Paul asked, "Want to do something Wednesday evening? It would help break up the work week."

Paying no attention to the distant voices inside her head, Michelle replied without hesitation, "I'd love to. What do you have in mind?"

"I don't have anything special in mind. We could go somewhere for supper, then do something, or, we could get together after we eat. We could go for another walk in the park or go over to the mall and people watch. I don't want to be out very late since it's a work night."

"That sounds good to me," Michelle replied, "I guess the possibilities are mindless, or, is it endless?"

Paul chuckled. One of the things he was really starting to like about Michelle was her tangential answers that often caught him off guard. "Mindless is probably a lot more appropriate, especially for us. I'll call you Tuesday evening or at work Wednesday."

"That's fine. I'll talk with you then."

"Great. 'Bye."

Michelle hung up the phone and once more tried to relax. Now she was even more disturbed than she had been. Though she enjoyed the way being with Paul made her feel and she really wanted to see him again, she sensed a deep feeling of uneasiness. As usual, the recurring thoughts darted through her mind causing Michelle to say to herself, "When he stabs me in the back I'll have no one to blame but myself. I know it's coming. It always does and I know better but this time I'll deserve it for being a fool." She closed her eyes and continued to dwell on what she some way knew would have catastrophic consequences for her. With a long sigh, she finally said to herself, "Get ready back. Here comes another sharp knife headed straight for you and this one will be the worst of all."

Michelle was acutely aware of the toll that the cumulative effects of life's blows had taken on her. She had always thought, even as a young girl, that there would be someone who would care whether or not she lived or died during the day, however, certain events had come to pass that now made her begin to doubt this concept. She was well aware that she was in great danger of letting herself put too much emphasis on this budding relationship. "If I proceed with this, I'm not sure I have the energy to deal with it when he leaves," she thought. Yet, her desire to love and to be loved caused her to lean in the direction of becoming involved--- just one last time. With that thought in mind, Michelle got up and went outside to sit on the porch.

Just as he had said he would do, Paul called her on Tuesday evening so they could finalize their plans for the next day. They decided to go out for a light supper and then to take whatever came their way.

Michelle was sitting on the front porch when Paul arrived at a few minutes after seven the next evening. He got out of his car and walked over and sat down beside her on the porch swing. "If your neighbors are nosy, you'll soon be the talk of the town," he said.

"I guess so but I really don't care. I doubt if they do, either. All my neighbors seem to be very relaxed. They're all friendly and helpful but nobody seems very interested in running anyone else's business."

"That's refreshing. Shall we go? I'm getting hungry." "I'm ready," Michelle said as she got up to close the front door. As they started down the front walk toward Paul's car his hand brushed hers and she felt a slight tingle shoot down her spine when, just a moment later, he took her hand in his. As they continued toward the car Michelle thought, "This shouldn't feel this good. I'm in trouble already."

As they drove across town toward The Greenhouse, a small restaurant that specialized in salads, Michelle's mind was racing. An entire gamut of feelings rushed through her from sheer ecstasy to a deep, unexplained fear.

"You're very quiet this evening."

Paul's voice jarred her back to reality from her inner war. "Sorry," she replied, "I was just letting my thoughts wander and I think they ended up lost in life's high grass."

"Nothing wrong with that unless they get really lost and can't find their way back home."

Michelle put her hand on the seat between them and Paul did what she hoped he would do, he put his hand around hers. Though her thoughts had made her anxious, feeling his touch made her feel more secure and she started to relax. "How was your day," she asked. After this opening into conversation, they engaged in small talk for the rest of their ride.

$IWHU WKH\ KDG fiQiVKHG WKHiU VDODGV, DQG ViQcH WKH\ ZHUH in no real hurry to leave, they just sat there sipping their raspberry tea. "Now what?" Paul asked.

"Like I told you, the possibilities are mindless," she said with a light chuckle. said with a light chuckle.

"No doubt about that," he replied. "We can take another walk in the park or we can go to the mall and chill out."

When Paul mentioned a walk in the park memories of what he had done to her on their previous walk made

Michelle tremble ever so slightly as she felt blood rush to her nipples. She had been hoping Paul would suggest another walk in the park and relieve her of having to make that decision since her actions on the last one had caused her some after the fact embarrassment. Michelle was afraid that if they went back to the gazebo that she would make a complete fool of herself by becoming Paul's lo-cal dessert under the stars. She knew that only the dog had saved her the last time and she really didn't want to come across as being an easy conquest. Paul rescued her when he said. "Let's go to the mall. I need to pick up a battery for my cordless phone."

Though this was not the answer she really wanted, Michelle was somewhat relieved because she needed more time to consider where her involvement with Paul might lead. She was relatively sure of where she hoped it would take her but she was also afraid of where it might take her. "That's fine. I might see something there I can't live without," she replied.

The mall was busy but by no means crowded. As the two of them casually strolled passed all the different shops and stores Michelle sensed that she was actually enjoying herself. Though she had no particular aversion to malls or to shopping, she just never spent a lot of time concerning herself with either one but this evening was different. She was with someone, really with someone, and it made her feel more a part of her surroundings. Usually, when she was in a public place, she simply noticed how few people were there alone and she was part of that small group. However, tonight was different. She was part of the other group, the group that says, "I'm accepted," and it made her spirit soar. As they passed the entrance to an electronics store Paul caught her by her finger and steered her through the doorway. She followed easily as he lead her to the back of the store to the telephone section. As he stopped to peruse the different batteries on display he turned loose of her finger. That action came as no great surprise to Michelle but she was a little disappointed. She liked it when he touched her and she also enjoyed touching him.

Paul reached into his shirt pocket and pulled out the dead phone battery. With that to go by, it didn't take him long to locate the one he needed on the display shelf. While he had been conducting his search Michelle had been wandering aimlessly around the store. She stopped to take a closer look at some digital clocks and thought, "Cute, but my old one works just fine and besides, it's paid for."

Paul stopped beside her and said, "I'm ready to go unless you need to look for something."

"Whatever. Did you find what you need?"

"Sure did. One just like the one that died," he replied, as he pulled both batteries from a small plastic bag. "These are the best ones I've tried," he continued, as he held them out for her to see. "They're small but potent. I guess they go to the battery gym, or something."

Michelle finished looking at them and Paul dropped them back into the bag. "What else do we need?" she asked.

"That's all I need," Paul replied, "do you want to look for anything?"

"No, I was out here earlier in the week and got the few things I needed then."

"Shall we go? Anything special you want to do?"

Michelle continued to walk without responding to his question. She knew exactly what she wanted to do but she wasn't quite ready to bring it up. "I need to know if there's any substance to us first," she thought. "No, not really. I'm up for most anything, or nothing."

They continued to walk slowly through the mall, occasionally pausing to take a closer look at something in a store window. When they stepped out into the night air Michelle became aware of how good it felt after being inside where she had found the temperature slightly too cool. "This feels better," she said, "I got cold in there."

"The temperature is much better out here," Paul answered.

As they walked toward his car he put his arm around her and gently pulled her closer. The pace of their walk slowed and Michelle responded by putting her arm around him. "We could go back to my house and chat or take a walk through the neighborhood. It's a nice place to go for a stroll." She paused, then added, "With just the right number of really dark spots." As she added that, she tried to pull him closer.

"Okay. That sounds like a good plan to me."

They arrived at Paul's car and got in. As they drove back across town toward Michelle's house there was very little conversation. Michelle wasn't sure what she wanted the next step to be. Her feelings for Paul were growing quite strong and she was both elated and afraid. "This next phase is the really tricky part," she thought, "I know he wants me, I've felt that much, and I know I want him. If we go in the house and he tries to put a bug in my ear I'm a goner and this time there won't be a strange dog to rescue me. I know we're headed toward bed but should it be tonight? We haven't even talked about being an us, or love, or anything. I guess I'll just see what happens. Will he call me tomorrow, does it even matter? This could be my last chance to be loved and I don't want to blow it, maybe him, but not it." With that thought Michelle got tickled and before she could regain her composure, she laughed.

"What's funny?"

"Oh, nothing. I just had a tacky thought and lost it before I could tuck it away again."

"What kind of tacky thought?"

"Nothing. Never mind. I might tell you sometime but not right now." Though Michelle tried to laugh it off to cover her embarrassment, just thinking about it had aroused her.

When they got to her house they went inside. She put her handbag on the couch and handed her house key to Paul. "Would you mind looking after this till we get back?" she asked.

"Not at all," he replied and dropped the key in his pocket.

They stepped outside and Paul closed the door behind them. He gave it a slight push to be sure it had latched, then the two of them stepped off the porch and started for the street. Michelle's house was situated between street lights and their surroundings seemed very dark at first. As they walked down the driveway their eyes started to become accustomed to the dim light and they could make out the shapes of things around them. At the end of the driveway Michelle veered to her right and Paul followed. She felt his hand brush her hand, then she felt his fingers slipping between her fingers. Michelle gave his hand a squeeze and let her head rest on Paul's shoulder as they walked. The warm night air and the faint scent of flowers in bloom had an intoxicating effect on them. They walked under a street light at the end of the block and she steered him around the corner. "There'll be a surprise down here for you," she whispered.

"I do like some surprises," Paul replied softly.

As they approached the shadows in the middle of the block, Michelle said, "Close your eyes, I'll guide you."

"You'll probably run me into a tree or something," Paul teased.

"I would never do anything to hurt you," Michelle said in a barely audible whisper and she was a little surprised at the seriousness of her words. "I know what pain is like, all kinds of pain, and I wouldn't do that to you, at least not intentionally. It's all about trust."

Paul had noticed the emotion in what she had said and was thinking about what a sensitive person she appeared to be. "Okay, they're shut. I'm in your hands," he whispered.

"Just a little to the left and we'll soon be there," she said.

The street they were on was one of Michelle's favorites. She liked it so much that she had made it part of her routine running course, especially during the warm months when the flowers were in bloom. As they crossed the street she began to make out the shape of their destination. In the corner of a neatly manicured lawn was a large butterfly bush in full bloom. Michelle knew from passing it during the daytime that it was lavender in color and was usually filled with butterflies, moths, and numerous bees. There had even been occasions when she had seen a hummingbird hovering over the blooms drinking in the nectar. Stopping in front of it, she said, "Here we are. Don't open your eyes, just take a deep breath through your nose."

Paul did as she had requested and his nose came alive with the sweet scent emitting from the shrub. "Wow! What is it?"

"You can open your eyes now. This is a butterfly bush.

My grandmother used to have one like this when I was small. I would drag a chair off her porch and put it as close as I dared and sit and watch all the little creatures come visit it." Paul stepped into the yard and put his nose close to another cluster of blooms. He inhaled deeply and said, "I don't think I've ever smelled anything like that before. No wonder the bugs like it."

Michelle stepped closer to it and put her nose next to a bloom. She also inhaled deeply and said, "I'm glad you like it. It's one of my favorites. Sometimes when I stop here and do this I go back to once upon a time."

"What a way to take a trip," Paul said, as he put his arm around her and pulled her close. She felt good to his touch, soft, but at the same time, firm. Each time he touched her, and that was becoming a more frequent thing, he was amazed at this contradiction and, while he knew he didn't understand it, he also knew how much he enjoyed it.

They stood there in the dim light admiring what was before them and Paul also looked around to see if anyone was walking down the street. They were all alone except for an occasional car passing. The butterfly bush was so large that they could have easily hidden behind it if they did not want to be observed. He pulled her closer and put his other arm around her. Michelle melted against him, trying to get as close as possible as she reciprocated by putting her arms around him. They swayed lightly from side to side like stalks of wheat in a gentle breeze. Paul moved his hands up and down Michelle's back in a light massage. He felt her body narrow as his hands approached her waist then he felt the flare of her slender hips as he moved them even lower. As he pressed lightly on her with his fingertips he found her to be firm everywhere Paul let his hands continue to move lower and tried to pull her even closer. Michelle responded by holding him even tighter. "Damn, she feels good," he thought, "where has she been all this time?"

As Paul held her and rubbed her back, Michelle started to struggle with her inner feelings. She liked being with Paul and she was well aware after their interlude in the park that she might like him too much. If the dog had not made its noisy appearance when it had, they might have continued in the direction they were headed and she knew she would have let Paul take her to wherever he wanted them to go. She was, at the same time, ecstatic and afraid. What if he comes in when we get back to my house? I'm safe here but will I be safe from myself when we get back there she wondered.

With her fingertips, Michelle started to draw designs on Paul's back. Finally, she stopped the finger tracings and just held him. They had stopped their silent dance and were just holding each other in the dark, enjoying the sweet scent of the blooms. Paul pushed her hair out of the way and lightly kissed her neck. His lips left a damp trail as they moved to her ear which he also lightly kissed and then flicked with his tongue. Michelle had been coping with the feelings that were going through her without becoming overly aroused but when Paul's tongue touched her ear she could no longer stifle the sensation and a prolonged shudder ran through her body. Michelle dug her fingernails in Paul's back and bit her lip to keep from crying out. Paul slid his hands up her body till he could feel the firm side swell of her breasts. Michelle moved her head back from his shoulder and they gazed into each other's eyes. He kissed her softly, at first their lips toyed with each other, then their tongues touched and it became a volcanic eruption of passion.

After several long, delirious moments Michelle broke the kiss and put her head back on his shoulder. As her feelings whirled on an emotional centrifuge, she trembled with a combination of excitement and fear. She thought briefly about what always happened to her in a relationship but she could not deny that this felt so good. "I think we need to continue our walk, don't you?" she whispered.

"Probably," Paul replied as he slipped his hands gently around her breasts and gave them a light squeeze. As he caressed her, he touched his lips lightly to hers and delicately ran a fingertip over her swollen nippes. Michelle bit her lip again as she put her hands around his hands and squeezed them. He followed her lead and gently fondled her as they silently looked at each other.

Paul knew she was right, they really did need to continue their walk because, though this might have been the right time, it certainly wasn't the right place. Without a word he took her by the hand and they stepped out of the dark shadows of the yard and walked quietly down the street. Neither spoke as they continued on their journey. It were as if they both seemed to know that the slightest noise would destroy the magic moment they had just experienced.

As they walked quietly along Michelle's emotions were starting to wage war again. She wanted to proceed slowly with what appeared to be a budding relationship that also appeared to have long term possibilities. She knew that was her mind talking about one aspect of it, her feelings wanted her to drag Paul back to her house, her bedroom in particular, and wake up beside him in the morning. Before they would go to sleep, though, she wanted him to take her on a journey through the stars. As they approached her house she still had not made the decision as to which way to go. When they finally got to her driveway Michelle cast the die, "Would you like to come in for a while?" she asked.

Paul gave her hand a squeeze and said, "Yes, I would like to do that but it's been a very tiring day so I think it would be best if I run on home. Maybe next time."

"Thanks for a fun evening," Michelle said but she wasn't sure whether she was disappointed or relieved. The only thing that she was sure of was that she wasn't sure of anything.

Paul walked her to the door and unlocked it for her. He handed her the key and pulled her close. They held each other for a long time without speaking then he kissed her lightly on the tip of her nose and said, "I'll talk to you tomorrow. G'night."

"Bye."

He turned and walked to his car as Michelle stood and watched. When he got in, they waved one last time and she stepped inside and closed the door. Without turning on a light she made her way through the darkened house to the bathroom that joined her bedroom. Michelle then turned on the bathroom light, unbuttoned her blouse and draped it over the back of a chair. Then she brushed her teeth and washed her face. She finished undressing and slipped into a tee shirt that had a picture of a large sunflower on the front. Michelle turned off the bathroom light and got into bed.

The sheets were cool against her skin but quickly warmed to her touch. Across the room the striking clock that had once belonged to her grandparents kept her company with its rhythmic ticking. As her eyes started to adjust to the darkness she looked around the room and her mind began to wander. She tried to visualize how things might be different if Paul had accepted her invitation to come in. Michelle was well aware that one evening soon, maybe even the next time they were together, that she would ask him to stay with her. "I must check to see if I have an extra toothbrush," she thought. She closed her eyes and ran her hands lightly over her body as she pretended they belonged to him. Finding this to be much too stimulating, she finally forced her hands to leave her body alone and started to relax. She wondered how having him share her bed, or her sharing his, would change things. Would it bring them closer together or drive them apart? Would she be used and discarded or would it be a gradual thing? Then the big question hit her. "If we have a problem, will he marry me or want me to solve the situation without him? Would he even want to know? Would I marry him? Do I even want to spend the rest of my life with him? Do I even want to spend the night with him? I don't know the answers to the other questions," she thought, "but I sure know the answer to that one."

Michelle realized that just thinking about these things had caused her nipples to swell and she touched them through the shirt. "If I don't have another toothbrush in the house, I'll get one," she decided. "I think I love him. Not a good sign, I know I'll get smashed again. What the hell, I've been smashed before but if it happens this time, it'll be far worse than any of the others." As Michelle continued to toy with these thoughts she noticed a change in her breathing, then sleep, like fog on a still valley, engulfed her.

Though she had gone to bed much later than usual, Michelle still woke up when the first rays of light came through the bedroom window. She didn't get up immediately, she wanted a few minutes to consider the events that had transpired just hours earlier so she propped the pillows against the headboard and relaxed in a reclining position. Michelle envisioned Paul lying beside her and wondered what the final outcome of everything would be. In a way she wished he had come in and that their first night together was over then she would have a better feel for the situation and, hopefully, be more able to answer some of her own questions. As she continued to lie there, she suddenly became very tired and the accompanying sadness that always came with it overwhelmed her. "Since I know better than to do this," she thought, "whatever happens to me, I deserve. I know I'll get the knife in the back again, don't know why, don't know how, I just know I'll get it." With these thoughts consuming her, she slipped back down into the bed and pulled the sheet back over her, then she pulled one of the pillows over her eyes so nothing was exposed except her nose. Michelle continued to ponder her questions until sleep once again crept into her darkened world.

This short nap, though much needed, didn't last long and this time when she woke up, she got up instead of letting her mind wander again. After splashing some water in her eyes, Michelle pulled on some lightweight sweatpants and went into the kitchen to see if she could conquer breakfast. This morning she chose the easy way out and settled for a small bowl of cereal with some grapes for dessert.

After breakfast Michelle remembered the toothbrush thought from the night before. It only took a few minutes of rummaging around until she found a blue one with the plastic seal still on it. "This should do just fine," she thought as she took it to her bathroom. "I won't beat round the bush, I'll just ask him if he would like to stay and tell him I have a toothbrush for him and that we can share the floss." Michelle felt a shudder of excitement go through her at the thought of what Paul might say and then do. "If he doesn't try to seduce me, I'm going for it," she said out loud, surprised at the amount of determination in her voice.

Michelle halfway expected Paul to call her sometime that day, after all, he had said he would call, just not when. Though her phone did ring on two occasions during the day, neither call was from him. She tidied up her house, not because it was in disarray but to be sure it didn't get that way. It was a routine with her and it didn't take very long for her to complete the task. After finishing the inside work, Michelle went outside and picked up twigs that had fallen from the trees and pulled some weeds from the flower beds. She briefly considered mowing the grass but it wasn't quite high enough and, due to the lack of recent rain, she decided it could wait a few more days.

Her thoughts stayed on Paul, the fun they had been having, and the fun she hoped they would have. She wondered about the toothbrush and whether or not it was the right thing for her to do. The questions and doubts that had troubled her earlier came back to haunt her and she had to force them from her mind. "He may not love me but I know he wants me," she thought, "and it's not like I haven't been pitched in love's dumpster before. If he calls, fine. If he doesn't, fine. I'd rather know now than after I get in even deeper." With that thought ringing inside her head, Michelle finished weeding the flowers and went behind the house to a corner of the backyard to a hammock that was in the shade of some trees. She climbed in and lay back with her eyes closed. As she relaxed she became more aware that all around her the birds were chirping, she heard the faint barking of a dog, and even the buzz of a bee now and then. Michelle opened her eyes to look around just in time to see a large, yellow swallow tail butterfly go floating silently over the fence into her neighbor's yard. Closing her eyes again, Michelle lay there just enjoying the sounds around her and feeling the light breeze that carried different scents on it. Someone in the neighborhood had a charcoal grill going and whatever they were cooking sure smelled good to her. Lying there with that in mind, Michelle drifted into a peaceful sleep and dreamed of dining out with friends.

Paul had said he would call and Michelle expected that he would. She really thought he would call the next day, surely within two, even three days, but he didn't. She thought about being upset but decided against it. "Not worth the time or energy," she thought, "anyway, I'd much rather get a pocket knife in the back than a dagger. A knife's a knife, just a difference in the length of the blade and the damage that's done."

The following Wednesday evening, as she sat on her front porch watching people take their after supper walks, Michelle was still in a quandary as to what could have gone wrong. In her mind she had replayed their conversations and the time they had spent together but nothing gave her any clues. So lost in thought was she that when the cordless phone she had brought outside with her rang, she jumped. Since it was prime time for telemarketers she almost decided to let the answering machine take the call. Michelle suddenly decided that she was slightly bored so she picked it up, punched the button, and said, "Hello."

Her pulse quickened at the voice in her ear as Paul said, "Hi, Cutie Boop."

"I was beginning to think you had died or maybe got snatched by aliens."

"No, nothing quite that exciting. I really meant to call you long before now but I had a bunch of stuff I needed to think about. We need to sit down and have an uninterrupted chat."

Michelle felt the blood drain from her face. "Here it comes again," she thought, "kiss off time." Trying not to sound concerned, she replied, "Okay. When do you want to talk?"

"Actually, I want to talk right now but Friday at supper will do just fine. Do we want to eat at your place or mine? I'll pick up something so neither of us has to cook. You pick the place."

Though Michelle didn't reply immediately, her mind was racing. If I'm going to get a knife in the back, damned if I'm going to go to any extra trouble, she decided. "Come on over to my house," she said. "We can eat, then talk, talk then eat, or talk while we eat. I don't care, any way you want to do it is fine with me." She wondered if Paul had noticed her lackadaisical response but really didn't care.

"Okay. I'll see you at seven Friday and I'll bring something for supper. 'Bye."

"'Bye," Michelle replied as she turned off the phone.

"I'm glad I found the damned toothbrush instead of going out and buying one," she muttered to herself. As her energy drained away, she lay back on the porch and thought about all the possibilities that she knew just got shot in the head. The thought finally hit her, "Maybe I'm jumping the gun. Maybe this isn't the old heave-ho. Maybe he's been offered another job. Maybe, maybe, maybe. Historically, though, anytime half of a relationship needs to talk, it's always bad. Not much I can do abut it now." She looked at the lengthening shadows, then checked her watch. "If I don't dawdle, I've got time for a run before dark and that always makes me feel better," she thought. With that in mind, she got up and went inside to change clothes.

Michelle did feel better after her run but she was still troubled. Upon finishing her shower she made herself a strong gin and tonic because she knew she wouldn't go to sleep without some help. She sipped the drink while trying to get lost in bad TV, knowing that it would soon be a respectable bedtime. It didn't take long for the alcohol to hit her and she felt herself start to relax. Michelle finally lost what little interest she had in what she was watching and decided it was time for bed. She gulped the rest of her drink, turned off the TV and the light, and walked through the darkness down the hall to her bedroom. When she lay back and closed her eyes the room started to slowly spin and she knew sleep would soon overtake her.

Though Michelle tried not to think about the approaching Friday evening, it was hard for her to keep it out of her thoughts. She had enough to do at work to keep them at bay but after work on Thursday they finally caught up with her and she once again became very sad.

Friday seemed to be in slow motion in spite of her work schedule. A deep feeling of impending doom simply would not leave her alone. When the work day was finally over she drove home wondering why she even cared anymore. "At least I haven't made a complete fool of myself," she thought, "and in a few hours I can go on to other things."

When Michelle arrived home she wondered about how to prepare for the evening. She gave some thought to not even showering and just slipping on some lightweight sweat pants. After a few minutes of considering it she decided to wash away the work day and jumped into the shower. "Why not look as good as possible," she thought, "and let him know what he's throwing away." Michelle decided on her favorite jeans, old and faded, but they fit her just right. She then chose a bright blue silk blouse to complete her ensemble. As she stood in front of the mirror Michelle decided that she really liked the contrast. "Nothing like being uptown and in the low rent district at the same time," she mused. Glancing at the clock, she decided she had a few minutes to relax before Paul arrived. Slipping on some sandals, then re-checking her hair, she went outside and sat down in a chair on the front porch.

One of the many things Michelle liked about Paul was that he was punctual and tonight was no exception. He arrived slightly early and, as he unloaded a box of food, Michelle went to offer any help that he might need. She wasn't sure what was in it but the contents of the box smelled good.

"Hi, Bugaboo. You sure do look spiffy," he said, then added, "hope you like it."

"It does smell good. What do you want me to carry?"

"It's all right here in the box," Paul replied.

Michelle closed the car door and they walked toward the front porch. "If he's troubled about anything, he sure is doing a good job of hiding it," she thought. She opened the door and they went inside to the kitchen. Paul put the box on the counter and gave her a big hug. He seemed very relaxed and genuinely glad to be with her.

He turned her loose and said, "Let's eat."

"Okay."

Paul had picked up quite a feast. He took out a roasted chicken, then containers of beans, potatoes, biscuits, and some deep dish apple pie for dessert. Michelle started to get plates from a cabinet. Paul stopped her. "Silverware only. We don't want to be bothered with dishes," he said. When he put a small bouquet of flowers on the table Michelle started to feel a little less anxious. She got a pitcher of tea from the refrigerator, poured them each a glass, and put them on the table.

Paul helped Michelle with her chair, then sat down across the table from her. They ate in silence for a while then Paul asked how her day had been. She told him and inquired about his day and the past week. They continued with the small talk even though the suspense was killing her. She wanted him to go ahead and get it over with so she could get on with her life. "Why is he doing this to me?" she thought, "at least the food is good."

If Paul had anything really earth shattering to say to her he continued to be exasperatingly slow in saying it. The small talk continued as they ate but nothing of any consequence had been said by the time they finished the main course. When they were ready for dessert Michelle dished out some apple pie for each of them. It was slightly tart and the mixture of spices, without overpowering the flavor of the apples, made it one of the better bought pies she had ever eaten.

After they had finished with dessert Michelle cleare the table and tidied up the kitchen. Paul had disappeared while she was doing that and she knew he had gone to floss. She was glad that neither of them could stand dirty teeth. When he returned she was finishing up in the kitchen and, as he sat down at the table, Michelle said, "I'll be right back."

"Okay. I'll be here."

As Michelle walked down the hall toward the bathroom she once again became anxious. "Won't be long now," she thought, "till I know one way or the other." When she finished, she returned to the kitchen and found Paul sitting at the table looking out the sliding glass door at the backyard. She sat down across from him and decided she had waited long enough. "What is it that we need to talk about?" she asked.

"Nothing big," Paul replied as he continued to look outside. After what seemed like forever to Michelle, he turned and stared into her dark eyes. Her hands were on the table and Paul reached over and put his hands on top of hers. He gave them a light squeeze as he continued to gaze into her eyes though he still hadn't said anything. The prolonged silence wasn't helping her at all. She couldn't tell if this was part of the game or if Paul was trying to collect his thoughts and carefully choose the words he wanted to use. She was about to explode with anticipation when he finally started to speak in a soft, but clear, voice.

"Michelle, lots of times when people say things it's either during a heated argument or during flame broiled passion. I've never really trusted those statements because I never knew how much the moment was influencing what was being said. I'd rather hear things that are in no way related to the moment." With that, Paul turned loose of her hands and put his hands together. Michelle said nothing. She had no idea what to say or what he would say when he continued, if he continued. After the pause, with the same soft voice, Paul continued, "Michelle, I love you."

Michelle said nothing, she didn't even twitch, she just sat there looking into his eyes. Her hands were still where they had been while Paul had been holding them. Her brain was trying to process what had just been said and not everythine was working correctly. "What?" she finally whispered.

"I love you," Paul said again, this time a little louder.

"I love you, too," Michelle replied in a whisper that was only slightly louder than before. It had finally started to register with her as to what Paul had just said. "I guess I should be doing cart wheels or something," she responded. "At one time I would have but this is all very scary. I do want someone, especially you, to care whether I live or die during the day but being stabbed in the back takes a lot out of me. I've been stabbed enough to know and each time it happens; it takes me longer to recover. I know my response must really seem strange to you but I really am terrified of all this. Love is very personal to me. It means so much to me that I have a hard time sharing it because, in the past, no one has ever had much respect for my feelings."

Paul made no effort to interrupt her, he continued to sit quietly with his hands still folded on the table. When she finished he said, "You have no idea how much I've wanted to hear what you just said. I really do love you, I've just been afraid to tell you. I've been afraid to tell you because I wasn't sure how you would respond. I, too, have been stabbed in the back and I know it's not a lot of fun. This may come as a shock, Michelle, but men have feelings, too. At least some of us do and I happen to fall in that category."

"This changes everything," Michelle said, "even though it all looks the same, it's all different."

"I know. It must be the endorphins or something." Michelle hoped Paul wanted to take her down the hall to her bedroom and tear her clothes off as much as she wanted to do it to him but she couldn't quite bring herself to voice her feelings. He suddenly got up and walked around the table and stopped behind her. He put his hands on her shoulders and began to massage her upper back and neck. Michelle felt some of the anxiety and tension start to drain away and she started to feel more relaxed. "Let's go into the living room and get a more comfortable place to sit," she said.

"Okay."

Paul pulled her chair back and she got up. She took him by the hand and led him into the next room. He sat down and pulled her down so she was sitting on the couch but her upper body was resting across his lap and her head was on the couch arm. Michelle closed her eyes and thought about how good it felt to be this close to someone, physically and emotionally. Paul put his arms around her and pulled her even closer. With her head on his chest Michelle could hear his heart beating. She found the rhythmic sound very relaxing and she began to fantasize about hearing it every night at bedtime. "With a few of the right moves, I bet I could make that sucker speed up," she thought.

After a few minutes of just holding each other in silence, Michelle said, "We must be getting old, or at least be in shock over what just happened. The normal sequence of events would be for us to run down the hall, rip off each other's clothes, and jump into bed. Anyway, that's the way it is in the movies."

Paul chuckled. "This isn't a movie and it's even more fun," he whispered and pulled her even closer. "This is nice but it is kind of scary. Maybe we are getting old but I want to get even older with you. Eventually, we can even get matching canes and rockers."

Michelle laughed and raised her head from his chest. For a few seconds they gazed into each other's eyes, then she raised her head a little more as she offered her slightly parted lips to his. Paul took what had been offered to him and he found her lips soft and clingy, he knew they would be, but now they truly were different . They where no longer just friends, someone to spend an evening with, take in a movie, or go to supper. What had just happened meant they were no longer just thinking of the moment but that they were considering the future and they wanted to be in it together. As their lips parted, they stuck together slightly. Michelle trembled as she tried to snuggle even closer to Paul and, though he tried, he couldn't hold her any closer to him.

Michelle felt safe and loved as she tried to sort out what was going on. She was wondering whether or not Paul liked children when a relaxed fog settled over her and she felt her breathing change. Some time later, she wasn't sure how long, Michelle awoke to find herself still in Paul's arms, just like she had been. As it dawned on her what she had done, she felt her face get warm with embarrassment.

With an impish grin, he said, "Nice nap?"

Her face grew even warmer and she was very thankful for the dim light so Paul couldn't see how much she was blushing. "I'm really sorry," she apologized, "but I was so relaxed. I could hear your heart beating and the next thing I knew, I was gone. It just feels so good to be held by someone special. I felt so safe."

"I better go, Sleepyhead. We're both tired and we need to think about some things."

"No, no. You can't leave," Michelle protested as she tried to hold him, "I'm too comfy."

As Paul wiggled out from under her and got her resettled on the couch, Michelle thought about telling him that he could stay if he wanted to and that she even had an extra toothbrush for him to use. Paul got down on his knees by the couch and kissed her. It was long and tender and she responded to it. As he was kissing her, Michelle once again unconsciously spread her feet slightly apart. It wasn't much and she was almost certain he hadn't noticed but she had and she knew what it meant.

Paul stood up as Michelle continued to hold his hand. "Are you sure you have to go? It's really not all that late and I'll try harder to stay awake," she said as they both laughed at her statement.

"If I stay, I'll join you in Nappyland and we'll both wake up with a stiff neck. Besides, I want us to think about our little chat and be sure this is the way we want to go. Let's not rush into anything we might regret later on. I'll call you tomorrow."

"I'll walk you out," Michelle said as she started to get up.

"No. You stay put. I know where the door is and I'll be sure it's locked." He bent down and gave her a light kiss on the end of her nose. Paul pulled back from her and walked toward the door. As he stepped into the warm night air he gave her one last look and said, "'Night, Bugaboo."

Then, the door closed and he was gone. Michelle was still comfortable on the couch so she decided to just lie there for a while and try to sort out the events of the evening. She had reached the point in life that she had started to wonder if love even existed outside of poetry and the movies. Now, here was someone she really liked expressing his love, whatever that meant, for her and she, like a fool, had reciprocated and expressed her love, whatever that meant, to him. She wasn't at all sure about this new turn of events. She had been quite comfortable being "in like" with Paul but being "in love" with him upset her emotional apple cart. Before tonight, had he walked away or simply failed to call her, so what. Now, the stakes were higher. She had expressed her feelings, the other party knew how she felt and she had been sincere.

Michelle shifted slightly on the couch and said out loud to herself, "I'm old enough to know better. When this is over I'm really going to take a tumble and I'm gonna' scrape both knees." She wished Paul had not left, she had felt very safe and secure as he held her. With that pleasant thought playing around in her head, she said to herself, "He cares whether I live or die during the day. That's nice to know."

A very faint noise roused Michelle from her light sleep. As she listened she recognized it as the clock in her bedroom striking. She wasn't sure how many "bongs" she had missed but she had managed to count seven. Knowing there had to be more, Michelle got up and walked across the living room so she could get a look into the kitchen at the clock on the microwave. It told her that it was three minutes after eleven and she decided that it was time to call it a night. She turned off the lamp in the living room and walked down the hall toward her bedroom.

True to his word, Paul did call her the next day. It almost surprised her that he actually did what he had said he would do because she had heard those words before. Though Michelle thought of Paul as being sincere, and he had never given her a reason to doubt him, her feeling of exhilaration continued to be tempered by a feeling of caution. She tried to keep it in the background because she was painfully aware of a big, empty place in her life and that Paul was just what she needed to fill it. Their conversation lasted for over an hour without discussing anything of any substance.

When they were talking, though it was by telephone, she simply felt connected to him and he seemed to feel the same way about her. They each had caused the other to chuckle numerous times with an occasional full fledged laugh. Neither was trying to be especially funny, they were just enjoying each other and reveling in the concept of someone who not only cares but is cared about. Michelle's brain had released endorphins that made her feel as if she had eaten way too much chocolate.

After they had said their good-byes over a ten minute time span and hung up the phone, Michelle flopped out on the couch and closed her eyes. Paul had told her that he had not been kidding when he had expressed his feelings the previous evening. As they had been trying to hang up he had once again told her of his love for her. Michelle had felt a glow when she heard those words. As she relaxed and replayed their conversation in her mind a feeling of utter despair began to settle over her. She tried to fight it off because it made no sense to her. Here she was involved with someone she could easily spend the rest of her life with and just moments before she had been floating on love's euphoric cloud. Now, everything seemed to be different. Her uneasiness only grew deeper as she wondered how it would all end, when it would end, and whether or not she would survive another devastating emotional upheaval.

For a while she wondered if she should simply tell Paul goodbye and get it over with or if she should wait for him to tell her. As this inner battle raged, she said in a loud voice, as if trying to be sure she heard it, "Michelle, you ignorant bitch, get a damn grip. You've barely gotten involved with someone who says he loves you and you're already ending it." With a heavy sigh she added, "I deserve whatever happens because I really do know better." With that final statement, her energy was spent and she slipped into the dark, quiet world of sleep--her only refuge when she needed to escape.

When Michelle woke up from her nap her mind had begun to clear and her thoughts were not so cluttered. Now, she began to think that it might actually work. She again visualized a small person or two running around the house that bore a striking resemblance to the two of them. She thought briefly of making cookies and attending school functions. This made her smile and she decided that she had better get up and be a little more productive around the house. "Productive," she laughed, "not reproductive--at least not right now." Michelle walked down the hall to her bedroom and stared at the basket of dirty clothes. "Nothing like a load of laundry to bring a person back to reality," she chuckled.

Though nothing had changed in the physical sense, everything had changed through her perspective. She started to pay more attention to the beautiful music the birds made, the colors of the flowers seemed brighter, and she noticed that situations and events that she had once found so frustrating and stressful really made no difference. Though she and Paul didn't always talk by phone in the evening, Michelle was happy just knowing that he was only a call away if she needed him for whatever reason.

Their weekends together were eagerly anticipated and she knew that one evening in the not too distant future that one of them would ask if the other really wanted to go home or would staying over be preferable. Michelle pondered that possibility and finally decided that it might be more comfortable for her if she took the initiative and asked him to stay with her. She had very little doubt as to his answer because she had often felt the result of Paul's passion as they held each other. She thought again of the evening in the park when the dog had interrupted them and remembered vividly that she was extremely close to taking off her clothes and removing all doubt about her feelings right there on the picnic table. Michelle thought of how that would have looked in the newspaper if the dog had not barked and gotten their attention. She went to check the medicine cabinet to be sure the tooth brush was still there. Sure enough, she found it right where she had put it days earlier.

No matter where Paul was, he always called her on Thursday evening so they could make weekend plans. With this in mind, Michelle started to think that she would at least drop a hint, if not come right out and ask him, if he would like to spend most of the upcoming weekend with her.

As the time went by and Thursday evening approached Michelle began to wonder if she were up to the task of extending some sort of invitation, subtle or otherwise. "What if he declines?" she wondered. Michelle laughed at herself as she remembered what one of her friends had said when several of them had gone out to supper one evening. Of course, men had been one of the topics of conversation and Pam had made a good point. She said, "Remember, girls, anytime you think a guy's big head will go against what you want to do, be sure to appeal to the little head. The small headed judge will always rule in your favor." Though this statement had brought a roar of laughter, everyone had agreed because they all knew it was true.

As she puttered around trying to tidy up an already clean house Michelle wondered about how their "first time" would come to pass. Would Paul be into some type of kinky activity or would he just love her? She tried to visualize what she could wear that would make her appear to be super sexy and even wondered if a special shopping spree might be worthwhile. Michelle was well aware that how something was packaged had a lot to do with potential interest, whether on the store shelf or in the bedroom. She finally decided that, as a woman, she would be able to convince the small headed judge to rule in her favor.

Thursday evening finally arrived and Michelle had just come in from walking around in the yard and pulling a few large weeds from around the flowers. All day she had looked forward to the quiet time of evening and Paul's call. While she was in the kitchen washing her hands, the phone rang. Rushing to dry them, she picked it up. The voice she had been waiting for all day was now in her ear, "Hi, Bugaboo."

Michelle smiled when she heard it. Their conversation started around how their respective days had gone and branched out into small talk about other things. Neither cared what they talked about, they only cared that they were talking. After they had chatted a while, Paul suddenly said, "I can't make it Saturday." Michelle felt stunned and she was just starting to visualize the "kiss off" banners flapping in a strong breeze when he continued. "I have to go to a seminar early next week. That's the bad part. The good part is, it's at the beach and I have an empty seat in my car. Do you want to fill it? We can leave Saturday morning and spend the weekend there. If you want to, we can stay even longer after the business part of it is all over."

As quickly as the "kiss off" banners had materialized they disappeared from her mind as her spirit soared. "Yes, yes. I'd love to go," she replied without hesitation. She could hardly contain herself. "There's hope after all," she thought.

Paul continued, "The seminar is at the Seaside Hotel. I've been there before. It's right on the water, plus two pools, one in, one out. The food's great and the company is picking up the room and most of the expenses. I've got to run now. I've got work to do before we leave. I'll call you tomorrow night and we can set times. Michelle, I really do love you."

Almost before she could respond with any kind of answer, Paul was gone. In Michelle's mind this travel offer both simplified and complicated the issue. Being gone from work on such a short notice would be no great problem since she always had vacation time saved up. The question of her place or his was now answered and the answer was neither one, it would be on neutral ground. By saying she would go with him, Michelle knew there would be expectations on the part of each of them and she was well aware that she wanted to be up to fulfilling any that Paul might have of her. As she thought about what the next few days and nights might have in store, she began to feel warm with desire. Closing her eyes, Michelle ran her hands over her breasts and noticed that her nipples were also anticipating what the near future held. A shudder of excitement went through her body and it jarred her from her reverie.

She went straight to her bedroom and started rummaging through her dresser for clothes that had just the right look. Michelle ignored all underwear that was only functional. She was on a quest for lingerie that made a statement and she wanted the statement to say in a powerful way, "I'm a woman and I'm going to rock your world." As she looked through the dresser everything Michelle chose was colorful, lacy, low cut, or a combination. She wanted to be sure that it would be a time in Paul's life that he would never forget. She not only wanted him to enjoy the present she had for him but she also wanted him to enjoy unwrapping it. Her swimsuit choices were much easier. She only had two and they would both be packed. Michelle laid all of her selections on the bed. She counted the number of days they would be gone, then added enough of everything for three extra days. Not really expecting anything very formal to happen, she mostly ignored that possibility. She did remove from the closet some clothes that would suffice, she thought of them as "casually formal," just in case she needed to accompany Paul to some sort of business function. She thought about putting them in her suitcase but decided against it. Instead, she made a pile in a chair in the corner. With her bed now clear of everything Michelle gave some thought to trying to get some sleep but she knew that, due to her excitement, it would be difficult. With this in mind she went into the kitchen and got out a bottle of coconut rum. She knew a stiff shot of this would make her drowsy and that sleep would soon follow.

Michelle's day at work on Friday moved along at a steady pace. Making the short notice arrangements to be gone only required minimal effort. Her supervisor was not only glad to see her come to work and take care of business, she was equally glad to see her take time off for whatever reason. Her philosophy was "all work and no play makes Jill a dull girl and a less productive employee." Michelle delegated to others the few tasks that had time sensitive deadlines and finished what she could. Her anticipation of the next few days kept surfacing and she did occasionally let her mind drift into potential scenarios. As the workday began to wind down Michelle caught herself humming a tune while she reviewed a document. She smiled as she pondered the positive impact Paul was having on her life and realized that she was actually the happiest she had been in a long time. She worked an extra half an hour to finish the final task because she knew that it would have been done on time if she had not let her thoughts wander on one issue that definitely was not work related.

During the drive home Michelle went down the checklist in her mind and realized that in the morning all she really had to do was to get up and go. She thought about the upcoming days and nights, especially the nights, with Paul. She knew she was looking forward to it all and wondered what it would be like to wake up and have him in bed with her. Michelle trembled with excitement at that thought. She turned down her street and once again caught herself humming an old tune. As she slowed to turn into her driveway Michelle could sense a tremendous smile on her face. "How nice it is to love and to be loved," she thought.

After she had changed clothes, Michelle went outside to see if any of the plants needed watering. Deciding that no water was needed, she continued to putter around a little longer just to get the office kinks out of her body. It was a warm, pleasant early evening so she moved a lawn chair close to a patch of flowers to watch numerous butterflies fluttering around as they searched for nectar before the sun set and the temperature cooled to end their day. Michelle had taken her cordless phone with her because she did not want to miss Paul's expected call while she enjoyed the backyard. A large Monarch was floating majestically by her when the phone rang. So enthralled with what she was observing, the sudden noise made her jump. Once again, the voice in her ear was the one she had been waiting for all day.

"Hi, Bugaboo."

Michelle felt her smile widen when she heard it and she responded, "Hi, yourself, Studmuffin."

Paul chuckled. "Blueberry or whole grain?"

"One each," and they both laughed.

"Are you ready to go tomorrow?"

"All ready. Anything that's not ready can be in fifteen minutes or less. I'm looking forward to it."

"Me, too."

"What time will you pick me up in the morning?"

"I should be there around nine. The drive will take us six to seven hours so we should be there in the late afternoon even if we stop along the way. No need to hurry. Let's make it all fun."

They chatted a while longer about how their respective day had gone and then went through their usual extended goodbye. After they hung up, Michelle got up and went inside, her steps as light as the butterflies she had been watching. After a light supper and a brief period of channel surfing, she closed up her house and went in the bedroom to read. This usually made her sleepy and she wanted to be rested for the adventure that lay ahead.

Michelle woke up as the first rays of sunshine peeked through the bedroom window. Since she had no desire to get up quite that early she continued to lie in bed with her eyes closed hoping for one more short nap. The excitement of her upcoming trip with Paul kept sleep at bay and she began to wonder about what she was reasonably certain would take place at the end of the day. Lying there, she made up several different scenarios for their first night together. As these thoughts played around in her head Michelle noticed that she was looking forward to it to the point that she felt flushed with desire and wished Paul would suddenly appear there in bed with her. She smiled as she thought about how their trip might be delayed.

The room continued to grow brighter and Michelle could hear the birds chirping. She knew the possibility of sleep was now history and that it really was time for her to get up and get her day started. She wanted everything sitting by the front door so, when Paul arrived, all they would have to do is throw her stuff in the car and go.

After Michelle finished breakfast she did her final bit of packing and moved everything from the bedroom to the living room. Having gotten up early and not having a great deal to do, she put on her running clothes for some early morning exercise. After a few minutes of stretching, she glanced at the clock and stepped outside into the warm morning sun. As always, her run started at a relaxed pace. It was a course through the neighborhood that she had run many times and she knew how long it would take her to complete it to within a few seconds. As she ran, Michelle looked around at the flowers and enjoyed the songs of the different birds. After about a quarter of a mile and feeling that her leg muscles were warm, she increased her pace.

Her breathing had stabilized and she settled on her favorite four step cruise count. "What a fabulous morning," she thought, "and I'm in love." Michelle was aware that she had a beaming smile this morning, even larger than her usual running smile. "I hope it lasts," she thought.

When she arrived back at her house she slowed to a walk and continued down the street as she cooled off. When the cool down walk was over she went inside and glanced once again at the clock. Lots of time she decided and headed down the hall to shower and finish dressing for the trip.

Michelle had everything ready to leave and had completed her pre-travel checklist. She had made up this list to be sure that she had everything she might need and to be sure that all the household items were covered. One item that had always been difficult for her to remember was the night light timer since Michelle did not like to leave her house dark for an extended length of time. The list was now complete and all she needed was for Paul to arrive. At seven minutes until nine Paul pulled into her driveway. Michelle was always impressed with his punctuality and she always tried to be ready. He was also wearing a large smile and he gave her a wave even before he got out of the car. She went to meet him and they held hands as they walked back inside. Once they were in the house, Paul pulled her close and held her. He noticed the softness of her hair against his cheek and how clean it smelled. Neither said anything as they stood there, they just enjoyed the touch in silence.

Finally, Paul said, "If we don't leave, we'll never get there."

"I know but this feels so good. Besides, I bet we could stay entertained even if we don't go."

"I'm sure we could but the conference is there, not here."

"I know. I'm all packed. All we have to do is throw it in the car and go."

"That's a good idea. We do need to save some of the good stuff till later. Are you sure you want to do this?"

"I'm sure."

With that, Michelle relaxed her hug and Paul turned her loose. They picked up her baggage by the door and walked toward his car. It only took a few minutes for them to load her stuff. Michelle was a light packer, taking only what she thought she might actually need plus just a little extra in case her plans got unexpectedly changed. Though her checklist was complete, Michelle took one last tour through the house. Satisfied that everything was as it should be, she closed the front door and walked with Paul toward his car. She squeezed his hand and said, "What a beautiful day to go somewhere."

"Yes, it is. We're going to have a boatload of fun."

As they headed out of town they were both very quiet. While Paul drove, Michelle was busy looking at the scenery. She would occasionally point out a really bright flowerbed or an exceptionally well maintained yard. As the houses began to thin out Michelle looked at Paul and said, "Do you know how to get there?"

"I think so. I looked at the map last night for a review and pretty much have it figured out. It's in the dash if you want to see it."

He briefly explained the planned route and Michelle agreed that it seemed like the best way to go. She put her hand on the console and it was only a moment till she felt Paul's fingers around hers. Just having him touch her brought about a feeling of contentment. Even though the countryside was beautiful, Michelle put her head back against the seat and closed her eyes.

With the sun beaming through the windshield and the hum of the road she had begun to grow sleepy. She imagined what it would be like to play the games that lovers play with Paul. Michelle found these thoughts quite stimulating and she hoped that he wanted her as much as she wanted him. After a few minutes in fantasyland she decided she should really be a more active part of the trip, besides it wasn't fair to Paul for her to be envisioning tangled sheets while he was watching the road. She opened her eyes and stretched. "If you get tired, I'll drive."

"Maybe later. I'm not tired yet. Did you take a nap?"

"Almost. I don't know why but all of a sudden I got sleepy. I really don't want to miss the scenery so I'm going to try to stay awake."

The miles continued to roll by. They went through small towns, large towns, bypassed the cities, and avoided the interstate as much as they could. In the early afternoon they stopped to eat at a little mom and pop cafe. They were both surprised at how good the food was and how little it cost them. After a relaxing meal they left the waitress a generous tip and a smile as they left to continue their journey.

By late afternoon the first leg of their trip was almost over. A sign informed them that they were only twenty- seven miles from their destination. Though their drive had been filled with beautiful scenery that was constantly changing and lively conversation, they were both ready to get out and walk around with the knowledge that they wouldn't have to get back in the car and continue their ride. The traffic began to increase and the roadside became more cluttered with billboards and businesses. Paul seemed to know exactly where he was going and how to get there so Michelle just relaxed and enjoyed the last few miles of the journey.

Paul made a turn onto a much larger road and Michelle could see an increase in the amount of water that was around them. A few stoplights later he had worked his way into the left turn lane and they were now headed toward a large hotel that she was able to catch an occasional glimpse of through the trees. Moments later they were there.

Michelle was instantly impressed with the appearance of it. The grounds were immaculate with well trimmed grass and flowers everywhere. Paul stopped under the covered entrance and they got out to go in and register. After sitting in the car most of the day Michelle got out and did some much needed stretching movements to get some of the stiffness out of her body. Then, after helping Paul unload the car, she watched their luggage while he looked for a parking place.

When he returned from moving the car they picked up their bags and walked across the lobby to the elevator. They were alone in their ascent to the ninth floor and the rode in silence, just happy to have arrived safely and to be together. When the elevator stopped they got off and walked down the hall to their room. It was a small suite with a kitchenette at the entrance, then a small sitting area, then the bedroom with a large sliding glass door that opened onto a landing that was shaded by the one above it.

They put the bags down and walked across the room and stepped outside. The view of the ocean was spectacular with the blue-green water and the palm trees at the edge of the beach. Michelle leaned into Paul and said, "This is nice. I love to listen to the surf crashing and the gulls fussing." He pulled her close and she melted into him. Neither spoke, they just stood there in silence holding each other and listening to the sounds of the beach.

Paul glanced at his watch, then whispered, "I'm getting hungry. Are you?"

"A little. Got any ideas on what to eat and where to eat it?"

"Yes, I do, and I definitely know what I want for dessert."

"Me, too," she replied, as she pulled him closer.

"I know where this little dump of a place is. It looks like it should be condemned but the food is great. It's right by the water and we can beat the rush if we leave now." As they walked down the hall toward the elevator Paul gave her a room key. "Here's one for you in case you want to go out for a walk while I'm doing the seminar thing," he said.

This time, when they got on the elevator, several people were already on it but it did make its way to the lobby nonstop. They held hands as they walked to his car. Michelle's mind wandered down love's potential dessert buffet and just what kind of treats were in store for her later that evening because she was reasonably certain that she had some treats he might like. She knew she loved Paul and that he certainly appeared to love her and tonight she was determined to back up her words with action.

When they got to the car he opened the door for her. A few minutes later they were headed south on a multi-laned road that ran parallel to the beach. The mischief in Michelle started to bubble over and she put her hand on Paul's leg. With an innocent smile she said, "I noticed that there is only one bed in our room. Is some sort of conspiracy in the works or am I the victim of a simple twist of fate?"

"Oh, no. No conspiracy. No victim. Remember, there is a couch in the sitting room."

"Well, as long as there's no devious plot on my honor. Devious being the key word. After all, it is a king size bed." She laughed as she squeezed his leg and then moved her hand.

Paul squeezed her leg and replied, "Aren't you the coy little tart? We're almost there. I hope you like seafood."

He slowed and pulled into the parking lot which was a large, unpaved area that surrounded the restaurant on three sides. On the fourth side was water from a large inlet that stopped several feet from the building but did not leave enough room to safely park a car. Several hundred yards in the distance the edge of a large marsh began and beyond it Michelle could see more beachfront hotels but they were reduced to the size of doll houses. As she sat gazing at the view the door suddenly opened and Paul was standing there offering her his hand.

"This is beautiful and kind of off the beaten track, isn't it?"

"You mean the setting or the building?" Michelle said as she shifted her gaze from across the water to the dilapidated brown structure where they were going to eat. There were lights on both in and around it, the requisite beer sign in the window, a half dozen cars scattered around the sandy parking area, and a dim neon sign that identified it as a place of business. The dim sign was what caused her to assume that it was actually open and a viable entity. "Is it safe?" she said and laughed. "Should we have a gun or, at least, a knife?"

Paul laughed. "Definitely safe. The food is quite good so most of the people are too busy eating to cause problems. Besides, they have this karaoke thing in there and folk actually give it a go. It's hard to start a fight when you're laughing. Once, when I was here, there was some girl trying to sing and I do use the term loosely, the bartender gave her a tiny bucket and told her to take it with her so she could carry her tune in it."

Michelle laughed. "You don't have to worry about me. I might make a fool of myself doing lots of things but trying to sing in public isn't one of them."

She took Paul's outstretched hand and got out of the car. As they walked toward the entrance she continued to marvel at the serenity of the setting. Gulls screeched and soared at the water's edge while cormorants sat idly on some barnacle encrusted pilings. As they crossed the sand and gravel parking lot Michelle put her sandaled foot down on a nettle and got an attention getting jab to her toe. "Ouch!"

"What happened?"

"That plant bit my toe," she said, as a small drop of blood appeared. They paused while she surveyed the damage.

"Shall I call 9-1-1?" Paul asked with an impish grin.

"No, not yet. Let's see if I can tolerate the searing pain and stop this outrageous blood flow, first," she replied.

As they continued their walk he squeezed her hand and said, "Oh, the drama."

"I'll live," Michelle replied, "but only if the crab cakes are good."

They went up the ramp instead of the steps and walked in. The room was well lit but not bright. Scattered around at small tables that had ample space between them, the people sat in groups of two except for one table that had four at it. Outside, on a large, screened porch sat two more couples. The bartender saw them and waved his hand over the room. "Sit anywhere you want. Someone will be with you in a minute."

Michelle and Paul looked around the room again. "Inside or out?" she asked.

"How about over there by the window?"

"That's fine." They walked across the room and sat down next to a large window that overlooked the porch and the water. Not too far from that side of the building was a small marsh that had three egrets patiently searching for a snack.

A few moments later a girl in her early twenties stopped beside them and put down two menus. "I'm Janice. I'll get you some water for starters and be back in a minute."

"Lemon with mine, please," Michelle said.

Moments later Janice returned with two large glasses of ice water and a tiny bowl with some plump lemon wedges in it. "Are you ready to order now or do you need a few more minutes?"

Paul responded, "I'm ready. You?"

Michelle nodded. Janice looked at her. "What would you like, ma'am?"

"I must try the crab cakes since I've heard such good things about them, plus the slaw with a baked potato, please."

Janice looked toward Paul. "What about you, sir?" "Make it the same for me," he said.

"What would you like to drink?"

"I'll stay with water," Michelle said, as Paul nodded in agreement.

"I'll put the order in and be back in a few minutes. Thank you." With that, Janice turned and was gone. Michelle looked around the room, pausing to briefly survey the people at the other tables. Everyone appeared to be relaxed and content. She turned her gaze to study the egrets waiting patiently in the shallow water.

"How do you like it?" Paul asked.

"It's different. Has it been condemned?"

Paul laughed. “The best way to describe it is as a dump with class.”

At that Michelle laughed. “At least you got part of it right. The class part is still open for debate.”

“Don’t worry, the food is great, especially the crab cakes. I rarely try anything else because they’re so good.” He put his hand on the table and touched her fingertips. With no more than this gentle touch Michelle felt a spark shoot through her. Just for an instant she let her mind project her into the near future. She knew that on Paul’s dessert menu there would only be one choice--her, with or without whipped cream, it didn’t matter. Michelle trembled slightly at that thought and tried to think about other things in order to divert the blood that had suddenly started charging to certain areas of her body while hoping Paul wouldn’t notice the lack of success she was having.

She turned and looked back out the window. “Aren’t those birds beautiful and so elegant looking?”

“Magnificent creatures,” Paul replied, “a lot like you.”

Michelle beamed. “I’m not sure I could stand in the water on one foot quite that well.”

“When we get back to the hotel you may not be standing anywhere very long.”

Michelle feigned shock and said, “You devil, you.”

Their conversational game was suddenly interrupted as

Janice returned with their food. She placed the platters in front of them and said, “Do you need anything?”

“No.”

“No.”

“I’ll be right back with a refill on the water,” she said as she scurried away. In just a few moments Janice returned with a condensation covered pitcher and topped off their glasses.

"I'll be back to check on you in a few minutes." With that, she moved on to the other tables with her pitcher.

Michelle and Paul began eating. The food started to take the edge off her flash of passion and for that, Michelle was grateful. "This really is good," she said after a few bites.

"I'm glad you like it," Paul replied, "this is my favorite place to eat when I'm down here."

"I can see why."

As she ate, Michelle watched the other people. A few more folks had come in but the room still wasn't crowded. Their arrival seemed to balance the number who had finished eating and left. She became aware of Paul's foot touching her foot. Michelle pressed it closer to his as she thought once again about what would probably take place back at the hotel. It had been a long time and she wanted it to happen--and for it to happen tonight with Paul.

As far as relationships were concerned she knew they were proceeding at a much slower pace than most other people but she still had a tremendous problem with the trust thing. Paul had displayed no sign of pressuring her or that he was anything other than sincere and trustworthy. Still, though she wanted it to happen, she couldn't fully relax. Michelle stopped eating as her mind started to wander and she became acutely aware of one thing--when this blows up, it's really going to hurt and that it would take a long time for her to recover, if she ever did.

Michelle was suddenly jarred back to reality. Paul was talking to her and, much to her embarrassment, she had absolutely no idea what he had just said, "Are you okay?"

That was the only thing that registered with her and she replied, "I'm fine. I was just lost in crab cake thought. Sorry.

What were you saying?"

"They really have a good key lime pie if you want dessert."

Before Michelle could stop herself, she blurted, "I do, and you're the dessert I want." "Damn," she thought, "I wonder if he caught it." Trying to regroup, she added, "I don't believe I said that."

"I don't, either, but you did. You just might get a two scooper tonight, whipped cream, cherries, big banana, the whole thing."

"Bring it on, big boy. I really like the sound of that big banana thing. You just might get a treat yourself," she said, as she ran her foot up his leg.

As they were finishing, Janice came back and said, "How was it?"

"Very good."

"Great."

"Dessert anyone? We have some good ones. The key lime pie is my favorite. It has a slightly different taste a little more pizzazz than most."

Paul looked at Michelle and said, "Let's split one."

"Okay, but I'll have to burn the calories later."

"Maybe you should eat the whole piece, then. Burn them, you shall."

Janice got tickled as she stood there listening to their exchange. "This sounds like a really fun dessert," she said, "I'll be right back." When she returned she brought two pieces of key lime pie. "Here's to energy and lots of it," she said as she put them on the table. As Janice put down the check she winked at Michelle and said, "Hope the rest of your evening is fun. Come back to see us." With that, she turned and walked away.

They sat in silence as they ate their dessert. Finally, Michelle said, "This really is good and it does have a slightly different taste."

"Told you it would be."

After they had both finished eating they continued to sit for a while sipping their water and looking out the window. The shadows were much longer now and some of the objects were getting hard to identify. After what seemed to be a long, pensive silence Michelle said, "You're right. This is a great place to eat. The ambiance isn't quite Fifth Avenue but I bet it's more fun."

"I think so. I've had crab cakes in a lot of places but never quite as good as these are. Shall we go?"

Michelle nodded. She had a pretty good idea how she would be burning more than just a few calories in a little while and a tremor of anticipation ran through her.

Paul reached for the check as he stood up. "I'll do the tip," Michelle said, "she sure added to the evening."

"Okay."

Michelle left Janice a generous tip and followed Paul toward the cash register at the end of the bar near the door. The bartender came over as they approached. "How was everything?" Then he added, "I know it went down. Do you think it'll stay down?"

The three of them chuckled together. "I think so," Paul replied, "anyway, I hope it does."

As he handed Paul his change, Moe said, "Thanks for stopping by. Come back to see us."

They both waved at Janice as Paul opened the door and they stepped outside. What few lights there were to illuminate the parking lot had come on. Along with them the multi- colored neon sign gave ample lighting to see where they were walking. As they walked toward their car Michelle slipped her hand into Paul's and gave it squeeze. "That was fun. Janice was a hoot and a really good waitress," she said, "thanks."

"Yu're welcome. It was quite nice; a great way to spend the early evening." He gave Michelle a slight tug toward him and put his arm around her as they walked. She leaned into him and he guided her across the parking lot as she looked up at the sky. When they got to the car Paul opened the door and she got in. Michelle reached over and unlocked his door. "I think I ate too much," he said.

"I know I did."

"Shall we go back to the hotel or is there somewhere you would like to go?" Paul asked.

"Hotel is fine," Michelle replied. "It's been a long day and I'm starting to fade."

"Well, don't fade out of sight because there may be some no-cal dessert later."

"Promise me," Michelle said, as she laughed and put her hand on his leg.

"Promise," he replied.

The drive back to the hotel only took them twenty minutes. Neither said very much and Michelle was well aware of the silence. One reason she enjoyed Paul's company so much was that he truly seemed to enjoy talking with her. Their conversation covered many different topics, from the light hearted and silly to the heavy philosophy of life.

Tonight though, neither seemed to have much to say and Michelle wondered if Paul was aware of the silence. Her mind was on what would transpire in a little while and she was sure that he was having similar thoughts.

When they arrived at the hotel they had to search for a place to park. Numerous people had arrived since they left for supper and the place they had originally parked had been taken by someone else. They parked in a corner of the lot and walked toward the main entrance. There wasn't a great deal of noise except for the waves crashing on the beach about a hundred yards away. A magnolia tree was in bloom not far from where they had parked. The breeze carried the scent of the blooms across that part of the lot causing Michelle to stop and inhale deeply through her nose as she tried to drink in as much air as she could. "I love magnolias," she said, "they're beautiful even when they're not blooming but when their blooms open, let me get downwind. They smell so good."

They stopped and Paul sniffed the air. "They do smell good," he said.

After standing there for a few moments savoring the aroma, they continued across the lot toward the front door. Three other people were waiting for the elevator and it arrived just moments after Paul and Michelle got there. Two stops later they got off on their floor and walked down the hall toward their room. Michelle knew she was a little nervous and hoped it wasn't too obvious. Other than Paul's lack of his usual conversation he showed no sign of being anxious. Michelle began to wonder if he could hear her heart pounding. They stopped and Paul opened the door, then he followed her in.

"After I do my teeth I'm going to take a splash," she said as she fumbled in her luggage for her toothbrush.

"Okay. I think I'll do that, too," Paul answered. Early in their relationship Paul had thought it odd that Michelle always said she was going to "do" her teeth instead of brush them. He had later discovered why her smile was so bright and why she had no fear of the dentist. Paul also noticed that he began to become more tooth conscious after they started spending more time together.

Michelle finished her tooth ritual and had once again started looking through her suitcase for sleep wear. Finding what she needed, she went back into the bathroom. Moments later Paul heard her turn on the shower. As Paul looked toward the bathroom door that she had left slightly open, the bathroom went dark. The harsh fluorescent brilliance had been replaced by a soft glow that he could barely distinguish with the lamp in the bedroom turned on. He quickly turned the light off and let his eyes adjust. The glow was a little brighter now and seemed to be flickering. Paul walked over to get a better look. On the counter by the sink two scented candles were burning. They put off enough light so he could see what was going on but not enough to be obtrusive. "Nice touch," he said through the slightly opened door.

"Thank you. I hoped you would like it. Do you do backs?"

"Fronts, too," he replied, "and all points in between."

Over the sound of the splashing water he heard Michelle say in a soft, shy voice, "Then, why don't you do mine?"

Seconds later Michelle saw a shadow moving across the room and the shower door slid open. As Paul stepped in and closed the door, he whispered, "Don't mind if I do." As the warm water splashed on the two of them, he turned to face Michelle and pulled her close.

Michelle's Goodbye

Michelle met Paul at Bud's Steakhouse for supper. Though they couldn't always get together on Wednesday evening for a mid-week rendezvous, she always looked forward to it when they could work it out. All day long she had let her mind wander about the upcoming evening and how much fun it would be. Now, even though she was a little bit tired from an exasperating day at work, Michelle tried to remain upbeat and perky.

Paul was waiting for her in the parking lot when she arrived. She parked and walked over to where he was standing. For a brief moment Michelle wondered why he didn't approach her but she cast it aside as insecurity. She said, "Hi," and put her arm around him as they started toward the restaurant entrance. Paul managed a faint smile and fell in step with her and though he also put his arm around her, he really didn't give her the squeeze she was expecting. Though Michelle tried to ignore it, to some degree it had troubled her. "Oh, well," she thought, "maybe his day was more aggravating than mine." However, it still gnawed at a corner of her mind. Michelle finally decided that she would simply have to feel good enough for both of them.

They stepped inside and waited for the hostess to seat them. Michelle was still trying to engage Paul in conversation but she was having very little success. He was not only very unresponsive to her efforts, she had also noticed that he seemed to be avoiding eye contact. This disturbed her even more because they usually had such a good time chatting with each other.

The hostess showed them to a booth in one corner of the room and placed a menu in front of each of them. As she turned to go, she said, "Your waitress will be with you in a few minutes." With that, she walked quietly away.

Paul sat there staring uneasily at his menu. Michelle sat across from him alternating between contemplating her menu and contemplating him. He was obviously preoccupied with something because he was fidgeting and seemed to be having a great deal of trouble concentrating.

It suddenly dawned on Michelle that she was very hungry and she pushed all other thoughts out of her mind and began to intently study the menu. About the time she made her selection their waitress approached to take their orders. Arriving at their booth, she smiled and greeted them. Michelle returned the smile and also spoke, Paul simply looked up and nodded but with a blank expression.

"Are you ready to order?" the waitress asked in a cheery voice.

"I am," Michelle replied. Paul just nodded to the affirmative.

After they had ordered and the waitress had departed, Michelle's thoughts once again returned to Paul and whatever it was that seemed to be bothering him so much. "I wish you would tell me what it is that's bothering you so. It must be something big because this just isn't like you," Michelle said quietly, as she reached across to touch his hand. She squeezed his fingertips but he did not respond, he just sat there with a blank expression looking at the surface that was separating them. Though the movement was almost imperceptible, Michelle felt his fingertips move slightly away from hers.

At that precise moment she knew what was on his mind and she also had a good idea as to who the other woman was. As she pulled her hand away from his Michelle felt a tremendous pounding in her chest. She immediately went into denial as her mind raced. "No," she thought, "I'm simply filling in the blanks with the wrong words. I'm jumping to conclusions. This is not related to us but to work or something else, not us. He told me he loved me. I must relax." With a great deal of effort, she finally composed herself and decided that she was simply being paranoid. As her pounding heart started to return to normal she began to feel better. "Why do I get so uptight over nothing?" she wondered. If Paul had noticed any change in her he had shown no sign of it. He was still just sitting there with a blank look as if he were in a hypnotic trance and didn't know what to do next.

Michelle was jarred back to reality by the waitress returning with their food. One whiff of the aroma and she was reminded of how hungry she was. It seemed to her that it was great effort that Paul moved his hands so his plate could be set before him. As they ate Michelle continued in her efforts to persuade Paul to tell her what was troubling him so much but she still had little success. Finally, he said, "This just isn't the time or place. After we finish eating we'll go to your house where we can talk in private."

Michelle thought what he said to be strange because it had never mattered before where they talked. She just said, "Okay," and let it drop. After that she made no more effort to engage him in conversation and though her mind was racing, she was having trouble concentrating on anything. All she knew was that she had a very heavy, foreboding feeling of impending doom.

When Michelle finished eating her grilled Cajun chicken salad she looked over to see if Paul was also through. He had barely touched his food, mostly he had just sat there toying with it and when he did take a bite, it seemed to take him forever to chew it.

Though he still had not looked up, Paul seemed to sense that she was finished and that she was looking at him. "Are you ready to go?" he asked.

"Wasn't your steak good?" Michelle inquired.

Instead of replying to her question, he just said, "I'm really not very hungry."

"It's Erika, isn't it?" Michelle said, barely above a whisper.

Once again there was no answer to her question, just, "If you're through, let's go."

Michelle felt her energy draining out of her. He had not admitted anything but neither had he denied it. Again Michelle grasped for anything that would give her hope and she decided that until he told her that it really was Erika, she would remain totally convinced that it was just a very bad day at work. Deep in her mind she knew that the only person she was kidding was herself but she clung desperately to this hope, it was all she had.

Paul beckoned for the waitress and asked for their check. She removed it from her apron and handed it to him. He quickly glanced at it and handed her some money. Noticing his mostly uneaten food, she asked if there had been something wrong with it. His reply was that he really wasn't as hungry as he had earlier thought he was. As he got out of the booth he said to the waitress, "Thank you," and to Michelle, "Ready?"

Michelle nodded and got up. As they walked toward the door she became acutely aware that though they were together, they were really walking out separately and when she thought about it, it was the same way they had walked in. Once they were outside, Paul said, "I'll follow you home, I think we really need to talk."

Though Michelle did not say it, she thought that it would certainly be the first time tonight. As she got in her car Paul walked over to his. She started the engine and backed out of the parking place. Michelle pulled into the street with Paul behind her. In the fifteen minutes it took for them to drive from Bud's Steakhouse to where she lived her mind tried to cover every possible scenario. Each time, after analyzing a situation, she always came up with the same result--it's kiss-off time.

By the time they got to her driveway she had decided that there was no other reason for what had already transpired during the course of the evening. In order to better brace herself for what she knew was about to happen, Michelle decided that she would accept it as a simple twist of fate and wish Paul the best in his decision. In order to give denial one last chance, she decided that one of his parents had suddenly become ill. Though it was a weak thought, it was a straw and for the moment she really needed something to hold on to.

Michelle turned into her driveway and, after a few moments, Paul pulled in behind her. She turned off her lights and got out of the car. For an instant she stood in the glare of Paul's lights and then suddenly she was in darkness when he turned them off. Michelle could almost feel the darkness around her and it seemed to match the feeling that something less than good was about to happen. She visualized herself as looking down a dark alley through which she needed to pass, one filled with overflowing dumpsters and being reasonably sure that she would not come out the other end unscathed.

Many times before she had stood by her car door as she waited for Paul to get out and walk over to her. All the other times had made her tingle with anticipation and excitement but not tonight. Suddenly she was so very tired, almost to the point that she didn't want Paul to come in and discuss anything. If all he had to tell her was that he was "stabbing her in the back," why go to the trouble, she decided. Michelle suddenly became aware that Paul was standing beside her and that was all he was doing, just standing there, not saying anything, not touching her, not anything, just standing there. In the past in situations such as this, he had often put his arms around her and they just stood there holding each other in the dim light. On at least one occasion they had gotten carried away and had almost undressed each other before a neighbor's dog had started barking and jarred them back to reality but that wasn't happening tonight, Paul simply said, "We can probably talk better inside."

Without either of them saying anything else they walked up the sidewalk to Michelle's front door. There they paused long enough for her to unlock it, then they both stepped inside. Michelle turned on a lamp as Paul closed the door. "It won't be long now," she thought, "everything will be all right or everything will be all wrong." Though she still did not want to face it, deep in her heart she knew which one it would be. Turning to face Paul, she said, "What do you want to tell me?"

Though he was looking at her, he would not look her in the eye. His eyes were focused on her neck and try as he might, he couldn't bring himself to meet Michelle's dark eyes that he knew had always held so much trust in him. He didn't mean to be cruel about it but he knew that what he was going to say would cut her to the heart.

In a voice barely louder than a whisper he spoke, "Michelle, you know I love you," and then he paused.

"There's still a glimmer of hope," Michelle thought, "he said he loves me."

"Sometimes things happen that we don't always count on. There's someone else." As he was saying this he finally looked her in the eye, his face showed absolutely no expression, no happiness, no sadness, not even a look of relief. For all the emotion he expressed, he could have had on a death mask. Paul just stood there as if waiting for her to make the next move or to say the next word.

Michelle also just stood there as if nothing had been said that would affect her in any way. Though she clearly heard the the words and knew exactly what they meant, her mind refused to register what had been said. Her brain reacted just like it would have if she had been severely injured and, knowing that the physical pain would be too great for her to bear, it simply short-circuited in order to protect her. With a trace of a smile, she said, "It's Erika, isn't it?"

Paul nodded and answered with a whisper, "Yes."

Though Michelle had never actually met Erika, she had seen her a few times when she would go to meet Paul after his aerobics class. From the first time she had ever seen her, Michelle had always thought that Erika was a real "looker", the kind that most men would go for. She appeared to Michelle to be in her late twenties and had apparently started out having all her curves in the right places. The many, many hours of exercise that she had taken as an instructor had only enhanced these curves even more. She wasn't as tall as Michelle but she was slightly heavier and, obviously, very firm. After seeing Erika for the first time, Michelle often wondered if the men in class were there for the exercise or if they just got their hearts pounding by drooling over her "spray-on" leotards. Paul appeared to really enjoy her class and since Michelle knew the exercise was good for him, she had never thought about him pursuing her as a love interest. Besides, not only was there a tremendous age difference where Paul and Erika were concerned, he had said that he loved her, they had even discussed the possibility of something permanent.

Finally, though her mind was fighting it, the meaning of his words began to sink in. Michelle felt as if she had been hooked up to a machine that was draining the energy out of her and she put her left hand on the back of a chair to help support herself. Her stomach felt as if someone had just delivered a tremendous blow there and for a moment she thought she was going to be sick.

Michelle put her right hand on the chair for some additional support. Her mind was racing but none of the thoughts made any sense. Finally, she said, "If this is some kind of a joke, it's not very funny." Paul did not answer, he just continued to stand there looking mostly at the floor but with a few furtive glances at Michelle's face. After what seemed like an eternity of silence, she said in a loud whisper, "Why?" Paul still did not reply. After giving him ample opportunity to say something, Michelle asked again in the same loud whisper, "Why?" She looked him directly in the eyes as she asked this short question, her eyes pleading in turn for an answer that she could understand.

Finally, just when Michelle thought she would scream, Paul said quietly, "I don't know. I wasn't looking. These things just happen."

"Well, it didn't just happen to me," Michelle blurted in a voice that surprised her.

Then the silence began once more, it was finally starting to sink in--Paul was walking out of her life because, once again, her best just simply wasn't good enough. Enormous, very viscous tears suddenly formed in her eyes but did not fall. They were so large that she felt as if her eyes were being squeezed in a vise. Had the "crack" in her heart not caused the tears to finally fall, the pain in her eyes surely would have. Michelle blinked several times to try to ease that pain and she finally succeeded—the tears started to flow. They trickled slowly down her cheeks, each one following the one in front of it like tiny, transparent toy soldiers and like a well trained toy soldier, upon reaching the bottom of her face, each one in turn leaped to its death on the carpet at the back of the chair.

Paul was not quite sure what to say or do. He started to go put his arms around her but finally ended up just staying where he was. "How do I ease her pain when I'm the one who caused it?" he wondered. Not knowing what else to say and being really uncomfortable watching her heart break and her dreams shatter, he said in a quiet voice, "Maybe I should go on home." Michelle nodded but did not answer.

Paul started for the door, then stopped. Somehow it didn't seem right to just walk out. He thought, "Surely I can say something to make her feel better but what does one say when he, or she, has just destroyed all the hopes and dreams of another person?" Then, it suddenly came to him. He remembered a magical incantation that is usually uttered when one symbolically stabs another person in the back in order to end an affair of the heart. Actually, it does nothing to help the "stabbee", it is said only to help assuage the feelings of guilt of the "stabber". Not that the "stabber" ever really gives a damn, he doesn't care, he saw it coming. He wasn't caught off guard, there were no suprises in his world.

Like untold numbers of "back-stabbers" before him and those to come after him, Paul looked at Michelle and said, "Don't worry, you'll find someone else." This incantation always comes out easily because the person saying it is going on to a new set of hopes and dreams. The one standing there with pieces of shattered dreams scattered around never says, "Don't worry, I'll find somebody else." It's always one sided. One party thinks, "I'm glad that's over," and the other party thinks, "What's the use?"

Michelle did not even acknowledge Paul's statement, she just stood there trying to organize her thoughts as she looked around the room through eyes that were still blurred with tears. She tried to focus her eyes on Paul but the tears refracted the light so much that she couldn't do it. Everything seemed to have very soft, fuzzy edges instead of the usual sharp, well defined lines that they had just a few minutes earlier.

By invoking the age old incantation, "you'll find someone else", Paul was trying to accomplish two things. First, he was trying to ease the tremendous guilt he felt due to destroying Michelle's dreams and breaking her heart simply because he had gotten what he perceived to be a better offer and now her love, caring, and all the other feelings she had for him were simply no longer good enough. It did not matter that he had expressed his "love" for her many times in a variety of ways. Neither did it matter that he had willingly, even enthusiastically, been a participating member in the building of these dreams with her.

Secondly, he simply assumed that Michelle would find someone else, or, that someone else would find her. Either way, he was sure that sje would have a "significant other" in her life in the not too distant future. In reality though, he really didn't give a damn whether she found someone else or not but thinking it made him feel better. What really mattered was that he had found someone else and he was off to bigger and better things, in his mind, with someone who excited him more, or, so he thought.

It wasn't that Michelle no longer excited him, it was simply that, because she loved him she always tried to meet him at least half-way, sometimes more. With Erika, it was different. Erika really didn't love him and he really didn't love her but there was the high voltage spark of infatuation, intrigue, and passion that fueled their mutual interest in each other. He had to chase, catch, and then conquer her, Michelle was just there. He could always count on her to do just what she said she would do. They trusted each other in every way and neither had ever given the other a reason not to do so.

Over the span of their involvement Michelle had been the recipient of numerous invitations to spend time with other men in a variety of situations. Her major mistake was that she had always taken affairs of the heart, especially love, on a very personal level. To her, it was not just a game and she had not been equipped with the "on-off" love switch that so many people seemed to have. It had always baffled her how someone could profess to be forever madly in love with a different person every few months, or, sometimes every few weeks. Because of these observations she had always tried to approach relationships very slowly.

When Michelle was in high school and in college she had been "dumped" several times and, though none of the guys ever had the nerve to tell her the real reason, some of her friends told her it had been because her legs were tied together at the knees. Though it had hurt her at the time, and the cumulative effects of these blows of life would not be fully known until years later, she had managed to recover rather quickly because she took pride in herself and because she took love very personally.

Having been treated in this manner still did not change her. Her philosophy was "first the love, then the bed" instead of the more popular concept of "first the bed and let's see how how we feel in the morning." Because she approached affairs of the heart so slowly and deliberately this sudden change in her life caused by what Paul had just said and done left her deeply disturbed.

There was an awkward silence that lasted perhaps a half a minute. Michelle quietly broke the tension with a loud whisper, "I thought you loved me. You said you did. I love you. Doesn't any of this mean anything or was it all just a game?" She was surprised that it came out so quietly, she had intended to say it in a normal voice but she suddenly just did not have the energy. "Look, if you want to be with Erika, go ahead and give it a shot but if it doesn't work out, you can come back. I'll still be here."

"Either way, I won't be back," he whispered. Paul just stood there looking back at her with a look on his face that expressed both hurt and bewilderment. "Bugaboo, you know I love you; I'll always love you," he replied.

"I can really tell just how much you love me. It's so obvious, how could I help but be aware of it?" Michelle responded. A sudden burst of anger had given her enough energy to get her voice back. "I guess you really should leave because, if this is love, I'm really not interested in it anymore."

Paul started toward her as if to give her one last hug or to touch her in some other way but she stopped him with a shake of her head and a quiet, "No."

He stopped and turned back toward the front door and opened it. Paul paused and looked back at Michelle who was still standing behind the chair. "See ya'," he said, to which she responded with just a nod. Then he closed the door and was gone.

Just like that he was gone. The same door he had walked through to enter her life, he walked through to exit her life. The door looked the same, the room looked the same, everything looked the same and though they all looked the same, they had all now become different. No longer would they be items that simply served a purpose, they would forever become symbols of her life and dreams being blown all to hell without even an explanation. Not only would her surroundings never be the same, Michelle sensed that something had changed not only in her heart but also in her mind. Standing there looking around the room she just wasn't sure to what extent. Though she wasn't sure about the feelings she had, Michelle was sure that her life where affairs of the heart were concerned would never be the same again. She knew that this much hurt would have a long lasting, telling effect on her.

Michelle wiped the tears from her eyes and walked over to check the front door to be sure it had latched properly. Looking around the room, she observed that it looked just as it had looked that morning as she was leaving for work. One would have to look closely to find any difference in the two scenes because the only change was very subtle; tears on the back of the chair and also some on the carpet behind it. This slight change would probably even be overlooked by the trained observer. Michelle didn't even see it though she knew it was there. Had she thought about it, she would have wondered how that one minor change could possibly be so major.

She looked at her watch and was surprised to discover that it was not at all late, early bedtime at best. What seemed to have taken forever had, in reality, only taken a few minutes. "Strange," she thought, "that building dreams is such a long, slow process while destroying them only takes a moment."

From the front door Michelle walked over to the lamp and turned it off. She dreaded the walk down the darkened hall to her bedroom but she could not bring herself to turn on the hall light. Though she had not been afraid of the dark since she was a little girl, now she suddenly was. Even as she stood there hesitating to enter the hallway, she still refused to turn on the light to illuminate her surroundings. With her fingertips lightly touching the wall Michelle started slowly could go no further in the darkness and she forced herself to turn on the overhead light, then she walked over and turned on a small lamp by her bed. After that, she returned to the doorway and flipped the ceiling light off, then she went into the bathroom to brush her teeth and wash her face. After completing these tasks, she turned off the light and went over and sat down on the side of her bed. Everything she did was very deliberate, almost as if she had never done these things before. Michelle fumbled with the buttons on her blouse. She discovered that the front of it was wet and she sat there wondering how that had happened. She stopped trying to unbutton it and concentrated on what had happened to it. Finally, it dawned on her, she had forgotten to take it off before she washed her face. "That was dumb," she thought, "why did I forget to do that?"

After several minutes Michelle at last had enough energy to complete the task of undressing. Instead of hanging her clothes up she simply laid them across the back of a chair and slipped on a short gown. The gown was very simple, no lace or frills, but very feminine. The soft, cool satin felt good on her skin and the slight flare at the bottom accentuated her slender hips. The bottom of the gown hung just above mid-thigh and, had there been someone there with her, that person would have found her most appealing. However, tonight there was no one there to admire how she looked or how good her soft, smooth skin would feel. Michelle was all alone except for her thoughts and she really wished they would go away. What had happened earlier had been such a severe blow to her emotions that her mind had failed to fully process all that had happened. By not fully processing all of the data, her brain had done her a tremendous favor but now more of what had taken place was starting to sink in.

Michelle turned off the light and got in bed. The cool sheets felt good and for that she was grateful. As she moved around trying to find just the right spot and position, she closed her eyes and hoped that sleep would soon overtake her. Tonight, however, sleep would not be kind to her. Each time she closed her eyes the words and places of the evening appeared in her mind like a loop film.

Once again she felt her energy draining from her and more large tears forming in her eyes. Finally, the tears grew so large and hurt so much that she had to blink to force them out. Since she was lying on her back a tear went down each side of her face. The tear on the right side missed most of her hair and found its way into her ear. "As if things weren't bad enough," she thought, "now I have a waterlogged ear." Catching a piece of the sheet on the tip of her right little finger she dried her ear the best she could and shifted her position to avoid having that happen again.

Michelle knew by now that sleep would be a long time coming, if it arrived at all. As the minutes dragged on she changed positions from on her back to one side, then the other. Nothing worked and she at last decided--toddy time. Pushing the sheet back, she sat up on the side of the bed. Reaching over to turn on her bedside lamp, she closed her eyes against the sudden brightness. With her eyes still closed, Michelle got up and walked in the general direction of the bedroom door. Only when she could touch the wall did she at last open her eyes to the glow of the lamp. Her eyes adjusted quickly and this time she turned on the hall light and headed for the kitchen.

Upon reaching the kitchen, she turned on the light and walked over to the cabinet over the refrigerator, opened it and removed a bottle of Canadian Mist which she set on the counter. She then removed from the refrigerator a half-filled bottle of Coke and poured a water glass about two-thirds full. Returning the Coke back to the refrigerator, she turned her attention to the other bottle and she finished filling the glass nearly to the top. Michelle put the cap back on the bottle and set it back on the counter instead of returning it to the cabinet. "No reason to make it hard to get," she thought, "I'll probably need it again." With a long plastic spoon from the dish drain she stirred her rather potent sleeping potion. Michelle rinsed the spoon and put it back in the drain with the other utensils. Initially, she just took a small sip to see how the drink tasted. A little strong, she decided, but then she really wasn't drinking it to be sociable, she was drinking it to relax, to forget and, mainly, to get drunk and sleepy. After the initial taste assault on her tongue, she took a deep breath and downed what was left. Michelle washed out the glass, took two drinks of water, and walked back to her bedroom, turning out the lights as she went.

She hardly noticed how good the cool, fuzzy carpet felt to her feet as she walked. She got back in bed and pulled the sheet back up over her. Taking one last look around the room, she reached over and turned off the lamp on the night stand. As Michelle snuggled in between the pillows she started to dwell on how much her life had changed over the course of the last few hours.

As Michelle lay there in the darkness on her back the earlier scenes of the evening began to haunt her. She went from having dreams and plans for the future to having nothing. It dawned on her that she was actually worse off now than when she had first met Paul. She had invested nearly two years of her time building a future with someone else and now that someone else was gone. As she tried to concentrate on what was on her mind she felt the rather stiff sleeping potion she had just consumed start to reach her brain. Her thought processes started to cloud and she actually felt as if she were growing longer as the tenseness started to leave her body. "I'm so limp I could pass for a wet noodle," she thought, as the alcohol powered rocket inside her head started to take her away in a slowly spinning, climbing trajectory.

Though her thoughts were becoming very muddled, she suddenly became very sad. Michelle felt tears start to form in her eyes again and she opened them to take one last look around the room. As best she could tell everything still seemed to be in place so she closed them again and continued her journey. The sensation of spinning wasn't rapid enough to make her sick, it was just fast enough to feel good, like a slow carnival ride. At last the troubling thoughts of what had just happened faded from her brain and she floated away into the blackness of the only escape she would know for a long time--sleep, that would usually be alcohol kick started.

As the ensuing days and nights passed Michelle continued to dwell on what had happened. Every waking moment that her mind was not actively occupied by something else was spent on what Paul had said and done and the changes it had brought about. Her thoughts were complicated even more by the fact that he had not given her any reason for saying goodbye. If he had only told her why she could have better understood and possibly, even changed, but there had been no, "Michelle, you're too fat," "Michelle, you're too thin," "You have a wart on your nose," or even, "I like blondes better." His only attempt at an explanation had been, "These things just happen" and this was killing her.

Here she was in her upper middle thirties and the dreams she had built with another person had once again blown up in her face. The family she had hoped to have was gone, the special friend she had hoped to spend her life with was gone, but what hurt her the most was that her dreams went with him.

Michelle had tried to enter this relationship with Paul very slowly for several reasons. First, she was tired of being hurt. Second, she really wanted it to work but most of all, she took love very personally instead of using it as just another adult bed game.

Her entrance, once again, into the world of affairs of the heart had been done with great trepidation simply because of the toll it always took on her body and mind. So fearful was she of what might happen that she often thought of herself as a small child that had moved away from the familiar neighborhood where she grew up to a strange new neighborhood. The thought of entering this strange new world initially kept her inside the safety of her house, daring only to look out a window or to sit on the floor and stare out the screen door. Eventually, though, she decided to venture outside and play on the large front porch but, for the time being, she could go no farther. For a long time, she remained on the porch or sat on the steps playing with her dolls, but she could not bring herself to venture into the yard, much too unfamiliar. At last, the beauty and mystery of the large front yard was too intriguing and she had ventured down the steps and out the front walk toward the street. Before she could go that far, her fear of what might happen took over and she decided, that for now, the front yard was just fine, so she became comfortable with her surroundings and learned to enjoy them before going forward.

Though Michelle was safe in her front yard of her, mind and enjoyed the beauty of the flowers and trees, she eventually found herself playing closer and closer to the street with its fast moving traffic and a sidewalk that paralleled it. One day she grew bored with playing in the shade of a large tree in her yard and, putting down her doll, she walked quietly over to the edge of the yard and out onto the sidewalk. For the first time since moving to her new neighborhood Michelle's vision was no longer blocked by the tall hedge that bordered each side of her front yard. She just stood there looking up and down the sidewalk, afraid of, but yet excited by, this strange new world.

Her mom was inside baking, thinking that her shy little girl was still content to play with her dolls in the shade. As Michelle stood there trying to put this strange new world in perspective, a car loaded with teenage boys turned the corner and headed down the street right by where she was standing, still lost in the innocent world of a small child. With no thought or caring as to what it might do to her, they decided to have a laugh at her expense. Michelle was still looking the other way as the car approached. When it got near her the driver suddenly gunned the engine, blew the horn and swerved toward the very spot where the quiet, shy little girl with dark eyes and dark hair stood totally entranced by this strange new world. With no warning her tranquil world was shattered by this dark object roaring at her with its occupants shouting and laughing and the horn blaring.

With her dark eyes wide, Michelle watched it approach. She neither ran nor screamed. Before it got to the sidewalk the car swerved sharply away from her and roared out of sight down the street. Only after the silence returned did Michelle begin to cry. She took one last look up and down the street through her tears and walked slowly back over to her doll that she had left in the shade under the large tree. Once again she was safe in her own little world. Though unknown to her at that time, as the years unfolded, she would fine that her only place of refuge from the blows of life was inside her head.

Michelle's Attack

P. J.'s Pub was a popular gathering place for Michelle and numerous other people from the office complex where she worked. Though she no longer frequented it as often as she once had, Michelle still occasionally got together with some of her friends to visit and to try to relax to get the weekend started on a high note. This particular Friday evening she had joined six others in what had become a regular routine for four of the group and it was not uncommon for them to be joined by several more.

Michelle usually did not drink very much away from her home but the past few times that she had joined them she had seemed to lose track of the amount of alcohol she consumed. She drank so much one evening that Lisa, the office receptionist, had insisted that Michelle not even attempt to drive home but ride with her instead. Now, when Michelle attended the happy hour gatherings Lisa would usually stop by to pick her up and then take her back home to be sure she got there safely.

This evening they had been sitting around the table laughing and talking for about two hours, just whiling away the time and nibbling on appetizers. Michelle was at least one drink ahead of everyone and two drinks ahead of some.

Occasionally, she would briefly join in the conversation but mostly she just sat there appearing to be an avid, interested listener. When the others would laugh, she would laugh, too. Michelle really didn't care whether it was funny or not, she was there to drink and since she didn't have to drive, she knew it was safer than drinking alone at home.

Though the others observed her mouth laughing, had they looked deep into her eyes they would have seen only sadness. The lips that laughed were only a facade for a heart that was filled with the pain of confusion and emptiness. The hurt in her heart hung there like giant clusters of ripe grapes on the vine when they are ready to be harvested. One major difference though, was that someone would come by and remove the grapes before their weight caused the vine to break but Michelle's heart was different. There would be no worker coming by to remove the heavy clusters from it. They would simply continue to grow heavier and heavier until the tender, young vine was destroyed by the burden of this ever increasing weight.

If her friends had peeked inside her heart they would have found it crying out in its emptiness because of shattered dreams that she could neither overcome nor understand-- much like a single wolf howling in the moonlight from the top of a snow covered hill. The one thing that they would not have heard was the answer to this lonesome call. Much like this wolf, Michelle was alone and her mind hurt.

Michelle had consumed three more drinks than it took to get her comfortably tipsy and she was glad she did not have to drive home. She was well aware that to attempt to do that could possibly add more problems to her life that was already buffeted by enough stressful, frustrating circumstances that she could barely cope with them. Also, she was unwilling to risk endangering the lives of others simply due to an act of irresponsibility on her part.

As if a switch had been thrown inside her head Michelle suddenly became very tired, almost to the point of exhaustion. She began to feel even more disjointed from the group and their voices and the background seemed very far away. "To just go away and not ever come back would be wonderful," she thought. Michelle looked over at Lisa to catch her eye, then said, "I'm really tired. Are you ready to leave?"

"Are you sure?" Lisa replied. "Things are just starting to happen. Maybe you'll feel better in a few minutes. If you don't, we'll go. How about another gin and tonic? That might help."

Michelle just nodded to the affirmative. She hated to be a party pooper and she really did appreciate Lisa coming by her house to pick her up so she leaned back in her chair and took another sip of her drink.

From his seat across the table Larry had been intently watching Michelle. He knew that she was drinking too much, that she usually did, and that Lisa usually went by Michelle's house to pick her up. He had also observed the short exchange between the two of them through a combination of lip reading and faint hearing. He knew Michelle wanted to go home and that Lisa did not want to leave just yet. Larry thought about what he had just learned and suddenly had an idea for something that could prove to be a very interesting evening, especially from his point of view.

Larry had been observing Michelle ever since he had started his job delivering the office mail to the different floors several months earlier. At times he had a tendency to dawdle if he saw her. He viewed her as an attractive woman, though at times very distant and quiet, especially in recent months. There had even been times when he had let his imagination run just a little bit wild where Michelle was concerned. He knew that she kept mostly to herself and, for the most part, avoided social interaction with very few exceptions. One of these exceptions was to come to P. J.'s with a small group of people and get really drunk. Larry had also learned that Michelle had been heavily involved with some man named Paul and that her strange behavior had started after he had suddenly walked out of her life. As Larry was hurriedly formulating a plan, he thought to himself, "She is a slinky wench, what a waste."

Across the table Michelle was staring off into space when Larry started looking at her and trying to catch her eye. Though he continued to participate in the conversation with the group, he mainly watched her. Finally, after what seemed like an eternity to him, Michelle's eyes focused on her surroundings and she noticed Larry looking at her. Before she could look away he slowly mouthed the words, "I'll take you home if you really want to go."

Michelle just sat there looking at him without a response so he tried once more. Still no response. He caught Lisa's eye and mouthed to her, "If you want to stay here, I'll be glad to take Michelle home. I'm getting ready to leave, anyway."

Lisa nodded and turned to Michelle and said, "Larry has volunteered to take you home if you want him to. He's getting ready to leave, anyway."

Michelle nodded and said, "Okay. It's too far to walk and I'm too bombed to drive, even if I had my car." As she stood up she held on to her chair for support and thought that she probably should not have had the last three drinks. Larry pushed back his chair and walked around to where she was standing, still holding on to the chair to keep from swaying.

Michelle was fumbling in her purse for some money when Larry placed several bills on the table. "This will cover mine and yours," he said, with a smile.

As he took her by the arm and started toward the door, she looked at him and said, "Thank you." Then she looked at the people still at the table and said, "Goodnight, everybody.

See you Monday." Everyone spoke or waved in return and continued their conversation. With Larry helping to support her, they started toward the exit.

Once outside they paused and Michelle took several deep breaths to try to clear her eyes and head. After a few moments they proceeded slowly across the parking lot. Larry had turned loose of Michelle's arm and had put his arm around her waist. This move was not solely to better support her but also to see how drunk she really was. Larry was slightly surprised to discover that Michelle seemed either unaware of his arm or that she just didn't care. This bit of information only served to heighten his interest.

In the dim light Larry saw a subtle means of ascertaining Michelle's state of awareness. There was a pothole in the paved parking area that was about one and a half feet across and approximately three inches deep in the center. By pothole standards it wasn't a terribly large one but it was plenty big enough to help him gather the information he was seeking. He steered Michelle toward it thinking, "If she stumbles, then she's drunk enough and if she steps around the hole, she isn't. I bet she is."

Larry guided her gently toward the hole with his arm still around her waist. He could feel the fimr flesh beneath Michelle's lightweight, slip-over sweater. He altered their path slightly so he would completely miss the hole and so that Michelle's left foot would also miss it.

Suddenly, Michelle's right foot dropped below where she expected the pavement to be. Though the hole wasn't deep, it had served Larry's purpose beyond all expectations. Michelle swayed and sagged to the right away from him. Had Larry not been supporting her, she would have fallen.

Since Larry was expecting this he was already prepared.

As the right side of Michelle's body dropped down Larry slipped his hand up the front of her ribcage. It closed over the firm softness of Michelle's right breast. It was only then that he realized that she was braless. Larry pretended to stumble slightly while he continued to fondle her. As they were regaining their balance he gave it a final squeeze and ran his finger over the nipple that he could feel was slightly erect. Not wanting to press his luck, he slid his hand back down to her waist. There had been no protest on Michelle's part. Their balance now fully regained, he said, "With what they charge for drinks you would think they would fix that hole. Are you all right?" Michelle just nodded and mumbled in response.

They continued their slow journey toward Larry's car.

Once there he opened the door for Michelle and helped her in. When she was seated he went around and got in on the driver's side. Larry reached across her and grabbed the shoulder harness. As he pulled it across her body he let his hand graze, ever so slightly, Michelle's left breast. As he was connecting the buckle he made up his mind about two things; first, he was really turned on and second, Michelle was really drunk. "A bad combination for her but a great combination for me," he mused. Before Larry started the engine he paused to look at Michelle. Her head was back against the headrest and her eyes were closed. He stared at her for a few moments then thought to himself, "She really is foxy looking. Wonder what she looks like without her clothes on—I think I'll go find out"

He started the engine and pulled carefully into the street heading toward Michelle's house. He had a vague idea where she lived and she was able to give him the rest of the directions he needed. It was about a fifteen minute drive and upon arriving there he eased into her driveway and stopped behind her car. Larry turned off the lights and the engine, then he unbuckled Michelle's seatbelt. He got out and went around to her side to help her out. "Which one is your door key?" he asked as Michelle fumbled with her key ring. She held the ring up by one key and handed it to him. Still helping to support her, they moved slowly toward the front door. When they got there Larry inserted the key, turned it, and pushed the door open. With his arm still around Michelle's waist, they stepped inside.

After having come in one evening in a slightly tipsy condition and bumping her left shin on the coffee table Michelle had started leaving a small lamp turned on on an end table next to her sofa. Though it did not put out a lot of light it was ample for her to see where everything in the room was located.

The room had the usual furnishings that one would expect to find and, though it wasn't elaborate, it was nicely arranged. Larry noticed that it was an average size living room with the couch in front of the picture window that was to the right of the entrance. Across the room was a large recliner and a large rocking chair.

After Larry pushed the door closed and checked to be sure it was locked, he turned to face Michelle. While Larry had been looking around the room she had made her way over to the recliner and stood there holding on to the back of it for support. He held up the key ring and said, "What should I do with these?" Michelle nodded toward the coffee table and Larry walked over to it and placed them there on a magazine.

As he straightened up, Michelle said, "Thanks for the ride home. I think I can make it from here since it's not that far to the bedroom."

"I'll help you in there," Larry replied.

The room was spinning in lazy circles and Michelle knew she could crawl if she had to. "Thanks, but my head is starting to clear a little bit and I think I can make it with no problem," she said, hoping he would just leave so she could go on to bed.

Larry walked over to her and, taking her by the arm, started leading her in the direction she was looking. As he thought about Michelle's head clearing statement he chuckled to himself. He was well aware that her last drink was just now starting to cloud her already fuzzy brain. Michelle swayed unsteadily as they walked across the room and down the hallway. When they got to her bedroom door she pointed toward it with her right hand. Larry steered her through the doorway and paused long enough to reach across her and turn on the light. As Michelle stood there leaning against the door frame he walked over and turned on the lamp on the night stand. Then Larry walked back over to her and turned off the overhead light. Slipping his arm around Michelle's waist, they started toward her bed. Larry was still supporting her when they stopped by the side of it. "Doesn't this give you a warm, cozy feeling?" he asked.

Still detached from what was happening, Michelle replied, "If you say so."

Suddenly Larry stepped forward with his left leg and pivoted slightly on his right foot. Now he was facing Michelle. His left arm encircled her waist and before Michelle's foggy brain could register what was happening, he pulled her close and kissed her forcefully on the lips. As Michelle tried to turn her head Larry only tightened his grip on her. His tongue was hard against her lips as he tried to force them apart.

In a far away corner of Michelle's mind some circuits were starting to make a very weak connection. They were sending a faint message telling her that something wasn't right. The room was still spinning lazily around Michelle and Larry still had her arms pinned to her sides with his embrace. Being unsuccessful in getting her amrs free, Michelle tried to bring up her right knee in order to get Larry's attention but it had no effect because he was smothering her body with his.

As suddenly as he had grabbed her, Larry turned her loose and stepped back. Michelle's eyes were still wide with surprise and she opened her mouth to scream but nothing came out. Instead, there was a sudden, sharp pain and she started to gasp for air. She felt her head and back slam into the wall then the room started to tilt at a crazy angle as she collapsed on the floor clutching her chest.

When Larry had turned her loose he had stepped back and slightly to his left. As Michelle attempted her desperate effort to scream for help he had slammed his right fist hard into her stomach. It had landed with an upward motion in the opening between the right and left sides of her ribcage just below the distal end of her sternum. As the blow pushed her diaphragm upward, so went the air.

There Michelle lay, coughing and gasping for her breath as Larry stood over her. He bent down and grabbed the bottom of her sweater, giving it a tug. It came over her head but since Michelle was still clutching her chest, her arms were still in it. Larry took her right hand and pulled her arm straight. He pulled the sweater over that arm and dropped her hand back on her chest. Then he pulled her left arm straight and repeated the process. Larry paused for a moment and ran the material through his fingers then he tossed it out of the way on the floor.

Still holding Michelle's left hand, he twisted her arm to straighten it even more then he turned her over on to her stomach. Keeping Michelle's arm twisted, Larry moved her hand upward toward the small of her back. From his shirt pocket he removed a woven fiber cylinder about three inches long and only slightly larger in diameter than the average finger. He pushed it over Michelle's left thumb up to the first joint then reached around in front of her and grabbed and also forced it behind her back. Then he pushed the other end of the woven fiber cylinder over her right thum just as he had done the left one. He stood up and watched her struggle to get free. Larry smiled, he had fantasized about this moment for a long time and now he had her—Michelle was held securely in a pair of oriental handcuffs, He was well aware that she could not escape this children's toy unless she could compress the small cylinder from one end or the other and since her thumbs were held tightly, that this would be all but impossible.

Larry squatted down by Michelle's feet and turned her over on her back, then he leisurely removed her sandals. He continued to hold her ankles as he stood back up. Slowly he pulled her across the carpet away from the wall. When he had dragged her away from all the furniture he turned her legs loose and Michelle's heels landed on the carpet with a soft thud. Larry stepped up to her waist and bent down. As he reached to unsnap her jeans he suddenly stopped. Too much light, he decided.

Standing up, Larry walked over to the closet and turned on the light switch. He partially closed the door to decrease the amount of light even more and then walked over to the lamp on the night stand. Turning if off, he paused to let his eyes adjust to the darkness. Larry could make out all the objects in the room, especially this attractive but helpless woman lying on her back on the floor. The light was just about right. If he looked closely he could barely make out the darker areas of Michelle's nipples.

Larry walked back over to Michelle and once again squatted down beside her. He unsnapped her jeans, unzipped them, and started pulling them down over her hips. When he got them to mid-thigh he moved to her feet and, grabbing the pants by the bottom of the legs, pulled them over Michelle's feet. Larry tossed them to the side of the room and then just stood there for a few moments.

As he contemplated the desirable woman lying before him at his mercy Larry felt a sudden, tremendous adrenalin rush. Very deliberately he bent down and grasped the waistband of Michelle's panties. Ever so slowly he pulled them down over her hips and thighs. He stopped when he got her panties to her knees to study what had been revealed to him. Totally satisfied with what he saw, Larry pulled them over her feet and threw them toward her jeans.

Michelle had regained her breath and was watching Larry remove her clothes. She had been totally unsuccessful in freeing her thumbs from the woven cylinder that held them and had finally stopped struggling. As a child she had played with these things for toys and she knew that the harder she pulled the tighter it held her. Michelle also knew that her only hope of getting free was to push the cuff from the end in order to get it to release its grip but with her thumbs securely held by it there was no way she could grasp it to do so. Michelle had an idea of what was in store for her and she knew that there was absolutely nothing she could do about it. She knew that Larry could and would do with her as he pleased.

As Michelle lay there watching him he started removing his clothes. It was obvious to her that he was in no hurry. Unlike her clothes that he had just thrown aside. Larry was placing his in a neat pile on a chair. As Michelle continued to watch him she thought, "I don't have anything to lose so I might as well give it a try." In a quiet voice she said, "Larry,

I don't want you to do this. This is rape."

Larry turned to face Michelle. He was now naked and his state of passion was obvious, even to the casual observer. Smiling at her, he said, "Michelle, who's going to believe a bunch of bull like that? A half dozen people saw you almost too bombed to walk and heard you say how glad you were that you didn't have to drive. What jury would possibly convict me after their testimony? Besides, a jury would probably think that you were so grateful to me for taking you home that some fun and games is how you decided to repay me. Don't worry. I doubt if we'll do anything tonight that you and Paul, I think that's his name, haven't done before. Yeah, that's it. Just pretend I'm Paul."

Though Michelle's mind was still foggy, at the mention of Paul's name she felt tears start to form in her eyes. "Larry is right," she thought, "we probably won't do anything that he and I haven't done but what he and I did, we did out of love, not power." She tried to fight back the tears. To have this happen was humiliating enough but to start to cry simply at the mention of someone's name, especially when that person had been gone for months, just made it more so.

Michelle's mind once again started to play tricks on her. "Had I been more of a woman, more exciting, more of whatever he wanted me to be," she thought, "Paul would still be here and this wouldn't be happening tonight." As her mind raced to heap more abuse and blame on herself, Michelle started to think, "Maybe I do deserve this for just being stupid, if for no other reason." Looking up at Larry, she said, "Get it over with," then she closed her eyes and moved her feet apart.

Michelle heard Larry's feet quietly brushing the carpet as he moved toward her. She sensed him standing over her but he still had not touched her. He said, "Michelle, Michelle, Michelle. What's the rush. We've got all night if we need it. Besides, I've thought about this much too long to hurry. There are so many games we can play, things we can do. Just relax, you'll love it."

Before she had closed her eyes Michelle had been watching Larry as he removed his clothes. Even in the dim light she had been able to get a pretty good idea of what Larry looked like with no clothes on. He wasn't a bad looking guy, she knew that much from seeing him at work and, had things in her life been appreciably different, she would not have objected to going out with him even though she was several years older. He was slightly under six feet tall and appeared to be physically active. As he had been undressing, Michelle could not help but look at the part of him that she knew she would get to know much better before the night was over. Now, as he stood over her, she was able to get a much better look and she grimaced as she thought, "If I'm not ready, this could hurt."

Having said that, Larry dropped down on his knees beside her. Michelle still had her eyes closed because it was her only defense. She felt his fingers tracing circles on her tummy. Then he started rubbing his hands over her, down her thighs and then on the sensitive skin on the inside of them. Larry's fingers trailed back up her thighs toward the dark area at their juncture. Then, suddenly, they were trying to reach under her to stroke her firm bottom. While his right hand was teasing her there, his left hand was rubbing her chest but he was careful to avoid the tiny, erect tree stumps that her nipples had become.

Just as Michelle was starting to wonder what was wrong with her breasts, a red hot mouth closed over her right nipple and started a slow, rhythmic sucking. Larry then tried to engulf all the breast he could and then Michelle felt his wet, sandpaper tongue rolling her nipple against the roof of his mouth. Though she was able to stifle a low moan, her hips responded against her will when Larry had detected her respons he did not show it and Michelle held on to the faint hope that her body had not betrayed her.

Releasing Michelle's right nipple from the hold his lips and tongue had on it, Larry quickly kissed and then licked her left nipple. Michelle's breathing started to deepen as her body started to respond to the very things her mind was fighting against.

Suddenly, Larry released her and straightened up. He caught her left arm and rolled her over onto her stomach.

Then he took Michelle by her shoulders and raised her up until she was in a kneeling position. Larry stood up and looked down at her. Though the alcohol was still affecting her brain Michelle tried to protest. "Please, Larry. No," she said softly, "Just rape me and go on home."

"Michelle, don't look at it that way," Larry replied. With his finger he traced the outline of her mouth. "You've got sensuous lips and it would be a real waste if they didn't join the party," he whispered. Larry grabbed a handful of her hair and forced her head back. Then he kissed her hard, like a captor who could and would have his way with the captured. Michelle did not respond to his kiss and, as best she could, tried to turn her head away.

Larry pulled his lips back from hers. "You better be a little more sociable," he said in a low, cold voice. "Let's try again." He bent down once again and raped her lips with his. Still Michelle did not respond. Larry stood up again and turned loose of her hair. "You just don't understand, Michelle," he said. "I'm trying to be nice to you. I've tried two times to kiss you and each time you've acted like you just don't care. You make me think that I might have bad breath or something. This is the kind of treatment that could give a guy a complex. You really shouldn't be such a prudent little bitch."

The left side of Michelle's face suddenly exploded in pain and her head whipped sharply to the right. As she fell sideways onto her shoulder she thought her left cheek bone must surely have been shattered. Large flashes of light were going off inside her head as she tried to focus her eyes and she struggled against the blackness that was trying to overtake her.

Larry stood over her with his fist still clenched. He walked over to his pants and, still in no hurry, removed his leather belt. Walking back over to where Michelle was still lying in the floor he said, "I'm sorry. I shouldn't have hit you. I should have done this to start with but I was really hoping you would be nice to me so we could avoid any unpleasantness. I do so wish you would have listened to reason."

Larry bent down and stretched Michelle out on her stomach then he pushed her hair into a pile on the floor at the top of her head and put his left foot on it. He then placed his right foot in the small of her back below where her hands were secured.

Doubling the belt and holding it by the two loose ends, Larry brought it down sharply across the downward curve of the left smooth, round mound. There was a sharp crack when it landed and the sudden sting made Michelle start to forget about the pain in her eye. Larry did not hit her nearly as hard as he could have and he really had not planned on hitting her at all but he was tired of her struggling with the decision to be nice to him and he simply wanted to expedite the process and get her to see things his way. Larry raised his arm and brought it down again. There was another sharp crack and the tight skin on the downslope of the right mound exploded in flames. Michelle bit her lip and tried to press her feet into the carpet to escape the stinging pain. Eight more times the doubled belt slapped sharply across Michelle's smooth, round bottom. The blows were unhurried with a pause between each one for maximum effect knowing Michelle could only lie there anticipating the next one and that she had absolutely no idea how many more would follow. By the fifth blow Michelle's tears had started to flow. "Stop, Larry," she pleaded, "I'll kiss you, I'll do whatever you want me to do. Just don't hit me anymore."

After the tenth blow had landed Larry paused and studied Michelle as she tried to stifle her sobs and catch her breath. Still standing with one foot on her hair and the other on her back Larry said, "If you would just cooperate things would be much nicer."

"I will," she sobbed.

"I bet."

"Really, Larry. I will. I'll do whatever you want me to do. You name it. Just don't hit me anymore."

"Okay," he said. "We'll find out in a minute whether or not you're kidding."

Just for effect Larry sharply smacked the floor right beside Michelle's stinging bottom. He saw her flinch and hear a low whimper. Satisfied that he now had her undivided attention, he took the belt back over to his pile of clothes and laid it on top of his neatly folded pants. Walking back over to Michelle, he took her by the shoulders and raised her up to a kneeling position in front of him. Larry put his hand under Michelle's chin and raised her head. Bending down he kissed her again, lightly at first and then more forcefully as his passion once again started to build. He ground his lips into hers. His tongue touched the underside of her upper lip. Following his every lead, Michelle touched Larry's tongue with hers. Their tongues fenced with each other and she caressed the inside of his upper lip. Larry finally broke the kiss and said, "Much better. We could have been doing this all along." He straightened up, his blood swollen passion only inches from her face. "Would you like to make me feel good?" he asked. Michelle nodded. "It would be nicer if you would reply so there wouldn't be any doubt," he said.

"I would like very much to make you feel good," Michelle whispered.

"What would you like to do first?" Larry responded.

Michelle knew exactly what he wanted, it would have been obvious to all but the comatose. Though she had resigned herself to the fact that she would be forced to participate in whatever creative ideas Larry had, Michelle knew she could not just give up. If her humiliation were not already complete, she knew that before Larry was finished with her it would be. She was well aware that, had Larry wanted to, he could have already had his way with her and been gone. Now, he was just toying with her in order to strip away any remaining shred of dignity that she might have left. Knowing this, Michelle was determined to resist any way she could in order to win small, personal victories, even though she knew she would most certainly lose in the end.

"You're calling the shots," she said quietly, "so you tell me."

"When you were a little girl I bet you liked Tootsie Pops, didn't you?" Larry said, looking down at her.

"Yes," Michelle replied softly.

"Do you remember what you used to do to them?" he asked.

"Yes."

"What did you do to them?"

"The same things that all the other kids did to them."

"Such as "

Michelle hesitated, there was nothing else she could do. "This is a game," she thought, "and I'm going to lose so I might as well get it over with."

"Well, Larry, let me see," she said. "My dad would sometimes bring me one. I would take it outside and sit down under my favorite tree. Then, I would unwrap it and just look at it for a while and think about how great it was going to taste. Then I would lick it but I never could lick it very long. I would always end up putting it in my mouth and start sucking on it."

Michelle thought that it would have been impossible for Larry to get any more turned on than he had been but as she described her childish escapades with the Tootsie Pop he had actually seemed to get larger.

Much to her surprise, Larry abruptly turned and walked toward the dresser. When he got there he rummaged among the items on it, picked one up, and walked back over to

Michelle and stopped directly in fron of her. "Look up,"he snapped. Obediently she complied. "Close your eyes." As she did so Michelle sensed something moving closer to her face.

Something moved lightly over her lips. Why is he putting lipstick on me, she wondered. Then it dawned on her, the print of her lips on a particular part of Larry's anatomy would surely be a tremendous boost to his already macho image. Satisfied with his work, Larry withdrew the lipstick, put the cap back on it, and tossed it aside. "Keep your eyes shut," he said, then added, "and just pretend this is a Tootsie Pop in your favorite flavor.

Something warm and firm brushed lightly against Michelle's lips. Larry was tracing the shape of her mouth with his blood charged appendage. There was no reason to hurry and he knew it. As he guided the path of his blood swollen organ with one hand he held on to her hair with the other and Michelle also knew that there was nothing she could do.

Finally, still with a low, cold voice, Larry said, "I want the lollipop treatment, just like you described." Michelle had long since resigned herself to her fate and she had decided to try to make him feel good. She knew that if he desired he could and would whip her some more and if he really lost control of things, that he might even kill her. However, if she lived through it she would at least have the option to consider some type of retaliation. With that in mind, Michelle gingerly stuck out her tongue and began to trace small circles and other designs on the sensitive skin of Larry's throbbing passion. She lightly flicked her tongue in and out from side to side while it left a damp trail that was having a telling effect on him.

Larry finally broke the silence and said, "What's next?" Michelle had known all along that this was where they were headed and she had been expecting it. He was also right, it wasn't anything that she had not done before except for one tremendous difference. In one situation, she was someone's lover, in the other, she was someone's prisoner. With her eyes still closed Michelle ever so slowly opened her mouth. The same firm, warm object that had traced the outline of her mouth now slipped easily between her parted lips. She lightly tightened her lips around it as Larry started a slow back and forth movement.

With one of his fingers Larry began to follow the curve of Michelle's mouth even as it engulfed him. Michelle was well aware that he was enjoying himself since she could feel his body trembling and jerking as her mouth worked its forced magic on him. "At least one of us is having a good time," she thought. After several minutes of this Michelle felt Larry get very tense and he started to moan. There seemed to be less room in her mouth and she thought, "This is it." Just when she had braced herself for the imminent explosion, Larry stopped. His hips were suddenly frozen in place and her head was immovable in his grasp.

Very slowly he moved away from her until her mouth was empty. She knew that her lips were wet and slippery from all the back and forth motion and Larry was obviously enjoying himself. Michelle was confused and she whispered, "I thought that was what you wanted." There was no answer, instead this same object once again bumped softly against her lips. Michelle opened her mouth wide to receive it and then tightened her lips and tongue around it once again. Abruptly it began to move back and forth in her mouth just as it had been doing. After another few minutes of this motion there seemed once again to be less room in her mouth. Just as she was getting ready again for what she knew was going to happen, all movement again stopped. Larry moved his hips back and pulled his swollen member over Michelle's wet lips and once again, her mouth was empty.

Just when Michelle was starting to be concerned that she had not pleased Larry and that he was going to hit her again, he said, "Don't worry Michelle, I'm going to leave my load somewhere else and I bet you will enjoy it as much as I do."

Reaching down, Larry caught her under the arms and let his hand trail around from her sides to lightly caress Michelle's breasts with their dark, pink, blood charged nipples. Since her hands were still fastened behind her, Michelle's breasts had been thrust forward, making them appear larger than their normal size. Larry continued to fondle them. After he had rolled her taut nipples simultaneously between his thumbs and forefingers, his hungry mouth attacked first one and then the other with teenage exuberance.

As his lips and tongue ravished them Michelle became aware that her breathing had deepened. Her legs threatened to betray her as she felt the embers of her passion being fanned ever closer to their flash point. She struggled against the bond that so securely held her hands in its grasp and also against this surge of pleasure she was experiencing. "This can't happen," she thought, "I'm a victim and what he's doing to me is against my will." Even as her mind conjured up all the reasons to resist, her body was starting to respond to what was being done to it.

Now, Larry was licking the underside of her breasts. He left kiss tracks from there down to her belly button. There he flicked his tongue in and out and drew little circles around it it leaving a wet kiss trail. Even as Michelle fought it her body trembled and pressed harder against Larry's exploring mouth.

Michelle's head was back and her eyes were closed when she suddenly thought she was falling. She opened her eyes to try to regain her balance only to discover the reason for the sensation. Larry had picked her up and was carrying her toward the bed.

As he carried her he was gently sucking her left nipple. Michelle could resist no longer and she arched her back to try to thrust it deeper into his mouth. Her body was no longer cooperating with what her mind told it to do. Larry whipped her nipple rapidly with his tongue and a low cry escaped Michelle's lips. That cry seemed to be the signal to her brain that it was no longer in charge and her hips began to move rhythmically against Larry's chest. There would be no more struggling and now they both knew it.

Larry placed her gently on the bed and then crawled over her to kneel on the other side. With his fingertips lightly exploring Michelle's body, he bent over and kissed her eyelids. His lips left damp tracks as they smothered the rest of her face with kisses. Finally, his mouth ravished hers. Their tongues darted back and forth, probing like two superb sparring partners.

As Larry continued to rain kisses on her, his left hand toyed with Michelle's swollen nipples. Then, leaving them begging for more, he trailed it slowly down her ribcage and teased her tight, flat tummy. Michelle's head was now title back as she tried to press her lips harder to his. Larry moved his hand down to massage her thighs. Involuntarily, she spread her legs so he could rub the tender skin on the inner thigh. As he continued to massage her there, Michelle spread her legs even more and Larry moved his hand up her legs to let it rest on the darkened area where they joined. Michelle pressed her hips against it and started to move them in a circular motion.

As her hips moved Michelle noticed a strange sensation. The initial fires that Larry's belt had started in the shapely, twin mounds of her bottom had subsided. All that remained were faint, pink marks and an erotic tingling that she found very titillating. She remembered having read articles about this very phenomenon and now she knew first hand the point they had been trying to convey. Realizing this, she became more active in her hip movement.

Larry had found her magic spot with his fingers and was gently rubbing it as Michelle continued to move her hips against his hand. Though her brain was still somewhat foggy due to the alcohol, Michelle knew that she could not blame all of what she was doing on Jim Beam. Her body had cried out so many times for this since Paul had left. It no longer made any difference, it felt so good and she had needed it for so long. Michelle was panting as she pulled her lips away from Larry's. Her eyes were closed and her heart was pounding. In a barely audible whisper she said, "Give me your ear."

Larry turned away from Michelle's lips so she could kiss his left ear and kiss it she did. Michelle knew what was inevitable and she decided that she might as well enjoy what was left of it. Her hot tongue seemed to singe the perimeter of Larry's ear as she first kissed, then licked it. When she plunged her tongue into it she felt Larry tremble to the very depths of his being. Withdrawing her tongue, Michelle put his earlobe in her mouth and bit it very lightly, just enough to hold him but not enough to hurt him. After what had happened to her earlier she was totally shocked when she heard herself whisper, "Spank me, just hard enough to keep the tingle going. Please."

After she said that, Michelle turned Larry's ear loose and with her eyes still closed, let her head drop back on the bed. Michelle knew that she should be embarrassed but her body was now in charge and it just didn't seem to care anymore. Larry raised up and looked down at her. After a pause of disbelief, he said, "I didn't know you had it in you. Of course, you don't, yet, but you soon will."

He grabbed the three pillows from the head of the bed and placed them to Michelle's left, one on top of the other. Then he helped her to her knees and she crawled over to them. Michelle fell forward over them with her face turned to the left toward Larry. Not having landed quite right, she wiggled around until the three pillows were under her and her firm, still tingling bottom was arched nicely in a suspended curve totally at Larry's disposal.

Sitting on the bed to Michelle's left, Larry ran his right hand over the sleek, twin mounds that awaited his undivided attention. In the dim light he could barely make out the delicate pink color that was still present from his earlier efforts but this time things would be vastly different.

As Larry was kneeling there contemplating what was before him and how the philosophy of the evening had changed, Michelle whispered, "If you had rather use it, there's a hairbrush on the dresser." Larry thought about it for a moment, then the bed creaked as he got off it and walked across the room. In the dim light he could make out the brush just as Michelle had stated. He picked it up and smacked it lightly against the palm of his left hand, then he grinned to himself as he walked back over and once more got on the bed. He crawled back over to his original position beside Michelle's arched bottom and studied it. Though he had not thought about this creative new game, he was sure that he would enjoy it and he reached down to fondle himself.

Michelle still had her eyes closed and she had started to wonder how hard Larry would hit her this time. She was reasonably certain that it would not be anywhere near like what had happened to her earlier. Michelle did not have to ponder this question very long. Raising his hand with the hairbrush in it Larry brought it down sharply across the apex of the mound closest to him. As he watched he could barely see the skin flush with color. He raised his hand again and struck the other side on its apex. It, too, flushed with color. Michelle squirmed and though she could have tried to protect her tingling derriere from the blows, her still restrained hands stayed high on her back out of the way. "Just a little harder," she moaned.

As Larry continued to rain blows on her, Michelle continued to squirm and moan but she neither tried to move off the pillows nor did she tell him to stop. After several minutes Larry changed the direction of his blows. Now they were landing more to the side where the two firm mounds joined her thighs. Michelle's feet kicked lightly against the bed and her hips began to move excitedly.

Michelle's entire bottom had become flushed with color and her restrained passion could no longer be held back. This creative new game they were playing had excited Larry to the point that his swollen member had begun to throb, almost to the point of hurting. He hit Michelle one last blow, the hardest since he had been spanking her and got up on his knees. As he moved behind her, Michelle sensed what he had in mind. Still arched on the pillows with her suspended pink mounds glowing in the subdued light, she spread her legs when she felt Larry move in between them and crawl closer behind her.

Michelle knew she had gone over the limit. She was now totally out of control and totally helpless. She felt the roughness of Larry's body against the smoothness of hers. He was very slowly moving closer. Michelle suddenly felt the same firm softness that had earlier bumped her lips rubbing against her legs. With a slight push against her, Michelle felt her very being parting as she was impaled on a hot spear. Deeper it went into her and she thought she would be ripped apart. Her entire body trembled with excitement and a low moan escaped her throat.

The coarseness of Larry's body lightly sanded Michelle's sensitive, warm bottom as her inner being was assailed by his spear of flesh. A continuous low moan escaped her lips and she trebled as Larry ground his hips into her. Michelle responded by trying to push back against him. As Larry moved back and forth against her he reached around in front and began to rub her swollen counterpart with his fingers.

With the assault on her senses coming from front and rear Michelle could no longer concentrate on her rhythm. Suddenly, from a distance Michelle started to feel as if she were tumbling through space. Her body stiffened spasmodically and an unintelligible cry escaped her dry mouth. Michelle jerked at the bond that restrained her hands as her body suddenly went rigid. After this brief jerking and struggling she collapsed on the pillows and lay there without moving.

The bed shifted and creaked and Michelle was vaguely aware that Larry was moving away from her. All her nerve endings seemed to be on full alert and concentrated in one part of her body. She almost told him not to move away from her but her thoughts were much too scattered. Before Michelle could collect them enough to speak, she felt herself being rolled off the pillows to her left and onto her black.

Michelle's supercharged nerve endings were again brought peak sensitivity as she felt Larry move between her legs and once again impale her on his swollen appendage. As he plunged deeper into her body he began to gently suck her swollen nipples. Michelle's body responded as she arched het back and involuntarily moved her hips. Larry started his back and forth hip movements and she aggressively joined hu rhythmic efforts.

His lips found hers and their tongues danced with each other, always trying to incite greater passion than before. As

Larry continued to hammer her body, Michelle felt him start to grow inside her. He suddenly stopped his movement and put his hands under her bottom so she could no longer move.

After two or three minutes of holding Michelle in this manner Larry released his grip on her and once again started a slow, rhythmic pounding to both the outside and the inside of her body. This movement soon alerted his nerve center again and Michelle once more felt Larry begin to swell within her. This enlarging on his part only caused her passion to increase. Larry suddenly began an unmerciful hammering of her body as he seemed to get bigger and bigger. Michelle also felt this swelling and, though she thought she would be ripped asunder, it felt so good that she arched her back to better receive the pounding her body was taking.

As her breathing rhythm started to get ragged, she felt Larry stiffen again. Sweat dropped off his body onto hers and ran into tiny, salty pools that had already collected on her chest and stomach. Larry had now become relentless in his efforts. Michelle thought that she would surely be split apart if he continued to grow.

Just when she was sure that she could no longer take it, Michelle once again felt herself starting a slow tumble through space. Larry's eyes were closed and some guttural sound escaped his lips as his body became spasmodically rigid. Michelle's body slapped hard against his as she once again teetered on the edge of oblivion. She was once more pushed over the edge and started her free fall through space by a sudden rush of warmth that rolled through her.

After a few more violent thrusts Larry collapsed on her with his head by hers. Michelle could feel the sweat still running off him onto her hypersensitive skin. They were both gasping for their breath and neither spoke. After several minutes Larry regained enough energy to move and rolled off Michelle onto his back. Except for the quiet ticking of the clock on the chest of drawers the room was silent. After a few more minutes their breathing became deep and regular, no longer the ragged panting that it had been.

After what seemed like eons to Michelle, Larry roused, swung his legs off the side of the bed and stood up. He walked to his pile of clothes, picked them up, and carried them into the bathroom. The silence was soon destroyed by the splash of water in the shower.

About fifteen minutes later Larry turned the water off and, except for the clock, the room was once again silent. Michelle still had not moved when Larry emerged fully clothed from the bathroom. He walked over to the bed and stood there looking down at her. Still, neither of them had spoken. There was an awkward silence that seemed to say, "Maybe neither of us should have done what we did." Michelle rolled away from him onto her side and, as best she could, raised her hands toward him. Larry bent over and grasped the woven fiber cylinder that had so easily restrained her. Pushing Michelle's right thumb deeper into it, he released the grip it had on her. Keeping the cylinder collapsed, Larry gently pulled her thumb out then he repeated it for her left hand. Michelle rolled back over onto her back and pulled her left arm from underneath her. It felt good to have her hands free again. She stretched her arms and worked her fingers to get the kinks out and to get some extra blood flowing to them. When Michelle had moved them sufficiently she put her hands on her stomach with her fingers interlocked. She made no effort to cover any of her exposed body. Subconsciously, she could think of no reason to cover anything. "Why go to the trouble," she thought, "he's seen and touched every part of me that his passions desired. Besides, I have nothing left to hide from him."

Since freeing Michelle's hands Larry still had not moved. From her still vulnerable position on the bed Michelle looked up at him and met his gaze. He suddenly seemed embarrassed by her nudity and appeared to want to say something. "Let him be embarrassed," she thought, "I'm not, "I'm not, I'm still his victim." Then, without speaking, Larry abruptly turned and walked across the bedroom and disappeared into the hall. Michelle heard the front door open and close. A few moments later she heard Larry start his car and back out of her driveway. Still, there in the subdued light, her tormentor no longer present, Michelle did not move. She just lay there listening to the clock ticking its steady rhythm. There's no need to hurry, she decided, what's done is done. Michelle also knew that there was no reason to call the police and that, unless she could come up with a way to retaliate, that there would be no justice.

After several more minutes of lying there Michelle's exhausted body and mind began to relax. The familiar surroundings and the quiet rhythm of the clock had a tranquilizing effect on her. She eventually slipped away into the world of much needed sleep.

It was nearly an hour later when Michelle awoke and, being appreciably more rested, decided that it was time to get up and assess the damage from earlier in the evening. Larry had not turned off the bathroom light when he left after his shower so she could see how to get around without any additional lighting. Rising from the bed, she slowly walked toward the half open bathroom door. Her eyes adjusted easily to the ever increasing glow of the light.

Michelle pushed the door the rest of the way open and walked over to the medicine cabinet to view her face. As she gazed into the mirror she only saw one thing that really disturbed her. She had expected her hair to be in disarray and for the heavy application of lipstick Larry had applied to be a real mess. These situations could be alleviated with very little problem. Sure enough, just as she expected, where he had hit her in the face was swollen and had begun to bruise. Michelle lightly ran her fingertips over it, wincing at the pain it elicited. She then pressed lightly on her stomach where Larry hit her when he had first knocked her down. Though this spot was also slightly tender, she was satisfied that nothing appeared to be broken.

Michelle turned on the water in the shower and let it run until it got warm, then she stepped in. The warm water felt good cascading down her back and shoulders. When the spray landed on the twin, round mounds that had been the center of so much attention earlier in the evening, it seemed even hotter. Michelle knew she needed some ice for the side of her face and she also wondered how she would explain the injury at work on Monday. Since some of them knew she was really tipsy when she and Larry left P.J.'s, she decided to just say that she had an accident. In a way that was true, she had been accidentally attacked and raped. As she stood there with the water beating down on her, Michelle thought about Larry's statement that, under these circumstances, no court would ever find him guilty of rape. She knew this was true and it only added to her feeling of emptiness. Backing closer to get the water to land higher on her back, Michelle closed her eyes and tried to give herself a hug. Then, as her mind raced and the last tiny bit of her energy drained away, out of confusion and loneliness, she began to cry.

Michelle's Vacation

Michelle accelerated down the "On" ramp as she glanced over her shoulder and in the rearview mirror for ann approaching traffic that might be in conflict with her space as she merged onto the interstate. Satisfied that there wasn't any, she maneuvered into the right lane and continued to accelerate until she reached her desired speed of sixty-eight miles per hour. Punching the cruise button, she checked to see if the green cruise control light had illuminated. Satisfied with what she saw, she removed her foot from the accelerator and let her right leg relax as she shifted in the seat to try to get a little more comfortable. Michelle felt a slight surge as the cruise mode took over and a quick glance at the speedometer confirmed that she had set everything correctly.

The traffic was sparse, mostly the long haul trucks with only an occasional car here and there. Everything was dark except for the soft glow of the instrument panel lights or headlights. "Not much traffic," she thought, "but why should it be at this time of day, or night." Michelle chuckled to herself, she never had fully understood just exactly when day and night switched places.

The pale blue numerals on the clock on the dash indicated 6:22 and in the dark sky the first faint streaks of light were beginning to become visible low on the eastern horizon. The beginning of the sunrise was beautiful, it had always been one of her favorite times of the day and this morning was no exception. Michelle was glad the traffic was light because it allowed her to watch the early morning picture that was being painted in front of her along with keeping track of her driving. Though she knew she would not relish the idea of having to get up that early each morning, Michelle was enjoying watching a new day getting started.

In the distance the fiery red sky was being subdued by some clouds that added streaks of deep purple to the sky canvas. The red got brighter and suddenly, there it was -- the top of the sun started to barely peek over the horizon. “It’s like the sun wants to peek at the world first,” she thought “then, depending on what it sees, make up its mind whether or not to continue rising.” The sun soon became a large, red ball in the sky and it surprised her at how quickly that took place compared to how slowly it seemed to move while getting over to the western horizon.

Michelle continued watching as the sky became brighter and started to illuminate her surroundings. The trees and houses now had distinct shapes instead of being unseen objects hiding in a sea of darkness. By now most of the other drivers had turned their headlights off and she followed suit.

For weeks Michelle had really needed to leave, go away, get away from it all, whatever was necessary to see if she could find some peace of mind. She had been to the beach numerous times in the past, occasionally by herself but more often than not, with others. She and Paul had spent some of their most enjoyable times together there. Now, she was going back to the scene of those happy days but she knew they would not be quite as happy this time. Paul's sudden departure from her life had thrown things into turmoil for her. Everything she had counted on had been forced to suddenly change and her mind had become cluttered with all manner of jumbled thoughts. All day and night the same loop film ran in her mind and, where her life was concerned, she had begun to lose her ability to separate reality from fantasy.

All the things she had worked so hard to cultivate in an affair-of-the-heart were now gone. The love, the trust, the caring, the fact that she had begun to need him, not just want him, but actually need him in her life -- all these things had been destroyed by him saying, "Goodbye." His no reason, no explanation, no nothing approach to it all had left her feeling totally confused and emotionally devastated. It were as if he had been equipped with an "on-off" love switch and because he had one, she should also have one but she didn't and that was the sad part for her.

Michelle knew that she was one of the unfortunate people who take life and love very personally and she had often wished she could view it as a game the way so many people seemed to do. A big problem of hers was taking the words "I love you" with the utmost of seriousness, she didn't say them out of habit like so many people do but when she did say them, they were from the heart and had all of her very being behind them.

The miles slipped by as the sun continued its journey above the horizon. The vivid sky colors had disappeared as it climbed higher and higher. Blue had taken the place of the crimson and the purple clouds had become white. The early morning coolness had begun to be replaced by the heat that Michelle knew would only intensify as the day wore on but she didn't care. "That's what summer is all about," she thought, "and I love it."

As she drove, she started to imagine how good the sand would feel on her bare feet. She especially enjoyed walking on the beach and feeling the warm water splash on her ankles and legs. Her mind started to drift as she thought about her previous beach trips, specifically, the ones with Paul. Though she was trying to remain upbeat about her trip, she suddenly started to be overcome with a feeling of extreme sadness and fatigue such that she could feel her energy draining away and her spirit sagging.

Michelle drove on trying to regain the high spirits she had earlier but she finally realized that it was a losing battle. Her eyes began to ache as large, viscous tears that would not flow flooded them. As her vision became distorted and the pain increased she blinked to try to ease both the pain and to clear her sight. A single large tear flowed from each eye and coursed its way down her cheeks.

"You stupid bitch," she thought, "why can't you overcome this? Why do you take it seriously, it's nothing but an adult bed game." Once again the war inside her head had begun to rage and she continued to slip further into the strange world of reality distortion that existed in a far corner of her mind. "Why," she thought, "can't I just take a vacation and not be there when I arrive? All I want to do is to organize the clutter inside my head and find some peace of mind."

Though Michelle had enough energy to maintain proper control of her car, she was thankful for the cruise setting because she doubted if she had enough energy to continue without it. No longer was she enjoying the drive. The trees and flowers that bordered the highway were just as beautiful as they had been earlier but she no longer noticed them. The miles continued to pass beneath her and though she had not been traveling that long, she was glad to see a sign telling her that a rest stop was only a few miles away. When it came into view Michelle pulled off the interstate and drove slowly into the parking lot. Spying a large shady area, she headed for it. She pulled into a parking space, turned off the engine, and lowered the windows just enough to let in the light breeze but not enough for someone to put a hand inside. After checking to be sure both doors were locked, she put the seat in a reclining position. Michelle then closed her eyes and relaxed as she listened to the little birds singing in the trees around her. In a very few minutes she slipped into a much needed nap that not only rested her but also let her escape.

So great was her need to rest that the cars passing through that part of the parking lot had no effect on her sleep. After about a half an hour Michelle was awakened by the laughter and squeals of a small child. Raising her head and looking around, she saw a little girl about three or four years old watching a squirrel. A man was sitting at a nearby picnic table keeping a close eye on her as she ran around the tree trying to keep the furry creature in sight.

It seemed to Michelle that the squirrel had been through this same scenario a number of times before. Instead of scampering up the tree, it had climbed about four feet up the trunk just out of reach of those little hands and was simply circling the tree as the little girl ran around the bottom trying to keep it in sight. Each seemed to be enjoying this impromptu game so much that Michelle wondered which was having the better time. She couldn't help but smile as she watched the simple pleasures of the innocence of childhood. At last the squirrel got tired of playing and scurried up the tree out of sight. The little girl watched it disappear then ran laughing to the man at the picnic table and crawled up on his lap. Then, in rapid chatter, she started telling him what had happened. When she had finished they both laughed and he put his arms around her and held her close.

Michelle smiled at this scene and even as she smiled, she felt a tear in her eyes. It had made her both happy and sad. The joy and exuberance of this small child had lifted her spirits only to have them deflate because she wanted so much to be the mother of the little girl. Without taking off her sunglasses she wiped the tears away and got you stretch.

Michelle walked slowly through the grass toward the neatly kept brick building that housed the visitor center. The walk relaxed the stiffness that had set in during the ride pa- her short nap. She inhaled the fresh air deeply, enjoying the faint, clean smell of the tall pines that surrounded her.

Inside the building Michelle admired some pictures of various sites throughout the state. She was familiar with some but not all of them. After a visit to the restroom and a quick stop at the water fountain, she was ready to be on her way again. The inquisitive little girl and her dad were no where to be seen. Suddenly Michelle seemed to be obsessed by the urge to be on the road again. She had been at the rest area much too long and now she had to be on her way. It were as if some inner voice was calling her to make haste to continue her journey and she had to answer. With this feeling running through her mind, Michelle walked back to her car, only this time her pace was much quicker. As she settled into the seat she suddenly trembled with excitement. "That's strange," she thought, "I've taken this trip several times in the past, stayed at almost the same place and yet here is this feeling of anticipation running through me. That's a change. I hope it's a positive one."

As Michelle pulled back onto the interstate and worked her way back into the flow of trafficon was no longer tired and that she actually felt quite refreshed. "It won't be long," she thought, "until I feel my feet on the warm sand and the ocean spray on me." Michelle was much more alert now and she was also delighted to have this sudden burst of new found energy.

As her car began to match the speed of the right lane traffic Michele duners tpeed enjoy the remainder of her trip. After about another hour on the interstate she saw the sign that told her it was time to turn off and slow to a less hectic pace. She always enjoyed this part of the journey the most. The road was four lane, almost as wide as the interstate but with very little traffic and a much slower speed.

The excitement that had come over her at the rest stop had not yet diminished. She knew that only about two and a half more hours was left of her journey and she was once again enjoying watching the countryside roll by. The Spanish moss was much more prevalent and it draped the trees like thousands of gray feather boas. There was more sand now and she had also started to notice some swampy areas with cypress trees sticking out of the black water.

Regardless of where she traveled, Michelle had always enjoyed watching the subtle terrain changes as she went from one region to another. This trip was no exception and what made it even nicer was that she knew she was nearly there. The thoughts of relaxing on the beach and fresh seafood tempted her to increase her speed but she steeled herself against that thought. She decided that being a customer at some roadside blue light special was not the best way to start her vacation. The miles continued to roll by at a restful pace. Michelle continued to enjoy the scenery as she wondered why she was so excited about getting to her destination. It seemed as if fate were sending her a message telling her to be prepared for whatever might be waiting for her. She felt as if she were getting ready for a blind date--lots of anticipation and some nervousness, but thinking about whatever it was that she was so sure would be waiting for her had lifted her spirits, and for that Michelle was grateful.

Suddenly a road sign came into view informing her that there were only another fifteen miles to go and she would be there. In the past Michelle had always stayed at a beachfront condominium but in the past she had always come with at least one other person, sometimes more. This trip would be different, this time she would be staying in a cottage by herself just a block or two from the ocean. Michelle had decided to change lots of things about her trip in order to, hopefully, ease the pain of some of the lingering memories. Anything that she could do to erase the memories that remained of Paul, she would do, she had finally decided that she no longer had a choice. Remembering what had happened had taken a heavy toll on her body and mind and though it still disturbed her because so many things in her life had changed, she had finally decided--so what.

Michelle slowed her speed a few miles per hour. There was no more need to be in any hurry. It was only late afternoon and the end of her journey was only a few minutes away. As she turned onto Ocean Drive, Michelle relaxed even more. Now, her day of travel was only blocks from ending and she suddenly became very eager to finish it. She wanted to be there.

Then, there it was. It looked just like the picture that the real estate agent had sent her. She pulled into the driveway and stopped her car on the hard sand. Before getting out Michelle leaned back in the seat and closed her eyes. After a few deep breaths she opened them and decided that she now had enough energy to take her bags inside and unpack the few things that she would need for the night and simply arrange the rest. She carried everything up the steps to the front door and set it on the deck in a pile. Sure enough, just as the rental agent had told her, she found the key in a small magnetic holder sticking to the inside of the mailbox.

Opening the door, Michelle carried her stuff in and deposited most of it in the bedroom closest to the beach. The house wasn't elaborate but, she decided, it would serve very nicely as an escape from reality for the next few days. It was only a two-bedroom cottage but the owner had planned ahead and put a bath in each bedroom. The front door opened into a comfortable living room with a small eat-in kitchen adjoining it on the left. Though the furniture wasn't new, it was clean and completely functional.

When she had finished carrying her stuff to the appropriate room Michelle closed the front door and went into what would be her temporary bedroom. She opened a window and then went across the house to the kitchen and opened a window there. Immediately a pleasant breeze drifted through the house and brought with it the relaxing faint sound of the surf crashing on the beach.

Removing a pastel fitted sheet from one of the boxes, Michelle quickly slipped it over the mattress and collapsed on the bed. Though her trip for the most part had been pleasant, it had still been a long drive and she had gotten up very early.

The bed was simply too inviting and she let herself succumb to the temptation that it offered.

Michelle's nap lasted about an hour and she woke up feeling refreshed and rested. While still lying on the bed she stretched, reminiscent of a large cat, took a deep breath, and got up. It was only really late afternoon which gave her more than enough time to finish unpacking and then go for a walk on the beach before it got dark. Though Michelle enjoyed the beach after dark she thought it might be unwise to take one by herself, especially the walk back to her cottage at night.

After she had put nearly everything in its proper place, Michelle slipped on a pair of old running shoes and headed for the beach. As she walked she could see the water through the open spots between the houses. Michelle walked slowly along the side of the street being careful of what little traffic there was and admiring the flowers growing in the yards. The reflected heat from the packed sand radiated to warm her bare legs even more. It felt good and it made her feel even better. The combination of her mode of dress, the slow walk, the sound of the surf, and the warmth all around continued to help her relax as she made her way slowly toward the shore. "This is what a vacation should be like," Michelle thought, as she began to softly hum a tune while she walked.

Traffic was light so she had no problem crossing the street to get to the beach. There were some steps that led down to the sand and when Michelle stepped off them she paused to remove her shoes. Tying the strings together, she draped them around her neck so they hung in front of her chest. Since this had been her plan all along she had purposely not put on any socks since they would simply have been more for her to look after.

The soft sand immediately squished between her toes and part way up her feet. This late in the afternoon it wasn't hot enough to burn her but it made her aware of how hot it must have been earlier in the day. Like a child, the first thing she had to do was to walk across the sand to the water so she could get her feet wet. The water was pleasant as it splashed over her ankles and Michelle paused for a few moments to watch the tiny pieces of shell roll back and forth as the waves first pushed them onto the packed sand and then pulled them off again.

Bubbles of foam clung to her ankles as she stood there in awe of her surroundings. The vastness and power of the ocean always made her feel so tiny and insignificant. The constant crashing of the surf as the waves ran up the beach and ended their journey so peacefully made her think about the irony of it all. The waves could be so pleasant and relaxing or they could be powerful and destructive.

Michelle ventured further out into the surf until the water came almost up to her knees. The spray, the water, the sounds, even the smell, she found very refreshing. Still in the water, she started walking down the beach. As she walked, Michelle slowly angled herself toward the shore where she would still be on the wet sand but the water could no longer reach her.

There were still numerous people enjoying the surroundings but this late in the day the sun worshippers had all gone inside. As Michelle walked slowly across the packed sand she noticed how most of the people seemed to be with at least one other person, if not a small group. Sure enough, just as she had been afraid it would happen, old memories came rolling through her mind. Like the unending waves that rolled up the sand washing everything in their path, these memories started to flood her thoughts. Without warning, Michelle's thoughts started to become as jumbled and unorganized as the ever changing order of the myriad of tiny shells that constantly swirled in the water. Though she was suddenly aware that the sand had gotten warmer and dryer to her feet, Michelle was so deep inside her mind that she had lost track of the people around her. They all seemed to be a distant blur as if they were fuzzy figures in an abstract painting. Though the water was just a few yards from her, the sounds of the crashing surf seemed no louder than the wind borne sound of a distant train.

Her pace was very slow now, almost as if it were labored. She felt her earlier energy surge rapidly dissipating and her steps became more of a shuffle. Realizing how tired she had suddenly become and how far she was from her cottage, Michelle had a brief struggle with a panic attack.

She had slightly altered her course so she was no longer walking parallel to the water but was moving slowly away from it. About fifty yards ahead of her the sand rose sharply creating a small, low dune. Michelle decided to head for it so she could sit down to rest without obstructing any of the remaining people who were also walking or playing on the beach.

When she finally got to the dune Michelle summoned what little energy she had remaining and started up the side. The soft, dry sand did nothing to enhance her climbing abilities but the dune wasn't very tall and she really wanted to sit down on top off it. After some slipping and sliding she finally made it to the top where she sat down facing the ocean. Putting her arms around her legs Michelle pulled them to her. There she sat in this upright fetal position, peering over her knees out at the water that went as far as the eye could see. All she could hear over the sound of the waves breaking was an occasional screech from a gull as it sailed over her head. As Michelle sat there observing everything going on around her she started to rock very slightly back and forth.

The feeling that had so overwhelmed her and drained her energy was still with her and it seemed to be getting stronger. As she sat there trying to figure out what was going on inside her head Michelle thought about why she was the only person on the beach who appeared to be alone. As far as she could see in the soft, early evening light everyone seemed to be part of a couple or a group. The memories of walking along the shore with Paul suddenly pushed everything else out of her mind and she propped her chin on her knees. She became acutely aware of how her life had changed since he told her goodbye. Her emotional ties were still much too strong and she began to cry very softly. Everything became a blur as, one by one, the tears lined up and trickled down her cheeks ending their short life as they splashed on her legs. She was relieved that no one was close enough to see them. She briefly wondered if Paul still cared and whether or not he ever thought about her. Whenever this strange phenomenon happened Michelle was always unkind to herself and this time was no exception. With a heavy sigh, she said in words loud enough for only her to hear, "You are one stupid bitch."

As she sat there looking out over the ocean Michelle tried to put the jumbled pieces inside her head in order; she really didn't care what order, just something that made sense. In her mind she could accept the reality of Paul having said "goodbye" even though her heart had yet to turn loose. Now, what bothered her most was the ever present thought that no matter what she did, her best would just never be good enough.

Over time this thought had started to grow on itself and the only time it left her was when she was totally occupied with some kind of task or when she was sleeping and even with some kind of task or when she was sleeping even then she occasionally had flashback dreams that left her very disturbed and confused. Over the years most of her involvement with men had been pleasant with a mutual, noncommittal air about it. When she had finally been able to override her fears of getting married, her husband had left her. He had added insult to injury by dumping her, not for another woman, but for a male friend of his. Though this had hurt her deeply, she had, with the passing of time, learned to accept it. Michelle knew that she had loved her husband but at the same time she also knew that he had not been the great love of her life--Paul was. It had taken a long time to let Paul get to know her because she simply did not want to experience again what she was now going through. Michelle also knew that her entire life had changed forever when Paul had left her. She had been forced to suddenly go from having someone in her life that she wanted and needed to once again being alone. So much for caring for and trusting other people she had decided.

Dreams that she was about to become a major part of her own small family were broken as suddenly and as surely as fine crystal that had been dropped on a concrete floor. The child that she had started to think about having had also vanished. Though Michelle knew that women older than she were having children, in her own mind she had become too old. Occasionally she had even thought about enlisting the services of one of her male friends to help her in this respect but she just did not have the courage to raise the child by herself.

Michelle was acutely aware that even the possibility of marriage for her was now remote, much less having her own family. Now her main goal was to try to avoid having a similar situation ever happen to her again. Even though she knew that it meant putting distance between herself and others, Michelle no longer had the emotional strength to undergo it anymore. The ability for her to care and to trust had been damaged so severely that she was even afraid to make the effort.

It were as if she had been given a load of bricks with which she could build a bridge or a wall. If she built a bridge, it would connect her to the forest--a place that she now was afraid to go. So, Michelle had opted to build a wall and, though it kept her in, it also kept other people out. However, she simply did what she had to do in order to survive. She no longer had any interest in getting ahead, Michelle knew she would be doing well to simply keep up.

As she sat there Michelle had become lost in her own little world of thoughts. She had become oblivious to her surroundings, especially that there were fewer people on the beach and that it was getting darker. Suddenly she returned to reality and looked around. The soft light of evening bathed everything with a peach tinted glow. It started to dawn on her that it would soon be quite dark, that she was still very tired, and that she had a rather long walk back to her cottage. Michelle quietly chastised herself for not paying closer attention to how rapidly the sun was sinking. As she stood up, still facing the ocean, she became aware that someone was coming up behind her and was very close. Startled, Michelle turned around to see who it was.

Relief flooded over her when she realized that the approaching person was a woman who had stopped about six feet away from her, close enough to be personal but far enough away so as to not invade her space. In a quiet voice the stranger said, "Sorry, I didn't mean to frighten you."

"That's okay," Michelle replied as she brushed the sand from the back of her shorts, "I really shouldn't be sitting here in a coma, someone might trip over my IV's."

The stranger laughed. "Everyone needs to go into a coma occasionally, it's about the only way we can escape. I'm Traci," she continued, "I've been watching you and you haven't moved. I was beginning to think something might be wrong. Besides, it's getting dark and these condo parking lots give me the creeps at night. Too many police movies, I guess."

Michelle extended her hand and said, "I'm Michelle. Thanks for inquiring. You're right, someone is always attacked in a parking garage. I really better go. I'm staying in a cottage two or three streets over and I don't even know how far down the beach I've walked. I do remember the address, though."

Traci looked around. The last remnants of daylight were quickly turning into darkness. Michelle was disgusted with herself for not keeping better track of the time. "Come on," Traci said, "I'll take you. My car is right over there." She pointed to a well lighted lot adjacent to a large condo building. Michelle hesitated. She had no desire to get into a car with a total stranger but at this particular time she had even less desire to walk back to her cottage. "Besides," she thought, "Traci isn't dressed in a manner that would hide any weapons and she certainly seems pleasant enough." As Michelle found herself agreeing to the offer, she was also thinking about all the stories she had read about serial killers--they, too, were all very nice.

"Great," Traci said. "Let's go. I'll have you home in no time and I'll be back here before it gets really, really dark. I don't mind the parking lot if there are lots of people around." As they walked toward Traci's car Michelle was reminded of just how tired she actually was and she was thankful that she would not have to make the long walk home in the dark.

During the short walk from the beach to the car Michelle made a special effort to keep up with Traci. Though she was slightly taller and her legs a little longer, she lagged behind because she was simply too tired to hurry and Traci slowed her brisk pace when she noticed Michelle wasn't walking beside her. When they got to the edge of the parking lot Traci said, "It's the green Honda about half-way down this row," gesturing with a sweeping motion and an extended forefinger. In just a few moments they arrived at her car. She unlocked her door and punched "up" on the door lock switch. Michelle heard a light clunk as the right side door unlocked. Opening the door, she got in and collapsed in the seat. Traci got in and closed her door. Before starting the engine, she turned to look at Michelle. "Are you sure you're all right?" she asked.

There seemed to be genuine concern in her voice and Michelle was a little surprised at this expression of compassion. That a total stranger would offer her a ride would have certainly been kind enough but to also have this person express an interest in her well being made her relax a little bit. Without looking toward Traci, Michelle nodded her head to the affirmative.

Traci started the engine and backed out of the parking space. As they headed toward the street she said, "Just tell me where to turn." With a soft voice and hand signals Michelle directed Traci's driving. In less than five minutes they were pulling into the driveway behind Michelle's car. Traci stopped the car but left the engine running. Michelle opened the door and started to get out, then she stopped. She looked back at Traci and said, "This was a real life saver. Thank you."

"Glad to," came the reply. She paused, then continued, "Is it okay if I come by tomorrow to check on you?"

Michelle paused for a moment, then replied, "Sure, just don't do it too early. I'm going to take a sleeping potion and they usually knock me for a loop."

"How about mid-morning?"

"That'll be fine. Goodnight, and thanks again."

As she was closing the door Michelle heard Traci say, "You're welcome." Michelle turned and walked across the yard and pulled herself up the porch steps by the hand rail while Traci sat there with the head lights illuminating the way for her. When Traci saw a light come on inside the house she started backing out of the driveway. Michelle turned to wave one last time and Traci responded with a light beep of the horn, then she disappeared into the night.

Michelle closed the door and shuffled through the living room into the bedroom and turned on the overhead light, then she turned the living room light off and returned to the bedroom and turned on a bedside lamp. Before turning off the ceiling light, she looked through her suitcase for some sleeping tablets. She took two of them with a small glass of water. It made no difference that she was physically and mentally exhausted, she had long ago learned that when her mind hurt this much that she could not sleep without pharmacologic assistance. She also knew that the worst thing she could possibly do was to lie in bed with her mind racing and not sleep.

Those times were the scariest of all. Her thoughts made absolutely no sense and all she would do was toss and turn and wonder why the best she had to offer was never good enough. Michelle knew from the earlier events of the day that this would be another one of those nights if she let it but tonight the two little white pills she had taken would be her friends. She turned off the lamp and collapsed on the bed.

As Michelle lay there it dawned on her that she had not yet taken off her clothes. She thought about removing them and then decided that it would simply not be worth the effort. Besides, she was comfortable and also starting to feel a little bit drowsy and she did not want to risk becoming more alert by moving around. The world of sleep was the safest place she could be and she was in a hurry to get there. Once she got there she would be safe from all the jumbled thoughts and anything that might result from them. As more of the chemicals hit her brain Michelle felt herself start to relax. She became aware that her breathing had changed and in a few more minutes she crossed from one realm to another.

The two little pills Michelle had taken transmitted her safely once again into a restful sleep that was filled with vivid, realistic dreams. In one of them she was once again a little girl playing in her grandparent's big yard. She watched with wide eyes as the numerous beautiful butterflies flew back and forth among the many flowers in her grandmother's large flower garden. In another she was driving a bright, raspberry colored tractor pulling a load of orange hay. Only once did she awaken in the middle of the night for a quick trip to the bathroom. Returning quickly to the bedroom, she pulled off her clothes and finally got in bed instead of on it. The sheets felt cool on her bare skin and in just a few minutes she was once again crossing the border into the safe world of sleep. This time there were no dreams, just deep, sound sleep.

The sun began peeping into her bedroom window at about 5:30 the next morning. As the room became brighter, it finally woke her. Michelle opened her eyes just enough to look at the clock and then decided that nothing was that pressing. The pills had done a great job for her--she was still groggy. She rolled from her side onto her back and positioned a pillow so it covered her eyes but left her nose and mouth uncovered. Soon she was floating away again into oblivion.

When Michelle finally returned to the world of reality her room was bright from the late summer morning sun. She looked at the clock and was mildly surprised to discover that it was almost 9:00. The haze that the pills had induced in her brain had mostly dissipated and she felt relaxed and rested. Deciding that it was now time to get up and face the day she did a tremendous stretch like a large cat just waking from sleeping in a sunbeam on a windowsill. After several seconds of stretching she once again collapsed on her back on the bed. The sounds of the street were already greeting her through the opened windows and she knew she really should get her day underway.

Finally, after another several minutes of listening to the outside world, interspersed with an occasional stretch, she decided to get going and sat up on the side of the bed. Her clothes that she had discarded in the middle of the night were lying on the floor in a loose pile close to the bed. Still sitting on the edge, she leaned over and picked them up. After folding them and smoothing out the wrinkles, she put them in an empty box that she had decided to use for her dirty clothes. As she walked toward the bathroom for her wake up shower she thought about what she had just done and found it to be rather strange.

When the needles of hot water began splashing on her back and then cascading down her body Michelle forgot about what she had done with her clothes and just enjoyed the exhilarating sensations of the water. She turned to let the stream hit her in the face and then stepped back slightly so it landed on her chest. She swayed gently from side to side relishing the titillating feeling of the individual streams landing on her breasts. Michelle put her soapy hands under her breasts and slowly pushed them up as her hands slid lightly over them. Her pink nipples were fully erect and sensitive to both the water and her fingers. She felt her light-hearted spirit start to sag slightly and she made a conscious effort to fight it off. "It's a beautiful day and I'm on vacation," she thought, then emphasizing it in her mind, she added, "and I'm going to enjoy it."

As she started to feel better, once again she knew what was missing. There simply did not appear to be any escape from it—she missed having someone to touch her. Specifically, she missed Paul. She thought of the fun they used to have washing each other's back and other parts. Though she tried to put her arms around herself to give her- self a hug, it just wasn't the same.

Finishin her shower, Michelle turned the water off and just stood in the tub for a while. The warm water felt good as tiny waves lapped at her ankles. Finally, she started to squeegee the excess water off her body with her hands. She stepped out of the tub onto a bath mat and picked up a bottle of baby oil. While the water droplets were still on her she poured some of the oil in her hand and, after lightly rubbing them together, she rubbed the oil over her still slightly wet body. Only after she had gotten the mixture all over her skin did she pick up her towel and begin to dry off. When she was dry she ran her hands over her body. Her skin was soft and smooth and as she stood in front of a full length mirror, she decided that she was holding her own in the war against gravity. She also decided that though she could no longer be considered, as her grandfather used to say, "A spring chicken," if she really were over the hill, she was simply picking up speed. Chuckling softly to herself she struck a pouty, erotic pose with her best come hither look. Deciding that she had played around enough, Michelle walked into the bedroom and slipped on a lightweight, mid-thigh length robe. As she was tying the belt around her, her stomach reminded her that it was well past her usual breakfast time and she still had not eaten anything. Slipping on some sandals, Michelle went into the kitchen to fix herself something eat.

Not knowing quite what she wanted and not having a very well stocked cupboard, Michelle decided on some of the mainstays of life--some crackers with peanut butter, a large pear, and a glass of ginger ale. Though it was approaching mid-morning, the time Traci had said she would come by, Michelle lingered over her breakfast. As she slowly ate she decided that it really was irrelevant when Traci showed up, this was her vacation and she did not plan to rush for anyone, not even the president.

A gentle breeze was blowing through the house moving the curtains as if they were dancing to some strange music that only they could hear. In the front yard, just outside the living room window, a mockingbird was expressing its appreciation for the beauty of the lovely morning. Michelle finished eating but instead of clearing the table and putting on some street clothes, she just sat quietly at the table enjoying some of nature's finest music while she flossed.

Mingling with the song from the little bird was the noise of the increasing activity from outside. As it approached mid-morning and the sun started to heat the sand, people started heading toward the beach. Michelle could hear the voices and the laughter of the people walking passed her cottage. From all the outside bustle she assumed that there were still quite a few tourists in town and that the beach would be crowded. Still in her robe, she got up and walked out on the front porch. Just as she had thought, there was a relatively steady stream of people walking by. Most of them carried a small cooler or a day pack and a few also carried some kind of ball or a Frisbee.

Michelle stretched long and slow and inhaled as deeply as possible. She could smell the ocean and she savored the aroma of it as she sat down in one of the aluminum folding chairs on the deck. "This is what a vacation should be like," she thought, "everybody having fun with some heavy duty relaxing simply adding the icing to the cake."

Michelle was still sitting there lost in people watching when Traci drove into the driveway. She was slightly embarrassed that she had let so much of the morning slip by and still had not gotten dressed. As she climbed the deck stairs Traci greeted Michelle with a perky smile. "Feeling better this morning?" she asked.

"Much better," Michelle responded. "Thanks again for the ride home. I'm not sure I could have made it without you."

"Glad to help you," Traci replied as she sat down in one of the remaining chairs.

"Sorry I'm not dressed but my sleeping potion really knocked me out. I slept kinda' late and all I've done so far is lollygag but I did eat breakfast."

Traci laughed and said, "That's what vacations are for."

Even though Traci had brought her home Michelle really had not gotten a very good look at her until moments before when she sat down on the deck with her. She wasn't as tall as Michelle but she was equally as attractive, just in a different way. Her sand colored hair was cut so it didn't quite come to her shoulders. Traci had combed it with the slightest outside flip, a style that would look fine even if tousled by a breeze. It seemed to match the carefree air that she had about her. She had blue eyes that seemed to be full of mischief. At the corner of Traci's right eye Michelle thought she could make out a lighter line on her skin. It was a thin line, about an inch long. Possibly a scar, she decided. Her light yellow shorts and shirt blended nicely with her golden skin tones causing Michelle to wonder about what type of work she did. It was obvious that she knew how to choose her clothes and how to look nice though be it extremely casual.

"Cute outfit," Michelle said, "I guess I should go put on something a little more presentable."

"Do you have plans for today?" Traci asked as they got out of their chairs.

"Plans. I haven't even formed a committee to study the possibilities."

Traci continued, "Good. You put on some clothes and we can go play putt-putt, ride around looking at the guys, go to a movie, play on the beach, whatever. There's a pool where I'm staying and a Jacuzzi. We have a ton of possibilities, if you're interested." Michelle didn't quite know what to say. Traci certainly seemed excited about what the day might bring and she also seemed pleased that Michelle might be spending it with her.

Michelle just stood there looking at her trying to think of a proper response. "It all sounds great. I really don't have any plans except to chill out," she finally said. Turning to open the screen door she began to think that it really might be nice to have someone to pal around with, besides, having someone to talk with would keep her from thinking about things she didn't understand. Michelle knew she needed to avoid doing that at all costs. "I'll go change," she said and walked inside.

Traci followed her but stayed in the living room as Michelle disappeared into the bedroom. As she went through the open door Michelle gave it a slight push behind her. Without looking back, she crossed the room to her boxes of clothes.

Due to the light breeze blowing through the house the door had not closed all the way and had actually been blown slightly open. Traci was looking at the pictures on the wall and the decor of the room. The movement of the door caught her eye and she looked through the opening into Michelle's bedroom. Michelle was oblivious to what had happened with the door and also to Traci's rapt attention as she stood in the next room watching Michelle's every move through her reflection in a large mirror on the dresser.

Traci knew that if Michelle looked in the mirror that she would probably be caught and that they would both be embarrassed, but especially her. She was afraid Michelle would say something that required an answer and due to its clarity, discover the open door. Traci had just decided that what she was doing was slightly tacky and started to turn away when she saw Michelle give the belt on her robe a tug to untie it. Traci stood there holding her breath, afraid to move for fear Michelle would detect her movement and catch her looking.

Michelle pushed the open robe over her shoulders and let it slide down her back and land in a pile around her feet. Traci let out a quiet gasp that she knew had to give her away but if it did, Michelle never let on. The mirror wasn't angled correctly to reflect all of Michelle's body and Traci could only see her from mid-thigh up. Her heart was pounding at the unexpected voyeuristic scene that was unfolding before her. "Michelle either has to be in a coma, or she wants me to see this," she thought. Traci felt the blood rushing to her nipples and for just an instant she thought about stepping into the bedroom just to see what Michelle's response would be. As she continued to watch, Michelle slipped on some champagne colored underwear. When Michelle had bent over, Traci had gotten more than a glimpse of her firm, teacup size breasts. Since she had observed no sign that Michelle was the least bit aroused, Traci decided that what she was observing was all purely accidental.

Still unaware that she was being watched, Michelle put on a matching bra and hooked it in the front. By now Traci was almost in a panic mode. How much longer could she observe and not get caught and yet she could not bring herself to look away. From another box of clothes Michelle removed some tan shorts and put them on, then she walked to the closet and removed a short sleeve, teal colored shirt. As she slipped it on, Traci knew that she could not risk getting caught any longer. Stepping out of view she went over to a chair and sat down. Though Traci's heart was still pounding and her breathing had not yet returned to normal, at least she was safe from being found out.

In a moment Michelle emerged and said, "I'm ready." Hearing her voice brought Traci back to reality with a start. She was still a long way from recovering from her voyeuristic journey and the last thing on her mind was playing a round of putt-putt. "Are you okay?" Michelle added.

"I'm doing great. Why?"

"You look kinda' flushed."

"Oh, really. No, I feel fine," Traci replied. "Let's go," she said as she stood up. She hoped Michelle could not detect her still swollen nipples, but just to be sure, she pushed her shoulders forward to try to move her shirt away from her breasts. As they walked down the stairs to her car Traci was thinking about Michelle's question as to how she was feeling. She grinned to herself and decided that Michelle really had no idea how good she felt or, for that matter, how good they both could feel.

They got into Traci's car and headed west toward the main north-south highway where the majority of the activities that would appeal to vacationers were located. As they rode they engaged in light conversation about the scenery and all the different possibilities that were available. After riding around for about an hour just seeing the sights they decided to pull into the parking lot of a formidable looking putt-a- round course that featured a pirate motif as its decor.

Though there were a few people ahead of them in line, they didn't have to wait long until it was their turn to start playing. They laughed and chattered like two high school girls who had been friends for a long time might have done. Their play was relatively even with neither being able to gain a real advantage. Michelle felt very relaxed, she was glad to have met someone to be with simply to occupy her mind and time. By the time they had finished their round they had had so many laughs at each other that they had gotten their scores confused.

After turning in their clubs they sat down on a small bench in the shade of a large magnolia tree. Neither spoke for several moments, it were as if they were both embarrassed by their shenanigans of a few minutes earlier. Traci was first to break the silence. "You must be recovering from something," she said quietly without looking toward Michelle.

"What do you mean?" Michelle replied.

Traci still did not look up, she kept her eyes fixed on a small crack in the sidewalk as if they could talk more freely without eye contact. "Well, you're attractive. You seem intelligent. You're fun to be around and you're at the beach by yourself."

Being reminded of that caused Michelle to let her shoulders droop forward. There was a long silence and Traci started to think she had really offended her. Without looking at Traci, Michelle said, "So are you."

Traci detected a change in the tone of her voice. "I'm sorry. I didn't mean to pry or to hurt you."

Michelle still did not look up. In a barely audible whisper she said, "You didn't. There's nothing you, or anyone else, can do to ever hurt me again. Most people just aren't creative enough to match the pain of a shattered heart."

Traci reached over and put her hand on Michelle's hand and gave it a light squeeze. "There's a lot of truth to that," she answered, "let's go get a glass of tea and try to forget about the mind games people play."

"Suits me. Let's do it."

They got up and walked over to Traci's car and got in. The air felt good blowing in on them as they pulled onto the highway and headed toward the nearest fast-food place.

"Let's get it to go and take a ride around the country side," Traci suggested.

"Okay."

Spotting a fast food restaurant, Traci turned into their parking lot and stopped at the drive-thru menu. She ordered two large, unsweetened teas with lemon and in just a few moments they were back on the highway headed out of town.

They rode in silence for several miles, their only sounds were made as they sipped the tea. It was refreshing and they both became aware of just how hot and thirsty they had become. Michelle finally broke the silence. "Thanks for taking me home last night. I really appreciate it. That's something most folks would not have done."

"I was glad to do it," Traci replied. "You looked kind of abandoned just sitting there, not moving." She laughed and added, "I was afraid you might have gone catatonic on me. Now, that would really have created a problem."

Michelle laughed with her. "I had no idea I looked abandoned. It must have been more obvious than I thought."

"Being abandoned is certainly no sin on your part. I know what it's like. I was abandoned big time--with a capital

A. That's how I got this scar and also why I have very little interest in being involved with men anymore except on a real casual basis." As she was saying that, she took her right forefinger and traced it down the side of her face by her right eye. "I got it all in one fell swoop." Michelle looked at the line Traci's finger was following. Sure enough, it was now obvious to her that what she had earlier noticed was a thin scar that appeared to be just under an inch in length. Though her curiosity was aroused as to how Traci had gotten it, Michelle considered asking about it to be prying and impolite.

Traci made no further mention of it, they just rode on in silence admiring the beauty of the day. After three or four minutes she said, "Are you hungry? The tea seems to have gotten my attention and now I'm starving."

Michelle agreed with her by saying, "Something to eat might be nice."

"Is there any place special you would like to eat?"

"No. How about you?"

"I know a quaint little place on the southside that I try to go to at least once when I come down here. Let's go there. You'll like it. It ought to take us about a half an hour to get there but it's worth it, unless you just can't wait."

"That sounds good to me. I might have eaten there on one of my other trips. What's the name of it?"

"Moe's Crabhouse. It's a dive but the food is excellent."

Michelle was slightly surprised at this coincidence but she did like the food so she simply said, "Okay."

It took about fifteen minutes for them to get to the main road, then they headed south. Before long, Traci had turned off on another road that lead toward numerous marinas and cheap motels. "There it is," she exclaimed. She pulled into the parking lot and stopped. Michelle looked around and began to wonder if it really had been a good choice. She knew memory ghosts would be waiting there to haunt her if she let them. Nothing had really changed at Moe's since her last visit and she made up her mind to fight against memories. There weren't many cars in the parking lot and Traci's description of the place as being a dive was certainly as she remembered it.

The building sat on the edge of a small inlet. It was made of wood and looked as if any stain that had ever been on it had long since weathered away. "No change," Michelle thought. As she got out of the car she could smell the faint odor of the ocean mixed in with the scent of spices and food cooking. The smells were not at all unpleasant and some of the apprehension she had initially felt started to dissipate.

Even though it was only late afternoon it was dark inside the doorway. They paused to let their eyes adjust before proceeding. As they were standing there blinking, a waitress appeared and asked, "Two? Follow me, please. Would you prefer a table or a booth?"

"Booth," Traci said, "where it's quiet, so we can chat."

The waitress showed them to a booth in the corner and said, "How's this?"

"Fine," Michelle replied.

Laying down two menus, the girl said, "I'll be back in a few minutes," and departed.

"Have you been here before?" Traci asked.

Michelle shook her head to the affirmative.

"Well, it's all good and the crab cakes are the best I've ever had anywhere. That's what I'm having."

"I think I'll have some, myself," Michelle answered.

"The story I started awhile ago about my scar, I didn't mean to leave you hanging but it's kind of long and I thought it would give us something to talk about while we eat." Michelle was elated though she tried not to show it. After all, she decided, it was obvious Traci had been injured some way and it did appear to be very personal but her curiosity was killing her just the same.

After a few minutes the waitress returned to take their orders. They both ordered crab cakes and a baked potato. Traci once again ordered unsweetened tea with lemon but this time Michelle chose sweet tea with lemon. After the waitress left they decided to make a trip to the ladies' room to wash their hands. As they were returning to their booth Michelle wondered aloud if Moe ever paid his electric bill since all the lights were so dim. They each got a chuckle out of that and Traci's reply that if he did, it must not have been on time.

They were still chuckling as they sat back down. During their absence the waitress had brought their drinks. Once she got comfortable again and had taken a sip of tea, Traci said, "Well, are you ready to sit through another tale of-- is it really worth it?"

"Sure," Michelle replied, "I may even add to it."

"Okay, but if you get bored, stop me."

"I will, promise."

"I was involved, I guess you could say as a significant other, with a guy named Steve. I thought we had a pretty good thing going, at least most of the time. It wasn't perfect but these things never are. Anyway, one night we went to a party that one of his friends had. Nothing super big or wild, just a nice, quiet get together.

I sell real estate for a living and at that particular time I had been selling for several years on a part-time basis. Steve and I had talked some about getting married. We each had our own place and we spent a lot of weekends together. I'd go to his house or he would come over to mine. Most people would probably have just lived together but for whatever reason, I've always struggled with that. Anyway, we went to this party and lo and behold, who would be there but a man named Reed Smith who just happened to own the biggest, fastest growing agency on the block. Lots of people wanted to work for him because of his reputation for being honest and for looking after his agents and his clients. Well, since Steve and I had been talking about getting married, I started thinking about going full time. Just working part time, I made a decent living but now I thought that a boost in my income would be nice. Neither of us had a really big house and we had talked about selling the two of them and moving into a larger 'our house'."

Traci was interrupted by the waitress returning with their food. She set it down and said, "I'll be back in a few minutes to check on you." They both thanked her and she departed again.

Traci continued, "I didn't know Mr. Smith even knew I was in the world, much less that he would ever consider offering me a job. Anyway, during the course of the evening he and I ended up chatting with each other. We did the usual small talk for a while and I just mentioned that I was giving some thought to going full time. When I said that, he asked me if I would like to come to work at his agency. Needless to say, if my Poli-grip hadn't been holding, I would have dropped my teeth." Michelle laughed. "Here I am, part time, a real nobody in the world of real estate, and the owner of the biggest agency in town just offered me a job. I didn't know what to say or do. So, I did the only thing I could think of. I said, 'I'd love to,' and threw my arms around him.

Let me put this in perspective. Mr. Smith is up in his sixties and is at least slightly rotund. Not exactly my first choice to be marooned on an island with but a super nice person. While he and I were talking, Steve was watching. I never thought a thing about it but apparently, Steve was not as secure as I thought he was. Neither of us was above taking a little taste, especially if it was good champagne, but as a general rule we didn't get drunk, either. I noticed that for the rest of the evening he always had a glass in his hand. I didn't think much about it at the time but looking back, I probably should have picked up on it because it was a bad sign of worse things to come. Aren't these crab cakes great? I don't care if they are fried, they're wonderful."

Michelle nodded in agreement and replied, "They really are delicious."

"Anyway, back to the party where it's starting to get late so I asked Steve if he was ready to leave and he just sort of grunted, drained his glass, and set it down. That's when I first noticed just how little pain he was actually feeling. We said our goodbyes and headed for the car. I'm trying to help support him so he won't fall down the steps and he's all over the place, really limber legged. When we got to the car he wanted to drive. Now, we're having words in the driveway. Finally, it dawned on me that no one has ever reasoned with a drunk, so I said rather forcefully, 'Damn it, Steve. Give me the car keys. You're in no condition to drive'. I couldn't believe it, his answer was typical alcohol induced logic. When I told him he was in no condition to drive he just looked at me like I was from outer space and said, 'I sure as hell can't walk.' I grabbed the keys and told him that he was still able to ride and nudged him into the car.

The ride home was tense, to say the least. When we got there I helped him into the house where he promptly sat down. I went to brush my teeth, thinking he would follow. I finished in the bathroom and went in the bedroom to get ready for bed. I pulled my clothes off and put on my favorite little red gown. It was light and comfy and, because it felt so good on my skin, I rarely wore anything underneath it.

Still no Steve, so I went back into the living room to see what had happened to him. Some way he had managed to get to the kitchen, pour himself another drink, and make it back. He was just standing there, kind of leaning on the back of a chair to keep from falling. I was already about half disgusted with the way he had been acting and seeing him with another drink in his condition really chapped my ass. I said, 'Come on, let's go to bed. You've had enough to drink for one night.' I started to walk away when he said, 'Wait, I want to talk to you.' I stopped and turned around. He finished what was left of his drink and dropped the glass on the carpet. I said, 'Okay, talk.' He said, 'Is that what this is all about?' He said, 'Ain't I good enough for you?' So I said, 'That old fart that you seem to think is trying to get me in bed just happens to be Reed Smith, the owner of probably the fastest growing real estate agency in town and he was

QRW WU\iQJ WR VcUHZ PH, KH ZDV iQ WKH SURcHVV RI R⊠HUiQJ me a full time job, which I accepted.' Steve said, sort of sarcastically, 'Well, just how do you plan to repay him for this full time job?'

All this time he had been moving around beside the chair closer to me but I didn't think anything about it. I said, 'Look, all I'm going to do is work for him. Let's talk about this tomorrow. I'm going to bed.' As I was turning to walk away, he grabbed me by my right arm and pulled me back around to face him. About the time I got turned around--wham! He backhanded me with his right hand, just happened to be the one he wore his big, old class ring on. Next think I know, I'm falling over the coffee table seeing stars that Galileo never even imagined. I really banged my head when I hit the floor and I was having some trouble collecting my thoughts. Got to give good old Steve credit, he was kind enough to help me up. I still hadn't really figured out what was going on when--wham, again from the other side. This time I landed on the couch and sort of rolled off in onto the floor.

By the time I got my eyes focused again I felt something warm oozing into my mouth and Steve was standing over me. I kept trying to get up but none of my body parts would listen to what I wanted them to do. He bent over me and took me by the arms and helped me up. I still wasn't sure I was in the world, I was just trying to keep from falling when I felt this big tug and the sound of something tearing. All of a sudden, I'm standing in front of him with nothing on. This red blur went flying through the air and landed in the floor behind me."

Traci paused and took a few bites, Michelle followed suit. She had become so wrapped up in what she was hearing that she had forgotten to eat. After a sip of tea, Traci continued, "Why did he have to tear it off? He could have removed it in a second but he didn't. The bastard had to tear if off me and ruin my favorite little gown. I guess he had to make a statement.

Anyway, back to the story. He caught me by my hair, it was much longer then, and started pulling me behind him toward the bedroom. I don't know which one of us was the least able to walk, him or me. Even though I didn't have all my faculties back, I knew what was going to happen next.

When we got there, he turned loose of my hair long enough to bless me with another good, stiff slap and when I stopped falling I was on the bed, once again trying to clear my head. It must really excite men to knock us around because all the alcohol he had consumed sure didn't have any ill effects on that part of his anatomy. About the time my head was starting to clear I felt him on the bed pushing my legs apart. Oh man, it hurt. I wasn't ready and he didn't care. He finally worked his way in me and then started pounding me like a jack hammer."

The thought of that made Michelle cringe and she unconsciously moved her knees together. She said, "This isn't a very fun story. You don't have to go on if you'd rather not." Michelle remembered much too vividly what Larry had done to her and she empathized greatly with what Traci was relating to her.

Traci shrugged and waved her hand. "Don't worry, I'm almost to the good part. Besides, it wouldn't be fair to you for me to leave you in suspense."

"Okay. It's up to you but if it becomes too painful, believe me, I'll understand."

"You'll like the ending," Traci said. "Anyway, when he finally finished pile driving me into the mattress he didn't get off. He passed out, still on top of me. To put it mildly, Michelle, now I really was screwed, literally and symbolically. There I was being mashed by a hundred and eighty pounds of dead weight on top of me. I could barely breathe and I didn't know which part of me hurt the worst since both ends had really taken a pounding. Blood was still oozing out of my mouth and eye. Needless to say, I was in a real predicament.

I finally squirmed around enough that I got my shoulders out from under him and that let me free both arms. I used his left arm as a lever and I finally moved him enough that his upper body was beside me. After I did that, I rested a minute to try to catch my breath. From there I kept squirming and pushing till I managed to slide out from under him, off the bed and onto the floor. That about wore me out. Anyway, I rested again before stumbling into the bathroom. I turned on the shower and then looked in the mirror. My face looked like it had been used for a soccer ball. My eye was cut. That's how I got this scar that you noticed earlier. My hair was matted with dried blood, my lips were split, both eyes were black. I looked like a raccoon. My right eye was nearly swollen shut and my nose was bloody. I spoke at great length with the marble throne."

Michelle chuckled at that but said nothing. Traci continued, "I got in the shower and did my best to wash away everything that had happened. After I was as clean as I could get, I let the cold water splash on my face for a long time. I really needed an industrial size ice pack but I didn't have one. All this time I just knew Steve would wake up and I had no idea what he would do next. I guess I should have gone home right then but I really didn't feel like driving and I thought the shower might revitalize me and it did.

After I got dried off, I cut some pieces of adhesive tape and tried to close the cut by my eye, then I got dressed. Steve was still on the bed, dead to the world. I found his pants and got out his key ring and removed the key to my house that I had given him. I tried to be as quiet as possible as I got the few clothes that I kept at his house out of the closet. I almost died when I dropped a coat hanger but it never even phased him.

I carried my stuff into the living room and put it in a pile by the front door. I decided that a grocery bag might help me keep my stuff together so I went into the kitchen to look for one. That's when I saw it. There it was in the dish drain-- a wicked old butcher knife. I decided right then that I would kill him, or at least cut off part, or parts, of his anatomy. I picked up the knife and went back into the bedroom and went right over to where he was still sprawled out on the bed. I could see my face in the dresser mirror and the longer I looked at it, the madder I got. I raised the knife up and thought--this is it, right through the throat. Then it dawned on me, he probably wouldn't feel a thing. He would simply be alive, then he would be dead without really experiencing the transition phase.

Then I decided that, though no jury would convict me after the members saw pictures of my face, I still didn't want to go broke having to pay some big buck lawyer to defend me so I ruled out killing him. Then I decided to call the police. Then I thought, why? All they will do is arrest him, maybe, and even if they do, he'll be out the next day but I simply could not bring myself to just walk away.

I took the butcher knife back into the kitchen. I couldn't decide what to do but I knew I had to do something. Then I saw it. There it was on the stove just grinning at me, the answer to my quandary--a ten inch, cast iron skillet. Those suckers can be used for more things than just frying chicken and baking cornbread. I picked that jewel up and, as best I could, waltzed my ass right back into the bedroom. There was good old Steve right where he had been, except now, he had turned over on his back.

None of the lights that we had turned on since we got home had been turned off so every time I went passed a reflective surface I got a good look at what was left of my face. The longer I stood in front of one looking at the damage the higher my blood pressure went.

The next Monday morning I was supposed to show an expensive piece of property to a real hot-to-trot client and there was no way I could do that in my present condition. I knew I would have to get someone else involved and that would mean splitting my commission if it even sold. That really torqued me big time because the only crime I had committed in the first place was to want to work full time to make more money so Steve and I could start a nest egg for the future. That's when I decided again that I would kill him after all. I would simply bash his head in and take my chances in court. About that time, he moved around on the bed and I chickened out but I knew that even if I couldn't kill him, I couldn't let him get away with this scot-free.

So, while I was standing there trying to decide what to do next he shifted in bed and bent his right leg slightly so it was off the bed with the knee sticking up--it made a nice target. You've got to understand, mind you, Steve took great pride in his tennis game and he really did do a nice job playing. So, I just decided I would simply slow his game down a little.

I raised that big old skillet up ôver my head with both hands, like this." Traci became more animated as she really began to get involved in the retribution part. Michelle had stopped trying to eat and had even put down her fork because she did not want to miss anything. Traci had her hands together up over her head like she was holding something by the handle.

"I brought that frying pan down as hard as I could swing it right on the point of his knee. It landed with a dull thump. Well, that woke him up and he sat up in the bed grabbing for his knee and yelling like he was being killed and he almost was. I hit him so hard that the frying pan bounced off leg. Now, I'm in the driver's seat of a great situation, one that everybody who's ever been knocked around ought to be in at least once. I hadn't planned to do this but as the skillet was bouncing off his knee and he was trying to sit up in bed, I drew back again and met him half-way. Actually, he came a little over half-way but it still counted."

Michelle was now laughing uncontrollably as Traci re-enacted this tragic scene. Traci was even having some trouble telling it because she was laughing, too. Finally, she composed herself and wiped the tears from her eyes. She put her hands back together and extended them beside her to her right, then she brought them over the top of her plate like she was hitting a baseball.

"The bottom of the pan was almost perfectly vertical when it made contact. What made it even better was that the pan was going east as his head was coming west. It went whump and he folded up like a wet noodle under pressure. I felt his nose give and the blood flew everywhere. It looked like I'd hit a ripe tomato. He flopped back on the bed and didn't move. I thought then that I really had killed him. Boy, he was a mess. His old nose was looking sideways and both of his eyebrows had been peeled. He looked like he was having cosmetic surgery in the low-rent district.

I didn't quite know what to do. I just stood there holding the frying pan watching him bleed. I even started to call 9-1-1 then I thought about all the compassion he had shown me and that idea soon passed. I knew he was dead and I was just standing there trying to think of a good lawyer when I heard him groan and gurgle. I really was relieved that he wasn't dead, honest. That's when I decided not to bash him in the head anymore but I did whack him on his good knee before I dropped the skillet between his legs and decided to leave well enough alone and go home and go to bed. So, I picked up my stuff that I had put by the front door and did just that. And that, Michelle, is the whole story of how I got this little scar.

Wait! No, it's not, either. There's one more kicker that you absolutely will not believe. Several days later Steve called and left me a message on my answering machine. He wanted me to call him so we could get together and talk about our problems, you know, patch things up. I ignored the call but he was persistent. Every few days he would call again and leave the same message. He must have thought I was in a coma and I would had to have been to even consider thinking about putting myself back in that situation.

After several weeks of this foolishness, I got really disgusted and decided to see if I could put a stop to his nonsense. I thought about what to say and it finally came to me. So, one day while he was at work, I called his house and left this message on his machine.

'Steve, it's over. I didn't like being your punching bag and I didn't like what else you did to me. So, just in case you have any doubt about my feelings for you, you son of a bitch, I wish I had a damn thousand room hotel and found you dead in every room. Goodbye.' I was afraid I had been too subtle but he must have understood because he didn't call back after that." As Traci was saying this, Michelle was taking a sip of tea which turned into a fine mist as she sprayed it over the outside portion of the booth. She quickly grabbed a napkin and wiped her mouth and cleaned up the mess she had made. Neither spoke. They just sat across the booth in the dim light laughing at each other.

Traci continued, "It also fills in the blanks as to why I'm at the beach by myself, sitting here talking with you instead of being with some man. I'm kind of afraid of them now and I really don't like to be alone with them anymore. What happened to me, simply because I wanted to improve my job-- it's no longer worth it to me. You're at the beach by yourself so you must have at least a little insight into what I've told you."

Michelle nodded. "I didn't get beaten up nor was I mistreated. He just got a better offer and couldn't get rid of me fast enough. We went from house shopping and talking about setting the date to 'what did you say your name is?' It really doesn't matter, she was younger and she had bigger knockers than I have-- I guess that counts for something."

Traci laughed. "I guess it's a good thing we only have one head, that way if any thinking does take place, at least we know which one is doing it."

Michelle chuckled. "So much for love and affairs of the heart," she said. "After I got the knife in the back I gave a lot of thought to all the words that are used and to what they really mean. The accepted definition of words totally changes when men and women are involved. For future reference, just so I would never forget again, I got my dictionary out and added the real meaning of some words. Take the word 'always' for instance. The dictionary implies that it means 'perpetually or forever'. I added a fourth definition, 'in affairs of the heart, till I get a better offer."

"That's pretty good," Traci responded, "and it sure makes sense to me."

"I like it," Michelle answered, "but not nearly as much as I like the ninth definition of love. This one is kind of long. I hope I can get right. You'll love it." She doesn't long. I hope I can get it right. You'll love it." She closed her eyes and thought for a few moments as she tried to recall the words she had written ages ago. Finally, she said, "I think the heart, as opposed to one's feelings about chocolate, the socially accepted form of the verb to bullshit, which is not socially acceptable in all circles. Everyone will accept the phrase I love you but some people struggle with the literal translation which is, I'm bullshitting you and you're stupid enough to fall for it.'"

Traci just sat there for a few moments without saying anything. Then, she started laughing and said, "That pretty well sums it up. I don't think I've ever heard it put more realistically. I like that." Then she picked up her glass and extended her hand toward Michelle. "I propose a toast to some great definitions and to the thought that went into them." Michelle picked up her glass and they lightly clinked them together, then took a sip. "What happened to you still bothers you a great deal, doesn't it?"

Michelle nodded. "It changed my whole outlook on a lot of things, especially those related to men and to the love thing. You said that you're afraid to be alone with them. Well, I have a great deal of difficulty trusting and caring about all this stuff anymore. I'm not afraid of them, I just don't have the desire to take the chance of ever being treated that way again. There's just not enough of whatever I need left in me to ever want to go through that anymore so I avoid them."

"Don't you miss touching and being touched? You know, all the things it's supposed to be about."

"Yes, I do," Michelle said quietly, "but I simply can't take the chance again. What about you, don't you miss it, too?"

Traci didn't answer, she appeared to be lost in thought and didn't even look up. After a long pause, she raised her head and grinned. "Steve used to say something that I've changed slightly to fit my needs. He used to say, 'There's women, other men, and sheep". I changed it to say, 'there's men, other women, and," she raised her clenched fist for exclamation, "Mr. V."

"Mr. V.," Michelle said with a confused look. "Who's Mr. V.?"

"Mr. V. is not a who. Mr. V. is a what and he's quite nice when it comes to helping put out fires of passion that burn within my loins," Traci laughed. At Traci's explanation Michelle got tickled. It dawned on her what Traci was talking about and she was slightly embarrassed that it hadn't registered sooner. They sat there laughing as they held up two fingers toward each other.

When Michelle finally stopped laughing, she said, "Mr. Churchill would really be impressed if he knew just how versatile his victory sign can be." They laughed some more. Michelle had almost forgotten how good it felt to laugh that hard. After a break in the laughter, she looked at Traci and said, "You are kidding, aren't you?"

"Not in the least," Traci replied. "Just because I'm afraid of men doesn't mean I'm no longer a woman. I have feelings. I have desires. I just have to be more creative. Look at it this way, Michelle, Mr. V. has never hit me. He's never raised his voice. I don't have to cook for him. I don't have to wash his clothes. No unwanted children. No gifts that keep on giving. I don't wonder if he's telling me the truth or if he's having an affair. Speaking of affairs, I actually have three Mr. V's of different sizes. That way, I can be involved in an ongoing relationship with one and, If I get the urge, I can have a fling with a stranger simply by grabbing a different box."

Michelle just sat there listening with rapt attention. She didn't know for sure whether Traci was serious or if she were going to be the object of some kind of tall tale Traci was telling. She thought about laughing but she hesitated because Traci seemed so serious.

"Look at yourself, Michelle, you avoid involvement with men so that only leaves you the other two possibilities." "There is another possibility," Michelle said, "I could simply do without."

"Yes, you could, but I doubt it. If you're not involved in any other way, you must be involved with yourself by playing yellow pages and letting your fingers do the walking."

Michelle hoped that in the dim light Traci couldn't see how red her face had become because she could feel it tingling. She had to admit to herself that sometimes the fires of passion were so hot that she could no longer ignore them and that there had been occasions when she had let her fingers do the walking, especially when the hot water was beating down on her in the shower. Though some might consider the extra time Michelle spent there a waste of water, she thought it was fun and it did solve her situation.

When Michelle looked up again her face had cooled substantially. She asked Traci her own question, "Don't you miss touching and being touched?"

"Yes, I do, a great deal. Sometimes I need someone to touch me so much that I almost cry. Not being touched can actually hurt, sometimes I think more than being touched the wrong way; like what Steve did to me. Maybe that's why people, especially women, stay in an abusive relationship. At least they're touched and when the abuse is over, the other party feels guilty and touches them in the way they really need. Michelle, our conversation has gotten much too heavy. Let's lighten up. Mr. V. may not be much of a conversationalist and he isn't worth doodle when it comes to rubbing your back but he can sure rub other things that will make you forget your back hurt to start with."

Michelle chuckled at what Traci had just said. She was trying to make up her mind which way Traci would swing if she were on the his or her pendulum but she couldn't decide. Certain statements had been said that made Michelle think one thing but other statements had been said that made her think something else. She finally put the question to rest by deciding that it really didn't matter. Traci was pleasant and fun to be with and it sure beat being alone.

"Are you ready to go?" Traci asked.

"Let's do it," Michelle replied. "That sure was tasty. I'm stuffed."

Traci nodded and said, "Me, too."

"Our waitress did a nice job, don't you think?" said Michelle as she placed some money by her plate.

"Yes, she did," Traci answered as she fumbled in her bag for her billfold. She also put some money by her plate and they made their way toward the cash register by the door. They paid their checks and stepped outside into the early evening light.

There was still plenty of daylight left even though the sun had dropped considerably in the western sky, softening the shadows and letting the air start to cool. As they walked toward the car Michelle said, "I should have brought my camera. This light is a photographer's dream for portraits, or anything else."

"What do you mean?"

"Well, it's light enough to shoot without a flash yet there aren't any harsh shadows."

"Oh. I never thought about that," Traci said as she looked around.

"Put a reflector or two up, hand me my Kodak, and you would think you were some high fashion super model doing a shoot."

"You really did eat too much. I think it's gone to your head." They both laughed. When they got to Traci's car she unlocked the door for Michelle. Michelle opened it, got in and reached across to unlock hers. Michelle left her door open and when Traci opened the other door a tunnel-effect breeze blew through the car taking some of the trapped heat out with it. Traci got in and left her door open as she started the engine. She punched the air conditioner button and they soon felt cool air blowing on them. They rolled the windows down slightly and closed the doors. The hot air continued to be forced out and the interior of the car became relatively comfortable.

Traci had driven several miles before she realized that their conversation had grown one sided, she was the only one talking. "Do you feel okay, Michelle?" she asked.

Michelle nodded in reply and Traci had to look at her to get her response. "Are you sure. You're very quiet."

"I feel all right except, all of a sudden, I got really tired."

"Oh. I thought that maybe you had eaten something that was having a super quick effect on you."

"No. I feel fine physically. When we came outside I guess something triggered some old memories and my mind, or what's left of it, crashed and burned."

"Is Moe's a place you and your friend used to come to?"

Michelle nodded. "Sometimes my thoughts get all jumbled and nothing makes any sense. A doctor I went to see several years ago seemed to think that it was caused by a chemical imbalance in my brain but he wasn't quite sure what to do about it and I never pursued it any further. I just know that when it happens I can go from being full of energy to being totally exhausted in a matter of seconds."

"Really. That is strange."

"I know. An example of how quickly it can happen is like the time some friends had invited me to join them at one of the local clubs back home one evening. I looked forward to it all afternoon and hurried home from work to get ready. While I was taking a shower the chemicals, or whatever it is, shifted from one side to the other and I ended up struggling out of the shower and going to bed. Sleeping seems to be about all I'm good for when it happens. Also, in case you haven't noticed, I'm not very good company, either."

"Is there anything I can do?"

"No. I guess I'll just go on back to my cottage and take a nap."

"You can take a nap at my place. I've even got a Jacuzzi in my condo that might make you feel better. Besides, I've got three bottles of cheap champagne in the fridge just waiting for a reason to be opened."

"I don't think so, Traci. At times like this I seem to do better when I'm by myself. Plus, I have no idea how long this will last. It may be a few minutes or it may last for months."

"Have you ever tried being around other people? Maybe that would make you feel better."

"I've thought about it but knowing how obnoxious I can be, I avoid them because I don't want to offend anyone."

"Then why don't you give it a try. You should have realized by now that I'm not easily offended. Besides, I'll even rub your back. That always makes me feel better, regardless of the problem."

Though Michelle really felt uncomfortable being around other people when she sank into that far away place inside her mind, she also hated to be by herself because she never knew what she would do next. Besides, this unreal world inside her head was a very scary place and she was always uneasy there because her thoughts were so jumbled that nothing made any sense. "I still need to go by my place and get my bathing suit," she said in a quiet voice.

"Wear one of mine. Hell, Michelle, it doesn't matter whether you wear one or not. There won't be anybody there but us. Relax, let'em hang out. I might even join you in running bare."

Michelle had reached the point that she was really too tired to care. The idea of a back rub had sounded good. It sounded even better when mixed with some champagne and she hoped that the combination would relax her enough to put her to sleep. She had discovered that the world of sleep was the safest place for her to be when this unsettling phenomenon took place. After a short period of silence, she said, "Okay. I'll give it a try. Besides, nothing else helps and I don't have enough energy to argue about it." After another short pause she added, "By the way, Traci, are you trying to seduce me?"

Traci did not respond; she didn't even look at Michelle. She kept her eyes focused on the road ahead and concentrated on her driving. After a long pause, Michelle began to think she really had offended her. She was getting ready to offer some statement of apology when Traci finally answered. Without looking at her, Traci said in a quiet voice, "I really don't know. I like men and so do you but I'm afraid of them for physical reasons and you're afraid of them for emotional reasons. Either way, the result is the same--we both avoid them. Anyway, in answer to your question, I really and truly do not know. I've thought about it but instead of a seduction plan, I guess I'll simply wait and see where the evening takes us." She paused for a moment, then added, "Do you want me to?"

Now it became Michelle's turn to be hesitant with her answer because Traci's response had taken her completely by surprise. She would have had to struggle with the answer even if her mind had not become so jumbled a few minutes earlier but now, with her thoughts in such a state of disarray, Michelle was totally confused as to how to answer this question. Something that added more to the confusion was that when these particular circuits inside her brain shorted out she had absolutely no desire to be around other people, she even went out of her way to try to avoid them. Due to this, the possibility of an encounter with another person, even a casual one, much less an intimate one, with either sex, had virtually no appeal at all to her.

Michelle was exhausted. All she really wanted to do was get in a dark room and go to sleep. She knew Traci was waiting for an answer but she still had not come up with one. "I don't know, I'm just so very tired," she mumbled, "I won't be very good company for you or anybody else."

"That's okay. Relax in the Jacuzzi, have some champagne, and if you go to sleep, so what, there are two beds in the condo. I just don't think you should be alone right now. Besides, maybe some of the bubbly and the bubble jets will make you feel better."

"Possibly, but the point you're missing is that it's not my body that hurts, it's my mind and I have no idea how a bubble jet can help that."

They were rapidly approaching the condo and Michelle knew that she was running out of time if she wanted to change her mind. It finally dawned on her that what they did or did not do that evening really made no difference to her, anyway. She just knew that her mind hurt so much that if Traci wanted to drive head-on into a concrete wall that it would make no real difference to her. With that in mind, she said, "Why don't we start with a large glass first?"

"Great. Now you're talking. Like I said, I've got three bottles and if that's not enough, we'll get some more."

As they pulled into the condo parking lot Michelle began to wonder just what she had gotten herself into but quickly decided that it really didn't matter. She figured she had probably spent better evenings and she was positive that, unless Traci killed her, she had spent worse. Traci pulled into a parking space and turned off the engine. She looked over at Michelle and said, "Let's go get some bubbly."

They got out of the car and walked through the lengthening shadows into the lobby toward the elevator. The lobby was clean but by no means elaborate. There was a large potted ficus benjamina on each side of the sliding glass doors. Behind the registration counter were two pleasant looking girls who appeared to be in their early twenties. They smiled and spoke as Michelle and Traci walked passed them. Michelle and Traci returned their greeting and continued toward the elevator.

"A place to set your luggage and a place for them to take your money, these people are definitely out for the buck," Michelle thought, as the elevator door opened. They stepped in and Traci pushed the button for the fifteenth floor.

Michelle leaned back in the corner opposite the control panel and closed her eyes. The cool metal felt good on her shoulders and upper back. The elevator was so smooth and quiet that she wasn't certain they were moving when the floor indicator bell quietly chimed her back to reality. Only then did she realize that she had almost gone to sleep as she propped in the corner.

The door opened and Traci said, "Walk this way," as she stepped out into the hallway and tried to imitate a gait that Michelle was sure she must have seen in a B-grade horror movie. As Michelle stepped out behind her, she did her best to copy the strange example that Traci set. They bounced along through the hall looking like two line-dancing zombies. Even as tired as she was, Michelle had to laugh.

Traci turned the corner and went to the last available doorway. There they stopped and she unlocked it. Spreading her arms for exclamation, she said, "Home sweet home away from home, about once a year."

Traci stepped inside and turned on a lamp as Michelle followed her. She looked around the room and walked over to look out the sliding glass doors at the sun deck. "What a view. This is nice."

"I like it. I always try to get up high in this wing when I come down here. This way I can see the beach, the marsh, and part of some golf course. It's really not a bad view."

Looking at the room from the front door, it curved slightly to the left, sort of like the end of a hockey stick. There were two full size beds separated by a chest of drawers. Toward the foot of each bed was a Queen Anne's chair. Where the room turned there was a small kitchenette with a tiny glass table with four ladder back chairs around it. In the center of the table was a surprisingly realistic silk flower arrangement. Situated around the living room was a love seat and two matching recliners.

"This is what I like," Traci said as she pointed to the area at the end of the room, "Ah one and ah two, the bubble machine." They laughed at her poor impression and she finished the tour with, "And here's the bath. Not a bad little spot to relax and just try to recover from the blows of life. How about a glass of nectar of the gods?"

"Sure sounds good to me," Michelle replied.

Traci reached into the cabinet over the counter where the sink was located. She removed two of the short, fat water glasses like the ones so often found in motels and ran some water in each one. She swished the water around to rinse them out, then poured it into the sink. Setting them on the counter, Traci opened the refrigerator and removed a bottle of champagne. She peeled the foil off the top of the bottle exposing the convoluted plastic stopper and the fine wire that was twisted around it as a sagety precaution. She untwisted the wire and removed it, placing it on the counter.

"These bottles are a pain in the ass to open but they're worth it. Besides, I remembered to bring a secret weapon." She reached into a small flat box that was on the counter and held up a large pair of pliers for Michelle to see. "Meet Jaws, a life simplifier," she said. "Hold the bottle while I twist."

Michelle put both hands around the large part of the bottle and pressed it firmly against the counter. Traci put the pliers around the top and began a back and forth motion as she pushed up. In a few seconds the top came off with a resounding pop and a small cloud of vapor wafted upward from the now open bottle. Traci put down the pliers that were still holding the top. She filled each glass about three fourths full and then put the top back in the bottle and returned it to its place in the refrigerator. Traci picked up both glasses and took a sip of one as she offered the other to Michelle. Michelle used both hands as she accepted the glass, her left hand underneath it the glass to support it and her right hand to stabilize it. She said, "Thank you," and took a sip. Then she added, "This just hits the spot." They walked over to the small glass table and set their glasses down, then they sat down across the table from each other.

Neither spoke for a couple of minutes. It were as if they had just met and really didn't know quite what to say. They just sat there across from each other watching the tiny bubble floating to the top of their drinks. The condensation on the outside of the glasses made an acceptable palette so Michelle drew a happy face on hers. Following Michelle's lead, Traci drew a flower on her glass.

Each was aware of the silence but neither seemed to be quite sure of the best way to break it. Each thought the other might be slightly embarrassed about what might come to pass and neither really wanted to force the issue. They would just let whatever was going to happen, happen, without any real push from either of them. At last the silence started to become awkward and Traci said, "Look, Michelle, I don't want you to feel like you're under some kind of obligation to participate in any fun and games that might come to pass. This isn't for everybody, and yes, I also wish the circumstances were different but they aren't. If I could have my way, Steve would never have used me for a punching bag and he would be here now instead of you but that's not the way it is. He's gone, your friend is gone and here we are. Like I told you earlier, I really miss not having someone to touch and someone to touch me. I've learned that if I close my eyes and pretend, I can put someone else's image in you. I know you think that I'll be using you by doing that and I suppose you're right but I'll be willing to bet that you'll be doing the same thing where I'm concerned. So we're using each other, not abusively but because right now, we're it. We're all we have."

Michelle remained quiet. She continued to doodle in the condensation on her glass which was by now half empty. She didn't know quite what to expect, to do, or to say. The one thing that she knew for certain was that Traci had told the truth. She, too, wished that things had not gone the way they had, that it was Paul sitting across the table from her sipping champagne the way they had done so many times in the past but it wasn't him and it never would happen that way again. Everything Traci had said had hit her right in the heart. Michelle felt a tear start to form but she fought it back. She wondered if it really did matter who was touching her as long as it was done in a tender manner? Instead of a sip, this time she took a rather large drink from her glass. As she let it trickle down her throat she was acutely aware of how good it tasted and how good it felt. The champagne was starting to make her feel giddy and more relaxed. She was beginning to discover that the possibilities of this unique situation were at least, slightly titillating.

Neither of them seemed quite sure of what to do next. They still seemed to be waiting for some kind of sign to move them to the next level and though neither knew what it would be, they were both well aware that it would be easily recognized.

"Are you feeling better than you were on the ride home?" Traci asked.

"I don't know. I'm not feeling much of anything right now. This stuff is not only good, it's potent," Michelle replied. "My mind is about half numb but I'm still a little tired."

Though their glasses were not empty, Traci got up and retrieved the bottle from the refrigerator. She set it on the table and picked up the pliers. Without either of them speaking, they went through the original ritual of opening the bottle. Michelle held it while Traci twisted the top and once again there was a hollow pop when it came off. She refilled their glasses and returned the nearly empty bottle to the fridge door.

This time when Traci got back to the table, she didn't sit down. Instead, she took a big drink and set her glass back on the table. Then, she walked over and stopped behind Michelle. The champagne was also beginning to make her a little woozy and Traci was enjoying the dulled edges of reality. She put her hands on Michelle's shoulders and started kneading the muscles. She moved her hands from her neck out toward the points of her shoulders and back. Then, Traci put her hands under Michelle's hair and massaged up and down her neck.

This would feel good regardless of the situation, Michelle decided, but after the day's activities, the heat, and the champagne, it was nothing short of wonderful. Traci hooked her fingers on top of Michelle's shoulders and pushed her thumbs deep into the muscles just below the base of her neck. Now, instead of just feeling her muscles relaxing, Michelle suddenly felt a tingling sensation shooting down her spine. As Traci continued this deep thumb massage Michelle started to squirm. It almost hurt but it also felt very good. She tried to keep her head balanced as the muscles relaxed but it was becoming harder to do. It bounced around for a few seconds, almost like a cantaloupe rolling down a washboard road, then suddenly stopped. Traci was no longer massaging her. Though she had stopped the rubbing part, her hands still rested lightly on Michelle's shoulders. Traci moved her hands in unison up each side of Michelle's neck and stopped. With the forefinger on each hand she started lightly tracing the outline of her ears. To Michelle it was a combined feeling of being tickled and being titillated. Traci seemed to be attuned to what would make her feel good and it made Michelle wonder what other sensations the evening might have in store.

Traci started massaging again and moved Michelle's head back and forth toward one shoulder, then the other. As her neck was being manipulated in one way or another, Michelle felt the tension and apprehension slowly dissipating. She was starting to enjoy this non-aggressive touching when she was suddenly jolted back to as close to reality as she could get, under the circumstances, by a spark that shot the length of her spine and caused her to tremble. While her head was pushed nearly to her left shoulder, Traci had planted a very long and passionate kiss on her right ear, flicking it with her tongue as she pulled her lips away. It had taken Michelle so by surprise that she had jumped and nearly knocked over her champagne glass when she banged into the table.

No one had done that to her in ages and she could not stop squirming as one impulse after the other shot down her back. Her nipples felt hot and swollen and for a moment she was afraid that she was going to fall out of the chair. For an instant Michelle considered putting up some kind of protest, if for no other reason than just to appear slightly more respectable, but she decided against it because it simply felt too good.

When Michelle regained her composure again she felt her hair being raised from the back of her neck only to have Traci move her lips from her ear to there. Soft kisses made the tingling sensations continue to shoot down her spine like tiny laser beams. Michelle had no idea how far she wanted this to go, or even if she really wanted it to go anywhere at all but she also knew if she were going to put a stop to things, that she would have to act soon. Traci left warm, moist kiss tracks around her neck and started to direct her attention to Michelle's left ear. She traced the outline of it lightly with her tongue and then, with the same light, sensuous touch, licked it.

Before Michelle could stifle it, a low moan escaped her throat. Traci whispered in her ear, "Just keep your eyes closed and pretend I'm anyone you want me to be." Michelle was starting to have trouble concentrating on anything except the wonderful sensations coursing through her body and mind.

As Traci continued to nibble on her ear and neck, she let her left hand slide down the front of Michelle's throat until it came to rest at the top of her sternum. She traced tiny circles with her fingers and then moved back up her throat of trace the outline of Michelle's lips with one finger. After a few tracings she moved her finger very slowly down her upper lip and paused where Michelle's lips were slighted parted. Traci felt a light kiss on her fingertip, then the lips parted a little more and the tip of Michelle's tongue came out and touched her finger. The lips opened more and the tongue seemed to pull Traci's finger inside. Michelle's mouth closed over it and she started a gentle sucking.

Now it was Traci's turn to tremble with excitement and Michelle felt it both through Traci's finger in her mouth and through the hand on her neck. As Traci moved her finger in and out of Michelle's mouth she let her right hand move slowly forward and down Michelle's chest until it stopped at the top button of her shirt. She deftly undid the top button and then moved to the next one which she also undid with no problem. Putting her hand inside Michelle's shirt, she gently cupped her left breast through her bra. Traci could feel the hardness of her nipple through the material. As she lightly kneaded the resilient flesh she felt Michelle tremble once again. With that, she slipped her hand inside the cup and rolled the erect nipple betweem her finger and thumb.

The sensation was almost too much for Michelle to bear. Her head sagged back against the back of the chair and her lips went slack. As Traci slid her finger out of her mouth, Michelle did manage to five it one last kiss and flick it with her tongue before it was out of reach. Traci slid her hand down Michelle's throat and then, removing her other hand from inside Michelle's bra, she easily undid the front hook and pulled the cups to the side. Michelle shivered slightly when the cool air flooded over her hot breasts. Traci undid the remaining buttons on Michelle's shirt and pulled it open.

Michelle no longer cared that it wasn't Paul who was doing these things to her. She had taken Traci's advice and kept her eyes closed and just pretended. Her body and mind had been craving these sensations for so long and she knew that she was now a willing participant in whatever the evening held. Traci was now fondling a teacup size breast with each hand and rolling each blood charged nipple back and forth.

A long, low moan escaped from Michelle's throat but she neither cared nor made any effort to stop it. Though she had become acutely aware of how dry her mouth was and how much she would like another sip of champagne, Michelle was hesitant to move for fear this might really be a dream and she would wake up. Traci's fingers continued to caress her and she became aware that she had unconsciously arched her back in order to thrust her breasts forward to make them more accessible.

Michelle was having enough trouble staying in her chair due to being slightly tipsy and having her body flooded by these sensations when Traci kissed her. At first it was just a light kiss as if it were an experiment to see how she would respond. Michelle had often wondered what it would be like to be kissed by another woman and whether or not she would be repulsed by it but as the kiss became heavier, she met it hungrily as the needle on her passion indicator continued to climb.

Traci probed Michelle's lips with her tongue and, using the tip of it, dragged it along the inside of her upper lip.

As the sparks shot through her body Michelle tightened the grip she had on the edge of the table until she thought she would surely break it. Traci ground her lips harder against hers and touched the tip of her tongue to Michelle's. They both trembled with excitement and it dawned on Michelle that she wasn't the only one whose passion was rising; Traci neede her as much as she needed Traci. Traci finally broke away from Michelle's lips and kissed her on the tip of her nose. From there she kissed Michelle's closed eyes and then flicked her tongue into her right car.

Though her body was limp except for an occasional shudder, Michelle still had such a death grip on the edge of the table that her hands were starting to ache. Since the assault on her senses had begun, neither had spoken. Traci broke the silence with a whisper, "Keep your eyes closed." Michelle felt a hand behind her head as Traci propped it up, then she felt a glass being placed lightly against her dry lips. In just a moment she felt a tiny stream of cool, sweet champagne trickle into her mouth and down her throat. It felt wonderful and she tried to suck more out of the glass, making slurping noises like a small child. Traci removed the glass from Michelle's mouth and Michelle heard her take a drink before she heard the glass clink back on the table. A drop had remained on Michelle's lips and Traci lightly kissed it off, then flicked her again with her tongue.

Michelle wondered how much more she could take before she totally lost control. She knew that if Traci didn't do it for her, that she would have to let her own fingers do the walking in order to find some much needed relief. Though Michelle did not know what to expect next, she sensed the passion would be turned up quite a bit.

Michelle's hands had just started to relax when a champagne cooled mouth closed over her right nipple that was already almost at its boiling point. Ice met fire, each side won. The sensation rolled over Michelle causing her body to jerk. She turned loose of the table and put both hands behind Traci's head so she couldn't move it. "Oh, Traci, don't stop," Michelle moaned as she tried to push her breast deeper into Traci's mouth.

Using her tongue, Traci pressed the taut nipple against the roof of her mouth and rolled it from side to side. Michelle let out a slight gasp as she tried to arch her back even more. By now her breathing had become ragged and in an uneven whisper she said, "I'm not sure now much more of this I can take."

Without removing her mouth from its sensuous attack, Traci replied, "Me either." Then, turning loose of Michelle's right nipple, she went hungrily after the left one. As her mouth closed over it she made more soft sucking noises and she felt a shudder go the length of Michelle's body. Traci moved her head back slightly, letting the nipple slide slowly out of the warm, wet cavern that had engulfed it. As it slid between her lips, Traci gave it a light kiss and one last quick flick with her tongue.

Michelle's eyes were still closed. She was trying to get her brain to sort out all the sensations she had been experiencing in hopes that it would send her some feedback on what to do next. She was still trying to regain some semblance of composure when Traci kissed her again directly on her slightly parted lips. Once more it started as a very light, soft kiss, like one might expect if two people were just getting to know each other but it didn't stop there. Traci cradled Michelle's face in her hands and turned the kiss into a thing of unbridled passion. She flicked the tip of her tongue against Michelle's and ground her lips hard against hers. It now became Traci's turn to tremble with excitement, and tremble she did. It coursed through her body and left her feeling flushed with desire.

Traci pulled her face back from Michelle's and laid her head on Michelle's shoulder. Lightly fondling Michelle's breasts, she whispered, "Let's jump in the shower before we get in the Jacuzzi. I'll even wash your back."

Michelle did not respond immediately. She was still having trouble with cognitive thought but one thing she did know for sure was that getting her back washed was way down on her list of things to consider. Traci's whisper seemed to come from far away and the question rolled around inside her head while she tried to think of the proper answer. Traci had begun to think Michelle either had not heard her or just did not want to respond when she heard a quiet, "Okay."

Traci got up and offered her hand to Michelle. Michelle reached up and grasped her hand and Traci helped pull her up from the chair. The combined effects of the champagne and the sensations she had just experienced left Michelle's knees weak and she put her left hand on the table to help steady herself. Traci said, "Stand here a minute and relax. I'm going to go start the water." Michelle swayed slightly when Traci let go of her and she also put her other hand on the table in order to help maintain her balance. Traci disappeared and in a few moments Michelle heard water splashing in the shower when Traci turned it on. In a few seconds Traci returned and, putting her arm around Michelle's waist, said, "Let's go."

Neither of them spoke as they walked toward the sound of the splashing water. When they got to the door Traci stepped back so Michelle could go in first. After she had started the water and adjusted the temperature Traci had turned the light off so the small room was dark except for the light that was coming through the doorway. Michelle leaned against the counter at the sink while she waited for her eyes to adjust to the subdued light. Her head was slowly spinning around due to all the champagne and with nothing to focus her eyes on, she decided to just wait to see what Traci was going to do. Besides, Michelle was afraid she would fall if she tried to stand in the dark with no support. As her eyes began to adjust to the dark she started to see things around her. She could make out items that Traci had left on the counter and she felt more confident about maintaining her balance.

Since most of the evening's activities were all new to her, Michelle was glad Traci had left the light turned off. The darkness helped to hide some of her anxiety about what was going on. It wasn't the first time she had been in the shower with another person. On numerous occasions she and Paul had washed each other's back, and other parts, much to their mutual satisfaction. However, this would be her first time at letting another woman wash her back and she could only imagine what else.

Traci said, "Last one in is an old maid but then, who gives a damn?" and started removing her shirt. Since Michelle's shirt was already unbuttoned and her bra unhooked she should have had the advantage but Traci's challenge had caught her off guard. She gave her shirt a tug, slipped it off her shoulders and let it fall by the sink. Before either of them was really aware of what was going on, they were standing in the dark, naked and giggling, each trying to be the first to step under the refreshing stream of hot water. The friendly competition had made them forget any inhibitions they had and at last, here they were. Traci could probably have stepped through the open sliding glass shower door first, it was a close race, but she didn't. Instead, as Michelle headed for it, Traci stepped back and said, "Go ahead, I'm through with'em, anyway."

As Michelle stepped in, Traci steadied her by holding her arm. After a quick turn in the water she stepped back so Traci could enter. Traci closed the door and also took a quick turn under the cascading stream. "Doesn't this feel great?" she said softly.

"Sure does. I just hope it doesn't put me to sleep."

"For some reason I really think sleep will be way down on your list," came the reply. They both laughed and Michelle decided that what Traci had said was probably correct.

Traci picked up the soap and faced Michelle. "Turn around. I'll do your back," she said. Michelle did as she had been instructed and in just a moment she felt her back start to become slippery as Traci's small hands rubbed the soap over it. Traci put the soap down and continued to rub it in what was turning into a slippery massage. After washing Michelle's back, Traci picked up the soap again and, getting close behind her, she put her arms around Michelle and started rubbing the soap over her stomach. After she worked up the suds Traci moved up to Michelle's breasts where the dark nipples were still standing at attention. As her slippery hands slid back and forth over them Michelle tried to back up, forcing Traci closer to her. Michelle could feel Traci's soft features pressing against her and she knew that Traci was also enjoying it because she could feel her erect nipples pressing into her back.

Traci's hands slipped softly over Michelle's breasts as she not only washed them but sensuously caressed them. She rolled Michelle's swollen nipples between her thumb and forefinger, occasionally pausing to pull her nipples outm only to let them slide slowly from between her fingers. Michelle's senses were becoming overwhelmed by the amount of stimulation she had received and she began to wonder how much more she could stand and just what Traci had in mind to do next.

Michelle did not have to wonder long. Traci picked up the bar of soap again and once more started working it into a sudsy lather on Michelle's stomach. Michelle knew her upper body was as clean as it had ever been and she trembled slightly with excitement as she considered where Traci's small hands might go next. She was right; with a handful of soapsuds Traci moved into the darkened area below Michelle's belly button. Michelle almost fell as Traci's fingers started their combination of washing and caressing. She put her arms around Traci in a reverse hug and let her head roll back until it rested lightly on Traci's forehead. Michelle tried to pull Traci even closer to her when she felt Traci rubbing her hips against her as she moved from side to side.

Michelle knew that she was quickly becoming a more and more willing participant in this erotic escapade and she gave brief consideration to becoming embarrassed and calling a halt to what was happening. Though she wasn't a total stranger to having her back, or other body parts washed by someone else, the previous washings had always been done by a man and she found it slightly disturbing that what was happening to her felt so good and that she was enjoying it so much.

Traci's slippery hands were now moving up and down Michelle's thighs. They moved deftly from inside, to front, to outside, and then behind her. They slid lightly over Michelle's firm bottom and lingered there momentarily as she not only washed, but caressed it.

When Traci moved her hands back to the front of Michelle's body and once again started the combination of washing and caressing, Michelle unconsciously spread her legs until her feet were touching opposite sides of the tub. Realizing what she had done, Michelle rationalized it by thinking that it helped her to maintain her balance but deep down she knew she had done it in order to allow Traci's caressing fingers easier access to another part of her body that was craving attention and, since it was already swollen with desire, it was easy for her to find. Traci's exploring in an alternating up and down, then circular motion.

All this stimulation was beginning to overwhelm Michelle and as her legs grew more and more unsteady, she held on tighter to Traci. As Traci's fingers continued to send delicious sensations coursing through her body, Michelle started to move her hips back and forth, then in a circular motion, in opposite rhythm to what Traci was doing to her. Traci had turned Michelle's head slightly and now she began to kiss and lick her right ear. With her free hand Traci once again began to fondle Michelle's nipples. Michelle's breathing had started to become ragged and uneven. Her mouth was open as she tried to suck in enough air to kee[her nerves firing in order to keep the sensations as intense as possible.

Finally, the combined stimuli to these three sensitive areas caused Michelle's erotic planets to align and she started a slow tumble through space. She pulled her arms even tighter around Traci and gasped, "Don't stop. I'm falling." As she pushed her hips forward against Traci's fingers something unintelligible escaped her throat. Her body jerked spasmodically as it finally found much needed relief. Michelle's knees started to buckle and Traci tightened her grip on her as they banged into the fiberglass at the front of the shower.

Michelle had released her hug on Traci and put her hands against the wall to protect her face when she felt them falling forward. On weakened knees she leaned against the wall trying to catch her breath. Traci said, "I've got you," as she continued to fondle Michelle's breasts. "That must have been a good one," she added.

Michelle's head was still spinning and her thoughts were as scattered as dandelion seeds on a breezy day. After what seemed like an eternity her breathing started to become more regular and the weakness in her legs started to subside. Michelle raised her head and took one final long, deep breath. In a low whisper she said, "What makes you say that?"

"It was just a wild guess." Traci put her hands on Michelle's hips and with a little push on one side and pull on the other, she got her to turn around until they were facing each other. Their eyes had long since adjusted to the dim light and though they could not see real well, they could make out each other's features. The water splashed on Traci's shoulders and ricocheted into Michelle's face. Traci still had her hands on Michelle's face. Traci still had her hands on Michelle's hips; Michelle was still trying to figure out what to do with hers. She was unsure whether she was supposed to reciprocate and do what had just been done to her or not. Traci sensed the awkwardness and said, "If you want to touch me, it's okay. I won't break."

Shyly, Michelle put out her right hand and gently touched the bottom swell of Traci's left breast. Traci put a hand over Michelle's and gave it a light squeeze. Michelle felt the soft mound of flesh conform to the shape of her hand. The only thing that resisted her touch was the dark, erect nipple that almost seemed out of place in the presence of all the other softness. She lightly fondled it and then put out her other hand in order to caress the right one.

Traci placed her hand back on Michelle's hip and stood there with her eyes closed, swaying slightly from side to side. Not knowing what else to do and because it seemed to be in keeping with the events of the evening, Michelle bent over and closed her mouth over Traci's left nipple. She alternated between a gentle sucking and flicking it with her tongue. After a minute or so she let it slide slowly out of her mouth and then turned her attention to the other one and gave it the same treatment.

Michelle finally turned it loose and straightened up. "That felt good," Traci whispered, "you don't have to stop." She moved closer to Michelle so their slick, warm bodies were touching. Traci moved from side to side as she rubbed her breasts back and forth over Michelle's chest. She rubbed soap over Michelle and they slipped across each other even easier. As they stood there with their eyes closed enjoying all the sensations Michelle sensed Traci's face close to hers. Traci tightened her arms around Michelle and pulled her closer. Then, she kissed her. It was a light kiss at first, squarely on Michelle's slightly parted lips. Though it taken her by surprise, Michelle did not find it at all unpleasant. She responded by putting her arms around Traci and holding her tight.

The kiss that had started out with tenderness had now begun to take a new direction. It had now become one of roaring passion and Traci touched Michelle's lips with the tip of her tongue. Then, she managed to get it passed Michelle's parted lips but instead of attacking her tongue, Traci turned hers up on the end and moved it from side to side, caressing the sensitive area on the inside of Michelle's upper lip. At this, Michelle trembled and responded by opening her mouth wider and flicking Traci's tongue with hers.

From one mouth to the other their tongues flicked back and forth leaving tiny electric sparks in their wake like a welder who was dragging a rod across a piece of metal but was having trouble sustaining the arc. After several minutes of their sensuous game Michelle broke the kiss and laid her head on Traci's shoulder. Traci followed by resting her head on the front of Michelle's shoulder and for some time they just stood there holding each other as the water splashed down on them. Traci finally whispered, "Why don't you go get in the Jacuzzi and I'll finish in here and join you. There are more games to play if you want to."

Michelle whispered back, "Okay, but before I go, is there anything I can do for you?" After what Traci had done for her Michelle felt a little guilty about leaving her in the shower--unsatisfied.

"No, you go on. I'll join you in a minute."

Michelle stepped out of the shower onto the bath mat and reached for a towel. As she began to remove the water it suddenly hit her that it was kind of silly to dry off, only to walk a few feet and get into the water again. She paused but then decided to dry just enough to keep from dripping water on the floor. It only took a few moments to remove the excess then Michelle stepped off the mat onto the cool tile and walked out of the bathroom.

Prior to leaving the bathroom Michelle had wrapped the damp towel around her and tucked it in at the top just the way her mother had taught her to do many years earlier. Her bare feet made no noise at all as she moved across the floor and without observing her, one would not even have known she was in the room. The silence was broken as Michelle laughed out loud at the irony of the moment. There she was with a towel wrapped around her even though no one was looking at her and the only other person anywhere close by had just finished exploring her with eye and hand and had even implied that there was more to come. Even as she laughed Michelle said out loud, "What the hell," and gave the towel a tug. It unwound from around her and she held it by one corner at an arms length beside her. Michelle raised her other arm up beside her so they looked as if she were going to give someone a giant hug. "I should have had a drum roll for that," she thought. Then she turned the towel loose and it fell silently by her feet.

Michelle stepped carefully into the Jacuzzi and sat down so a bubble jet was right at the base of her spine. The steady stream of bubbles felt good on her and she leaned back to enjoy the relaxing feeling caused by the swirling water.

She heard Traci turn the water off and then slide back the glass shower door. Traci also dried off just enough to keep from dripping and in just a moment stepped out of the bathroom. Traci did not even feign modesty as she walked toward Michelle. It was much lighter than it had been in the bathroom and Michelle got her first really good look at Traci in the nude. She was obviously a natural blonde and, though she knew exactly what the female body looked like, Michelle caught herself staring at Traci. Though this embarrassed Michelle, if it bothered Traci the least bit, she never let on. Michelle decided that Traci was a lot less inhibited than she was. This was fine with her because it let her be the follower instead of the leader and since she did not know what was going on anyway, it made her role simpler.

Traci dropped the towel she was carrying close to the side of the Jacuzzi and stepped into the water across from Michelle.

She sat down and extended her legs so they touched Michelle's. "Doesn't this feel great?" she asked.

"Sure does. I love these bubbles."

There was a long silence during which they played a mutual game of footsies. At last Traci said, "Michelle, I don't know if this has crossed your mind or not but I'll clarify it just in case it has. I expect nothing from you in return. I don't want to pursue a relationship with you, or any other woman. Like I told you earlier, I like men, I'm just afraid of them. I'm not some over sexed butch predator on the prowl but sometimes I just need to touch somebody and to have somebody touch me. Most of the time I cope with it pretty well but sometimes it all catches up with me and I've got to feel some real, live skin on mine. I think you need that, too, and there are more games we can play if you would like. But, please remember this--I'll take you back to your place right now, or, at anytime you would like to go. It's that simple and the ball's in your court."

Michelle had not expected this so she hesitated to respond. She thought for a while as they continued their footsie game. Everything Traci had said applied to her, also, and she did find the possibilities exciting. She had not only wanted what had already been done to her, she had needed it. She finally replied, "You will have to kind of lead me because this is all new. Besides, it might be nice--no smashed faces, no smashed hearts, just fun and games."

"I was hoping you would say that. I'll get the champagne and punch your ticket for inter-galactic, erotic travel," Traci said as she stood up and let the rivulets of water cascade off her body back into the tub. She reached over and got her towel and finished removing the water, then she dried her feet one at a time as she stepped out. Hanging the towel on the back of a kitchen chair, she padded silently to the refrigerator to get some more champagne.

Michelle watched her as she worked and in a matter of moments, Traci returned with a glass of bubbly in each hand. "For you," she said as she proffered a glass toward Michelle who took it with a smile and a quiet, "Thanks."

Michelle took a rather large sip and, setting down her glass, she stood up and said, "I think I'm done with the water. I don't want to look like a big, white prune."

Traci bent down and picked up Michelle's towel and started to dry her. Michelle held up her arms and slowly turned around to make Traci's task simpler. She thought it strange as to how much better the same towel felt just by being in the hands of someone else. As she climbed out Michelle took the towel from Traci so she could dry her lower legs and feet. With her free hand she picked up her glass and took another sip as she walked toward the kitchen table. Michelle set her glass down and then hung the towel on the back of another chair the way Traci had done.

Now that she no longer had the subdued light of the bathroom or the water of the Jacuzzi to shield her from the eyes of another, Michelle became slightly embarrassed though Traci exhibited no sign of being the least bit bothered. When Traci had come from the shower she had approached Michelle from behind and, though Michelle had gotten a relatively good look at her, Traci had been moving and the look had been more like a prolonged glance. The light they were in now would not have been considered bright but it was ample for them to observe each other's body and it was the first really good look Michelle had at her.

Though Michelle had earlier experienced the succulence and firmness of Traci's breasts with her tactile sense, she had really not gotten to see them very well. They were a little larger than hers, somewhere in the "C" range instead of Michelle's "B" range. They were high and full and the bottom of each one rested lightly on Traci's chest without flattening out. The nipples that Michelle's mouth had earlier ravished still stood erect like dark centurions standing watch over the mily flesh that supported them. Traci wasn't quite as tall as Michelle but she did appear to be in excellent physical condition. Her stomach was flat and her hips flared nicely into the tight skin on her thighs. Michelle had already observed how Traci's firm bottom bounced as she walked and she had wondered what kind of exercise she took. "She certainly is an all around attractive woman," Michelle thought, "every bit equal to me and maybe even more so."

Michelle was jarred from her musings by Traci taking her by the hand. Traci then picked up one of the cold glasses and pressed it lightly against Michelle's left nipple that had still not yet fully recovered from its earlier stimulation. When the cool surface touched her Michelle felt a shudder of anticipation and excitement course through her body and she was certain that it had not gone unobserved. Traci suddenly moved the glass to the other nipple and pressed it into the surrounding tissue with the cool, damp surface. After a few seconds she moved it away and pressed it against the slight swell of Michelle's tummy, just below her belly button. Still holding Michelle's hand, she removed the glass from her and took a sip. "Let's go in the bedroom and see what kind of entertainment we can dream up. The possibilities are mindless," she whispered.

Hearing the invitation and feeling the tug on her hand, Michelle picked up her glass and followed Traci. Though the bedroom was dark there was enough light entering through the open door for Michelle to get a general picture of the room. She could make out some of Traci's clothing on hangers and a suitcase on the bed farthest from the door. Traci steered her slowly toward the side of the nearest bed and she set her glass on the night stand by a small digital clock with red numerals. Michelle took another drink and did likewise. "Wait right here. Don't go 'way," Traci said, "I forgot something."

Traci turned loose of Michelle's hand and gave her a light pat on her bottom as she turned and walked across the room toward the dresser. Michelle heard a scraping sound and Traci was suddenly outlined in the glow of a match as it exploded to life. For an instant that side of the room was engulfed in a brilliance that soon died to a subdued light. The light became a little brighter and then Michelle heard Traci blow out the match but a soft, flickering glow remained. Traci stepped away from the candle and walked silently over to the door and closed it. The room was now bathed in the yellow-orange light of a flame from a small candle. Michelle was already interested in what the immediate future might have in store for her and this only added to the intrigue.

Michelle reached for her glass and took another sip. As she was once again setting it on the night stand she nearly dropped it. Without making a sound Traci had walked from the door and now stood behind her. From the rear she put her arms around Michelle's waist and made tiny circles with her fingers as they worked their way up the front of Michelle's body. Traci paused to fondle Michelle's breasts and to roll and pull lightly at her nipples. Traci moved her hips from side to side, rubbing against Michelle's firm, round bottom. She dragged her own hard nipples across Michelle's back, much to their mutual satisfaction. She turned loose of Michelle's right breast and slid her hand slowly down her tummy--and even lower. Traci stopped her hand's movement when it was over the soft, dark fleece at the juncture of Michelle's legs. Patting it gently, she said, "I've got something special for this, I think you'll enjoy it."

Michelle felt Traci's arms tighten around her and she was pulled down toward the bed. She ended up sitting on the edge of it while Traci balanced on one knee on the bed besider her and one foot on the floor. The bed felt good on Michelle's bare skin. The spread was cool and, due to the champagne she had consumed, it was a relief to no longer have to concern herself with keeping her balance.

Traci grabbed the spread and the top sheet and gave them a tug. She pulled them down from the corner until they could go no further due to Michelle sitting on them. Feeling the cover pulled next to her, Michelle raised slightly off the bed and Traci pulled it underneath her. When she sat back down she felt a crisp sheet against her skin where the spread had been. Michelle let the champagne take charge and she toppled over, landing on the bed on her left shoulder and the side of her face. "This feels good. I'm afraid I'll go to sleep," she said.

"Go ahead but I think you'll wake up when things start to happen."

"I sure don't want to miss anything and it really does feel good," Michelle yawned.

Traci picked up Michelle's legs that were still hanging off the side of the bed and helped her move closer to the middle. Michelle had consumed enough bubbly that she was starting to enter the giggly stage that always preceded her being too relaxed to function. With Traci's help Michelle finally got situated somewhere close to the center of the mattress where she rolled over on her back, gave a tremendous stretch and held it, then she went totally limp.

Michelle lay there with her eyes closed. Since this was all new to her she wasn't quite sure what to do or say so she decided to just follow whatever lead Traci took. Her eyes weren't closed very tightly and she could still detect the flickering of the candle flame. The bayberry scent of it had started to permeate the room and it only added to the ambiance of the evening. Michelle could barely hear Traci moving around the room but she didn't open her eyes to see what she was doing.

Michelle sensed Traci moving closer to the bed and then felt it give as she sat down on the edge. Opening her eyes ever so slightly she could make out a fuzzy image though the narrow slits. The bed creaked as Traci leaned over and kissed her lightly on her parted lips. She felt Traci's hair tickle her face and she raised her hand to move it. Traci caught her hand and pressed it back down on the sheet without breaking the kiss that had now begun to be increasingly more passionate. Michelle felt the tip of Traci's warm, wet tongue lightly probing the sensitive area inside her lips so she opened her mouth slightly and offered the tip of her own tongue as an invitation for Traci to continue, which she did.

Traci finally broke the kiss with a flick of her tongue as she raised up. She gave Michelle's hand a squeeze and said, "Let's not just get physical, let's get mental."

With a puzzled expression, Michelle said, "What?"

"Let's let our minds, especially yours, get involved, as well as our bodies. Once again, especially yours."

"Just exactly what do you mean?"

"People play games when they're children. Why can't we play them as adults?" Traci said.

"I suppose we can. We just don't seem to do it very often, at least not the fun ones."

"I know but if you want to, and, if you trust me, that's the key word, we'll play a game you won't soon forget. Do you trust me?"

"I guess so. I never really thought about it one way or the other," Michelle whispered.

Traci began to trail her fingertips along Michelle's tummy as if her skin were paper and her own fingers were pencils. She drew numerous geometric figures as she continued to titillate Michelle without touching any strategic spot. Michelle started to squirm on the sheet as Traci continued with the finger doodling. Though she didn't have any idea what Traci had planned for her, Michelle certainly did the prelude intriguing.

Traci seemed to be content with what she was doing and she went no further than to draw designs on Michelle's body. Now, Michelle not only wanted Traci to go to the next level, she was really beginning to need her to do so. She was starting to become concerned that the evening was going to fizzle when she remembered Traci's statement about trust. Not knowing what else to do or say, and without opening her eyes, she arched her back and whispered, "I trust you."

These words suddenly entered the magical realm of please and thank you. The first indication that this was what Traci had been waiting for manifested itself in the form of a warm, wet mouth latching onto her left nipple like a tiny vacuum cleaner might do. It would not let go, it stayed there with a continuous, gentle sucking interspersed with light tongue flicks. Michelle tried to press her chest upward in order to thrust more of her breast deeper into Traci's hungry mouth. She was having so much trouble keeping her hips still that she had unconsciously begun to move them up and down and from side to side. Her body was starting to take over and Michelle decided that it simply felt too good to fight. "Maybe this girl thing isn't so bad, after all," she thought.

The bed creaked again as Traci moved over closer to Michelle. Suddenly, all movement stopped and Michelle became more than a little disconcerted when she discovered that Traci was now straddling her chest. "This certainly isn't what I had in mind," she thought, and had just started to protest when she felt Traci's soft lips once again on hers. Michelle still had her eyes closed and was almost afraid to open them for fear of what she might discover. It were as if keeping them shut protected her from something, she just didn't know what.

Traci covered Michelle's hands with own and extended her arms as she pushed them up the bed until Michelle's arms were straight and stopped them at a point about halfway between Michelle's shoulders and the top of her head. As Traci held them there she moved slightly to her right and positioned her left breast with its swollen nipple directly over Michelle's mouth. She lowered herself and moved from side to side as she dared Michelle's lips to do more than they had been doing. After a few moments Traci felt Michelle's mouth open and her tongue flick out to caress her. Michelle stopped her tongue under the end of Traci's breast and opened her mouth wide. Using her tongue, Michelle guided the nipple inside her mouth and began first to lick it, then to suck it in a slow, rhythmic manner. Traci let out a low moan at how good it felt. After two or three minutes of this treatment she forced herself to raise up and change her position enough so that she could offer the other swollen nipple to Michelle's willing mouth. Michelle went after it with the same exuberance that a hungry baby might display and she even made soft sucking noises as the sensations shot through Traci's body like tiny electric sparks.

Now Michelle was the one holding Traci's hands in place. Traci's strength started flowing out of her as if she were Supergirl and Michelle's mouth were kryptonite. She continued to sag lower and lower until she finally collapsed beside Michelle with a long, low moan. As Traci collapsed the distance had become too great and her nipple at last escaped the hold Michelle's lips had on it. Sensations continued to course through Traci's body as she tried to regain enough composure to continue with what she had in store for Michelle. Finally, some strength started to return and she was able to raise up. She turned loose of Michelle's hands and lightly caressed her upper body by drawing unseen designs with her fingertips on Michelle's soft skin. Michelle just lay there enjoying the sensual sensations of being used as an erotic chalkboard. Traci seemed to be in no hurry to do more than to just titillate her and it felt so good that Michelle made no effort to move or to change what was being done to her.

Michelle found these tracings to be both relaxing and very stimulating. With her eyes closed the champagne caused the bed to spin slowly and Michelle imagined herself to be on a small merry-go-round. Traci moved her hands from Michelle's upper body and leaned back slightly. Now her fingers were drawing the crazy patterns on top of Michelle's thighs. She seemed to be in no hurry as she moved them between Michelle's knees and hips. She let them slide to the outside of Michelle's thighs and moved them suddenly to her knees. Lightly digging in her fingernails, Traci pulled her hands slowly up Michelle's legs leaving very faint, white streaks that soon flushed to a very pale red. Michelle squirmed as Traci's nails came up her legs and stopped even with her hips.

The way Traci was straddling her had created an obstacle and she could go no further without taking her hands off Michelle's body. Traci slid her hands back down Michelle's thighs and started to pull them up her legs again, only this time she moved them to the soft, sensitive skin on the inside of Michelle's thighs. As Traci's fingernails moved up her legs Michelle could not stifle the shudder that coursed through her body nor could she keep herself from spreading her legs a little more in hopes that Traci would drag her nails as far as possible. She was not disappointed when Traci did just that and then let her fingers linger for a few more titillating moments.

The bed creaked again as Traci shifted her weight to the side and stood up. Michelle opened her eyes and looked up at her. The flickering candle made the shadows move and also made Traci's skin even more golden than it was. Michelle rolled her head slightly to her left so she could get a better look at Traci. Neither spoke, they just let their eyes trace the other's body. Not knowing quite what else to do, Michelle reached out and put her right hand on Traci's left thigh. Her skin felt soft, smooth, and very resilient to Michelle's fingers. She drew little designs on Traci's skin, much like what Traci had earlier done to her.

Reaching down, Traci took Michelle's hand in hers and gave it a light squeeze. As she held Michelle's hand Traci looked into her eyes and in a low voice, said, "It's time to get the mind involved in what we're doing, it'll be a lot more fun. You do trust me, don't you?"

Michelle's mouth moved to say, "Yes," but no sound came out. Traci had to get her answer through lip reading. "Good. Don't go 'way. I'll be right back." She turned and walked away from the bed and disappeared from the room. Without appreciably changing her position Michelle gave another tremendous stretch and then relaxed on the bed. The champagne was still having a wonderful time deadening her senses and Michelle was on the verge of going to sleep when she heard Traci's feet slipping across the carpet. She sensed her standing by the bed and opened her eyes. Traci was holding a small bundle of stuff but in the dim light Michelle could not see it well enough to make out what it was. "Want to let the good times roll?" Traci asked.

Michelle replied, "Why not. It's been fun so far."

The bed creaked as Traci once again sat down on the edge. "Close your eyes, Michelle, and relax. That's especially important because we need our psyche involved with our soma in order to experience sensations to the fullest. Now, in order to get the maximum benefit from what is about to happen, you must first shut out as much outside stimuli as possible."

From the bundle she was holding Traci removed a dark object and leaned toward Michelle. "Raise your head and close your eyes," she whispered. Michelle did as she had been instructed. Just as her eyes were closing she got a look at what the dark object was--a blindfold. Traci slipped it over Michelle's head and made some minor adjustments, then said, "Is that comfy?"

"Yes, it's comfy but it's also kind of strange, even a little bit kinky."

"I know but it helps do away with distractions so you can better concentrate on feeling things. Remember, trust is the key word." Michelle put her head back down and silently agreed that it did add to the mystery of the evening. She had started once again to relax when she felt something brush against her left hip. "Raise your hips," Traci said. She complied and felt something being positioned underneath her. "Relax." Michelle did and discovered a different feel beneath her. The surface wasn't as smooth as the sheet had been and when she touched it with her fingers Michelle discovered that it was a towel. "The plot thickens," she thought.

Michelle felt Traci pick up her left hand and slip something over her wrist. Just then part of what Traci had in mind dawned on her. Visions from movies and the news of victims who had been lured into this situation, only to be found days later and days dead, flashed through her mind. She pushed the blindfold up with her right hand and looking at Traci, said, "I don't know about this. Couldn't you just do whatever it is you're going to do without all this other stuff?"

"Yes, we could do away with all this other stuff but this is where the trust part comes in. If you trust me, I'll take you on a journey to Eroticaland that you won't soon forget." She fondled Michelle's breasts as she continued to talk. "Most people simply go through sensuous escapades with their body. For whatever reason, they prefer not to get their mind involved. This is where the trust part comes in. You really don't know what's going to happen next, will it be a burning tongue licking your nipples or will it be the hot sensation of an ice pick in your chest? So, you get an air of mystery that's charged with an adrenalin rush to stimulate the senses."

Traci bent over slightly and kissed Michelle gently on her soft lips. Her added weight pushed Michelle back down on the bed where Traci felt her relax once more. As she was raising up, Traci paused long enough to treat each of Michelle's still swollen nipples to a warm, wet kiss.

Michelle thought about it for a moment as she felt Traci once again adjusting the lightweight cord around her left wrist. Everything Traci had said made sense and she had exhibited no characteristic of being the least bit devious so, Michelle decided, why not, I'm not getting that much out of life, anyway. "I really do trust you, Traci."

"You won't regret it."

Traci positioned Michelle's left arm out straight and slightly above her shoulder. Michelle repositioned the black velvet blindfold so it was comfortable and stretched out that arm so it was in roughly the same position as the other one. Traci leaned over her and looped another lightweight cord around Michelle's right wrist. She crawled lightly across Michelle and sat on the other side of the bed. Michelle felt her pull the cord snug and then let it relax so there was a little slack in it. "If I'm going to do something about this, I better do it soon," she thought. Michelle gave a tug with her right arm to see if she could get free but it was too late, Traci had already secured the other end around the bed frame.

A sudden wave of panic shot through Michelle as she remembered what had happened to her the last time she had been held against her will. She tugged on both cords but neither budged. Michelle was just about to tell Traci that it wasn't fun anymore when she felt Traci's hands caressing her thighs and the slight swell of her tummy. Traci bent over and kissed Michelle's belly button, then flicked it with her tongue. "Just relax. I've punched your ticket and you're going to take the nickel tour of Eroticaland like I promised," she said quietly. Michelle felt a hand under her head and a glass being placed to her mouth. She took a small sip and was relieved to discover that it was more champagne. She took several more swallows before Traci removed the glass and kissed away the remaining drops from her lips. Then Traci moved her hand and Michelle let her head drop back on the bed.

Traci straightened up and drank what little remained in the glass, then she set it on the night stand. Carrying two more pieces of the cord that were each about four feet in length, Traci got up and walked to the foot of the bed. There she stopped and reached down to lightly tickle Michelle's left foot. Michelle bent her leg to try to escape. Traci put her hand on the other foot but she did not tickle it. Instead, she started to massage the instep and to knead the sole of it. Michelle let the other leg relax hoping that Traci would decide to give it some of the same gentle treatment. Traci made a small loop and put it over Michelle's right foot and pulled it snug. Michelle's leg followed the direction of the tug and Traci soon had the cord secured to the frame at the foot of the bed.

Michelle's mind was continuing to imagine all manner of dire consequences and she knew that she was totally at Traci's mercy. As Traci started to secure the other leg, Michelle thought, "How did I get myself in this predicament- too damn much champagne." Traci tugged lightly on the cord to pull Michelle's legs apart then she relaxed the tension. She tied the cord around the frame on the opposite side from the first one. Michelle started to squirm in order to test the security of the cordd but all her effort only proved one thing--Traci must have been a Girl Scout. Traci had left enough slack that Michelle could move her legs away from her body but not toward it no matter how hard she tried. It dawned on Michelle that she could spread her legs but she could not bring them together.

Traci briefly watched her struggle and then said, "Why don't you just trust me. You said you did. Well, it doesn't matter. You're mine to do with as I see fit and I see fit to give you a night of pleasure you will probably remember as long as you live."

"I hope so, because I'm planning on being around quite some time."

"Maybe you will but only if you don't OD on pleasure tonight."

Hearing this made Michelle feel a little better. "Maybe Traci isn't a serial killer, after all," she thought.

Michelle felt the bed shift again as Traci sat back down on the edge. She put her hands on Michelle's chest and started to lightly rub her. It wasn't hard enough to be a real massage but it was certainly suitable for titillation purposes. Traci let her hands explore every inch of Michelle's soft, smooth skin. She ran them along her restrained, outstretched arms and back, then down her chest with some strategic pauses along the way. She traced the rim of Michelle's belly button and then let her fingers trail slowly down her legs to her feet and then back up to her hips. As her hands returned to the juncture of Michelle's legs Traci paused. Michelle squirmed and tried to position her hips under these exploring fingers but the restraints on her ankles kept her from doing so. She realized that in this situation Traci could deal her pleasure or pain, in any amount she chose, and there was absolutely nothing she could do about it. She hoped it would be the former because the latter had never been her strong suit.

As Traci sensuously explored Michelle's body she talked quietly to her. "Michelle, do you remember your high school biology class?"

"Some of it," Michelle replied.

"Well, we have five senses to help us survive in this world but when we go to Eroticaland we really don't need all of them. First off, we won't be there too long. Then, there's nothing dangerous waiting on us. And, last, with too many senses in operation, they interfere with the one that went there to be stimulated. The one we're interested in is the sense of touch. The blindfold took away your vision but there's no practical way to take away your sense of taste and smell. That's probably good because they can sometimes add to the pleasure in this particular world. That only leaves hearing to be considered. Music or soft words can add to the ambiance but we're not here for that. All we're interested in is pleasure, pure, unadulterated, no water added, sheer, pleasure. So, with that in mind, I'm going to take away that sense with this set of shooting muffs."

"This is weird enough not being able to see," Michelle said.

"Give this a try and see how you like it. Remember, pleasure is in the mind and this will help us isolate it."

Michelle sensed Traci bending over her and then she felt something slipping over her hair as Traci pushed it back away from her ears so they were better exposed, then she felt a light pressure on each side of her head. Traci moved the muffs around slightly and said, "Are they comfy?"

"Move the left side up and forward just a little." Traci complied. "How's that?" she asked.

"Much better. My ear was being pinched before but that solved it."

Michelle played with the cords that restrained her arms as she slowly started to adjust to this strange, new world. After a few minutes she started to lose track of time. Now she could neither make out the shadows of Traci's movement nor could she tell what Traci was doing or where she was by sound. "This isn't so bad after all," Michelle mused, "now I know why she kept stressing trust."

As Michelle lay there wondering what was going to happen next she was roused from her reverie with a start and an audible gasp. Knowing that Michelle had no idea what she was doing, Traci had slipped into the kitchen and gotten some more champagne and some ice cubes. She put the champagne on the night stand and, holding an ice cube between the thum and forefinger of each hand, Traci placed them simultaneously on Michelle's nipples. Michelle shuddered and squirmed but could not escape. Traci held them there until her fingers got so cold that she could no longer stand it. Only then did she remove them and drop them in the glass on the night stand.

When the ice was removed Michelle stopped squirming and lay quietly on the bed. In the candlelight Traci could barely see the drops of water that remained but those few drops looked extremely inviting. The ice cubes had caused the desired effect so she leaned over and sucked the water off the soft mounds of flesh. Satisfied that all the water was gone, in turn, she held each swollen nipple in her mouth until all the cold was gone and they were warm once more. Michelle trembled with anticipation and excitement at what had just been done to her. She knew there was more to come and Traci had implied that it would only get better.

The bed creaked when Traci's weight shifted as she moved around. Michelle detected the movement through the mattress but she could only imagine what Traci was doing.

She felt more movement as Traci shifted her weight back toward her original spot. Michelle waited for something to happen but nothing did. Though she could still feel the springs compressed in the mattress, it appeared to her that Traci was sitting there motionless. Michelle began to imagine that Traci was sitting there holding an ice pick, or a very sharp knife, and she was halfway trying to prepare herself for the sudden, stinging pain that would mark the end of her life. Still, no movement. Michelle was really starting to regret allowing herself to be enticed into this totally defenseless position and was trying to think of something to say that would persuade Traci that they should do something else for entertainment.

Michelle had just shaped her mouth to speak when she felt something lightly touch the inside of her right knee and start moving slowly up her leg titillating the sensitive skin on the inside of her thigh. She decided not to say anything just yet and she really doubted that it would make a difference if she did.

It didn't feel like Traci's hand or even one of her fingers. It seemed slightly rigid, firm but yet giving, and a little cooler than the surrounding air as Traci, Michelle thought, she even hoped, moved the object ever closer to the dark shadows between her legs. In her dark, quiet world Michelle was no longer sure that it was Traci sitting on the edge of the bed. A panicked thought went through her mind, "What if Traci had gotten her in this position so someone else, man or woman, respectable or derelict, could take advantage of her and then leave without her ever seeing who, or what, it was." Though these thoughts did unnerve her to some degree, Michelle knew she was at someone's mercy.

The object got as far as it could up Michelle's right leg and then jumped to the top of the left inner thigh. From there it started its slow journey down the inside of that leg until it got to her knee. There it stopped and was removed from her skin. In just a moment it was on her again. This time it started just below her belly button at the edge of the soft fleece where her legs joined. It started inching its way slowly up her tummy and paused only briefly to trace the outline where her ribcage started. It came slowly up her sternum and only strayed from its path long enough to caress each nipple for a few seconds, then it continued up toward her throat. When it got to her chin it was once again withdrawn from her skin.

Michelle still had not figured out what was being used to stimulate her but she had decided that it was in no way an unpleasant experience. As she pondered this she detected a faint, sweet smell that had not been there moments before. Something very light barely touched her lips. Michelle was just putting out her tongue to investigate when whatever it was, was pulled back from her so she had to raise her head to follow it. She put out her tongue once again and could just barely reach more of the mysterious substance. This time it did not move away and she strained to raise her head as much as possible.

When Michelle flicked out her tongue the object moved a little closer and she was able to get a bigger sample of it. As she savored the flavor and texture it dawned on her that it was some kind of a whipped cream type substance. Michelle continued to lick until it was pulled out of reach. When it did not reappear after a few seconds she relaxed and let her head fall back on the bed. Suddenly, there it was again and more whipped cream brushed her lips. This time she did not have to raise her head to pursue it. As she continued to lick the whipped cream off, Michelle decided that it was much nicer not to have to strain her neck muscles by chasing it. "This is kinda' fun," she thought, "I hope it's low fat."

Michelle had begun to think that the whipped cream had been offered to her in a small cone when she felt the thing that she had been licking brush her lips. She opened her mouth to take a bite only to have the cone, or whatever it was, slide between her lips into her mouth and stop. She felt two or three inches of something and she started exploring it with her tongue. Michelle remembered having this same shape in her mouth before and she realized now, in no uncertain terms, that it definitely was not a small ice cream cone.

The object started to move back and forth, never out quite far enough that she could close her mouth or in far enough that it bothered her. The smooth object was made slippery by her wet mouth and she discovered that it was not at all an unpleasant sensation as it moved back and forth over her lips and tongue. Michelle opened her mouth wider and then pursed her lips in order to make things more comfortable for herself. Though Michelle wasn't sure what this game was called, or who the other player was, she discovered that she was enjoying it. Her body had started to respond and she knew that if things kept going as they were that it would soon take over completely and then there would be no turning back from having the other person do these things to her.

Since she had experienced no pain Michelle assumed the other person, she still hoped that it was Traci, was also having a good time without hurting her but she also knew she was still at her, or someone's, mercy. Michelle decided to just relax and roll with the flow. "This really isn't bad at all," she thought, "no distractions from sight or sound, just total concentration on the pleasures at hand. Maybe Traci was right."

Suddenly, the object pushed further back into her mouth and stopped just short of making her gag. After it paused a few seconds it started ever so slowly in the opposite direction. It seemed to take forever before it slipped gently from between her lips. As it moved slowly away from her Michelle raised her head to try to follow it as she showered the end of it with kisses. Finally, her bonds restrained her from following it any further and she flicked out her tongue to touch it as a final farewell.

For a few seconds Michelle remained in that position hoping it would come back. When it did not, she relaxed once more on the bed. Michelle detected no movement and started to think that this part of the game was over when something lightly brushed her lips. Before it could move away she opened her mouth and raised her head to engulf this familiar shape that was still slippery from moments before.

"Someone is just teasing me," she thought, as she moved her head back and forth making soft sucking sounds like a hungry baby. The object lingered in her mouth for a few moments and then began a slow withdrawal. When it was again out of reach Michelle lowered her head back to the bed. This time she had trouble relaxing and she knew she was panting because she could feel her chest heaving. Michelle started to be embarrassed over her passionate attack on the object a few moments earlier but she decided that this was exactly what someone had wanted her to do. Though she still hoped that it was Traci sitting on the bed, she really no longer cared.

Soft, warm lips touched hers and pressed her head into the mattress with an impassioned kiss. A tongue touched hers and she started to squirm as the kiss became harder. Michelle tugged at the cords that held her but they did not give at all, she was still held securely. Finally, the unseen lips pulled back from hers and she knew that whomever it was could detect that she was visibly shaken. Her hips would not stop moving and she could sense the swelling in her nipples.

Michelle's hips were still moving when warm, wet lips closed over her left breast. Involuntarily, she arched her back to try to thrust it deeper into this unseen mouth. As she did that, a low whimper escaped her throat and she knew that her body had completely taken over and that she both wanted and needed more. Michelle was now ready for the next level and, unknown to her in her dark, quiet world, this had not gone unnoticed by the other person.

The strange lips released her left nipple and attacked the right one with the same flicking tongue and gentle sucking motion. Michelle continued to squirm even after the hungry mouth had turned her loose. She lay there trying to catch her breath and wondering how much more of this game her body could take.

The bed creaked and shifted as the person who had been sitting on it got up. Still, Michelle could discern nothing. No one touched her and she was finally able to bring her rhythmically moving hips under control. After two or three minutes she had regained most of her composure and had begun to relax again when she felt the mattress give at the foot of the bed.

Someone had returned, she still had no idea who, but someone was definitely on the bed between her feet that were still firmly secured to each side of the bed by their thin cords. Michelle was reasonably certain what would happen next, or at least in the near future, she just had not figured out all of the details. The bed creaked again as the unseen person shifted her, or his, position. Now she could feel someone touching her legs as whomever it was moved slowly up the bed. This person was no longer between her feet but was now between her legs. Even if Michelle had been quicker, she still could not have brought them together because of the way they were restrained but now there wasn't even the opportunity to attempt it.

Michelle felt her legs being forced even further apart by what appeared to her to be this unknown person crawling up the bed in a kneeling position. She knew that her only hope for any semblance of modesty, that's a joke, she thought, was that the room was still illuminated only by the candle that she had seen earlier as their game was just beginning. Though there was nothing she could do about it, she even hoped that it had burned out. This thought struck her as odd because of the things she had already experienced earlier in the evening. Michelle pushed it from her mind and waited to see what would happen next. She did not have to wait long.

Michelle felt someone's fingertips touch the soft, sensitive skin on the inside of her right thigh. A slight tremor shot through her body and then she felt fingertips on the inside of he left thigh. The fingers were drawing lazy circles and other designs that she could not make out, she justknew that it felt wonderful. Soon the fingers turned into hands that were gently massaging her. Michelle noticed that they were working higher up her legs but each time, just when she thought they would become more intimate, they retreated and the entire process was started all over. She knew that it was simply a tease and nothing more. She also knew that it felt very good and that her body had started to respond accordingly. Her breathing started to deepen and she tugged at the cords that held her hands. Michelle was aware that her hips had started to move again and that she wanted to be embarrassed, but she wasn't.

The unseen hands suddenly pulled back from her legs. Though they were no longer touching her, Michelle's body continued to respond as if they were. As she squirmed Michelle had unconsciously spread her legs further apart. She had no idea whether the other person was looking at her or not but she took a chance and mouthed the word, "Please."

Suddenly she felt something touch her at the juncture of her long, slender legs. Feeling it push lightly against her, Michelle tried to spread her legs even more as something smooth and firm started easing its way inside her. A low moan escaped her lips as her body took total control. As this thing slipped deeper inside her, it began to dawn on Michelle that this must be the same object from which she had earlier licked the whipped cream. It started a slow in and out movement and her hips moved with it. A sensation suddenly shot through her body like an electric spark and some totally unintelligible sound escaped her lips.

Michelle tried to collect her thoughts. Now, it all made sense to her. She remembered what Traci had told her about Mr. V. and now she knew that she, too, was enjoying having an affair with him. The tingle continued to course through her body as someone helped Mr. V. maintain a steady back and forth rhythm.

Michelle's lips were dry and she had now begun to pant. She heaved and thrashed on the bed, tugging at her bonds and driving her hips in sync with Mr. V. Suddenly she felt as if she had started tumbling through space and her bouncing on the bed increased to a fever pitch. In one final effort she arched her back until she was barely touching the bed. Mr. V. stayed with her through each gyration, sending shock waves through her body with its tingling motion. With an indecipherable, guttural sound, Michelle's entire body went rigid, then she collapsed on the bed. Though her hips continued their rhythmic motion, their movement was growing weaker. Finally, even that movement stopped and she no longer tugged at the cords that bound her. She felt Mr. V. being slowly withdrawn from her.

Michelle lay motionless, her energy spent but she could still feel the bed shifting as the unseen person moved from between her legs and got off it. She felt warm lips touch hers and someone gave her breasts one last caress, then nothing. She was alone in her dark, quiet world.

Time passed but Michelle had no idea how long. She became aware that something was tickling her nose and she was surprised when she discovered that she was able to scratch it. She moved her other hand and found that it, too, was free. Michelle moved her feet and discovered that they had also been set free but when she tried to open her eyes, she found that the blindfold had not yet been removed. As she raised her hands to remove it, she felt the ear muff's still in place and she removed them first, then the blindfold.

When the muffs were removed, she heard soft music from the next room. She opened her eyes and looked around. Nothing had changed except the length of the candle--it was appreciably shorter. She gave a big stretch, like a cat often does upon awakening, and held it for a few seconds. Then she collapsed on the bed once again.

As Michelle lay there trying to get it all to make sense she noticed that she really did feel good--the world really seemed like a nice place. Someone had covered her with the sheet and the bed felt great. Michelle wondered who had helped Mr. V. ravish her and decided that it might be best if she didn't know. She moved around on the bed and swung her feet over the side so she could sit on the edge. From the other room she thought she heard Traci talking to someone and she quickly pulled the sheet around her to cover up. Very faintly, she heard Traci say,

"Thanks for coming over. Goodbye," and the sound of the door closing.

"Traci," she said in a voice loud enough to be heard only in the next room.

"What?" The bedroom door opened slightly and Traci peeked in. "Hi. Did you have a good nap?" she asked with a perky smile.

"I thought I heard you talking with somebody."

"So."

"Were they here very long?" "A little while."

"I mean while I was aah, you know."

"It doesn't matter," Traci replied as she stepped into the room. "What matters is whether or not you had a good time playing. You sure seemed to."

"But, those people, I don't even know those people. I thought it would just be the two of us. Were they playing with us or, should I say, me? Did they see me making a fool of myself?" Michelle protested.

"Relax, Michelle. Did you enjoy yourself?"

"Yes." As Michelle answered she felt her face flush with embarrassment, "But those people."

"Did you see anybody?"

"No, but I heard voices."

"You can hear voices on the radio but you can't see the people," Traci said.

"But, I'm not on the radio."

"Michelle, it doesn't matter. It only adds to the mystery."

"But," Michelle stammered.

"Were you hurt in any way?" "No."

"How do you feel?" "Great."

"Then what seems to be the problem? You don't even know for sure that anybody but me was in here watching you bounce on the bed like a bucking bronco during an eight second ride, do you?"

"No."

"If the opportunity ever comes up again, would you go for it?" Traci asked.

"I'd have to think about it," Michelle said, but she knew she would because she had never experienced anything as intense as this ever in her life.

"Let's go in the living room and watch TV."

"Okay. But, first, I want to take a quick splash in the shower."

Michelle stepped into the bathroom and started the water. The hot spray felt good and it helped to bring her back to reality. She wasn't exactly sure what had taken place, or who had done it, and the more Michelle thought about it, the more she wondered if she really wanted to know. It all seemed like a dream to her, and if it had been, she had to admit that it certainly was one of the better dreams she had experienced in a long time.

Finishing her shower, Michelle stepped out onto the bath mat. Taking a large towel from the rack, she began to rub it over her smooth, wet skin. As she moved the towel over her body Michelle discovered that she felt as if she were in a state of euphoria, like she had eaten way too much chocolate and caused the release of too many endorphins in her brain. As she continued to dry off Michelle was surprised to discover that she was humming one of her favorite songs.

When she was completely dry, Michelle wrapped the towel around her and stepped out of the bathroom. When she walked into the bedroom she saw that Traci had laid a long, white satin robe on the bed. Assuming it was for her, she unwrapped the towel and placed it on the back of a chair. She picked up the robe and slipped it over her shoulders, pulled each side until they overlapped, and then tied the sash around her waist in a half bow. The material felt soft and cool against her warm skin. Picking up the towel, she carried it into the bathroom and draped it over the shower door to dry. Then she walked into the living room.

Traci was propped up on one end of the couch watching television. Michelle sat down on the other end, swung her legs up, and covered them with the robe. For several minutes neither of them spoke, they just sat there watching CMT, each waiting for the other to break the silence. Michelle had no good idea as to what to say so she was really hoping Traci would speak first. After several music videos Traci finally spoke. "I've had a great vacation and meeting you made it even more fun and exciting. I'm really glad I ran into you and that we could do some stuff together," she said quietly.

"It has been fun and very different from any other vacation I've ever taken," Michelle replied.

As Traci continued to talk, Michelle noticed that she had a sad, far-away look in her eyes. "Everything I told you is true. Even though I had a great time being with you and I hope you had a similar time being with me, I wish we could both have been here with our friends from once upon a time. I wish a lot of things. I wish I didn't have this little scar on the side of my face, not because it's unattractive but because of what it symbolizes. Every time I look in the mirror I'm reminded of the price I paid for trusting and caring about someone. The only difference in us is that your scar doesn't show. I can cope with the physical pain. That stopped hurting a long time ago but the hurt inside my head and my heart never stops."

"I know," Michelle said in quiet voice totally devoid of any emotion or inflection.

Traci continued, "I don't know how or why all this happened. I really didn't plan it when I met you on the beach. Maybe it was something we both needed, at least until we can do better." There was another long silence as they both just continued to sit on the couch watching more videos. The silence was broken again when she added, "I'm tired. Do you want me to take you home or would you like to spend the night here?"

Michelle hesitated. She wasn't quite sure she knew how to respond. Finally, she answered, "I'm tired, too. It's late. Let's go to bed. I'll go home tomorrow."

Traci picked up the clicker and turned off the television Michelle got up and walked into the bedroom and turned on the light as Traci turned off the one in the living room.

Traci then joined her in the bedroom and turned the light off. Only after it was dark did Michelle slip out of the robe and lay it over a chair. In the dim light Traci made her way over to the bed and took off her robe. They were both tired physical and emotionally had passed and, though they wanted physically and emotionally and there was a silent agreement that the moment had passed and, though they both wanted desperately to reach out to someone, it wasn't to each other.

Michelle pulled down the cover on the unused bed and crawled between the sheets. They were cool and crisp on her skin and she immediately started to relax. "What a strange evening this has been," she thought. There was no sound in the room and in the silence Michelle heard Traci's breathing change and she knew that Traci had gone to sleep. As Michelle waited for sleep to overtake her she thought about the big, empty spot in her heart that only one person could fill. She knew exactly for see what was broken, she just didn't know how to fix it. As she lay there in the dark she thought of a quotation she had read years before by T.E. Kalem, "The heart is the only broken instrument that works," and she felt big, viscous tears start to form in her eyes because she knew it was true. She was just starting to chastise herself for being fool enough to care, love, and trust when sleep overtook her and her world went black. Once again Michelle had entered the only realm where she would ever truly be safe.

Michelle's Revenge

In the ensuing months sice Larry had taken her home from PJ's Pub, Michelle's mind had continued to race, her major problem though was that none of her thoughts made any sense. At times her already dark mood would sink even lower. Often she would wake up in the middle of the night with a start and just lie in the bed trembling. The memory of those events was still much too vivid to allow for peace of mind, even when she was sleeping.

Usually, upon awakening with her heart pounding and her mind unable to sort out her thoughts, the abject humiliation of what had happened would cause her mood to swing violently from dark depression to white hot hatred, both for herself and for Larry. She already had enough on her cluttered mind without having to deal with this and it only added to her inner turmoil.

Michelle rarely slept very well due to the all too real dreams and all the tossing and turning. She was exhausted when she went to bed and equally exhausted when she got up. She often thought, "I was struggling enough without this. Why is life such a never ending uphill climb? I don't even have to have a downhill stretch but I would dearly love to just have some level ground for a change." As these thoughts kept her mind spinning, Michelle drew ever closer to mental and physical exhaustion.

Early one Thursday afternoon Michelle was walking slowly back to her office from a meeting in the conference room down the hall. Though she knew she was dawdling, Michelle simply could not make herself rush straight back to her office. She had a strange feeling that something was detaining her but she had absolutely no idea what or why.

Suddenly, the elevator bell rang and the door opened jarring her from her trance. From the elevator, out stepped Larry pushing his mail cart in front of him. It was still piled high with boxes and mail yet to be delivered. It suddenly dawned on Michelle that he had reversed his route today. Usually his cart was nearly empty by the time he got to the fifth floor offices where she worked and, though she had observed him doing this before, she had never really given it much thought. As long as the mail got delivered no one really cared how Larry went about doing it so he would occasionally reverse his route and start on the upper floors and work his way down toward the basement simply to break the monotony.

This reversal of his usual route suddenly gave Michelle and idea. Though she wasn't sure she could bring it into fruition, she knew she had to give it her best shot. She paused for several seconds to be sure she wanted to try this spur of the moment plan, then decided that the worst thing that could happen to her was that she would look like a sex-starved bitch who had gotten what she deserved and wanted, and who now wanted more. "However," Michelle mused, "if I can pull this off I'll feel a lot better and Larry will learn a great lesson in life, besides, what else can he do to me that he hasn't already done?"

Right after the incident had taken place Michelle had tried to avoid or just ignore Larry but there were times when that was simply impossible. When she did encounter him he was always pleasant but it was obvious to her that he was thinking about what had happened. Invariably, he would give her an innocent look as he mentally undressed her with his little smirk that always made Michelle burn with a desire to let him know what it felt like to be treated the way he had treated her.

She had not even gone to the police to report the incident. What Larry had laughingly told her was true and who would believe her anyway. At least a half dozen people had heard her say how glad she was that he was taking her home since she'd had too much to drink. So upset had she been that Michelle had not mentioned what had happened to anyone. Why add insult to injury by being put on trial by my friends or by the court system, she had decided, all I wanted was a ride home, not what I got.

Larry had stopped his cart by the receptionist's desk and had just placed a bundle of letters and a small package on it. From where Michelle stood observing, he and Lisa, the receptionist, appeared to be engaged in casual conversation and Larry did not seem to be in any hurry to continue his mail delivery. "Good," Michelle thought, "but I still must be very careful and relaxed about this."

Earlier that morning as she was dressubg for work Michelle had first moved a mid-calf length dress from the closet. It was quiet floral print with a zipper up the back. She had even started to unzip it to take it off the hanger when she had suddenly stopped. "I don't think I'll wear this today," she thought, "for a change I feel foxy." It now dawned on her that she must have had an even earlier premonition of things to come because after her morning shower she had donned a matching set of underwear. It was a black set that she had chosen after passing over the usual workday garments, the kind that would be acceptable if she were in a car accident. This particular set was one her favorites. The panties had high cut legs that were open to the crest of the ilium and the bra was a decolette style with soft, lacy cups that allowed her nipples to show darkly through the lace. "I look suitably slinky," she thought, "and it sure would be nice if someone wanted to see me in, or out of, this."

Returning the dress to the rack in the closet, Michelle selected a black skirt that would leave a considerable amount of her lower thigh showing. She hung it on the door facing and then selected a silk fuschia colored blouse. Michelle took the skirt down from its perch and held the blouse over it as she looked in the mirror where she studied it intently, pursed her lips, and then nodded approvingly to herself. Michelle donned the blouse and proceeded to button it all the way to her throat, then she stepped into her skirt. She pulled it up over the tail of her blouse, zipped it, and then buttoned it. Though the skirt was not "street walker" tight, it was snug and it left no doubt that she took pride in what it covered. Michelle stood there in front of the mirror for a few moments scrutinizing herself then she unbuttoned the top two buttons on her blouse. Though she knew she was modestly covered, she also knew that if someone happened to look at just the right moment that it would not be too difficult for that person to see the black lace and maybe a little more. For some reason she found the possibility of being a random peep show in heels slightly erotic. "What a great feeling," she thought, "I haven't felt like this in ages. I just know something good is going to happen to me today."

To complete her day's apparel, Michelle slipped on some black pumps with a medium heel, then she removed her shoes and pulled on some black hose, put her shoes back on and decided that she was now ready for work. Taking one last look in the mirror, she laughed as she thought to herself, "Today I'm a power chick." As Michelle started out the door she paused long enough to put on a gold tennis bracelet, then she departed for the office.

Now, as she stood looking across the room, Michelle understood why she had put the floral dress back in the closet.

Though it was very pretty and she looked very attractive while wearing it, she knew that the sensual impact of it couldn't compare with what she had on. Michelle smiled to herself and thought, "I wonder if I was being guided for this very moment?" With her heart pounding, Michelle paused and took a deep breath, then she started slowly over to where Larry and Lisa were chatting. As she moved toward them she was careful to try to stay relaxed and to put her feet in front of each other as she walked. With her feet oriented like this Michelle could feel the extra sway in her hips and she was well aware that this was much more titillating than her normal walk and she fully expected Larry to take the bait she was offering.

Her movement was soon detected by Larry's peripheral vision and he then rolled his eyes to the side to better observe her approaching. Even while doing this he was continuing his conversation with Lisa. Michelle knew that he had already undressed her in his mind and that knowledge caused the fires of her smoldering anger to blaze once again, even higher than before. Though it was a struggle, she forced herself to remain calm and to maintain a pleasant but seductive smile. "I'm going to shove that smirk up his ass," she thought to herself. Michelle halted behind Lisa and slightly to her left.

"Hi, guys," she said in her perkiest voice.

Lisa turned her head slightly in Michelle's direction and said, "Oh. Hi, Michelle."

Larry straightened up and offered a quiet, "Hello."

"Are you reversing your route today or are we just being blessed with this industrial size load of mail?" Michelle asked.

"Oh, no. All you're getting is what's on Lisa's desk," he replied matter of factly, "the rest of it goes below."

Michelle fought hard to control her mounting anxiety and excitement. She now knew what she was going to do if she could only get Larry to unwittingly cooperate. If he had too much mail to go to the fourth floor it wouldn't work; neither would too little. "Please let it be the right amount," she whispered to herself. Michelle knew she would only get one chance at this and she would have to appear to be sincere in everything she said and did.

Next to the elevator door was a large umbrella stand that contained five umbrellas of various colors and sizes. The largest umbrella of the bunch was a green and white striped one with a heavy wooden handle. It resembled the larger than normal type that many golfers attach to their golf bags to protect them from sudden showers. The nylon fabric had been rolled tightly around the shaft and was held in place in the usual manner, by a short strap with a snap on it.

Lisa had turned her head back to face Larry. She could no longer see Michelle but she continued to tell Larry about the movie she had seen the night before. Lisa appeared to be finishing her discourse about the movie and Larry had already started inching back toward the mail cart. It's now or never, Michelle decided. "Larry, do you have much mail going to the fourth floor," she inquired.

"Yes, I've got this large box, two smaller ones, and a pack of letters," he answered.

Michelle saw her opportunity quickly slipping away and almost started to panic. Lisa was still facing Larry, watching him point to the different items as he called them out. Michelle thought, almost out loud it seemed to her, "I better pull out all the stops." She moved slightly to her right to get even more behind Lisa. As Larry looked up from the cart she said, "Rats. I need to return an umbrella to the fourth floor and I was hoping we could walk down together."

"I better take the elevator," he replied. "The boxes aren't real heavy but they are clumsy."

Smiling demurely, Michelle said, "What a shame."

As she was saying this Michelle raised her right hand and deftly unbuttoned the third button down on her blouse. Since she had left the two topmost buttons unbuttoned when she dressed that morning her blouse was now half unbuttoned. No sooner had the button disappeared through the button hole when she hooked her fingers inside the material and pulled it down and to the right. This movement exposed an ample portion of her right breast that appeared to want to burst out of the black lace that was holding it so sensually in place. Not knowing if that would be enough of a come-on to get him to decide to walk down the steps with her, Michelle slowly ran the tip of her tongue over her upper lip. Hoping this would be a suitable enticement, she quickly pulled her blouse back together and buttoned it. All of this had only taken a few seconds and Lisa had observed nothing out of the ordinary as she sat looking the other way.

Michelle ventured a quick glance down at the front of Larry's pants and noticed a slight bulge that had not been there just moments before. "It worked. I've got him now," she thought, "he remembers what happened and I'm going to give him something else to remember me by, the horny bastard."

She was still looking at him and smiling when Larry said, "Well, maybe I will walk downstairs with you. After all, I could use the exercise."

"Great," Michelle replied. "You pick up the large box and I'll put one of the other boxes and the mail on top of it and I'll take the remaining box and the umbrella."

Larry removed the mail bundle and the two smaller boxes from the cart and placed them on Lisa's desk. Michelle walked over to the umbrella stand and removed the oversized green and white one. Before she turned to walk back toward the desk she paused and took an enormous slow, deep breath, held it briefly, then exhaled quietly. Slightly more composed, Michelle returned to where Larry was waiting for her. Leaning the umbrella against the desk, she picked up the larger of the two small boxes and placed it carefully on the right side of the largest box. Then, she said, "I'll put the bundle of mail on after you pick up these two. No need to risk hurting your back."

Larry grinned, grabbed the two boxes and straightened up. Michelle picked up the bundle of mail and placed it on the large box but to the left of the other one. With the boxes stacked in this manner Larry could see where he was going but he had to look to his left in order to do so. Very calmly, Michelle picked up the remaining box and the large umbrella. "I'll be back in a few minutes," she said to Lisa, then added, "Shall we go, Larry?" and started toward the light brown metal fire door that led to the steps.

As Larry turned away from the desk Michelle fell in beside him on his left. Upon reaching the door she stepped slightly ahead of him and, pushing the door open, held it for him to follow her through. When she had closed the door he said, "This was a great idea. My arms won't be full when we come back up the steps."

"I thought it was a pretty good idea, myself," Michelle replied. To herself she thought, "Actually, it's a grand idea but you won't be coming back up with me."

The concrete landing where the steps made their turn was about four feet wide and eight feet long. The cinder block wall to the right had been painted a light shade of yellow except for the area about a foot above the floor and steps. This area had been painted a dark, contrasting brown. The stairs were well lighted with fluorescent light fixtures attached to the ceiling. A metal handrail was anchored to the wall and around the edge of the concrete surface. The rail to keep people from falling off the side of the steps was about three and a half feet high and the vertical supports were evenly spaced about three feet apart. There were ten steps to the first available landing and then ten more to the next landing that contained the entrance door to the fourth floor office suites.

As they crossed the landing toward the first set of steps Michelle admonished Larry to be careful. He had just grunted his answer when they started down. After she had closed the door, Michelle had moved to Larry's right where he could not see her even though he could still see the top of the guard rail.

"Did you like what I showed you awhile ago?" she asked.

"It was very nice. Want to show me some more?" he answered.

They had just started their descent and had negotiated the top three steps when Michelle dropped her box. In one motion she stooped and thrust the tip of the oversized umbrella several inches through the uprights of the guard rail. Her positioning of it had been exactly where she had intended. It caught Larry's legs midpoint between his feet and his knees. Wanting to be sure that he could not correct this out of balance situation, Michelle put her left hand as high on his back as she could reach and gave a sharp push forward.

With no where for his feet to go and his hands full, Larry fell face forward toward the concrete and metal steps below. Flinging his load, he extended his arms to try to catch himself. His right arm impacted with a muffled crunching noise on the front edge of a step while his nose absorbed more punishment as he slid downward over them. In a matter of seconds he had come to rest with his head and shoulders on the landing below and his torso and legs diagonal across the stairway. Michelle quickly glanced at the upper and lower doors to see if anyone had heard the commotion and she was much relieved when no one appeared.

Larry just lay there moaning and he seemed to be only semi-conscious from the impact of his forehead on the steps. Since he was unable to get up with his feet above him on the steps, after a few seconds as his head tried to clear he started slowly trying to work his way forward so he was totally on the landing. Observing this, Michelle grabbed his left hand and pulled him forward onto the smooth concrete. His feet made a dull thud each time they fell from one step to the next.

When Michelle finally got him off the steps she rolled him over on his back. Larry was still trying to focus his eyes on Michelle as she stood over him. A thin trickle of blood oozed out of his nose and he was clutching his right arm with his left hand. Michelle said, "I'm going to catch you under your arms and prop you up against the wall but I need you to help me."

Though Larry's eyes were still glassy, he managed to mumble, "Okay."

Michelle took his left hand and pulled him into a sitting position. Then, she bent over behind him and, with her hands under his arms, she locked her fingers in front of his chest. As Michelle tugged him backward toward the wall, Larry pushed with his left hand as his right arm rested useless across his stomach. Michelle got him as close to the wall as she could and loosened her grip on him. As she stepped out from behind him she eased him backward until his upper back and shoulders rested against the wall. "Is that better?" she asked.

By now Larry's eyes had started to focus to some degree and he looked up at her and said, "Yes. What happened?"

His nose was no longer straight but angled slightly to one side and light bruise had already started to discolor the skin over a swollen place about three inches back from the wrist on his right arm.

"Does that place on your arm hurt very much?" Michelle asked.

As Larry nodded to the affirmative, he mumbles, "Yes,

I think it's broken."

He had started to lean slightly to one side like a ship that was taking on water so Michelle gently helped him back into an upright position. She straightened his legs and left them slightly parted. Then, Michelle moved to the bottom of the steps and picked up the big umbrella. She held it by the tightly rolled fabric around the shaft and walked back over to Larry. Michelle stepped over him with her left foot and planted her right foot on the concrete between his legs. She stood there straddling his right leg about midway between the hip and the knee. The handle of the large umbrella rested on the floor by

Larry's right thigh. Michelle looked down at him and said in a cold, quiet voice, "You remember taking me home, don't you?" He nodded. "Do you remember what you did to me?" Larry nodded again.

Using the umbrella as a support, Michelle drew her right foot back and brought it forward sharply. Her toes were pointed down and this made the top of her foot nearly flat when it was jarred to a sudden halt at the juncture of Larry's legs. When it landed Larry's body convulsed violently and his mouth flew open but no sound came out. Expecting another kick, he turned his broken arm loose and put his hand between his legs to try to protect himself from another excruciating blow. Michelle took the umbrella and, holding it like a golf club, brought it swiftly around toward his head. The large wooden crook of the handle crashed into his already broken nose whipping his head violently to the right. Seeking to shield his face from another painful onslaught, Larry turned loose of his throbbing groin and put his hand in front of his face to protect it.

In one motion Michelle withdrew the umbrella and balanced herself with it once again. Her right foot snapped back and then whipped forward in a blur. Her toes were still pointed down when the nearly flat surface of the top of her shoe landed with another dull thud precisely where the first blow had landed. Not wanting another blow to his nose, Larry simply tried to turn his head to the right to get away from what he knew would be another painful blow from the umbrella. Trying to avoid another kick, he had crossed his legs in order to try to trap her foot but due to the existing pain, he had trouble squeezing with his thighs.

As best he could, Larry now had the two prime sources of his pain protected. Michelle was trying to wiggle her foot free from between his legs and was having some difficulty doing it due to the partial grip of his thighs. Then she vividly remembered something. When he had taken her home Larry had hit her twice and each time it was with his right hand. In a flash Michelle stopped the struggle to free her leg. Now, balanced steadily on both feet, she raised the umbrella over her head like it was an axe and lying in front of her at her feet was a piece of wood. Raising her left hand to grip the shaft and add maximum force to the blow, she brought it down as hard as she could swing. The large wooden handle streaked through the air and impacted with all her might on the swollen bruise on Larry's right arm.

When this blow landed, the hold he had on her foot with his legs suddenly relaxed and she was able to step out. Michelle stood there straddling him. "Larry, Larry," she said in a cold voice, "Look at me." Expecting to be hit once again, Larry very slowly turned his head toward her and with glassy eyes tried to look up at her face. Looking down at him Michelle continued, "I haven't forgotten what you did to me. This is what it feels like to have someone take advantage of you. Not much fun, is it?"

Still holding the umbrella, she turned and climbed the stairs back to the fifth floor entrance door. There she paused, tucked in her blouse, and took several deep breaths.

Regaining her composure, Michelle walked through the door and over to Lisa's desk and stopped. In a deliberate voice she said, "Lisa, dial 9-1-1. Larry has fallen and he can't get it up, or something like that. You know what I mean." Still carrying the big umbrella, she turned and walked toward her office. Though she still did not feel great, Michelle had to admit to herself that she did feel a lot better.

MICHELLE'S END

Michelle had a small combination radio-tape player that sat on the left side of her oak dresser. She walked over to it and rummaged through a box of cassettes sitting next to it. Finding her favorite tape, she inserted it and turned it on. She let it play for several seconds and then slightly adjusted the volume. It was already adjusted for her to listen to while she was in the bedroom but, knowing she would be moving back and forth to different parts of the house, she increased the volume so she could still hear it as she moved around. She then started to hum softly with the music. Closing her eyes, she listened intently as the relaxing melody seemed to almost put her in a trance. Michelle leaned lightly against the dresser and let her upper body begin to sway slightly as if she were dancing with someone who was very special.

Suddenly she remembered that she was neither here to listen nor to dance but to perform a task. She continued to hum along with the music as she turned and walked across the bedroom and down the hall to the hall closet. There Michelle pushed back the pocket door and pulled the string that went to the overhead light. Neatly folded and pushed between two cardboard boxes was what she was looking for--a large piece of black polyethylene. It measured about eight feet wide and nearly fifteen feet long. Michelle had often used it as a drop cloth when she painted or as a dust catcher when she did numerous other messy tasks. However, tonight this piece of plastic had a different job to do for her. Though it would be the last task it would ever perform for her, it would certainly not be one that was very pleasant. She pulled it from its resting place and started back toward her bedroom.

About the time Michelle walked back into the bedroom it dawned on her that she had forgotten something. She gave the plastic a pitch onto her bed and turned and walked back toward the hall closet. She continued to hum softly with the music as she walked and as she rummaged around in a cardboard box for a roll of masking tape. Finding it, she turned out the light again and closed the sliding door. This time, instead of going back to the bedroom, she went the other way down the hall toward the kitchen. As she stepped into the room Michelle turned on the light and walked over to the counter. She put the tape down and opened the cabinet door under the sink. Removing a can of spray wax and a cloth, she walked over to the kitchen table. Except for the two earthtone place mats the round wooden table was uncluttered and spotless. She picked up the two mats and sprayed a light mist of wax on it. Then, Michelle took the soft cloth and rubbed the top until all the wax had disappeared and the surface had returned to its previous high luster. Then she put the place mats back on the table, picked up the wax and dust cloth and returned them to their place under the sink. Next, she picked up the tape and inspected the countertop. It was also spotless so she turned and and slowly walked back toward the bedroom, turning off the kitchen light as she left.

The music coming from the bedroom grew louder as she drew closer to the door.

Michelle entered the room and walked over to turn down the music. Then she walked over to the bed and flopped down across the foot of it on her stomach. The soft, fuzzy fabric on the inside of her sweatsuit felt good against her otherwise naked skin. "This feels good," she thought. The wine had made her slightly lightheaded and since no one was watching, she rubbed her chest over the bed. The slight irritation of the sweatshirt made her nipples start to become erect as the blood rushed to them. Michelle kept moving back and forth until they were swollen to their maximum size. As she continued the movement with her upper body, she suddenly realized that her hips had started a rhythmic movement of their own.

Suddenly she stopped and collapsed motionless on the bed. She felt a tremor that started in the pit of her stomach and worked its way upward causing her entire body to tremble. She looked over her shoulder toward the bedroom door and said in a barely audible whisper, "Paul, I need you." Her surroundings started to distort as her eyes filled with tears that were so large that they hurt but the tears would not flow. They seemed to be clinging to her as if they could postpone the inevitable by not falling. Finally, they got so large that there was nothing else for them to do but fall. They trickled out of her eyes, the left one falling slightly before the right, and landed quietly on the bedspread. In a few seconds they had soaked into the material and the only remaining evidence that they had ever existed was the tracks on her face and the two small wet spots on the bed.

Suddenly Michelle sat upright as she swung her feet over the foot of the bed and wiped her eyes with her index and middle fingers. "You stupid bitch," she screamed out at herself, "he's gone, he's been gone, and he won't be coming back. Get over it." With that outburst, the sadness and hopelessness of the moment overcame her again and the tears started to flow in earnest. This time she did not try to stop them and they flowed freely for several minutes.

After many tears had fallen, it once again dawned on her that she still had a task to complete and that the time she had spent lying across the bed and then sitting there crying had done nothing to accomplish what was ahead of her. She got up and walked into the bathroom to get a tissue so she could blow her nose. After doing this and dropping the tissue in a trashcan, she patted some cold water on her eyelids making them feel a great deal better. When she had finished this she walked back into the bedroom, her bare feet hardly making a perceptible sound as they moved lightly over the carpet.

The tape was still playing and she paused momentarily to listen once again to the quiet, peaceful music. Michelle savored each word and note with her ears as a person who is about to go on a diet might savor a perfectly cooked filet. In either case it would have to last for a long time and she wanted the memory fresh and distinctly imprinted in her mind.

She continued her walk over to the bed and picked up the three pillows that were there and stacked them so they would be comfortable for her to prop against. From many hours of reading after she got in bed Michelle knew just how they should be arranged. One of the pillows was larger than the others and that was the one that she placed on its side with the flat surface against the headboard of the bed. She then took one of the other pillows and placed it on one end so it was resting in the center of the first pillow and protruding a few inches above the top of it. Then she placed th third pillow horizontal over them. In this configuration she would have good support for her back and head.

With the pillows in place, Michelle turned her attention to the next part of her adventure for the evening. Picking up the masking tape, she put it on the night table. The black plastic was next. She unfolded it and smoothed it out over the bed as if she were going to paint the ceiling and did not want to risk dripping paint on the bedspread. However, she didn't stop there. Michelle then pulled the plastic up over the pillows and the headboard. When she had pulled enough polyethylene that it would cover the wall about two feet above the headboard she knew she had enough. It was held in place on one side with the masking tape and as far out into the middle as she could reach. She then walked around the bed and secured the other side of the plastic to the wall.

To keep from pulling the drop cloth off the wall when she got on the bed, Michelle pulled more of it up from the foot of the bed and put a fold in it that was about a foot wide at the head. This she decided, would give her enough slack for when she got on the bed. Michelle really did not want to have to stop and go back to redo anything, therefore she would just do it right the first time.

Michelle did have a pretty good idea of what she wanted to do and how to do it. For several months she had been having a recurring dream that had, at first, greatly disturbed her. After much thought she finally figured out what the dream was all about. It happened at no particular time of night or frequency but it always came to her just as she entered the in-between zone of really being awake and really being asleep.

The dream was always the same. In it she would see herself lying on her bed on top of a piece of black polyethylene that totally covered her bedspread. She was doing nothing more than just lying there motionless with her arms folded across her chest. Everything would always be peaceful and serene when suddenly a very loud noise would invariably awaken her with a start.

As a general rule she would wake up trembling and her heart would be pounding. Michelle would look around the darkened room and listen intently for a follow-up noise. Always, after lying there for a few minutes listening intently, she would then turn on her bedside lamp and then look around some more.

The first time it had happened she had very quietly pulled open the drawer in the night stand by the bed and retrieved her old .38 caliber Colt pistol. As loud as the noise had been, she was convinced that someone had broken into her house and knocked over a vase, or lamp, or some other small piece of furniture in the dark. On occasion, she had even gotten out of bed and slipped quietly down the hall, checking each room as she went. Eventually, each room had a light turned on and the entire house had received a thorough inspection that had revealed everything to be in order. Though still disturbed, she had turned out the lights and gone back to bed, only to toss and turn for what seemed like hours before finally falling into a troubled sleep. Even more disturbing to her, the same dream continued to return at no set interval to wake her with the same loud noise. Even though she no longer got up to check the house, she still woke up trembling with her heart pounding. Then, there were times when she would go back to sleep only to experience it a second time.

Over several months Michelle had given much thought to this unnerving, but recurring, phenomenon. It both troubled and fascinated her. It almost seemed that somebody, or something, was trying to communicate with her and that this dream was the only medium that could be used. After much thought, she interpreted it to mean that she was being beckoned from another realm. Anyway, she finally decided that her idea of what the dream appeared to mean was the only plausible explanation. This, and the cumulative effect from the blows that life seemed to take so much pride in dealing her, had caused something in her thought processes to go tragically awry. The hardest blow of all was the one that Paul had dealt her when he had suddenly dumped her. It had not only shattered her heart, it had broken something in her mind.

She thought about the many plans that she and Paul had made and the dreams they had discussed. Michelle often wondered how she could have been dumb enough to put herself in the position of actually needing, not just wanting, but needing, another person in her life. She even decided to never be that stupid again and, if through some lapse in sound judgment that she should be, that she deserved whatever would befall her for being a fool. It was now beginning to look doubtful that she would ever have to deal with that particular situation again. Very simply put, she had entered a darkened tunnel in her mind and there was no light at the other end, just darkness that seemed to have no boundaries.

Michelle contemplated what she had done up to that point and decided that it deserved a "thumbs up" for how it looked. Now, she only needed a few more things but they were very specific items. She walked across the bedroom and into the hallway. Turning the hall light on, she continued down it and turned left into the living room. From its place on an end table she picked up her Sears catalogue. It was one of the big, fat two inch thick editions that must weigh at least two or three pounds. Though she was certain that one of the other not so thick versions would be suitable, she decided not to take any chances.

On her way back toward the bedroom Michelle stopped once again in front of the hall closet. “I will eventually get everything I need. It may take a while but I will get it,” she thought. Somewhere in one of the boxes was another necessary item--a piece of quarter inch wooden dowel that was approximately eighteen inches long. She put the catalogue on the floor and rummage through the boxes until she found it. Tidying up the storage boxes, Michelle turned off the closet light, closed the door, and walked slowly back into her bedroom. As she passed the hall light switch she flicked it off. “Won’t be needing that anymore,” she thought. Michelle placed the piece of dowel and the catalogue on the night stand and walked over to her dresser. Lying on the top next to her hair brush and comb were two brown, covered rubber bands that she sometimes wore in her hair. She picked them up and went back over to the night stand. Placing them on the catalogue, she went over to the chair and sat down. “Why rush,” she thought, “everything is right here waiting for me to put it to use.”

Michelle relaxed against the back of the chair and closed her eyes. Though she tried to make her mind go blank, thoughts and visions of Paul kept running through it like a never ending loop film. Here it was, over two years since he had carried this weight of wondering why and of being totally confused by what had so suddenly happened for so long that It had finally overpowered her. Tonight, she had decided, would be the night that she would finally put down weight and end the myriad things that had made her mind hurt so intensely since that evening that had forever changed her life.

The soft music relaxed her and she knew that everything would fo off just as she had planned. She could even visualize how it would all go. The bed was all arranged and just waiting for her. She had solved the problem of the possibility of chipping her teeth by incorporating the piece of dowel but she really had not decided what to do about her ears. Michelle found it baffling to her as to why that thought would even enter her mind but it had. Loud noises had always bothered her, usually by giving her the headache, and she loved to listen to quiet music, the chirping of birds, and the summertime bugs making their night music. Now, she had a dilemma--how was she going to protect her ears from being damaged.

As Michelle sat listening to the music she tried to formulate a viable plan. The earmuffs that she used when she went shooting were in the hall closet hanging on a nail in plain view. "I should have thought of them sooner," she mused, "but how do I get them off after they have fulfilled their task." Something could pull them off after they're no longer needed, she decided. Then it came to her; a string tied to the earmuffs and attached to a heavy object. "I could balance a brick on the headboard that will fall to the floor when I turn it loose," she said out loud. This idea caused Michelle to smile and nod her head slowly with approval.

She got up and once again returned to the hall closet that contained so many of the miscellaneous items that she had collected over the years. Tugging at the light cord again, Michelle immediately spotted the hearing protectors. She removed them from the nail on which they spent most of their time resting, picked up a ball of heavy string from the shelf, and went back to the bedroom.

Suddenly, the perfect heavy object caught her eye. Several years earlier a friend had given her a decorated brick for a doorstop and there it sat in front of her bedroom door as if it were holding the door against the wall. This will do quite nicely, she decided. Picking up the brick, Michelle carried it over to the night stand and placed it on a magazine so there would be no chance of marring the glossy finish on the wood.

She removed a pencil from the night stand drawer where she kept it with a small note pad in case she ever needed to make night notes. With it, Michelle carefully punched a hole in the black plastic just above where it covered the headboard and as close to the center of the bed as possible. She then went into the bathroom and got a thick washcloth. This she placed over the headboard underneath the plastic and held it there securely with a piece of masking tape on each side. Now, she decided, there was no danger that any furniture would be damaged from anything that was going to come to pass.

The top of the headboard was about four feet from the floor so Michelle cut off a piece of string that was about five feet in length. She pushed one end through the hole that had been punched in the plastic and then ran it through the center hole of the brick. Tying the string in a square knot, she set the brick on the washcloth on the headboard. Holding tightly to the other end of the string, Michelle gave the brick a push. It fell as planned and when it could fall no farther due to taking up all the slack, it snapped the string sharply against her hand causing a very faint bruise on her soft skin. She reached behind the bed and, grabbing the brick, once again set it back on the washcloth protected headboard. After she tied the other end snugly around the center of the earmuffs, she stepped back and surveyed what was before her. It all met with her approval.

Only one thing remained to complete all the needed items for the evening. One last time she pulled the night stand drawer out and pulled back a soft, slightly oily cloth.

Nestled down in the soft material was the only thing that her maternal grandfather had ever given her, with the exception of a large stuffed bear and a few childhood toys that had long since been lost. Michelle still had the bear and she had discovered that it made a good conversation partner. For years she had kept it on one of her two bedroom chairs and tonight she looked at it for some moral support.

Michelle reached into the drawer and her long, slender fingers wrapped around a checkered piece of walnut. From the soft cloth she removed the old Colt pistol. It was really too large a gun for her but it had been a gift from someone who had loved her very much, even as much as she had loved him.

Lots of times, especially in the warmer months when she had visited as a child, her grandfather would carry it with him when he took his numerous walks through the woods on his large farm. As a child Michelle would usually spend several weeks each summer visiting there and when she had grown big enough to do so, she would accompany him on his excursions.

They had been rambling trips with no set pattern, path, rhyme, or reason and she had grown to love the outdoors and the tall, work hardened gray haired man who taught her about it. She had eagerly learned about the different forest creatures and their habits. He had taught her to identify many of the birds by sight, a few by sound, and she was no stranger to the many wildflowers they encountered.

This old man had been so patient and understanding of his granddaughter's youthful curiosity and exuberance for life that a bond had been forged that would never be broken. On one of their walks he had even helped her carve her initials in the smooth, light gray bark of a large beech tree. However, his love and respect for nature had been so profound that before he would let her begin carving, he had her explain to the tree what she was going to do and to ask the tree to forgive her for any pain that she might inflict. Only after they decided that the tree understood and a symbolic shot of Novocain was administered, was she allowed to proceed.

Not far from where her grandparents' home was located was a grassy knoll in a large pasture. From this knoll Michelle had spent many hours flying kites that this man with his large, gnarled hands had helped her make. His hands were such a stark contrast to the delicate, fragile kites they made, that the casual observer would never have suspected they were made by him.

The first time they had made one had been on a hot summer afternoon during her sixth year. Earlier in the day Michelle had taken a tumble while playing and scraped her knee. Knowing that the fresh wound had to hurt, after her grandmother had cleaned the place, sprinkled it with sulphur, and applied a bandage so big that Michelle had laughed, she had brought out some fresh tea cakes and had gotten Michelle to help her make real lemonade, the kind with fresh sliced lemons and real sugar.

After the three of them had relaxed on the large front porch with the refreshments for a while, her grandfather had asked Michelle if she would like to fly a kite. Michelle had replied that she would love to but that she did not have one. Just as her dark eyes started to fill with a look of sadness, her grandfather had picked her up and was moving her around over his head. She felt as if she were a kite buoyed upward on a gentle breeze performing the waltz of the wind. Still holding her, he sat back down in his chair with her on his knee and said, "Let's make one."

Michelle laughed gleefully at the thought of it. "Out of what?" she squealed.

Close to the fence at the edge of the pasture not far from the house was a small area of weeds that were about five feet tall. They were dried golden rods that were still standing from the previous summer that he had simply failed to mow down. He and Michelle walked over to them and he broke two of them off close to the ground. They were very dry and light and he knew they would serve the purpose.

"How can we make a kite out of these?" Michelle asked.

"They're just part of what we need," he replied.

As they walked back to the house, in her mind Michelle could already see visions of her kite dancing on the breeze. They went into the house and walked into the kitchen and put the two dried, brown weeds on the table. To Michelle's surprise, there were several sheets of tissue paper, some string, and glue already there. While they had gone to get the weeds, her grandmother had gotten out a collection of blue, green, red, and white tissue paper. "I want a red one," Michelle bubbled.

Her grandfather pulled out his large pocket knife and trimmed the rough ends from the weeds. He cut one about thirty inches long and the other about eighteen inches in length. With the string, he tied the two pieces together to make a cross. Michelle put her tiny finger on the know as he tied it. He then cut small notches in the ends of the two dried weeds to hold the string in place. Then, he put string around the two pieces so he had a frame with string around the outside. Once again Michelle put her small finger on the knot as he tied it.

Michelle took the red tissue and smoothed it out on the table. Her grandfather put the delicate frame on the paper and turned it so there would be a minimum of waste. Taking the scissors from her grandmother, Michelle carefully cut around the outside of the string leaving about an inch to fold over. When she had finished cutting, she removed the remaining tissue and, left there on the table was a bright red piece in the shape of a kite.

Her dark eyes grew large with excited anticipation as she beheld her kite actually taking shape in front of her. When her grandfather placed the frame on top of the piece of tissue it was almost more than she could bear. He helped her take some glue and run it around the paper next to the string. Then, with his help, she folded the paper over the string and onto the glue. She carefully smoothed out any tiny wrinkles in the paper and there it was, right before her eyes, her very own bright, red kite. Michelle lovingly picked it up and stared at it. It was so light that she could hardly tell she had anything in her small hands. "Can we fly it now?" she giggled.

"Let's let the glue dry for a few minutes while I get some more string," her grandfather replied. While he went to look for string that would be suitable for kite flying, Michelle helped her grandmother clean up the mess they had made.

Just as they were about to finish tidying up the kitchen her grandfather returned with a fishing reel, minus the rod, filled with lightweight fishing line. The glue had now dried sufficiently for the final step. He tied the end of a piece of string around each end of the long piece of the kite frame leaving about a foot of slack. He then tied more string to the short frame section in a like manner. Picking the kite up by these crossed strings, he made a small knot where they overlapped.

On the end of the fishing line was a small snap swivel that was used to hold the loop in the leader of some fish hooks. This, he snapped around a loop protruding from the knot.

Michelle had been watching all of this with amazement. "Doesn't it need a tail?" she asked.

"Only if you want one but it will just make it heavier," her grandfather replied. He handed the kite and the reel to her and, opening the screen door, the two of them stepped outside and walked toward the grassy knoll.

The breeze was very light, just enough to blow Michelle's dark, brown curls around. She held the kite out and the gentle wind immediately tried to snatch it from her grasp. "Let it go," her grandfather said softly.

Helping her operate the reel, they let out some line and the bright red kite floated up and away from them. They continued to walk slowly toward the low hill with the kite tugging lightly at the reel in Michelle's small hands.

When they at last arrived at the top of the knoll he helped her release more line and the kite started to dance merrily away. The excitement and uninhibited exuberance of his granddaughter caused him to smile. He sat down on the grass beside her and put his arm around her small body and pulled her close to him.

"Do you want to fly it?" she asked.

"I'd love to," he said.

Michelle handed him the reel and he let out some more line. The three of them were all having a grand time, this man who had seen and done many things who knew that his life was mostly lived, this small girl whose life was really just beginning, and the kite whose construction and flight had brought them so close together that a bond had formed that would never be broken.

Unnoticed by either of them as they watched the red speck waltzing against the blue sky, Michelle's grandmother had walked quietly up behind them. "Your kite seems very happy," she said, then added, "supper will be ready before too long just in case either of you would like to eat."

That night Michelle's dreams were filled with kites of every color, shape, and size, some with tails of bright ribbon and others with no tails at all but always just above them was this simple red one that in her dreams became known as "Sunset Cloud".

Over twenty years had passed since the summer when her grandfather had helped her carve her initials in the bark of the large beech tree and had built the simple red kite for her. Once again the two of them were on a slow walk through the woods they both loved so much. On this particular excursion the pace was as leisurely as it had been on that day so many summers before but this time the pace wasn't slow because of the short legs of a six year little girl. Their roles had been reversed and now it was her grandfather who moved at a slow, deliberate pace.

The ravages of time had not chosen to spare him anymore than they choose to spare anyone else. Without saying anything about it, they both knew that their remaining walks through the woods to the magnificient beech tree on the side of the hill would not be nearly as many as they had been. Though they were both only too aware of this inevitable fact of life, neither was willing to mention it as if by not doing so, it could be avoided. Deep in her subconscious mind Michelle knew that when the two of them could no longer make the journey to

Beech Tree Hill that she would never return there alone. The memories would simply be too overpowering for her to face by herself.

At last they arrived at their favorite spot on his farm. In the shade of this majestic old tree there were numerous large rocks that had served them well as seats down through the years. Many years ago they had each chosen their favorite rock on which to sit as they talked and also as they listened to each other and to the woods surrounding them.

This time it had taken them much longer than usual to make their journey. Michelle had stopped many times under the pretense of looking at wildflowers or trying to spot a bird. They both knew that neither of these things was the real reason for their frequent stops but it allowed this old man she loved so much to save face and for that he was most appreciative.

At the base of the tree Michelle ran her hands over the smooth, light gray bark. With her fingertips she traced the shape of the letters that had been carved there so many years before. They were larger now than when they were first carved because they had grown along with the tree as it grew. She lingered with her hands touching its mighty trunk as if she were trying to draw strength from it to face the inevitable and also to etch indelibly in her mind what this beautiful tree looked and felt like. Michelle tried desperately to take in everything about this wonderful place that meant so much to her because something told her that she would never return here again.

Her grandfather had been sitting quietly, watching her as he rested and tried to catch his breath. Michelle finally finished communing with her favorite tree and walked slowly over to her rock seat and sat down. Neither spoke, they just sat there enjoying the cool shade and the gentle breeze that was nearly always present in this particular spot of woods.

It seemed that neither of them wanted to speak out of fear that this magic spell that enveloped them would be broken by their slightest noise. Finally, after what seemed like an eternity, her grandfather's voice broke the stillness of the moment. Instead of looking at her as he spoke, he continued to look into the woods as if he might miss something if he looked at her.

Michelle had started to speak but hesitated; she did not know why, she just did. Something told her that her grandfather had something he wanted to tell her and that she should remain silent until he did.

"Michelle," he finally said in a soft voice, "there's no reason for us to try to hide from, or deny, the inevitable. I know you stay so busy most of the time and it's a long ride for you to come see us. I don't blame you for only coming to visit in the summer, never have. Most likely we'll never pass this way again and that makes me sad because your grandmother and I love you so much. It's simply a fact of life--we're old and nobody lives forever in this world."

He paused and took a deep breath as if trying to decide what, or in this case, what not, to say next. He wanted Michelle to enjoy what he was reasonably certain would be their last visit together. Though it was a struggle, he was determined to project an image that everything was normal. He had told no one, not even his wife of many years, about his most recent trip to the doctor or what the x-ray of his chest had revealed. He simply knew that due to the rapid expansion of the shadow on the lower lobe of his left lung that when Michelle left this time, they would never see each other in this world again. His struggle against this overpowering sadness was a valiant one and he hoped he could pull it off. After all, there was no reason to spoil her visit.

Michelle still had not spoken. For some reason she could not bring herself to do so. It were as if some unseen being had sealed her lips because he needed to talk and she needed to listen. Finally, after a long pause, he continued. "Little Bug," he said looking at her. Michelle smiled at being addressed by this particular term of endearment that she had not heard for many years. It was one that he had reserved for use only during extra special moments. "I've watched you grow up, not everyday mind you, but during your stays with us in the summertime. I've watched you grow from a little baby that I thought I would break if I held you to what you are today. You're not a little girl anymore, you're a woman, and a mighty fine one, at that. I really don't have much of anything to leave a lady like you when I'm no longer in this world. I wish I had a lot of money so I could buy you something nice but I don't. In thinking about it, I've really only come up with one thing that you might like to have. On all of our walks over the farm, and most of them that I went on by myself, I've carried this with me."

He reached down to his hip and carefully removed from its soft leather holster a pistol. As he handed it to her he said, "Like always, it's loaded. It wouldn't be much good if it wasn't."

Michelle reached out and took the gun from his hand. As she admired the craftsmanship that had gone into its construction she asked, "Won't you need it for when you take your walks or for when I come back next summer?"

"No," he replied softly. "I don't venture too far from the house anymore and you can always bring it back with you when you come." As he said this his voice almost broke but he was able to cover it by clearing his throat and looking away from her.

Michelle had admired this old .38 Colt Army Special for a long time and when she was in her early teens she had been taught the proper way to handle it. Due to the large size of the gun and the small size of her hands, she always used both of them to hold it while shooting. Over the years she had gotten relatively proficient with it and it was not at all uncommon for her to out shoot her grandfather in their yearly "kill the can" matches.

He said, "I'll carry it back to the house and give it to you when your grandmother isn't looking. She doesn't think a modern lady has any use for a gun, especially one this size."

Michelle suddenly grew very sad and she looked away to wipe the tears that had formed in her eyes but had not yet fallen. She knew there was something that he wasn't telling her but she couldn't bring herself to ask him about it. More tears started to form and Michelle knew she had to do something to break the hold this thought had on her so she said as she stood up and pointed, "Look, there's a nuthatch."

Her grandfather turned to look in the direction she was pointing and replied, "Strange little birds aren't they, but very pretty. Sit back down, Little Bug, and I'll tell you the story of how I happen to have this old gun then you'll know how you happen to have it." Michelle had managed to stifle her tears so she once again turned her attention to him.

"It was way back in the late thirties," he began, "and I went on a trip out west with three other fellows. We made it all the way to California. Seemed like it took forever; the roads sure didn't have much to offer compared to what we have today. Anyway, after a few days we got tired of the west coast and decided to head back east. We still weren't in any big hurry, we just wanted to be moving in the right direction. Eventually, we ended up in El Paso, Texas. None of us had ever been to Mexico so we decided that since we were already in the neighborhood we might as well go across the border.

We had a problem, though. One of the other fellows had this old gun and he didn't want to take the chance of getting caught with it while trying to cross the border. We had heard that the Mexican jails weren't very nice places to visit. So, he decided he was going to throw it in the Rio Grande. I thought that would be a tremendous waste so I told him I'd give him five dollars for it. Well, he thought about it for a while and finally decided that he didn't have anything to lose and took me up on my offer.

There was desert everywhere, nothing much but sand and cactus. I found an odd shaped rock on the side of the road outside of town away from everything and, using it as a landmark, I walked out in the desert maybe a hundred yards or so. There was a strange looking clump of cactus growing there so I took a big screwdriver and dug me a little hole in the dry sand. It was soft, easy digging. I wrapped the gun in one of my shirts and then in a piece of old newspaper, covered it up, and we were ready to go to Mexico. I don't know why he didn't think of something like that. It seemed to me to be a simple solution but I guess it just never crossed his mind. We were all anxious to go over to visit the saloons and look at the senoritas. I reckon that must have clouded his thinking. Anyway, it was still there when I came back the next day to dig it up and it's been with me ever since and when we get back to the house, it'll be yours."

Michelle picked up the piece of dowel and held it under the barrel. She nodded her approval and then put everything down, picked up one of the covered rubber bands and wound it around her thumb and the first two fingers of her right hand. When it was sufficiently tight, she put it around the gun barrel and pushed it back toward the cylinder. Then she slipped the piece of dowel through it. The dowel was now attached to the barrel using the rubber band to hold it in place. She then took the second rubber band and did the same thing to it. When it was tight enough she slipped it over the dowel and then down over the barrel and positioned it just behind the front sight. Michelle worked the dowel under the barrel so they were both lined up. Holding the gun out as if she were pointing at a target, she sighted down the barrel. She tweaked the dowel ever so slightly and smiled to herself. Wherever the end of the dowel touched was right where the bullet would impact. So true was the alignment of the dowel and the barrel that, had the dowel been dark, the combination would have looked like a long, stack barrel pistol.

Michelle swung the cylinder to the side and pushed the springloaded ejector rod. The six bullets slid easily out of the cylinder and she caught them in her hand. She put them in a small box in the drawer of the night stand and removed one El Dorado .38 Special Starfire. As she looked at the end of the bullet Michelle decided that it looked like peering into a small tunnel with five bright fins attached around the circumference of it and evenly spaced at seventy-two degrees apart. Designed in this manner, the bullet would start mushroom when it struck something that offered any appreciable resistance thereby making the exit hole much larger than the entrance hole.

Though what Michelle had in mind should have caused her grave concern, she had entered an area in her mind that was totally made up of reality distortion. Had she spoken with a psychiatrist that evening she would probably have been told that she was experiencing a psychosis brought on by depression. The doctor would possibly have even prescribed a mild dose of something to elevate her mood. However, she had spoken to no one and had no intention of doing so. She just knew that the cumulative effects of the blows life had delivered to her had taken its toll. Due to this she had reached the end of her rope. Problem was, she had no desire to tie a knot in the end and hang on, Michelle was simply going to turn loose and start the long fall into oblivion.

All she knew for certain was that she was so unbelievably exhausted. Her energy level had dropped so low that, had her pulse and respiration not been pretty much involuntary, they would have probably stopped. She was not only physically worn out, her mind was also very tired and it hurt constantly with thoughts that were so cluttered that they made no sense. Ever since Paul had said goodbye she had been replaying every facet of their relationship over and over inside her head. She was still as much in the dark about why it happened as she had been when he had dumped her nearly two years earlier. Michelle had been searching inside her head all this time for a clue to cast some light on what had happened and why it had happened. Though she did not quite understand just where she was deficient, in her mind she just knew that, had she been the woman she should have been, Paul would still be in her life. Now, she had resigned herself to the thought that she was an undeserving bitch with nothing that anyone really wanted, needed, or could use.

This was certainly not the first time in her life that she had to deal with a dream blowing up but it was the first time that they had all blown up at the same time. Now, she didn't have any dreams left and she lacked the courage to try to build them with anyone else and the energy to try to build them by herself. Michelle had no special desire to die, she just couldn't think of any special reason to live. She just knew that she was so very tired and this was the only idea she had come up with to get some relief from the cluttered thoughts inside her head. Though her mind had been racing since Paul left, tonight it was very calm. At last she had begun to relax because the light at the end of the tunnel that had been hidden from her for so long had finally come into view.

There was one thing that Michelle did not like about her plan and that was the part about the brick that would pull off her ear protectors. She did not like the idea of having to hold the brick to keep it from falling because she knew she would not look relaxed when she was found. An idea came to her to change the original plan. Cutting another piece of string, Michelle ran it through the plastic and tied it to the brick. Then, she tied a loop in the other end. Now, she could push the brick off the headboard and support it with the loop around her finger. Then, when her finger relaxed the brick would continue its descent. By doing it this way she would not have her left arm in an awkward position. I'll look natural, she decided.

For some unknown reason Michelle looked at the clock. She chuckled softly to herself when she realized what she had done. "It must just be habit," she thought, "because time is the last thing on my mind." Then she remembered that she had forgotten to unlock the front door. She padded silently through the house and did so.

Returning to the bedroom, Michelle got on the bed and got everything adjusted so she was comfortable. When she put the catalogue behind her head it had a tendency to slip between the pillow and the headboard. This caused her to have to get up and reposition the bottom pillow by turning it from a horizontal to a vertical position. Getting back on the bed, she once again put the catalogue in place behind her head where her soft, brown tresses hid all but the very top of it. She wiggled around slightly to get as comfortable as possible.

After doing this, she went over an unwritten checklist in her mind. After much thought Michelle decided that everything was in order and in place. The only two things she could think of that were yet to be done were to turn out the light and to pull the trigger. The one thing she had forgotten to do was to turn off her answering machine but that one small oversight really would not interfere with what she had planned for the rest of the evening.

To be sure things would go the way they were supposed to go, she decided to try some practice sessions. Michelle removed the one bullet from the gun and placed it on her chest between the two shallow mounds of her firm, braless breasts. Pushing the cylinder back in place, she put her head against the catalogue and opened her mouth. She let the dowel rest lightly on her lower teeth and gently touched the back of her throat with the end of it against the roof of her mouth right where it started to slope forward. By looking down and crossing her brown, almond shaped eyes, Michelle could just barely see the front sight, the top of the barrel, and the cocked hammer assembly. She moved the handle from side to side very slightly in order to get just the right feel. When it was in the proper position she lightly pushed the trigger with her thumb. All she heard was a quiet click, sort of like a dry stick breaking. Michelle tried this several times with her eyes open. Once she had the hang of it, she tried it several times with her eyes closed. With the dowel to guide her, Michelle soon had this mastered and she decided that the next time would be for real.

All evening long as she had been preparing everything she had seemingly been detached from the situation. Suddenly, the gravity of what all of this had been leading up to hit her. She let the gun rest gently across her chest. She still had no idea what was going on inside her head, or why. Then she remembered that she was neither rich nor exciting and for what appeared to be one, or both, of these reasons, the person she had needed and trusted most had said goodbye. Since Paul had never told her just where she was deficient, Michelle had spent an awful lot of time filling in the blanks herself without ever knowing whether or not her answers were even the right ones. The toll her cluttered thoughts had taken on her had put her so deep into a reality distortion that nothing made sense to her anymore.

The bedroom was silent except for her breathing and the steady rhythm of her clock ticking. She thought briefly about the silence of her grave and it slightly unnerved her. Then she forced it from her thoughts and replaced it with the worst possible one she could have had at that particular time: what was it that she lacked? Michelle knew she was at least averagely intelligent and, though she had never been vain enough to consider herself beautiful, she had always tried to do the best with what she had.

Trying to understand what had happened and why, had always left her completely confused and tonight was no exception. It was almost as if when her heart had shattered that it had done so in the literal sense of the term and when she had picked up the pieces to try to put it together again she had overlooked one. That was the empty spot that never seemed to be filled. Since it happened, Michelle had tried everything she knew to try--she had laughed, she had cried, she had been silent, and she had screamed. Nothing worked, it remained empty.

Though Michelle had enough of the parts to make it work, it wasn't complete and never would be because the unseen piece had been sucked up by life's vacuum cleaner and had been unknowingly thrown away. Michelle reached over and turned out the light. As she waited for her eyes to adjust to the darkness she felt a tear start to form in each of her eyes. They did not flow, they just stayed where they were until they got so large that her eyes started to hurt. She looked toward her other clock, a digital with red numerals. Michelle used this clock to tell time during the night and the ticking one to keep her company. "Doesn't matter," she thought, "I can do this with my eyes closed." As she picked up the ear protectors and put them on her chest, she blinked. The two enormous tears slid slowly down her cheeks leaving their tell tale tracks of sadness. Michelle found the loop in the second piece of string that went to the brick and put around her thumb.

Across town at 750 Plaza Drive, Apartment C, there had been a discussion going on, if not heated, at least highly animated but now things were much quieter. The apartment had the usual things that one would expect to find. It was carpeted throughout except for the bath and the kitchen. The living room had a couch against the wall to the right of the front door. Across the room, separating them from the couch by a coffee table, were two chairs, a recliner and a rocker.

Erika stood behind the rocking chair with her hands on its back. As she leaned on it she was rocking it slightly back and forth. Paul sat on the edge of the sofa and was anything but relaxed. As they faced each other from across the room neither seemed to know quite what to say or do, or what to expect from the other person.

"I just don't think I'm ready for a commitment to a permanent, long term situation. I really think we would be better off to see other people for awhile and see what happens. Who knows, we may find someone like better or we may decide that we really are right for each other but right now, I just don't know," Erika said in a much quieter voice than it had been just a few minutes earlier.

Paul had already learned that when one party or the other thought it would be best for them to see other people, most of the time that person had already picked out one of the other people to see. He was well aware that it was a smoke screen that was used to try to hide what was really taking place which was the act of dumping. He briefly remembered saying similar words to someone in the not too distant past.

"You're sure this is what you want to do," he replied.

Erika nodded to the affirmative and just kept leaning on the chair rocking it slowly back and forth.

"It's the new guy down at the club, isn't it?" he asked.

"Yes," she said, without looking up.

"Why did you say all the things you said to me? Did you mean them or were they just another part of the game?"

"No. I really meant all those things, at least I think I did. I know I wanted to mean them at the time."

"Where does this leave me? I counted on you. I thought we were making plans for the future," Paul responded as he looked across the room into her eyes.

"Look," Erika said, "I'm sorry. I didn't mean for this to happen but it did."

Paul had known that something wasn't quite right earlier in the evening and, as it had progressed, he had begun to put it all together. Not only had he known what was taking place, he had been reasonably certain who the third party was. As he stood up to leave, he walked toward her and said, "I wish you the best."

Erika stepped out from behind the chair and walked toward him. "You, too," she replied.

They put their arms around each other for one last hug and then they walked toward the front door. As Paul stepped through the doorway he turned to look at her. "Bye," she said, so softly that he could not hear her and knew she had spoken only by reading her lips. He turned to walk away and heard the door close quietly behind him.

As he walked toward his car he mused aloud, "Nothing like a good back stabbing to make life fun." Paul wasn't quite sure how to feel since there was a combination of hurt from being rejected, anger at someone who had no respect for the feelings of others, and disgust at having it happen to him.

When he got to his car he opened the door and got inside. As he sat there in the dark he suddenly had a very strong thought of Michelle, quiet, shy Michelle who had loved and trusted him. "Ah, hell," he said out loud, "now I know how she felt when I did this to her." His thoughts began to whirl. Michelle had been his special friend at one time, simple and shy, but caring and sincere. He knew her only crime had been to care and to trust him and he had rewarded her in the same manner that Erika had just rewarded him. "I screwed up big time," he thought, "I traded somebody who just wanted to love me for somebody who was more exciting with a bigger chest but a smaller mind. Damn you, little head, for doing the thinking."

Paul pounded the steering wheel until his hands hurt. Finally, only slightly more composed, he started the engine and pulled into the street. He drove passed a bank with a large combination clock and thermometer outside. It was 9:42 and 76º.

A vivid picture of Michelle came to his mind and stayed there. Not only would this image not go away, it was followed by a very strong, foreboding feeling that something bad was about to happen but what it was and to whom it was going to happen, he had no idea. Was it to him or to someone else? The vision of Michelle just would not leave his mind.

I've got to call Michelle, he decided. He looked anxiously for a telephone as he drove down the street. Since he was overtaking all the other cars and no one was passing him, he glanced back inside at the speedometer. So strong was his feeling of panic that he was doing nearly sixty in a forty-five zone. He knew that there was a twenty-four hour convenience store about two blocks ahead of him. "Surely they have a phone," he prayed.

On her bed in the dark, Michelle lay very quiet and calm. Though she knew what would soon be happening to her, the desire to remove the hurt in her mind was still stronger than her desire to hold on to life. She ran her fingers over the smooth metal. It was cool to her touch. With a finger she traced the flutting in the cylinder and then pulled a neatly filed fingernail lightly over the checkered walnut handle. Had she not had the hearing protection on she could have heard her nail clicking softly as it jumped across the gaps in the checkering only to catch on the next piece.

In her now muffled world Michelle could no longer hear the friendly ticking of the clock that had kept her company for the last several years since her last remaining grandparent had died. She glanced again at the red numerals of the digital clock across the room. It too, had been her friend for quite a number of years but it had never been as close a friend as the other one simply because digital clocks do not tick. She picked up the gun and put the end of the dowel in her mouth. Running her tongue over the wood, she could feel the slightly rough texture and she could also, ever so slightly, taste it. "It doesn't taste all that bad," she thought, "but I bet it would be tough to digest." Just for a moment a faint smile played on the corners of her mouth and then vanished into the blankness of her expression. "The rest of this should be simple," she thought, "just push the brick and pop the cap."

Paul saw the sign he had been looking for and turned into the parking lot, almost hitting the curb in his haste. He slammed on the brakes and had the door open before the car had come to a complete stop. No real effort was made to close the door or turn off the lights. Paul fumbled in his pocket for the correct change as he ran toward the telephone. He jerked the receiver off the hook and put it to his ear as he tried to get his quarter into the coin slot but with no success. Someone had either been upset at the telephone company or had just decided to agitate some future caller. That unthinking person had stuffed a piece of cardboard in the slot and stopped it up and, most likely, never gave it a second thought.

"Damn," he exclaimed loudly, drawing stares from the people standing close by. Paul darted inside and stopped in front of the store clerk. "Do you have a phone I can use?" he blurted.

Without looking up, the clerk replied, "Pay phone outside."

"I know," he responded, "but it's broken and this is an emergency."

"Everybody got a 'mergency," she said. "Next."

Paul turned and started back toward his car. The vision of Michelle seemed to be even stronger than it had been and so was the foreboding feeling that went with it. He jumped in his car and in just a moment had the engine going. He hurriedly backed up, almost bumping into another car that had just pulled in behind him.

As Paul sped down the street again he was trying to watch traffic and look for another phone at the same time. After what seemed like forever he finally saw one outside a fast food restaurant. He turned in the parking lot and skidded to a stop in the closest spot to it that he could find. Jumping out of the car, he ran toward it as he pulled all the change out of his pocket. "This phone just has to work," he silently prayed again.

Paul was now obsessed with reaching Michelle. "If I can just talk with her things will be okay, please be home," he thought to himself. He shoved a quarter in the slot, heard the familiar "ding" and hurriedly punched out her number that he still remembered after all this time.

On the fourth ring he heard a familiar voice come on, "Hi. This is Michelle. I'm not available to take your call but if you leave your name and number, I'll get back to you. Have a ducky day."

At the sound of her voice Paul's heart started to pound in his chest like a small jackhammer. He suddenly discovered that the feelings for her that he had tried to suppress were really alive and well. He realized that he had been all too willing to trade love for the excitement of someone who was different, nothing more, just different. Speaking quickly, but yet quietly, into the phone, he said, "Michelle, it's Paul.

I screwed up big time. You'll never know how sorry I am for what I did or how much I love you. I realize that now. Call me as soon as you get back, whatever the time. Bye. I love you."

By just looking at the old gun that Michelle was holding one would hardly consider it to be a delicate piece of machinery. Complicated, maybe, but hardly delicate. After all, it was made from steel and had to be strong enough to withstand small explosions, possibly many of them in rapid succession. However, beneath the side plates and inside the handle is a complex puzzle of finely machined metal parts that must work together in order for the gun to fire. Maybe guns are in some way related to life because, as in life, timing is everything and it also is inside this particular weapon.

In order for it to be in time, and it was, perfectly, several things must happen. The hammer, trigger, and cylinder must all lock simultaneously. If these things do not happen together, one of two things may happen. The firing pin may not land on the cap and the bullet will not fire. If the pin lands to one side of the cap and the cylinder isn't lined up, it may fire but the bullet may strike the side of the barrel and cause a piece of the projectile to separate from the part that goes through the barrel. This dangerous phenomenon is known as lead shaving and the consequences can indeed be dire. However, due to the initial meticulous workmanship and the care it had received through the years from her grandfather, and now from her, this fie old Colt worked as smoothly and as surely as it had when it had left the factory nearly eighty years earlier.

The trigger assembly in it resembles two quarter moons that are connected at one end with a tiny hole drilled where they join. When placed in position with a pin through this hole, it can move back and forth as needed. On the back of the trigger, beneath the side plate, there is a slender piece of metal about an inch in length. As the trigger moves rearward, this piece, known as the hand, moves upward and pushes against a raised rib on the bullet ejector mechanism and causes the cylinder to rotate, in this case, sixty degrees to the right. If the hammer is pulled back it also causes the previously mentioned things to happen due to interconnecting parts.

On the bottom of the hammer is a rounded piece of smooth metal that terminates in a point. This is the solid sear and almost at the tip of this hardened point is a tiny depression, the cocking notch. Once cocked, the upper part of the trigger rests in this shallow indentation. Due to the craftsmanship of this particular gun, it only took a very slight rearward pressure on the trigger to release it from this stop in order to get the hammer to fall.

As Michelle contemplated the gun on her chest she really wasn't sure why it functioned as it did, she just knew how much her mind hurt and how much she longed to escape this never ending pain. Raising the gun to an upright position, she studied it carefully in the dim light. With the dowel attached beneath the barrel, it was about twice as long as normal and the entire assembly looked out of place in her small hands.

"The woody taste of the dowel really isn't that bad," she thought, "matter of fact, it tastes kind of good. Enough practice, this one is for real." With that, she laid it gently back on her chest.

Holding the string around her thumb with her first finger capped over it, she extended her arm and pulled the string snug. Michelle then reached back over her head with her right hand and gave the brick a slight push. As it tried to fall she felt the string dig into her thumb with constant pressure as the brick dangled. She placed her left hand low on her chest and got comfortable.

The gun was slightly more awkward to manipulate using only her right hand but she still managed. Before putting it back in her mouth she cocked it. Through the ear protection she could barely distinguish a faint click as she pulled the hammer back to the cocked position. Both the metal and the wood were pleasantly cool to her touch. They felt refreshing on this warm summer night.

Being careful not to touch the trigger, she twisted her small hand around the checkered walnut grip and swung the barrel around toward her head. Michelle opened her mouth and put the end of the dowel in it. She moved the handle until it was over her sternum and let it rest just below the xyphoid process. With the handle there, the dowel resting over the crack between her two lower center front teeth and the end of it lightly touching the back of her mouth just forward of the uvula, she knew that there was absolutely no way she could possible survive to be a burden or a vegetable. She took one last look around the room, opened her mouth as wide as possible, and pushed her head back against the catalogue. Closing her eyes, Michelle removed her thumb from the trigger guard and placed it lightly on the trigger.

By opening her mouth fairly wide Michelle knew she could get the proper angle for the path of the bullet. With the dowel resting on her bottom teeth and the end of it touching the back of her mouth just as it started to slope forward, she knew she had about a thirty-five to forty-degree angle that would put the bullet on the proper path.

Her goal was to shoot through the medulla oblongata and thereby shut down her vital involuntary bodily functions. The one thing she really wanted to avoid at all costs was being unsuccessful in the effort and becoming a vegetable, or worse, being severely crippled. For this reason she would not shoot herself just anywhere, it had to work right the first time.

The medulla is an enlarged part of the spinal cord that connects it to the base of the brain. It is situated just slightly above the first cervical vertebra and about level with interior base of the skull. If the bullet happened to hit this piece of bone it would only help make the task more efficient for two reasons. First, upon hitting bone, the bullet would start to flatten out and therefore make a larger and more ragged hole. Second, pieces of bone would become projectiles adding to the potential damage to this extremely delicate area.

This part of the brain is so sensitive that even an external blow to the base of the skull can cause death by shutting down pulse and respiration and by letting the blood vessels relax causing a severe loss of blood pressure. Michelle knew any one of these situations could be fatal but the combination of the three would most certainly bring about her desired result.

At almost the same time the quarter Paul had dropped in the telephone went "ding", there was a brilliant burst of orange flame that was bright even through Michelle's eyelids. Though the hearing protection had muffled twenty-six decibels of the noise, it was still loud enough to startle her. The powder in the one hundre-twenty grain Starfire bullet burned smoothly and the bullet sped away from its brass casing at nine hundred-fifty feet per second.

From the cylinder to the front of the catalogue was only about eighteen inches. The bullet got there in a millisecond. However, in the short time it was in transit it did a considerable amount of damage. It went through the soft palate in the back of her mouth without even slowing down. Had Michelle tilted her head back just slightly more the bullet would have missed the first cervical vertebra. As it happened though, it struck the upper front section almost dead center. This caused the bullet to alter its course about ten degrees higher than it would have been. This slight change in course, plus the addition of bone fragments, put it nearly through the middle of the medulla. From there it went through the lower portion of the cerebellum and tore a large, jagged hole in the occipital bone as it exited.

Had she been alive, Michelle would have been proud--she had finally been good enough at something. Everything worked just as she had planned it. The rubber band mounted dowel on the end of the barrel had protected her teeth from the possibility of being chipped due to the recoil of the gun. Gravity and the brick slipped the loop of string off her thumb when it relaxed and as the brick fell toward the floor; it pulled the hearing protectors off and out of the way leaving her soft, brown hair only slightly tousled.

The bullet struck the catalogue and flattened out appreciably more. It destroyed the sheets all the way to page 173 where it came to rest against an attractive blonde modeling a white sun dress that could also be ordered in robin egg blue or peach. The black plastic on which she was lying kept the blood that was oozing out of her mouth and the gaping hole in the back of her head from staining her favorite butterfly print bedspread.

There were some pieces of her skull that had slammed against the catalogue and then bounced to her left. Had she been able to scrutinize them she might have even been amused, possibly even a little disturbed, because among the thick, brown curls that were still attached to one piece was her first gray hair. She had never even seen it but there it was, growing right along with the others.

After the gun had gone off it had fallen to Michelle's left and was now lying on her chest with her right hand still touching the handle. The bullet had done exactly what she intended it to do. With the medulla oblongata destroyed her heart received no nerve impulses to make it contract, her blood vessels relaxed and her blood pressure plummeted.

There was no contraction of her diaphragm to bring any oxygen into her lungs.

The room was very still and quiet. The only things breaking that stillness were the quiet ticking of her clock that would eventually wind down and the flashing of the message light on her answering machine that someone would eventually turn off.

After hanging up the phone Paul had gone inside and ordered some iced tea. He sat down and sipped it for awhile as he mulled over what he should do next. He was relieved that he had left Michelle the message and was considering going home to wait for her to call him. Suddenly it dawned on him, when he had told her goodbye two years earlier he had failed to give back the key to her house. There was no real need to go home and wait for her to call. After all, he really wanted to see her so he could say in person what he had said on the phone. As he walked toward his car he decided to just drive over there and wait.

ABOUT THE AUTHOR

A former educator and personnel manager, J. Gunter has spent the past several years in the field of aviation. While in elementary school, J. discovered the enjoyment of writing and pursued it while acquiring two degrees from a major university. Other than academic and business writing, J.'s writing interest has included essays, poetry, and short stories. J. lives outside of Christiansburg, Va., with two ceramic cats.

www.ingramcontent.com/pod-product-compliance
Lightning Source LLC
Chambersburg PA
CBHW060902190726
48286CB00002B/342

* 9 7 8 1 9 5 7 0 0 9 4 6 9 *